PRAISE FOR AIDA ZI[...]

All the Ways We Lied

"*All the Ways We Lied* is an exquisitely-told family story, a jewel box filled with unique prismatic characters, luminescent in its exploration of love and betrayal among three Armenian American sisters and their cataclysmic mother. Aida Zilelian masterfully navigates their complex, interconnected emotions with compassionate precision as the women alternately confront and turn away from the disappointments in their lives, as they reach for each other even as they struggle to find their own way. Ultimately a story of bravery during a time of grief, *All the Ways We Lied* will draw you in to vulnerable moments across continents and cultures, leading you to the most tender, comforting, and insightful definition of the word 'home.'"
—Nancy Agabian, *The Fear of Large and Small Nations*

"At last! A terrific novel about a modern-day Armenian family, fraught with the chaos, capriciousness, and conflicts you can find in Armenian families and beyond, bringing to mind the best parts of Lahiri's *The Namesake*, Tan's *The Joy Luck Club* and a twist of Franzen's *The Corrections*. Zilelian's memorable work challenges the taboos of traditional cultures with unflinching honesty. At the same time, she measures the breadth and depths of kinship, self-sacrifice and ultimately the sense of autonomy. A must-read exploration of familial love and heartache."
—Arthur Nersesian, author of *The Fuck-Up*

"Reading Aida Zilelian's clear-eyed and captivating new novel – *All the Ways We Lied* – reminds me, once again, that specificity is universal, and that strong storytelling is anchored to our core humanity. Page after poignant page, I found echoes of my own life in the characters of Kohar, Lucine, Azad, and the entire Garabedian clan. This panoramic family tale cuts to the heart of what it means to forgive each other and, ultimately, ourselves."
—Jared Harél, author of *Let Our Bodies Change the Subject*, Winner of the Raz/Shumaker Prairie Schooner Book Prize in Poetry

"Zilelian takes a fascinating micro look at an Armenian American family suffering from collective generational trauma. Her writing captures the wildly different personalities of the main characters, depicted with compassion and deep psychological acuity. With *All the Ways We Lied*, the Manoukians join America's First Families of Literature as Zilelian's wry prose draws the reader in for an intimate portrait of contemporary America."

—Chris Atamian, award-winning author
of *A Poet in Washington Heights*

"*All the Ways We Lied* is a masterful, engrossing novel depicting the perfect storm of generational trauma and complicated family dynamics, and the strong women caught at the center of it, all yearning at their core to love and to be loved. Zilelian captures the burden and overwhelm of the eldest immigrant daughter expertly, along with the relatable resentments and grievances of a life spent straining against one's prescribed role in the family ecosystem.

With gorgeous prose and a page-turning plot featuring characters you won't soon forget, this is necessary reading for all children of immigrants."

—Christine Kandic Torres, author of *The Girls in Queens*

"The dark and light of tangled family relations are depicted in the pages of *All the Ways We Lied*. The book is a warm, entertaining and heart-rending read with a cast of endearing, albeit flawed, characters. Aida Zilelian understands how people are pinned together. How they're shaped by their parents and their parents by the generations before them and, in the case of this Armenian family, by a tragic history of loss and displacement."

—Eve Makis, author of *The Spice Box Letters*

"Aida Zilelian's accomplished second novel unfolds with rare grace and tenderness. The raucous imperfections of the Armenian-American family depicted in its pages, the way they spiral out and inevitably back into each other's lives, their unstinting patience and ultimate kindness towards each other, will remind us of our own. I wish I could spend many more pages with Kohar, Lucine, Azad, and yes, even Takouhi."

—Arif Anwar, author of *The Storm*

All the Ways We Lied

All the Ways
We Lied

a novel

Aida Zilelian

KEYLIGHT
BOOKS
AN IMPRINT
OF TURNER
PUBLISHING

Keylight Books
an imprint of Turner Publishing Company
Nashville, Tennessee
www.turnerpublishing.com

All the Ways We Lied

Cover painting by Amy Kazandjian
Cover and book design by William Ruoto

Library of Congress Cataloging-in-Publication Data
Names: Zilelian, Aida, author.
Title: All the ways we lied / by Aida Zilelian.
Description: First Edition. | Nashville, Tennessee : Keylight Books, an
  imprint of Turner Publishing Company, [2024]
Identifiers: LCCN 2022033428 (print) | LCCN 2022033429 (ebook) | ISBN
  9781684429516 (hardcover) | ISBN 9781684429523 (paperback) | ISBN
  9781684429530 (epub)
Subjects: LCGFT: Novels.
Classification: LCC PS3626.I4865 A44 2024 (print) | LCC PS3626.I4865
  (ebook) | DDC 813/.6—dc23/eng/20220721
LC record available at https://lccn.loc.gov/2022033428
LC ebook record available at https://lccn.loc.gov/2022033429

Printed in the United States of America

For Sophia
And to Brian for everything and more

Part 1

Chapter 1

KOHAR RACED UP THE STEPS TO HER BEDROOM, KNOWING THE doorbell would ring at any moment. She pulled open her lingerie drawer, her fingers still lightly dusted with confectioners' sugar, and combed through the contents nervously. As she reached back to the hollow recesses, from where some old underwear—a pair of stockings and a bra—reappeared, she heard two short rings from the front doorbell.

"Jonathan!" she cried out. "Can you please get that?"

She swept her hands toward the back of the drawer one last measure and slammed it shut. Despite her irritation, she remembered not to run, easing herself down the steps.

Both her mother's and mother-in-law's voices carried from the kitchen. Kohar walked in as they each gave Jonathan a gift bag.

"Presents?" he said. "I wasn't expecting anything. You didn't need to do that."

Kohar paused by the entrance of the kitchen, regarding her husband's tall, lean frame, wanting to hug him from behind. She noticed the living room was cleaner and less cluttered, the rug freshly vacuumed; he must have tidied up when she was in the shower.

The banana cream pie she had made that morning sat on the granite countertop. She hadn't had time to find the cake stand.

"Hi, Mary," Kohar said as she leaned in to hug her mother-in-law lightly.

"Hi, Mom," she said, noticing that her mother was already sitting at the dining-room table.

"Hi," her mother said. "Where's the cake stand? I thought you had one."

"I did. I do, but I didn't have the chance to find it," said Kohar.

"I'm going to come over one day and reorganize this whole mess for you," her mother replied, pointing to the slate-blue hutch behind her. The shelves were lined with pie plates, wine glasses, and formal dining ware. "Then you'll be able to find everything."

Kohar regarded both women. Taking in the differences of their physical appearances as if for the first time, she noticed that they were antithetical counterparts. Mary, blond-haired and blue-eyed, wore her hair in a sensible bob with bangs, dressed in a wardrobe of pastel colors. Takouhi, whose dark hair fell to the middle of her back, wore the colors of a fading bruise. And black and gray.

"You're getting up there, aren't you?" Takouhi teased Jonathan, who was turning thirty-seven.

"I guess so," said Jonathan. "It doesn't feel like it, though."

"It never does," replied Takouhi. "And then the next thing you know—"

The doorbell rang again. Takouhi's husband, Gabriel, was outside the screen door. Jonathan went to greet him and let him in. The men gave each other a mighty hug.

"I was starting to feel outnumbered," said Jonathan. "Were you looking for parking?"

"No," said Gabriel. "I had to take a quick walk. This is for you." He extended a decorative bag with a wrapped bottle inside.

"Aw, you didn't have to," said Jonathan. "Thank you."

Immediately noticing the banana cream pie, Gabriel stepped back in admiration. "You made this?" he asked Kohar.

"Yes," she said, and went to him for a hug.

"*Very* impressive," he said.

"I remember the dinner parties from when you and your sisters were little girls," Takouhi said. "The things I would make. One year, I made that tower of cream puffs—the French dessert. What's it called?"

"I'm sure Lucine would know," Kohar replied.

"Yes, your sister the pastry chef," Takouhi commented wryly.

"Why the face?" Kohar asked. "Did you two have a fight?"

"No," Takouhi said resignedly. "I just never hear from her. *Nobody* calls me."

"What's that supposed to mean, Mom?" asked Kohar. She never knew if she was taking the bait or holding her mother accountable when she made those comments.

"Nothing," said Takouhi. "I didn't say anything."

But you did. You did say something. "Do you hear from Azad?" Kohar asked, referring to her youngest sister. She did not hide the tinge of accusation.

"Don't start, Kohar." The words strung together melodiously, belying the warning in her voice. "Let's not fight."

Not realizing that she had been holding her breath, Kohar exhaled slowly and went to prepare a pot of coffee. She wanted to scream.

"Hey, where's my mimosa?" Gabriel barked jokingly. "A Sunday and a birthday celebration. What kind of service is this?"

Kohar went for the pitcher she had prepared that morning. Hiding behind the refrigerator door, she filled one fluted glass with only orange juice and set it aside. The rest of the glasses, she poured from the pitcher of mimosas at the kitchen counter.

"I'll make the toast," Gabriel insisted.

Kohar took the glass she had set aside. Everyone stood by the dining-room table, and Jonathan, now the focus of attention, blushed slightly and leaned against Kohar, kissing her cheek.

Gabriel lifted his glass and smiled brightly, turning to Jonathan. "Jonathan, you're a true gift to this family," he said. "May this year bring you all the joy and happiness you deserve. Happy birthday!"

"—And," Takouhi broke in. They held their glasses mid-air, awkwardly suspended. "May this year also bring you everything that you have been wishing for. Happy birthday."

As they sipped their drinks, Kohar and Jonathan exchanged a glance. He winked. She smiled. If only they could fast-forward through lunch so Jonathan could blow out the candles and they could announce their news.

Kohar was in her tenth week of pregnancy. The fertility specialist would be calling later to confirm that her hCG levels were rising. They would learn the gender of the baby at her next scheduled visit.

It was her third pregnancy. After two failed years of trying to conceive and two miscarriages, Kohar had made an appointment with a fertility specialist last winter. The sonogram had showed her uterus and fallopian tubes infested with cysts and growths that had been secretly harvesting and breeding, quietly tampering with Kohar's sanity and their sex life, which had become a joyless chore for both her and Jonathan. After her laparoscopic surgery, they had waited three months for Kohar to heal before trying again. Though she and Jonathan had been hopeful, they were both shocked by the good news when she suspected she was pregnant and the test was positive.

Kohar knew what the mothers would do upon hearing the news; they would launch into planning for the baby shower. Or, rather, her mother would claim the planning for herself and include Mary, to be polite. Her sister Lucine would high-five Jonathan and say "Good job. Your guys can swim." Azad would be excited to be a *morkoor*, an aunt. What Kohar was looking forward to most of all was the look on Gabriel's face. His ear-to-ear smile, the pure joy in his eyes.

Kohar's phone rang, jolting her from her thoughts. Her stomach lurched with excitement as she picked up the phone.

"Kohar?" The voice sounded like it was coming from far away, the *r* slurred. It was her father.

"Hi, Dad," she said, walking away, specifically from her mother's earshot.

"Can I talk to Jonathan?" her father asked.

"Sure," she said. "How are you feeling?"

"Fine," he replied.

He had suffered a stroke several years ago and was still bedridden.

"I'll come and visit soon," she promised.

"How's Lucine doing?" he asked. He always asked.

"She's good, Dad. Very busy with work," Kohar said, offering the stock answer.

"As long as she's okay," he said.

"She is. Hang on a second," said Kohar.

She went to the kitchen and found Jonathan. "It's my dad," she said, her voice dropping, though she knew her mother could hear.

Jonathan took her phone and disappeared upstairs.

"Hetch hayruh guh heratsayneh?" asked Takouhi. *Does his father ever call him?*

"No," Kohar replied in English for Mary's sake. Though she and Jonathan had been married for eight years, she still had to remind her mother to speak English in front of non-Armenian–speaking people. She found it rude and passive-aggressive when her mother conveniently forgot.

Kohar found her mother's question to be especially offensive, given the occasion and the fact that she had told her mother about Jonathan's estrangement from his father—and, more specifically, that his father had abandoned both him and Mary after they had divorced.

"I'll help set the table," Mary said, and went to collect the silverware that Kohar had stacked on the countertop.

Time passed tediously slow. Kohar kept glancing at the clock through lunch. By the time she had loaded the dishwasher and taken out the dessert plates, it was three o'clock, the time the fertility clinic closed on Sundays.

Resigning herself that she would not be hearing from the office until Monday, Kohar placed the banana cream pie on a serving plate and lit the candles. They sang for Jonathan, as she slowly made her way to where he was sitting at the head of the table and set it in front of him.

"Make a wish," Mary said; and, as she spoke the words, Kohar's phone suddenly rang.

"Wait! I have to get this," Kohar said, trying not to sprint to the phone.

"But you just lit the candles," Takouhi protested. "Let it ring."

Jonathan sat patiently, the array of candles illuminating his smile. His eyes followed Kohar as she answered the phone.

"I'm calling for Kohar Garabedian," a female voice spoke.

"This is she," Kohar said, feeling the tremble in her voice.

"Please hold a minute. Dr. Cheng would like to speak to you."

She glanced at everyone and held up her finger, signaling them to wait a second. Takouhi cast her a look that said *Do you really need to be on the phone right now?* Jonathan's mother raised her drawn-in eyebrows.

"Hello, Ms. Garabedian? This is Dr. Cheng."

"Hello," said Kohar.

"Ms. Garabedian, I wanted to speak to you myself about your blood-work. Typically, we like to see the hCG hormone levels between forty-four and one-seventy at this point. But your test shows that your levels dropped. I'm sorry."

"What does that mean?" Kohar asked. She guessed she would need hormone supplements to maintain her levels through to the second trimester.

"Unfortunately, the number is too low. It indicates that you will eventually miscarry. I'm very sorry."

Kohar held the phone for several long seconds, unable to listen. She took a small, inarticulate breath while Jonathan sat waiting, the candles now melted into tiny solid puddles. The doctor continued speaking, something about a pill to induce the miscarriage. Kohar hung up.

"Who *was* that?" Takouhi asked.

Kohar avoided Jonathan's gaze as she carried away the cake and replaced the candles, lit each, pretended to be too absorbed to answer.

As they sang for Jonathan, all Kohar could think about was the guest bedroom they often referred to as the "maybe baby room." They had painted it a cautious eggshell white. The only piece of furniture was a full-sized bed. They had reasoned that it would be the only necessary item regardless of the outcome. But in Kohar's bureau drawers, under the folds of precious scarves and clusters of pretty underwear, she had saved different treasures, ones of hope and desperation. Namely, a pair of winter white booties her mother had impulsively knitted when they had announced Kohar's first pregnancy. Kohar was glad now that she hadn't been able to find them. She had wanted to place them in a gift box for her mother and Mary to open, to announce their news.

For days Kohar ignored her doctor's voicemail messages recommending she take the pill to induce the miscarriage. Instead, she waited. The pain tugged at her insides; the small of her back ached. She bled more than the last two times. Like a smug fortuneteller whose prophecies unfailingly came to pass, Kohar's thoughts preyed on her: *You didn't deserve it in the first place. Nothing great will happen to you.*

Without asking, Jonathan rented a house on a private beach on the North Fork for three weeks. They drove to the beach house on a hot August Sunday. During the car ride, Kohar sat pensively, staring out the window and looking at nothing as Jonathan bounded down the Long Island Expressway, holding her hand. When they pulled off the highway, a winding two-way road came into full view. Farm stands dotted the roadsides with charming wooden signs boasting freshly cut sunflowers, bundled firewood, heirloom tomatoes, piles of corn snug in their husks, bins of stone fruit, oversized watermelons. There was the road ahead of them and the one they had left behind, and on either side were farm fields, bright and green, stretching far and wide.

Jonathan glanced at Kohar and saw her sit up a bit, her eyes bright and alive. He let out an inaudible sigh. Allowed himself to smile.

"Maybe we can drive back this way later. That one stand looked nice," she said. It was the first time she had spoken in miles.

Jonathan leaned back in his seat and massaged the back of his neck, momentarily at ease.

The road narrowed. Tall maple trees shaded the pebbled path that opened into a driveway. The cottage came into full view, with the blue horizon of the ocean behind it. From afar, it resembled a watercolor painting. Jonathan cut the engine. Kohar left her sandals in the car and walked barefoot across the lawn, the sun-soaked grass grazing against her feet.

The house was one of many along the shoreline of the Long Island Sound. Kohar went down the short, weathered steps to the sand and the homes that wrapped around the long wide curve of the beach. The Sound was vast and empty, the outline of the Connecticut shore faintly visible from where Kohar stood.

From the enclosed porch, Jonathan watched her single figure. The long stretch of sand was unmarred and inviting, the calm bay water undisturbed by Jet Skis or motorboats. Jonathan realized that the last time he had felt such peace was the morning after they had found out Kohar was pregnant. He had woken up and turned to her, surprised to find her still sleeping, given that she usually rose early and made coffee. He had imagined Kohar in the later part of her pregnancy still scurrying around the house baking, cooking, reorganizing the space in preparation for their new life, undaunted by her protruding stomach. Now, as he watched her walk along the lip of the ocean, his regret in having imagined such things left him feeling remarkably fooled and foolish.

He climbed down the beach steps and caught up with Kohar, who was now at least ten houses away. She walked cautiously and stared at the sand, crouching down to quickly peer. Sometimes she would extract a small piece of something and put it in her pocket.

"Hey," said Jonathan.

Kohar turned. "This is so nice," she said. "I wasn't expecting this."

"I wasn't either," he said. "It's like our own private beach."

"Where is everyone?" she asked.

"These are all private homes, so I guess everyone is working or away on vacation. But if you look way past to the left, you'll see the public beach. It's filling up now," he said.

"Away on vacation? I can't believe no one is here," Kohar said again. "And look." She held out her hand and opened her palm. Sea glass shimmered in her hand, frosted pieces of blue, green, and white in various sizes. "Do you want to walk and look with me?"

Kohar slipped her hand into his and they walked slowly, exploring. Firewood, carefully arranged, rested in dug-out firepits in front of some homes, promising an evening campfire. Rows of overturned kayaks lay before some of the larger houses. "Have a happy day" was spelled out with pebbles in front of another. Kohar hunted for more sea glass. They walked, an agreeable silence between them. Dusk was close behind. Finally they turned back, remembering that shops closed earlier on Sundays.

As Jonathan drove along on the main road heading farther into town, Kohar noticed the wineries that were soon to close. Then she spotted a cheese shop. By the time they headed back, they had bought a collection of food that would last them until the following afternoon: two baguettes (Kohar immediately froze one to keep it fresh), Stilton cheese, fig jam, half a pound of Hungarian salami, and a fresh peach-and-raspberry pie.

That evening, they ate on the enclosed porch, the soft lapping of the ocean waves only steps away. They had drained a bottle of wine between them before Kohar set out the charcuterie platter. From where they sat, the ocean was obscured in darkness. Small campfires burned along the sandy beach, illuminating shadowy figures.

"We should build a fire tomorrow," Kohar said.

"We should," said Jonathan.

"I want to look for more sea glass, and you can collect some kindling," she suggested.

Jonathan nodded with mock flattery. "*I* can collect the kindling? Thanks."

"You go on that camping trip once a year," Kohar said, smiling. "I imagine you're good at building a fire."

"You know the headache of building a fire with three other guys, right? Everyone's an expert. I've learned to sit back and watch them obsess over a pile of sticks," he said. "I've seen it done a dozen times. I'm sure I can figure it out."

Kohar took another sip of wine. And then it came to her with sudden clarity. The answer was so simple and obvious that it hadn't occurred to her until that moment. "I want to let it go," she said.

"Let it go?" Jonathan asked.

"All of it. What we've been trying to do." Kohar struggled to form the words, trying to avoid the most painful ones. "We've been here for one day. Just one. It's been so lovely. We don't need anything else."

Jonathan grew quiet.

"I've wanted to tell you the same thing," he said finally.

"Why haven't you, then?" asked Kohar.

"Because—I wasn't sure how far you wanted to take this," he said.

Had they taken it far enough? Jonathan couldn't once again surrender himself to having perfunctory sex, enduring the withdrawn self of Kohar when she got her period, carefully navigating their conversations to avoid the topic of babies, the taciturn evenings with Kohar when she would return from work with the news that another co-worker was pregnant. The memory of Kohar's two miscarriages felt like watching someone slowly peeling off their own flesh, how savagely the two losses had left her raw and hollow. And now this one.

"I'm done," she said. "I feel bitter right now, and I feel relieved by not living in the gray area. It's probably what's drained me the most."

She had been holding her breath, waiting to readjust her life. Nothing had happened, and everything had come to pass.

If she heard one more time that being a teacher was the ideal profession when becoming a mother, she could claw her eyes out. The irony was that she had fallen into teaching after a few disappointing years of working in the publishing industry. Now, fourteen years later, she had withstood the handful of difficult years at a failing school and was teaching high school English close to her neighborhood. While having all this freedom, she and

Jonathan had traveled, she had carved out time to pursue her writing, and she had continued playing the piano and the guitar. She would certainly have the time to take off from work and spend at least a year at home with a baby. Resist as she might, she could almost feel the light, reassuring weight of a newborn in her arms.

"Fuck having a baby," she told him now, wincing inwardly. "If it's already this difficult, I can only imagine what life will be like after."

"To think how long it took us to realize we wanted this," Jonathan said.

"I know," Kohar said, remembering their conversation when he had proposed to her. They had both agreed that they didn't want the burden of being parents. "We waited too long," she said.

"Don't," Jonathan said. "We've gone over this. So many times."

"I always thought I'd be terrible at it, anyway," Kohar continued. *At being a mother.* "And then . . . I don't know. I didn't like that I wasn't doing something because I was too scared." She wanted to tell him how terribly it weighed on her, that her body was to blame. That she was thirty-eight and too old now anyway. She had wanted a baby all along and hadn't admitted it—most egregiously, to herself.

They sat in silence, smoking. Kohar uncorked a second bottle of wine and poured another glass for each of them. Now from the distance came the sound of a chorus of singing. *"Keep your eyes on the road, your hands upon the wheel! Keep your eyes on the road, your hands upon the wheel! Let it roll, baby, roll! Let it . . ."* Laughter. Kohar and Jonathan sat together in the grim silence of the porch, listening intently to the carefree, disembodied voices coming from below. The image of a burning fuselage came to Kohar, glowing in the night and then slowly snuffing out like smoldering embers.

"Have you ever thought about adoption?" he asked. "Or what your friend did—the one you work with?"

"IVF?" Kohar asked. "IUI?"

"What is that? I'm sorry," he said, "I don't know the difference."

"With IVF they fertilize your sperm and my egg and put it inside me. With IUI they take your sperm and put it inside me," Kohar said. "I don't know if I can go through either. It's *a lot.*"

"A lot, like, how? Money?" Jonathan asked.

"No! On *me*," Kohar replied hotly.

"I'm not trying to upset you—I'm sorry," said Jonathan.

"Next thing you're going to say is we should find a surrogate," Kohar said.

"That's when someone else carries it for you? I mean—for us," Jonathan said.

"*Yesss*," Kohar replied, her voice rising. "Unless my eggs are rotten. Then maybe we can get someone else's embryo. Even better—and someone else can carry it, too."

"Kohar, stop," Jonathan said. "I just asked one question. I asked if you'd thought about adoption."

"I don't want to adopt!" Kohar burst. "I want a baby. To carry it in *my* body. To feel it. To love it. To give it what was never given to me! Why do I have to spell this out for you?"

"Kohar—please. It's going to be okay," Jonathan said and leaned across the table, taking her hand. He pressed her hand between his. "It's just not meant for us. At least not now."

It's not going to be okay, she wanted to tell him. Maybe she and Jonathan would always be okay. But *she* would not be okay. Her hesitation had prolonged them from having a baby, which was now impossible. Ultimately, it was her fault.

"Let's enjoy ourselves here," Jonathan said. "We've always been good at that. I don't want this to change us. I love you."

Kohar relented. "I love you, too."

It was the last they spoke about it.

THE NEXT MORNING, THEY WOKE TO A BLUE, CLOUDLESS SKY. They sat on the open deck that overlooked the beach and drank strong coffee. Kohar spotted a hare darting across the lawn behind them and a deer along the pebbled driveway. The empty clothesline swung against the mild breeze. On the sand, the thick hunks of wood in the firepits were now black bits of cinder. As if the merry chorus from the evening before had been a mirage, there was no human sound. The surrounding quiet fell so softly that time paused at its heels.

The three weeks stretched before them invitingly. Sea-glass–hunting, kayaking, shopping for antiques, driving through small towns on rainy days. They considered buying a beach house. Jonathan haggled with the owner of the house to stay on for another week.

On their last day, they packed up and left in the late morning and stopped off at their new favorite winery before heading home.

"I'm not ready to go back," Kohar said as Jonathan followed the main road that would lead them to the highway heading west.

"Me neither," said Jonathan. "I can't believe it's the first of September."

"It feels like it, too," Kohar said. The air had seemed a bit cooler when she had loaded her suitcase into the trunk. "Maybe it's because classes start next week, but it feels like fall is coming."

"Our vacation doesn't have to stop," he said. "When we get home, let's make a nice meal later and relax."

He took Kohar's hand in his, kissed it.

Hours later, Kohar had set a pot of short ribs braising in the Dutch oven. She grabbed a pair of shears and headed outside to the hydrangea bush. The last bit of sun silhouetted the oak trees. Only two weeks ago, she would have felt the warmth on her shoulders. Now the air whispered coolly against her skin as she clipped the discolored flowers that were neither pink nor green.

As she breezed through the house and headed toward the back yard, music erupted from the speakers in the living room. The dark plodding bass of a piano burst and then stopped. Kohar smiled.

Jonathan sat in the middle of the living-room floor with a rectangular box of old CDs, slowly flipping through the long row of jewel cases.

"You're trying to find that song," she murmured.

"Uh-huh."

"There are so many renditions," she said.

"Tell me about it," said Jonathan. "Hundreds, I'm sure. But I think I've found it. It's the one with Juan Tizol."

"Yes!" Kohar turned away from the stack of gathered flowers and loose petals that had fallen on the countertop. "That's the one. Did you guess what I'm making for dinner, or did you look?"

"Short ribs," said Jonathan.

He went to the dining-room table and pulled out two bottles of wine from a brown paper bag. He uncorked a bottle of Rioja and filled a wine glass.

The dramatic rhythm of "Caravan" came to a brief halt, and the big-band orchestration of the melody filled the room with the wild syncopation of drums and trumpets. Kohar sank into the leather armchair and threw her legs over one of the bulky arms, deciding to leave the front door open. She took sips from her wine and observed the pink glow of dusk filtering through the parted curtains of the windowsill, where rested an assortment of succulents in their colorful clay pots.

"I miss the beach house," Jonathan said.

"Me, too," said Kohar.

She could see the sidewalk through the screen door. The voices of passersby faded in and out as the sky darkened. Suddenly came the plaintive cry of a baby. Kohar glanced up. She saw a woman bent over a carriage.

Kohar's thoughts halted. There they were again: babies. Goddamn babies. For the last four weeks, it had been a great relief to not think about trying to have a baby or that she and Jonathan had decided to give up trying, but here it was. Maybe the next woman on the street would be pushing a two-tiered stroller with a toddler *and* a baby. Had she not seen babies while they had been away? Or pregnant women? Kohar hadn't cared enough to notice.

"—boiling and you should probably take a look. I lowered it just in case."

Jonathan was standing over her, saying something. "What?" Kohar asked, and, as if she were hearing a delayed echo, the words formed meaning. She went over to the stove and lifted the lid off the Dutch oven. She lowered the flame to a very low simmer, staring into the pot for a few seconds to shake the irritation of Jonathan interrupting her misery. Then she poured herself another two inches of wine.

"Hey, why so quiet?"

Kohar felt Jonathan's hands on her shoulders. She blinked three times, as if that would magically erase her dark thoughts. Jonathan's bloodhound perception of her moods, like imminent thunderclouds, was impeccable. Maddeningly so.

"I'm not," she said and headed to the back yard.

"By the way, your phone rang," he said. "I think it was your mother."

"Why?"

"Because then my phone rang and it was also your mother," he said, not bothering to hide the irony. "I didn't pick up," he added before she could ask. He had seen three missed calls from Takouhi on Kohar's phone.

Kohar sighed. "I spoke to her this morning," she said. "I hope she's not starting up again."

She sat on the steps of the back yard, feeling a familiar dread in her chest. Before going away, Kohar had met with her therapist to specifically talk about the phone calls.

"You can't control how much she calls you," her therapist had reminded her. "But you can talk to her when you feel like it."

"No, I can't. She knows exactly when to call me," Kohar had explained. "She manages to catch me between leaving the house and driving to work. *Every* morning. Then she calls at night, asking if I've spoken to Lucine and Azad—which makes no sense, because she calls them after she hangs up with me. It just never ends."

"I'm going to say it again: You can talk to her when *you* feel like it," her therapist had replied.

"But then she'll keep calling until I pick up," Kohar had countered. "She'll start worrying. By the time I call her back, she'll be freaking out. It's just easier to pick up the phone and get it over with."

"You're not responsible for her feelings." She would also say this often. "'Mom,' you say, 'I was in the middle of something and couldn't get to the phone. Next time, just leave me a message and I'll call you back.' You can say that. And if it gives you any peace of mind, tell her the reception out there is going to be tough. Can you do that?"

Kohar had nodded, feeling the relief of this solution warming through her until she was almost limp.

Now, sitting in the back yard with a glass of wine in her hand, Kohar felt fortified. "I don't feel like calling her back," she said out loud.

Their month-long vacation had thrown the entire pattern off-kilter; Kohar had called her once a week while they had been away, feeling like a teenager at her first sleepover, reassuring her mother that she was alive and breathing. Unrealistic as she knew it was, Kohar had hoped this would reset her mother's inclinations somehow. After they had returned home, Kohar had waited three days before calling her.

Jonathan had gone back into the house. She was talking to a tangled bed of overgrown herbs she had meant to cut that afternoon. "I'm not calling her back," she said, promising herself.

Chapter 2

THE ALARM BELL SOUNDED. TAKOUHI, AWAKE FOR HOURS BEFORE dawn, lay with her eyes open as the ringing blared in her skull. Upon her waking, the list of daily tasks, items that needed desperately to be completed, had grown steadily. They varied in so many ways; it was difficult to organize their chronological importance. First and foremost, she would have to wake Gabriel soon to drive her to the markets only ten blocks away; while he sat in his car reading, she would wade through the aisles to buy all her groceries for the evening's dinner party. The grocery list, which she had written the week prior, was on the dining room table. One could admire Takouhi's cleverness in compartmentalizing the items into quadrants: dairy, produce, protein, miscellaneous. But to her it went beyond the matter of expedience: the list was a necessity, the items rearranged and erased half a dozen times over.

She left the bedroom with Gabriel still sleeping. By the time she made coffee and dressed for the supermarket, he would be up. The answering machine in the kitchen blinked. Takouhi hit the PLAY button. "*Hi janig. It's Mariam. I'm sorry but Harout's caught a cold, and we won't be able to make it, I'm afraid—*" Takouhi hit the FORWARD button. The nape of her neck burst with perspiration. "*It's Lily. I didn't realize tomorrow is the same night as Mary's piano recital. I hate to do this, but we have to cancel.*" Takouhi hit the FORWARD button again. "*End of messages.*"

"It's only his goddamned retirement dinner," she muttered.

Takouhi stomped through the foyer to the dining-room table and squinted at her list; she had left her reading glasses on her nightstand. Now, her arms pumping like a fast-walker on a treadmill, she hurried into the bedroom and grabbed her glasses. She swung the door behind her, letting it slam shut. Four fewer people. Four fewer portions. She scanned her menu, reconfiguring. She took a sheet of paper from Gabriel's printer and began rewriting her list. Should she change the menu altogether now? There was quite a difference in cooking for eight guests instead of twelve. Perhaps something more decadent? But how long would the preparation take then?

The sound of running water came from the kitchen. The refrigerator opened and closed.

"Gabriel!"

Takouhi took in the silence for a moment, admiring the prewar apartment they had lived in for nearly twenty-five years. She and Gabriel had bought the apartment as newlyweds. They had redesigned the sprawling space with Prohibition décor, stripped the floors with a warm camel finish, wallpapered the parlor and dining room with soft, tasteful pastels. Juxtaposed to this era were the traditional Armenian accents that had been passed down to them from their families. Among them was a bust of Gomidas, the famous Armenian composer, a three-foot hand-carved cross made of stone—the *khatchkar*, a hand-knotted tapestry of the Armenian alphabet, each letter forming the shape of a bird. On most any day of the week, one could hear Armenian music spilling into the vestibule of the apartment building and smell the enticing aromas of Takouhi's cooking.

"Gabriel!"

Heavy footsteps ambled to the dining room. From the shadowed corner, the tall and burly figure resembled a bear—of the honey-seeking species, not its dangerous cousin—who had risen from a brief and necessary hibernating sleep. Gabriel paused in the doorway, wearing nothing but his underwear, which was threadbare and practically transparent. Takouhi wanted to ask why he hadn't thrown them away yet, why he hadn't put on the fresh pair that she had left on the bed from the night before. Glassless, he resembled a helpless tortoise with an eagerness to please.

"The Parikians and the Boghossians aren't coming," she reported. "I'm thinking of changing the menu. What do you think?" Before he could interrupt, she continued. "For appetizers I was going to make a mezze platter—I marinated the olives two nights ago, so maybe I should keep that. But instead of the stuffed pork loin and pilaf with the asparagus wrapped with prosciutto, I'm thinking maybe jumbo shrimp stuffed with crabmeat? I also have this lovely potato recipe I haven't tried before. It's French. You cut the potatoes and layer them with butter in a springform pan—"

The coffeemaker beeped, its sterile noise generating a gravitational pull; Gabriel turned on his heels and called back. "I'm listening. Hang on."

He returned with two filled cups and set one on the dining table for Takouhi.

"Can I say something?"

"What?" Takouhi wore the expression of someone who had just tasted sour milk.

"Nothing. Both sound good to me," he said, easing himself on the couch. He wanted to ask why a retirement dinner was necessary when his retirement party was several weeks away. A grand affair in the city that was being held at the Armenian General Benevolent Union.

"What kind of answer is that?" Takouhi asked. "I might as well not have asked you. Should I make our traditional food instead?"

"What time did you wake up?" Gabriel asked, hedging with accusation.

"I don't know. I don't check the clock the second I wake up," Takouhi said.

"Three o'clock? Four?" Gabriel needed to know. He needed to configure at what point in the day he would be in the direct line of fire. Her transmutations were disturbing and, depending on how little she had slept, downright destructive. It ranged anywhere from spontaneously opening and slamming shut all the doors in the apartment in successive three-lap intervals to threats of burning his collection of Armenian thesauri with a book of matches. Takouhi's chronic insomnia (and depression and anxiety) was one among many of her more toxic deviances that Gabriel accepted. In return, he expected the same; he had the right to two or three helpings of pilaf if he pleased, the freedom to unwrap a second pack of Camels by late afternoon, the privilege of nine cups of coffee. He had assumed, naïvely, that this had been their tacit agreement. He still wasn't sure if Takouhi had forgotten the agreement, didn't realize it had been made in the first place, or ignored it altogether because it only applied to her and not him. Regardless, he had to endure. The more she berated him for his overeating and smoking, the more he ate and smoked.

She thought for a moment, *The jumbo shrimp would actually take less time to make, although the potato thing may take longer . . .*

Abruptly, she stood up, remembering a dangling loose end her memory hadn't harnessed in the earlier hours of her day. Had the cleaning woman remembered to water the fern plants she had bought from the nursery? She opened the balcony door that overlooked the street and saw the four ferns in their pots. She bent over and lifted one up. It felt like a dead bird in her hand: empty and lifeless. She saw that the bright green leaves were now a graying mass. Disgusted, she gathered all the dead plants in the crook of each arm and dropped them in the kitchen dustbin, satisfied in her annihilation.

Takouhi grabbed the phone and dialed Kohar's number.

"*Who* are you calling?" Gabriel asked. At first, she ignored him. "It's *six-fifty* in the morning. No one wants to hear from anyone at this hour."

"Fine."

She hung up the phone. Kohar had said on several occasions that Jonathan liked to sleep in during the weekends. She thought of Azad, who was at a weeklong concert festival thing somewhere in the desert. Then she considered Lucine, but as an afterthought, accustomed to the hectic schedule of her job as pastry chef. Her living in New Jersey added another dimension of distance that Takouhi hadn't fully accepted.

"When you do speak to her, which I'm sure you will at some point today, can you ask her if Jonathan is still coming over to take pictures? For the write-up about me in the *Armenian Reporter*? They're really making a big fuss about my retirement," he said.

"I'm sure he is," Takouhi replied. "Now, can you drive me after you're done with your coffee?"

Gabriel glanced at her wearily. "Do you really think it's necessary at this hour?"

"If we wait until later, it's going to get crazy and I'm not going to be worried about feeding the meter when I need to concentrate on the list. That area is crazy, and you know it," said Takouhi. Little India was a small section of their neighborhood in Jackson Heights clustered with Indian, Bengali, and Burmese restaurants, and supermarkets selling produce, legumes, spices, rice at near-wholesale prices, where Takouhi often shopped on the weekends. "And it's no parking between eight and eight-thirty on Saturdays for street cleaning," she added.

"What's all that?" Gabriel asked, motioning to the legal notepad scribbled with Takouhi's elaborate penmanship.

"It's for the trip," Takouhi said. "I was on the phone with Hagop, writing down all the details," she said. "I told him we rented the apartment in Yerevan for three months. But we'll travel with the tour group for the first two weeks."

"How many people?" Gabriel asked.

"The usual," Takouhi said.

They had been to Yerevan several times with their friend Hagop Bedrossian, a professor of Armenian literature, who also organized tours through Armenia every other summer. A few weeks after Gabriel's retirement, they planned to travel there again, this time staying for an extended visit.

"So, you'll take me now?" Takouhi asked again, as if Gabriel would say no, or could.

While she would spend a good part of the morning and most of the afternoon cooking, Gabriel would be in his study translating a memoir he had recently undertaken. While she chopped and sautéed, marinated and minced, her husband, oblivious to all the lovely aromas wafting from the kitchen, would slowly drain a pot of coffee and smoke through half a pack of unfiltered Camels, Armenian dictionaries and books of grammar and idioms stacked around him like a fortress.

Takouhi folded her list and let out a long breath, as if trying to exorcise the memories of her three daughters when they still lived at home—or, rather, her disappointment at their leaving. One by one, like checker pieces, they had disappeared: Kohar first, by unexpectedly moving out, Azad second, when she graduated and left for college (Takouhi suspected that Kohar had persuaded Azad to leave since she hadn't been allowed to dorm at a college herself), and finally Lucine, who had met and married a chef she worked with after having known him for three months. Each of her daughters' departures had felt like roots being pulled violently out of the soil of her life. Out of the three, Kohar had stayed in New York. To make amends with her conscience for prematurely maneuvering Azad out of the apartment, is what Takouhi also suspected.

Revenge, in all its satisfactions, ultimately hurt the person seeking it. Takouhi would like to believe that Kohar's weekend visits to the apartment were out of sheer love and longing for them to spend time together. But Kohar had a great deal to make up for, a great deal to do in order to assuage her regret for the past. She was being punished now in ways that, although ordinarily they would have given Takouhi a private sense of justice, only pained her. Namely, Kohar's first two miscarriages and the surgery that had promised and not yielded results. And now this last one. It was no fault of Takouhi's. She had warned Kohar not to wait too long to have a baby. Until finally Kohar had blurted out—during one Christmas Eve, no less—that she had no interest in having children. *After* marrying Jonathan. Why get married at all?

"I'm parked around the corner—" Before Gabriel could finish his sentence, he began coughing.

Takouhi stood up, with indignation. "Stop. Smoking. These. God-damned. Cigarettes," she said, pounding her fist like a gavel on the dining-room table. "You promised you would quit when you retired. And don't say you haven't retired yet, because it's soon. So just stop already. Every year you have bronchitis. It's from the smoking." As Gabriel's coughing escalated, she continued, louder. "I'm not going to give you money anymore. You're going on an allowance again. That way, you'll have to pace yourself with how many packs you buy."

Gabriel, hunched over, now straightened himself and shook his head. He smiled at her wryly. "'Allowance',," he muttered. "Give me a break."

Takouhi put the list in her pocketbook. "We both know it's true. An allowance. You don't even know what we have in our bank account, do you?" she asked.

As if a joke between him and himself, Gabriel chuckled sheepishly.

"You don't know, do you?" she asked again, knowing this was his surrender. She stood on her toes to kiss him. "I love you," she said, and wrapped her arms around his sizable stomach.

Their marriage had survived twenty-seven years, though confronted with many difficulties: Through the aftermath of each of their divorces—Gabriel's ex-wife was a spiteful woman and Takouhi's ex-husband had married a woman who was a paranoiac, a traumatic bankruptcy, and the hair-tearing trials of raising three daughters through puberty and into adulthood. Life had changed them and not the love between them. And every morning when Takouhi lay awake in the fading darkness, absorbed by the intricacies of the coming day, Gabriel's sudden snoring would interrupt her thoughts. And she would smile.

"I'll walk to the car with you," she said, and waited for him to throw on a pair of pants. Takouhi grabbed her keys and let the apartment door close behind them. As they stood in the lobby, the sound of the ringing phone came from the apartment. Takouhi turned.

"Leave it," Gabriel said. "They'll leave a message."

"No. What if it's someone else canceling? I have to get it."

She unlocked the door and ran to the kitchen. "Hello?"

"Hi, Mom." It was Lucine.

"Hi," said Takouhi. "I had left the house but heard the phone ringing. Are you coming tomorrow?"

"Tomorrow? What's tomorrow?"

"Do you listen to your messages?" Takouhi asked. "I left you a message—"

"No," Lucine said. "I don't. I look at the missed calls and call back."

"Well, when I left the message, I asked if you and Steve wanted to come over for breakfast on Sunday. I'm going to try Kohar again—she just got back from vacation and—"

"She just got back like yesterday," Lucine said. "You don't spare a moment, do you?"

Takouhi bridled. "Well, I only tried her once—"

"Is Azad coming?" asked Lucine.

"No, she's not," Takouhi said. "She said she's going to some *thing* in the desert, I'm not sure where."

A noise of disgust emitted through the phone.

"What is it?" asked Takouhi.

"Nothing. Nothing. So, I can't come. I woke up very early yesterday, and then one of the bakers called in and they asked me to stay late, so I did. I have to go in this afternoon, later. Tomorrow's my day off," she said.

Exactly, thought Takouhi. "Whatever you think is best," she said. "Gabriel's waiting for me in the lobby. Have you spoken to your sisters?"

"Kohar and I texted for a while at some point last week," Lucine said. "And we just went over Azad's naked gallivanting in the desert, so no, I haven't spoken to her. She's probably riding a unicycle as we speak, on her way to some life-changing *drum circle*."

Takouhi shook her head. *Had Kohar driven to an area where there had been cell-phone service? To text with Lucine?* "I wish you texted or called *me* more often," she said. "And Azad isn't naked."

Another odd sound emitted from the other end of the line. It sounded like wheezing and then a staccato of cackles. Takouhi waited, drew in a breath. "'Azad isn't naked'—*that's* what you're worried about?" The subtext that there was much more Takouhi should be worried about jangled her.

"Why don't you call me?" Takouhi asked. She felt entitled posing such an obvious question.

"Do I have to hide from you how often Kohar and I talk on the phone?" Lucine asked. "She's my sister—"

"And I'm your mother. Who you should be calling every day," Takouhi said.

"Jesus—I can't. I can't do this. I just woke up and called you because I saw your missed calls. Mom, you don't give anyone a chance to call you— that's why it feels like we don't. I don't know what handbook you're reading about how often one should be calling their mother, but what you're asking for is unrealistic. I can't."

It was often this way. Having a conversation with Lucine was similar to navigating a minefield, careful to avoid detonating the bombs, bombs which Takouhi couldn't tell were intentionally laid out for her and her alone.

"You can't call me once a day? On your way home from work or on the way to work?" She paused. "Gabriel's waiting outside."

"Yup. Have a good day," said Lucine, her voice thin and tired.

Gabriel was double-parked in front of their apartment building, sitting in the driver's seat. He sensed from how Takouhi immediately clipped her seatbelt and locked the car doors that he should drive without asking.

As they drove down the quiet blocks with rows of prewar buildings, Takouhi stared out the window, trying to console herself. Her daughters' lives, a complicated skein impossible to disentangle, pressed upon her.

"I don't get it sometimes," she said. "I just don't get it." Before Gabriel could ask, she continued: "Armenian day school, Saturday school, Sunday school, the Siamanto Academy when they got older. We always said—*hay-eren khoseer,* speak Armenian in the house. There was A.Y.F., A.C.Y.O.A.—they quit. They married *odars.* You'd think I hadn't raised them at all."

She had magnanimously accepted Jonathan, despite his being American. But Kohar's refusal to have children had been a spiteful retaliation against Takouhi's hopes of her having the ideal family. And Lucine's husband, Steve—what was one good thing she could say about him? Nothing.

"At least we have a chance with Azad. Let's see. Krikor seems like a nice boy," she said, referring to the young man who Azad had been dating for several months.

Gabriel sucked his teeth. "*Stop* pressuring her," he said. "Do you think that boy is even her cup of tea?"

"How am I pressuring her? I'm just telling you. The parents, both professors—and did you know Hayganoush's father was Hampig Manuelian? The famous painter who—"

"I know who Hampig Manuelian is—c'mon. Hayganoush is a little dry," Gabriel said, referring to Krikor's mother.

"She's not dry. She's classy," Takouhi said.

Azad, born fourteen years after Kohar, was the joy of Takouhi's life. But since leaving for college, she had all but disappeared into a never-ending loop of parties and festivals. Takouhi had expected she would return home after graduating. Instead, Azad had rented a house in Fishtown with her college friends. That was before Gabriel's mother had died and left Azad the house in her will.

Gabriel exhaled smoke through the crack of the window.

"Maybe it was the divorce. That's what messed it all up. Or Antranig." Takouhi shook her head, reliving those long years once again. "He dragged us to church every Sunday. Then we would come home, and what would he do? Spend the afternoon gardening so the house would look nice. Image, image. Donating money to this and that Armenian charity—even for the opening of an elementary school in Yerevan. Mister Big Shot when we were in public. But in private—well, I don't have to tell you. He barely spent time with us."

"Well, there's no blueprint," Gabriel offered as a small token of solace.

"Did I ever tell you what Lucine picked when we did the *hadig* for her?" she asked.

"Yes," Gabriel said, "but tell me again."

He reached over and put his hand over hers.

"She was so little, could barely sit up. We had the bedsheet covered in hadig and of all the items she reached over, it was a dollar bill. You'd think she would have crawled over to the stethoscope or gavel with the hours she works as a pastry chef. She might as well be a surgeon or a lawyer, I see so little of her."

"What about Kohar?" Gabriel asked.

"I don't remember," Takouhi answered. "Probably a pen or something."

She leaned back and closed her eyes as Gabriel pulled into a spot. A memory transported her to another time. It was after her marriage to Gabriel, during Azad's younger years, when they could all sit together for dinner and share the details of their lives. When her three girls had been younger and more innocent, when she could hear giggling and bursts of laughter from behind a closed bedroom door. Now these rooms were storage spaces, hollow and foreign, and it made Takouhi wonder: Was this what it all amounted to? Why had the play ended and when? Because really, what was it all worth when you found yourself alone?

Chapter 3

THE ENGINE DIDN'T TURN OVER WHEN LUCINE TURNED THE IGNI-tion key. The dashboard lit up for a hopeful second and then faded. She turned the key again. A dying click emitted ominously. Baffled, Lucine looked around her wonderingly, as if a prankster was hiding inside the car or in a nearby bush. Long gone were the days when she believed the universe was a realm of enduring balance: when one fucked-up thing happened, she was entitled to another fucked-up thing *not* happening. Lucine's life, it seemed, was a series of fucked-up things.

"Are you *kidding* me!" she said, and then slammed her hands on the steering wheel. A sudden pain seared her palms. "Fuck!"

She glanced at her house, wishing Steve could hear her from the confines of the car. But even if he could, at most he would watch her from a window, just to see where the commotion was coming from, and then go back to playing his video games. Steve, though, was buried under a quilt in the basement, sleeping off an extended night of drinking.

In this rare moment, Lucine missed living in New York, where she could summon a cab or take the subway to wherever she needed. Having now lived in New Jersey for the past five years, she felt the rueful irony of living so apart from her family and, for all intents and purposes, civilization. New Brunswick, and the areas of New Jersey Lucine had driven through, seemed generic hubs of convenience shopping, with oversized Targets and Kmarts, one-stop supermarkets, and unremarkable neighborhoods where resided unremarkable people, who all lived and breathed the fumes of an indefatigable monotony.

Her rationale for moving had really been a series of lies she invented for herself and to tell others: New York stressed her out (her family stressed her out), the rents were too high (she had plenty of savings but was scared to live alone), she wanted to be in nature (she spent most of her free time watching television or reading), and—the most flimsy and pathetic of all—in New Jersey they pumped the gas for you and you didn't have to get out of the car. But at the root of it all, it was Steve's emphatic insistence that he needed to get away from her family—Lucine's mother, specifically.

She wished he didn't relish so much recounting the long, menacing list of her mother's faults and the stories that went along with them. Like the Saturday afternoon when a furniture truck delivered a dining-room set to their apartment in Sunnyside after they had first gotten married. It was after Takouhi and Gabriel had visited their apartment and she had made a comment about the retro bar table and matching stools being too small for family gatherings.

"She bought this dining-room set for *her*, not us," Steve repeated for months after.

"It's a wedding gift," Lucine insisted.

"She never even came to City Hall!" he said.

"Because we told her it was a formality, and we were having a real wedding!" Lucine reminded him.

"And where would she get that idea?" he asked.

"You said we would have a family wedding," Lucine said.

"I said I would think about it. It's not my fucking fault she didn't consider us getting married at City Hall a wedding," Steve said, and would quickly and brutally uncover truths that would leave Lucine's heart aching: "She only participates in things that are of interest to *her* or that she approves of. She expected a big Armenian wedding with three hundred people we wouldn't even know. But she didn't like the idea of City Hall, so she didn't come."

"If you're saying my mother doesn't love me—" Lucine began, trying to deviate from his point.

"This has nothing to do with if she loves you or not. It actually has nothing to do with you—that's the fucked-up part. All she cares about is what is of interest to her."

It amazed Lucine. How someone as ignorant, ill-bred, and uneducated as Steve could offer such depth of insight.

Sometimes he treaded too far. "And where was your father in all of this?" he would ask.

Her father, who Steve had met in passing, she called only twice a year: Thanksgiving and Christmas. He had remarried shortly after her mother and Gabriel's marriage, reclaiming his status in the community after suffering the scandal of being left by his first wife. Worse still, he and his wife had had a daughter, Beatrice, several months after Azad was born. A hideous competition. Since his stroke five years ago, his wife was now his sole caretaker.

When Steve saw Lucine's eyes pooling with tears, he said, "Kohar was the maid of honor and happy to be there."

Sometimes, according to Steve, Kohar was the best of the bunch. At other times, he despised her. Kohar thought highly of herself, Kohar liked to drink, Kohar was a bitch. If Lucine was feeling particularly fat or tired or overworked, it suited her to believe these things about Kohar, and less and less did she defend her sister or object to Steve's snide and ugly observations. The guilt of being a traitor to the one person who had never left her side weighed upon her.

A soft rapping came from the other side of the window. Lucine jumped. The person was speaking, but the words were muffled. The glare of the morning sun shone behind the figure, the face obscured in light. Lucine opened the door and saw that it was the son of one of their neighbors.

"Do you need a lift?" he asked.

"Yeah," Lucine said. "My car won't start."

"I saw," he said. "I was about to get on my bike to take a quick ride. I can drive you in my mom's car if you want. Where are you going?"

"To work," said Lucine. "It's a bakery about ten miles away."

They walked across the street to a gray two-door Nissan parked in a driveway.

"We just have to let it warm up," he said as Lucine settled herself into the passenger seat.

The morning sky was pale and gray, and a strong wind whipped through the trees. Their wet leaves showered rain from last evening's storm. Lucine felt a quiet, familiar sadness come over her. She pulled herself away from staring out the passenger window and briefly glanced at the boy. It occurred to her that she didn't know his name.

"I'm Lucine," she said.

"I know," he said. "You brought over some scones last winter for my mom."

"Your name?" she asked.

"Max."

As he fiddled with the radio, Lucine was able to take a closer look at him. The most she had seen of him was at a distance if she happened to be looking out the window when he was dragging out the trashcan or when he was walking with his friends down the block. His eyes were either blue or green or both—she couldn't be sure—and his hair, hanging almost to his shoulders, was a fine brown-blonde, still damp from a morning shower.

"What grade are you in?" she asked.

He turned to her sharply. "Grade? I'm a sophomore in college."

"Sorry," she said, feeling the heat in her face; "when you said you were driving us in your mom's car . . ."

"Mine's in the shop," he said, his smile revealing a charm and cleverness that Lucine would wholly experience in the weeks to come.

Now she wished for a cigarette, knowing she had none. "You don't have any cigarettes, do you?" she asked self-consciously. She didn't know if he was one of those straight-edge kids, touting their celibate, clean, and sober agendas to their parents and the general public.

"I do, but they're back in the house. Hang on."

Before Lucine could tell him not to bother, he had left the car. And before she could look at the time to check if she was going to be late, he was already back in the driver's seat. He threw a pack of Marlboro Reds—an old favorite of hers—in her lap and pulled out of the driveway. "Where to, exactly?"

THE NEW-HIRE BAKERS, SALLY AND JOSÉ, WERE STANDING OUT-side under the bakery's awning when Lucine stepped out of the car. Lucine, with the key ready in her hand, breezed past them and kneeled to unlock the iron gate. She could feel the wall of silence and judgment as they stood behind her. On her knees, it felt ludicrous to Lucine that in some way they were holding her accountable for being late, when in fact she had no reason to explain herself. Besides, she was going to be manager soon. By the coming spring, Hannah, the owner, had told her.

The security alarm wailed as they bustled through the front door. Lucine faced the keypad to obscure the code and punched in the numbers.

"Turn on the ovens and the proof box," she said gruffly and headed toward the back of the bakery to look at the week's orders.

From where she had hung her purse, she could hear the buzzing of her muted phone. Lucine dashed over and saw that it was Kohar. She walked back to the metal counter and started going through the slips of paper that Hannah had left them.

She called Sally and José to the front of the store. "We have four orders for tomorrow. Come."

As she sorted out the rest of the orders by date, she heard them shuffling toward the kitchen. She could hear the surliness in their steps.

"Hannah said we can open late today. It's shit weather anyway. José, you'll bake the cakes. Sally, make enough vanilla custard for three cakes and a lemon curd for one."

She paused and looked at the last order. There was a picture of a cake stapled to it. Lucine groaned. A unicorn? Seriously? There had been an outbreak of cake orders ranging in such absurd proportions that Lucine had begun missing the tedium of baking bread. Her first job after graduating from culinary school had been working at a family-owned bakery in Long Island City. Each week had felt like one very long day of kneading, proofing, kneading, shaping dough, baking, as if she herself were a machine.

"Your car broke down?" Sally stood across from Lucine.

"Not exactly," said Lucine. "But it might as well have."

She wished the girl hadn't brought it up. Lucine was trying to stave off her anxiety that she would have to take money out of her personal savings to buy another used car.

"I can drive you home later if you want," she offered.

Although Hannah had hired Sally only a week ago, this was the third time Lucine had worked with her. The first two times had been a frenzied day of filling last-minute orders and Lucine intermittently sitting in the back room to help Hannah with the accounting. Sally was short and pear-shaped, lending her a matronly appearance. She wore a severe pixie cut and had fair skin. Her plump hands and small wrists reminded Lucine of the three fairies in *Sleeping Beauty*.

"Thanks," Lucine said. "I should be okay, though."

Sally shrugged. "Well, if you change your mind . . ."

"Are you here tomorrow? I'm only asking because I may need help assembling the cake. And I need you to pick up fondant in the morning. Otherwise, I'll do it on my way here," said Lucine.

Sally raised her eyebrows. "You're back here *tomorrow*? Aren't you staying until after closing today?"

She stared at Sally without answering, letting her eyes press down on the girl. She wanted to tell her that it was none of her business, that she had been saving money unbeknownst to Steve. Hannah was letting her use the kitchen after the bakery closed for private orders. She had practically started her own business, not that Steve noticed her absence or questioned the long hours she was working.

When Lucine had married Steve, she'd had over fifteen thousand dollars in her savings account. Of the three sisters, she was the most prudent with money. In all fairness to Kohar, who had moved out after college, she had put herself in minor debt for fear of asking their mother for money, or, worse, moving back home. As for Azad, money was a means to an end, for which she was not responsible. It was only recently that their mother had stopped paying her cell-phone bill. Lucine, on the other hand, had been paying rent on a house she could barely afford and was making payments on a car she had cosigned for Steve because of his poor credit.

"Yes, I'm here," Lucine finally spoke. "Hannah said she only needed me for a few hours in the morning. I can pick up the stuff. Now go find José," Lucine told her. "What the fuck is he doing, anyway?"

Mercifully, the day was a long blur of churning out one cake order after the next. The kind of day when Lucine stood up and felt light-headed, realizing she had forgotten to eat since the day before. She stuffed a croissant down her throat, ignoring the crispy, buttery surface and soft, wispy interior, made with perfunctory precision that she now took for granted. Before she knew it, Sally was washing up and folding her apron.

As the girl was putting on her coat, Lucine could feel Sally cast her a guilty, sidelong glance. Then she realized. "Don't worry about the ride, Sally," she called out to her. "I'll be fine."

"I'm sorry! When I offered you the ride, I didn't realize you were working a double. Do you want me to come back? I can come back—"

"Sally. Get out of here before I kick you out," Lucine barked.

"Okay—and by the way, your phone has been buzzing all day. I figured you knew that, but just in case," she said.

Lucine let out a breath, then sat down for the first time in hours. The small of her back ached and a dull pain gripped her shoulders. She fished for her phone, which she had buried in the bottom of her purse. She grabbed a cigarette and lighter and took her phone with her outside.

The rain had stopped. The sky was a dull pale gray, and all at once the world to Lucine seemed a distant, faraway place. She could feel the gloom from the morning settle within her again.

The phone buzzed in her back pocket. Without looking to see who it was, she answered. She knew perfectly well.

"Hello?"

"Where are you?" Lucine couldn't decide if he sounded like an asshole teenager or a cranky old man who had lived for too long.

"On break," she said.

"When did you leave?" *I've been passed out all afternoon and I hope you didn't notice.*

"This morning."

"How? The car's outside." *I hope you're not bluffing and talking to me from somewhere in the house.*

"I had to get a lift. It won't start."

"I'll take a look at it later." *I'll say I did and that the car needs to be towed.*

"Thanks."

"What time are you coming home?" *Do I have time to drink a beer and smoke a joint?*

"Probably not until ten or so."

"Mike may be getting me later on. Watching the game at the Galloping Green." *Hopefully I can avoid seeing you until tomorrow.*

"Okay. Have fun."

Before putting her phone away, she noticed there were four missed calls and three voicemail messages. The first was from her father. He hadn't left a message. The second was from Kohar.

"Hi. It's me again. Just miss you and want to say hi."

The voicemail continued to the third message. "This is Jamie calling. The rent was due last week. Three months now. Please call me back."

By the fourth message, Lucine was only half-listening as she cupped her hand around the lighter with a cigarette in her mouth. "This is TD Bank calling to notify you that you are currently overdrawn in your checking account. Please—"

Lucine threw the cigarette on the curb and let the lighter fall with a clatter. Frantically, she scrolled through the message and dialed the contact number. After several automated prompts and being put on hold, she was relieved to hear a human voice.

"Hi. I just received a message that my checking account is overdrawn. Can you please help me? I don't see how that's possible."

Bracing herself, she began walking away from the bakery toward a residential street. "The account number is eight-nine-three, three-four-five, nine-eight-seven-four. Yes, I'll hold," she said.

"Hi, ma'am," the voice returned; "yes, it seems it's overdrawn."

"What does that mean? A deficit. I had about three thousand dollars in that account when I checked a few days ago," Lucine said.

"You're overdrawn by two hundred fifty-seven dollars," the representative said. "Do you have an ATM card?"

"I do," Lucine said, "but I don't use it. Can I please report—"

"Is yours the only name on the account?" the representative asked.

"No. My husband's name is also on the account. Can you check the last date? Like, the last activity on the account?" Lucine asked.

"Let me check. Please hold."

Masochistically, Lucine's mind whirred back in time. She recalled the evenings past midnight she had pulled up in front of the house, her eyes burning with fatigue, her feet sore from hours of standing, then climbing into a bed that was often empty because Steve complained he was tired of waiting for her and would go out with his friends.

"Ma'am? Thank you for holding. The last activity was this morning," the representative said.

"*This* morning?" Lucine shouted. "*This?* This morning? That's not possible. I've been at work since six-thirty. How does that much money disappear? I should have been alerted," she yelled.

"Did you check with your—with the person who shares the account?" asked the representative.

Then Lucine realized. She hung up the phone and ran toward the bakery. Sally was sweeping behind the counter as Lucine ran past her toward the kitchen. She dialed Steve's number as she grabbed her purse, knowing he wouldn't answer. After ten rings, her call went to voicemail. "Welcome to the Jungle" blared into her ear, followed by Steve's voice: "Hey, you know what to do, so do it."

"Steve," she yelled into the phone. She felt the hollowness of her words, the futility of her rage. "Pick up the phone." As if she were leaving a message on an answering machine. He would never bother listening to the message, she knew.

"I have to leave," Lucine told Sally. José was filling a cake box of assorted cookies for a customer.

"Uh . . . okay," Sally said. "Everything okay?"

"No," Lucine said, letting the door bang behind her, the bells jingling noisily.

THE UBER CAB WEAVED THROUGH HER NEIGHBORHOOD STREETS while Lucine lowered the window and let the cold air chill her face. A slow, steady panic gathered within her, sure as a brooding storm. As dusk fell indiscernibly behind the carcass of clouds, Lucine understood the seven long years of her life that had brought her here. She had married impulsively, moved away from her family, purposefully isolated herself, and suffered a husband who had been hired and fired from twelve jobs. A husband who alternately drank and pill-popped and lived in the basement jerking off to photos of underaged girls.

Kohar had tried bringing up the idea that Lucine should leave him. "Leave him and go where?" was Lucine's point. She had no money. And the idea of living at home again was impossible to bear. She would have to leave her job, she had argued with Kohar. It was too much of an upheaval; and, besides, drunk or not, Steve had outlined Lucine's dilemma in a hard little nutshell of brutal truth: she was fat and ugly now, and poor. No one would want to fuck her or pay her bills. At thirty-four years old, Lucine looked at her reflection every morning and let the words wash over her as if she needed to believe them.

"Here you go," the Uber driver said, pulling up to her house. She noticed immediately that Steve's car was not parked in the driveway.

Without thanking the driver, she left the car, realizing she should have asked him to wait, given that she needed to get back to the bakery. Clutching the key in her trembling fist, Lucine headed toward the front door of her house.

Upon entering, Lucine wondered if Steve was home after all. Rarely were there vestiges of human existence upon entering the house. In fact, there had been many occasions when Lucine, after having arrived home, had been scared to death upon Steve appearing out of nowhere.

"Hello?" she called out to the empty living room. The faint light from the window cast shadows on the dining-room walls. "Steve?"

She hoped he was gone. Yet her heart pounded wildly with rage; she was certain he had taken all their savings and run off. His phone call had been a ruse.

"Steve!" she called out again, anger now swelling in her chest, as she climbed up the stairs.

Their bedroom was empty, their bed unmade. The same as how she had left it in the morning, but without him in it. Lucine crouched down on her knees and peered under the bed to find his suitcase still there. She yanked the closet light. The bare lightbulb revealed his dusty duffel bag still perched on the top shelf.

A new thought occurred to her. A thought so alarming that the possibility seemed preposterous. Lucine grabbed the footstool from the bathroom and stood in front of her closet. She could see the blue-and-white crocheted purse leaning on the far right of the shelf. It had been moved from its hiding place.

"No!" she yelled. "You fuck! How? *How?*" she yelled again, reaching for it as she balanced on her toes.

She knew right away when she yanked it down. It was lighter than she had left it. And when she zipped it open, she saw that the old silver cigarette case was gone. Not emptied of its contents, but taken—two thousand five hundred dollars, to be exact. All the money she had collected since filling private orders at the bakery.

There was no time to cry. Lucine ordered another Uber to take her back to the bakery. She wondered, given how much he had taken from her, if he would ever return. And whether she wanted him to.

It was past ten-thirty when Lucine finally closed the shop. José, who had offered her a ride, was sitting in his car while she pulled down the metal gate and snapped the locks in place.

She eased into the passenger seat as he pulled out of the parking lot.

"Rough day," José said.

"Rough day," Lucine nodded.

"You coming back tomorrow, right?"

Lucine couldn't tell if he was offering polite sympathy or if he really gave a shit. "Yeah, I'm coming back."

She closed her eyes and heard him fiddle with the radio as he whizzed through the stations before leaving it on a local Rasta radio show. Bob Marley was singing . . . *let's get together and feel all right* . . .

"Take a nap," she heard José's voice. "I know how to get you home. GPS. It's all good."

Lucine inhaled the stale sweetness of pine car deodorant. It reminded her of when her father used to take her to the local car wash. She remembered sitting in her father's Cadillac as the massive, mechanized mops washed over the car, the thrill of being engulfed by wet soapiness without getting wet. She remembered her father in the driver's seat and her sitting next to him, the grip of his strong hand over her small fingers. And then again, a merciless sadness seized Lucine. Tears began to gather behind her closed eyes. A tear slipped down the side of her face. Then another.

Oblivious, José was listening closely as the GPS began navigating him through her neighborhood. "Here we are," he said.

Her block was now a somber row of houses, all the windows darkened. Lucine saw her car parked as she had left it that morning.

"Thanks a lot," she said, clearing her throat. "I really appreciate it."

"It's no problem," he said. "If I was working in the morning, I'd pick you up. Hope you get some rest."

"Thanks. You, too," said Lucine. She pulled out her house keys and jingled them as she got out of the car. "No worries. I'm good."

She watched his car slowly disappear around the corner. Her house was like every other, quiet and dark. A dim light came through from the back of the house. Although she had left in haste, she had remembered to leave a light on for herself for when she returned home; something Steve seldom remembered to do for her despite her late hours.

She undressed and turned on the shower, avoiding her nakedness in the mirror as she let her clothes drop to the floor. Long ago she had realized that time moved with fierce velocity, like a sweeping tornado, leaving behind the wreckage of what Lucine regarded with grim acceptance: prematurely graying hair, cellulite, and oversized sagging breasts. More often now, she avoided dressing in front of the mirror.

There had been a time when Lucine could slip on a miniskirt and a pair of tall black boots and conquer the world of unruly boys and men. It was a time when by choice and design she lived on cigarettes and coffee to stay slim; when she let her long, wild hair loose, and looked behind her to literally watch them lining up. Punk boys with liberty spikes and combat boots and flight jackets; aloof and lanky pale-skinned new wave boys; metal heads with MC jackets and hair long enough to rival hers; and the wayward boys with plaid peacoats and beat-up boots and chin-length hair—all a delicious assortment for Lucine's choosing.

She had relied solely on the prowess of her beauty. Art school had been a series of one-night stands with the occasional, intense, short-lived relationship during the uncomfortable pauses of boredom. Lucine had met Steve during one of those uncomfortable pauses. It was a pause that had stretched for too long, during which she convinced herself that getting married was the obvious thing to do, the hallmark sign being that they continued dating well past the point when most of her relationships abruptly ended, which were generally one or two months long.

Realizing that her degree in graphic design was useless, she had enrolled in culinary school and met Steve when they were students together. He was reckless and passionate and mysterious. And above all, he was consumed with a lust and jealousy that left Lucine feeling overpowered and intoxicated. At the time, she had not known or cared to know that Steve had been a heroin user and still treated himself to the occasional handful of oxycodone, which, in its absence, he replaced with binge drinking. She did not know that his mother, who Steve hated and lived with because his brothers refused to, had neglected and abused him until his parents' divorce when he was twelve.

Now, standing in the hallway as she towel-dried her hair, she looked at a picture of him hanging on the wall taken during his teenage years, long after the damage had permanently set in. His blue eyes hard, his smile sly and imperious. Lucine regarded the photograph with a sickening feeling of pity and contempt. *Where could he be?* she wondered. *How long would he be gone?* And more importantly, *What had he done with all that money?*

Fuck it, she was going to pour herself a glass of wine. Bundle up, sit out on the porch, and drink. As she settled into the tattered wicker chair worn more from weather than from use, she inhaled the smell of burning fire logs drifting from a nearby house.

"Care for an end-of-the-day cigarette?"

Lucine jumped and peered into the mysterious night.

"Here. *Hellooo?*" came the sing-song voice.

A shadow from the left-hand stoop. As the hand waved, the porch lamp lit up. Max was sitting on the front steps. "I didn't mean to be creepy. Our light is a motion-detector one. How was your day?" The light shone on him like an actor on a darkened stage about to deliver a soliloquy.

"My day—" Lucine labored to find the right words—"my day sucked," she said, still standing in the darkness.

"That's too bad. You'd figure since it started sucky, it would end well," he said.

"Well, not for me. Usually it doesn't work out like that for me," she said.

"Sounds like you're tired. Hope you get some rest," he called out.

Lucine could see that he was still wearing the clothes from the morning. His frame seemed more significant now, his voice warm and deep. Slowly she walked over, aware that her mouth was dry and that her hands were itchy with perspiration.

"I'll have a cigarette," she said. "I have my own if you want one."

The cool autumn air swept over Lucine, refreshing her senses. If she looked up, she would be able to count the stars dotting the surface of a black sky. She would see a full moon amidst a gathering of clouds, glowing translucently. Steve was somewhere, anywhere that was away from her. Even he could not find enough love in his heart for her. She walked carefully, as if she were prone to trip or fall, as if she were a young teenager, self-conscious of her longing. Into the night she stepped, leaving her house to disappear into the darkness behind her.

Chapter 4

AZAD PRIED THE GOGGLES OFF HER FACE AND ADJUSTED HER thong. There were deep impressions where the goggles had been tightened several times since sunrise. Her bare eyes, now exposed to the elements of the desert, were whiter than the rest of her face and made her look like a frightened owl. She wiped off a thin layer of dust from the lenses and placed them firmly over her face.

It had been the most disorienting six days of her life, every day of which she had berated herself for accepting the last-minute invitation from her two friends. Tickets sold out months in advance, they had told her. Someone had canceled at the last minute. She would be a fool not to go.

The dry, cracked earth beneath her feet felt reassuring in the chaos that loomed miles ahead of her. From where she stood, a small cropping of human figures arose silently, as if in a ritual awakening. Some walked, others weaved through the pathless surface on bicycles and unicycles, while the more valiant rode in vehicles painted and tricked out with an ostentatious ferocity. A silver metal rhinoceros glinted quietly. A red truck donned with bullhorns pulled up in the distance, topped with a makeshift oil well. A motorcycle lurched into speed, costumed as a menacing black rat. The drivers, the passengers, the itinerants, and the cyclists circulated in an understood harmony that Azad could not at all understand. And their smiles, all of them, conveyed the same absurd contentment: it was just another day in the desert.

To avoid the heat, Azad had been waking up early and retiring to her camp before noon, which seemed always nearly empty of people, where she slept fitfully on a damp cotton sheet as the sun blazed away. Her camp, Parea, was a nondescript Brooklyn-based camp juxtaposed in the epicenter of Party Naked Tiki Bar, Afterglow, Cats, and Then There's Only Love. The names, Azad had assumed, spoke for themselves. On her first evening there, deciding not to stray very far, she had visited these camps and realized quickly that they were not as aptly named as she had thought: only the men were shirtless at Party Naked Tiki Bar; Afterglow passed out glow sticks and glow-in-the-dark body paint; Cats, much to her relief, spent the majority of their time in cat costumes licking and grooming each other; and Then There's Only Love was a free-for-all orgy of any sexual orientation that did not mandate the use of condoms.

Regardless of how little or how much time passed, Azad would remember this trip as a long and bizarre string of days that faded in and out of one another. Days where dust crept into every crevasse of her body, her mouth and limbs hot and dry, her hair a matted nest, her insides parched no matter how much water she drank. She was unmoved by the massive art installations, the drum circle towers, the pervasive nudity and drinking and drugs and themed dance parties, and the orchestrated carnival of crazy.

"Hey."

Two girls walked toward the tent. Azad didn't recognize them at first. One had a shaved head and was wearing a pair of purple goggles; the other had only one side of her head shaved, and her eyes and face were painted with sparkly pink stars.

"Where have you been?" Purple Goggles asked.

"Yeah," said Pink Stars. "We haven't seen you since we set up camp."

Wanting to seem unruffled by her friends' transformations, Azad replied, "I've been around. I guess we keep missing each other. Where have you guys been sleeping?"

The pair looked at each other and smirked. "Everywhere," said Purple Goggles.

She was Kaitlyn, who Azad had met in her senior year at college. Kaitlyn's younger cousin Ariel—Pink Stars—was a lemming who tagged along with them regularly.

"Where have *you* been sleeping?" Kaitlyn asked.

"In our tent," said Azad self-consciously, sensing that her answer was unexciting.

"We're going to Make a Wish," Kaitlyn said. Ariel stood next to her, beaming with delight.

Azad caught herself before saying something profoundly unwitty, realizing it was a camp Kaitlyn was talking about.

"It's supposed to be this really chill place. Wish-making, apparently, is a whole *thing*, like they teach you *how* to make a wish," said Kaitlyn. "Come on."

Azad walked along with them toward the middle of the playa. Now they were surrounded by everything Azad had observed from a careful distance. Music hummed from all directions as if someone were flipping through the radio too quickly. Chaos, Azad sensed, was abounding. They weaved through the ocean of canopied tents.

"It's this way," Kaitlyn said. "Look for the wishing wall." She said this as if one might say to look for a fire hydrant or a stop sign. Ariel, at Kaitlyn's heels, began looking every which way frantically. She reminded Azad of a meerkat.

"There," Kaitlyn said, pointing to a wooden trellis tied with colorful rags and began walking towards it. "They're going to take it to the temple soon. So we have to make a wish before six o'clock."

"Do you want to find out your animal spirit?" they heard from behind them. Only Ariel turned around. A bare-chested man in a cowboy hat and sunglasses stood holding a large plastic container filled with something Azad couldn't see.

"We already hung out with that guy," Ariel said.

As they continued walking, Azad overheard him speaking to a young woman whose legs were painted orange. ". . . what you do is reach in, close your eyes, and take one. Then you put it close to your heart and open your eyes. And whatever you chose is your spirit animal that will guide you for the rest of the day. Eat it. The act of ingesting it will unite you with your spirit animal."

There were three women and a man standing next to the trellis, tied in rags. All of them were wearing sunglasses and smiling what Azad would refer to as the Burning Man Smile upon looking back at this moment in her life.

"Would you like wishing ribbons?" one of the women asked. She motioned to a pile of cutout cloth laid out in a small wicker basket. "We also have paper and tape if you'd prefer that."

"Yes, please," Kaitlyn said, taking a strip of cloth. Ariel took one.

"How many wishes can we make?" Kaitlyn asked.

"We get that question a lot," said the man. "We like to limit it to two wishes so we can leave room for others. Especially today. It's the last night."

Kaitlyn sat on the dusty ground, poising herself for the next steps. "So, what do we do first?"

"Just think of a wish you have—any wish—and write it down. We'll attach it to the wishing wall," he said.

"Should I repeat it in my head a few times before writing it down?" Ariel asked.

"You can," the man replied. "Everyone has their own process. It's really up to you."

Azad stood over them awkwardly, while Ariel lowered herself to the ground with a slip of cloth and pressed a pen to her temple in deep thought.

"How about you?" one of the other women asked her. "Would you like to make a wish?"

"I have lots of wishes," Azad said. She took a piece of paper and a pen and sat a few feet away from her friends.

But nothing came to mind. She had everything that one could wish for. It was just last year that she had moved into her grandmother's home in Pennsylvania—a home that had been left to her as the only granddaughter of four grandchildren after her Grandmother Helen had passed away. Her parents had given her their Jeep after buying the more sensible MINI Cooper (her mother's idea), and they had given her a reprieve on her student loans since she "had been working so hard at the art gallery," is how her mother had put it.

Azad remembered her mother's speech that Sunday afternoon while her father had pored over an essay he was translating as part of a Russian anthology. He sat at the dining-room table half-listening. Lucine and Kohar were in the parlor, helping Jonathan light the logs in the fireplace.

"We're so proud of you," her mother had said. "An internship at one of the most well-known art galleries in Philadelphia!"

Gabriel had looked up from his pen and smiled at Azad, nodding. She had wanted to remind them that she had squandered four years of college on a fine arts degree in sculpting that she would never use. In the corner of her old bedroom was her satchel of sculpting tools, boxes of clay, and odd creations, her adolescent whimsies an unsightly embarrassment. She had just come upon the revelation that she wanted to be a painter, a pursuit that had no clear path or goal.

She had hoped her sisters and Jonathan were too absorbed by the fireplace to hear as her mother had continued. "We don't want you to worry about the college loans. We see how hard you're working, and that means everything. We'll take care of it. You're already doing everything you can. We couldn't expect more from you," her mother had said.

Azad overheard Lucine echo parts of this speech later that evening. They were all sitting around the fire listening to their mother reminisce about Christmas in Beirut. No one noticed Lucine disappearing abruptly into the old bedroom the two had once shared. Except for Kohar. Azad, pretending she needed the bathroom, had left her glass of Grand Marnier on the table and walked toward the closed door.

"'We couldn't expect more from you.'" It was Lucine's voice, her hostility clawing at Azad through the closed door. "Then why the fuck did she expect more from us? Where the fuck is *my* house? Where the fuck is *my* car?"

"We have to go back. It's going to be obvious. Mom's going to walk in here. I don't want drama. It's been a nice day," Kohar had said.

"You think it's fair?" Lucine had continued. "She sees how hard Azad's working? I worked hard. I still work hard. This is bullshit."

"Listen, at some point everyone has to struggle. We've had our share of—"

"Ex*actly*," Lucine had said. "Exactly. Struggle. Where is her struggle? What's she ever going to struggle over? You and I have struggled five times over."

"It's been like this lately, when we've all gotten together. You have to let it go," said Kohar.

"Like you let it go," Lucine had said, her voice erupting. "It's not fair. Why can't she be to us what she is to her? Because she hated Dad and she loves Gabriel?"

"This is getting ridiculous. I can't do this," said Kohar.

Upon hearing the doorknob, Azad had flown into the bathroom and closed the door behind her. She sat on the closed toilet, her heart rising in her throat, her eyes burning. She felt like a child, eavesdropping on an argument between her parents she wished she hadn't heard, burdened by the cruel knowledge of what she had suspected for years: that her sisters hated her. Perhaps not *hated*, but certainly resented. As if they had been dealt an unlucky hand of cards and she had been holding a royal flush, certainly not hard-won. The differences in how Kohar and Lucine carried themselves in light of the years of inequity revealed a great deal to Azad. Kohar, in short, tried to be a good sport about it, whereas Lucine, who had been overthrown from her position as the youngest, was otherwise.

I WISH, SHE WROTE. FROM BEHIND HER SHE OVERHEARD ARIEL ask if her wish would still come true if she told it to someone after tying it to the wishing wall. *I wish. That Krikor is the right one? That I start painting again?* Azad labored over the task as if she were contending with a midterm exam. Her wishes, she knew, were superficial or lacking in substance. As she feared she was. In the midst of nearly seventy thousand human beings who at the very least had sought and found some kind of purpose in their time in the desert, she felt as vacuous as the day she had arrived. And when the small world gathered to watch the hundred-foot wooden figure of a man blaze into flames, Azad was on the other side of the desert, lying in her tent and listening to the din of chaos.

AZAD STOOD UNDER THE WARM WATER AS DARK BROWN RIVU-lets streamed down her legs. The floor of the shower was a pool of muddy water. It was the first time she had bathed in almost a week. She squeezed the water and conditioner out of her hair several times before the water ran clear. Finally satisfied, she climbed out. Having lost track of the time, she realized she would be late to dinner at Krikor's. She had learned in her brief time away from civilization that the hour of the day didn't matter. Keeping track of the time, abiding by a schedule, was a human construct and rather stupid. But now, having returned, she knew the jig was up, so to speak.

As she dried herself and brushed the stubborn knots and tangles out of her hair, she wondered what it would be like to see Krikor again. In the several months they had been dating, Azad was waiting. For a feeling, mostly. The first time they had kissed, his lips had felt slippery and slick, familiar in an uncomfortable way. She had hoped their conversations would stir within her a longing, a consuming passion.

After all, he was Armenian. Being raised by immigrants, they had suffered the same plights (although her father was first-generation): foreign-sounding names that eluded teachers, parents who were disconnected from American culture, their unrealistic expectation of their children marrying an Armenian or, at the very least, being part of the Armenian community. Not to mention that they were a culture whose tragic history had been largely ignored for over a century.

The problem was, Krikor had drunk the Kool-Aid. He *wanted* what his parents wanted for him. And Azad couldn't be sure if this was Krikor's sincere allegiance to his love of being Armenian, or if he had blindly abided by his parents' expectations.

They had met at an art gallery where Azad was interning. It was the opening for PAFA's graduate students, where Krikor's sister had recently graduated. He was with his family, admiring a sculpture, when she overheard them speaking Armenian. After introducing herself, she came to realize that their parents were acquainted and that Krikor's mother and father had attended her father's lectures at various literary events in Manhattan. He had asked her out so casually that at first she hadn't realized it was a date.

"I'd love to hang out with you sometime," he had said. "Do you mind if I call you?"

They had met at an Indian restaurant. Azad couldn't help noticing that he had chosen the standard chicken tandoori and avoided trying the egg curry and lamb saag she had ordered. To her, it communicated his lack of adventure. As for the movie they had gone to see, she had relented, sensing that he preferred *The Amazing Spider-Man* instead of *Silver Linings Playbook*, which she had mentioned over the phone.

One date followed the next and, despite his advances, she had not slept with him. She reasoned with herself that she wanted to avoid being impulsive, her past failed relationships a result of such hasty decisions. Most all of her college friends had moved on to long-term relationships, their texts and emails riddling her phone last Christmas with "fingers-crossed" emojis, alluding to the hope of a proposal during the holidays. The enduring assumption that she would eventually meet someone was replaced with the newborn knowledge that she would only attract men who, like her, were not self-sufficient or independent.

When she chronicled the men she had either dated or considered dating, each of them had the same elemental flaw as herself, and it echoed a remark Lucine had once made: they were not fully formed adults. Mark, who she had met on a dating app she had immediately unsubscribed from, was living with his father and had started his own painting business, relying mostly on the "barter system," as he had explained to Azad. Another young man, Tom, lived with his college friends and worked as a barista at the same local coffee shop where he had been employed since his senior year of high school. So many of them were content in their aimlessness, unbothered by their unmoored existence.

Krikor was completing his MBA and still lived at home to save money, the antithesis of anyone she had dated. And although her mother only made mention of her distaste toward Steve, Azad understood her mother's deep disappointment that neither Lucine nor Kohar had married an Armenian. Her father rarely communicated such expectations. The walls of his study were lined with books that her father had inherited from his father, a Genocide survivor. She only had to step into the smoke-filled room and look at the worn spines and yellowing pages of old Armenian texts to feel the weight she had to carry. For all her misgivings, Krikor could be a harbinger of a new life for her.

As Azad rang the front doorbell, she felt suddenly uneasy. Given that this was the second time she had been over for dinner, she wondered if there was already talk of an engagement. She glanced down at her Birkenstocks, realizing that they were inappropriate for the season and occasion. Not to mention that she hadn't bothered removing the chipped purple nail polish.

"Hey!" The door opened and Krikor leaned to kiss her, the Drakkar Noir filling her nostrils. "I was about to call."

"Sorry. I had to stop off to get gas," she lied. She was only ten minutes late.

She watched him disappear into the living room, hearing him call out to his parents that she had arrived. He was wearing jeans and a dark gray button-down shirt. Exactly the kind of guy she would walk past without noticing.

"Azad! Come in," she heard Krikor's father call over.

His mother breezed into the dining room with a covered Pyrex dish, the condensation obscuring the contents.

"Hello, Azad," she said, her tone cool and reserved. Azad couldn't be sure if this was her overall demeanor, or if she was put off by Azad's lateness. "Let's eat."

Krikor pulled out a chair for her and then seated himself beside her. Then she noticed the older woman at the head of the table.

"This is my Medz-Mama," Krikor said as Azad was about to introduce herself.

"Oorakh em," the woman nodded politely. *Pleased to meet you.*

Azad could feel the old woman's eyes on her, as if unveiling her, somehow aware of Azad's thoughts.

"I spoke to your mother the other day," said Krikor's mother as she passed along a dish of tabouleh. "She said you were at a festival? In the desert?"

"Yes," said Azad, immediately wanting to change the topic.

"Ansovor." *Out of the ordinary.*

Azad understood the subtext.

"What was it like there?" Krikor asked.

Azad knew he was attempting to normalize the strangeness of her trip. "Very different," she said.

Sitting at the dining-room table with his family, Azad felt like she was a visitor from another planet. Describing the last week of her life to anyone, especially to Krikor's family, was laughable.

"When I think of the desert, all that comes to mind is Der Zor," said Krikor's mother.

She was referring to the Syrian desert, where the Ottomans had sent Armenians on death marches during the Genocide.

"Ma—please. Everything isn't about the Genocide," Krikor said.

Krikor's mother paused and stared at him.

"I'm sorry," he said. "I didn't mean to offend you."

"Well. I *am* offended," she said. "We were forced to walk through the desert until we died of heat and starvation, and yet there are people that choose to go there for fun and entertainment."

Azad had to control the urge to excuse herself and leave. Instead, she said, "I went there for the purpose of a painting I'm working on. It wasn't recreational, though my parents think otherwise. I've been working on this for quite some time. Please don't mention it to my mother, should you speak to her again," Azad said, speaking only to Krikor's mother.

"*We*," Krikor muttered under his breath.

"What was that?" his mother's sharp tone silenced the room.

"*You* didn't walk anywhere," said Krikor, surprising Azad. She had expected him to balk at his mother's question. "And Azad was in *Nevada*. Which is hell and far gone from Der Zor."

"It's getting intense in here!" interrupted Krikor's father. He smiled at Azad, winked. "Dughas, get the oghee," he said.

Krikor went to the liquor cabinet and returned with a bottle of ouzo. His mother continued passing along the dishes, now at a mechanical pace.

"Don't upset your mother," Krikor's grandmother said in Armenian.

The old woman wore a maroon quilted housedress, her gray hair held in a tight bun. Azad could tell that she spoke very little English.

"Are you still working at the art gallery?" Krikor's father asked.

"Well, right now I'm interning," Azad said. Again, she was in the spotlight and Krikor's father had unwittingly placed her there. "I think in the spring there will be a position opening for assistant to the director, and hopefully they'll hire me."

She could have kicked herself. *Hopefully they'll hire me.* She sounded desperate, lacking confidence.

"Azad, tell us about your sisters," said Krikor's father.

"My sister Kohar is the oldest—she's a teacher and a writer. And Lucine is a pastry chef in New Jersey. Although there's a big age difference, we're all very close," she said.

"What age difference?" Krikor asked. "You showed me a picture of them. You all look the same age."

"Kohar's fourteen years older than me," said Azad.

"Fourteen years!" Krikor's mother exclaimed. "Why such a big difference?"

Though she had no reason to be ashamed, Azad could feel the heat in her face. "My mother was married once before, and Kohar and Lucine are from that marriage. Their father also remarried and had his own—"

She knew there was no reason to provide the complications of her family's dynamic or her sisters', but it was too late.

"So they're your half-sisters," Krikor's mother said.

"We don't think of each other that way," replied Azad. *I'm going to stuff that fucking dolma down your throat.*

"It all seems very complicated," Krikor's mother said, shaking her head as if it were too much to take in.

Azad knew the empty silence was for her to break. "My mother tells me your father was a famous artist," she said to Krikor's mother.

"Famous, well . . . one could say, yes," she said.

"And how about your mother?" Azad asked, turning to Krikor's grandmother. "Does she speak English, by the way?"

"Very little," Krikor answered. "But she understands almost everything. Right, Medz-Mama?" he asked, smiling at her.

The woman simply nodded and continued eating her meal.

"My mother has a different talent, if you want to call it that," said Krikor's mother. "She can read coffee cups. She'll read yours after dinner."

"No, that's okay," Azad said, the words leaving her so immediately that she wondered if she seemed rude in declining.

"You have to," pressed his mother. "Anyone she meets for the first time, she reads their cup."

This seemed implausible. A lie.

Yet, after dinner, Azad found herself sipping a cup of Armenian coffee. She drank it quickly, hoping to finish it and take it to the kitchen herself.

"Let me take a look," said the old woman.

Azad was almost done. She showed her demitasse cup to the woman. She nodded and gestured for Azad to finish. Dutifully she took the last sip and followed the woman's instructions.

"Swirl it around," said the old woman. "And then turn it over. Don't move it after that."

The old woman ushered them into the parlor while Krikor and his mother were in the kitchen. Azad didn't know whether she wanted Krikor to join them, but knew it was a private affair.

"Hayeren guh khosees?" the old woman asked. *Do you speak Armenian?*

"Yes," said Azad.

"Then answer yes in Armenian," the woman scolded.

"Ayo," said Azad.

"Ayo. Good," the old woman nodded and lifted Azad's overturned cup off its saucer.

Azad, perched on the couch, waited in the uncomfortable silence as the woman held the cup in her hand, circling it back and forth.

"Toon eench khent deg katseres es," the woman commented. *What a crazy place you've been to.*

She continued speaking in Armenian. "You're not going on any trips for a while," she said. "You don't have anyone visiting your home either. But there are two pairs of eyes. Like a pair of foxes. They're looking at your home. Like they are hungry for it."

Azad had learned the first rule of having your cup read: You never ask questions. You listen.

"There is lots of fighting in your home. Not the one you live in now. Another one. Lots of fighting," the old woman said. She shook her head, bewildered.

Then she paused slightly, furrowed her brow, and looked deeply into the dried coffee grains.

"You are going to experience a very big change in your life," the old woman said finally. "There will be an ending and a beginning. Something significant in your life is going to end. It's going to end quickly. Before you realize it, it will be over."

"What else?" asked Azad, unable to stop herself from asking.

"Then a beginning, like I was saying. Something new that you've never experienced. Something new for everyone in your life. A blessing. A flower. A brilliant red flower."

"When?" asked Azad.

"It will happen at the same time. Almost simultaneously."

Azad was about to thank her, and then remembered a second rule: You never thank a coffee reader. As she stood up, the old woman spoke again.

"But these fights," she continued, surprising Azad. "It's like two enemies. Nobody can win."

Azad waited, hoping the old woman would move on.

"Vicious." She gazed at the cup as if she was watching a disturbing scene in a film. She shook her head again. "Normal che," the old woman said, borrowing from her limited English vocabulary. *It's not normal.*

Again, Azad waited. It was the second time that evening she'd found herself fighting the impulse to spring out of her seat and leave.

"Hasgutzar?" the old woman asked. *Do you understand?* Azad knew the woman was looking for acknowledgement of the truth. But who was she to ask? How was it any of her business?

Azad felt the heat rise in her face. She shrugged her shoulders. "Chem keeder," she said. *I don't know.*

"Ayo," the woman insisted. "Toon keedes. Shad lav keedes." *You know. You know very well.* As if Azad was responsible.

She held the cup in her hand, her eyes probing Azad. She wondered what else the woman was able to discern.

"Ankayn," said the old woman, lowering Azad's coffee cup and turning it over on the saucer.

Relieved, Azad gave her a small smile and rose from the couch. Quickly, she headed to the hallway for her coat, hoping Krikor wouldn't have time to intercept.

"You're not leaving, are you?" She felt him standing behind her as she opened the coat closet.

"I have to," Azad said, relieved to find her parka hanging in plain sight and grabbing it.

"Why?" he asked. "Did my grandmother say something? She's a little abrasive, but it's how she is. Don't take it personally."

"Not at all," Azad said. "I have to go in early tomorrow and I'm tired from the trip."

"Let me walk you to your car," he offered.

"It's fine. I'm right outside," she said and went to thank his parents and leave.

"Wait. Azad." His voice rose with slight alarm. She turned to him. "I wanted to take you out next week. I made reservations at that Italian place we keep seeing. How's Saturday night?"

Azad noticed the beads of perspiration that dotted his brow. His cheeks were flushed. "Sure," she said and kissed him. "I'll call you soon."

Sitting in her car, she looked out at Krikor's house, taking in the details of the evenly trimmed hedges and the neat row of chrysanthemums. The exterior of the home looked like a photograph that could be listed as one of the many sought-after homes in Wayne County.

She started the car and turned off the radio. She needed, desperately, silence. A quiet mind. And as she drove down the block, Azad remembered why you never thank a coffee reader: It will undo their prophecy. She wondered if maybe she should have thanked the old woman after all.

Chapter 5

"BADMEH NAYEENK," GABRIEL SAID.

Jonathan smiled, lifted the camera, and aimed it at Gabriel. The early-morning sunlight illuminated the bookshelves that ran around the circumference of the room.

From his crash-course years of listening to Armenian and deciphering mysterious idioms, Jonathan understood. Literally, it translated to mean "tell me." What it really meant was: Tell me what's going on in your life.

"Not much," he said. He pointed the camera at the cherrywood step-ladder, then at the vintage candlestick phone. "I love this room."

Gabriel looked at the space he had occupied during the span of his career with fresh eyes, appreciating the worn leather chair he had sat in for so many years, making a living as an Armenian translator, among other things. His office, the smallest of all the rooms in the apartment, was where everyone gravitated. Perhaps it was the odd charm of the custom-made bookshelves, the glass amber ashtray filled with unfiltered cigarette butts, the old digital clock-radio that perpetually emitted jazz music, his over-sized writing desk, and volumes of books.

"How's Kohar?" Gabriel asked.

Jonathan held the camera and leaned in closely. "I'm just testing right now," he said. He snapped two photographs and then looked at the digital image. "The lighting is nice this time of day. How many do you need?" he asked.

"Just one," said Gabriel.

"She's doing good," Jonathan said. "The trip was beautiful."

"Should I ask the big question?" Gabriel asked.

"What big question?" Jonathan asked. He paused. "No. Nothing to ask."

"Why? What's going on?" asked Gabriel.

"Nothing," said Jonathan. "We've decided to stop trying. It's too much."

"That's such a shame," said Gabriel. He shook his head. "For what you've had to go through. Maybe for now, that's all you can do."

"Yeah."

"Sit," said Gabriel. He extended the soft pack of unfiltered cigarettes. Jonathan took one, lit it, and sat on the lowest rung of the stepladder.

"Do you want to know something?" he asked.

"What's that?"

"I wanted a girl. Not a boy," said Jonathan.

"Girls are great," said Gabriel, smiling appreciatively.

This was their way. Upon their first meeting, when Kohar had brought Jonathan to the apartment for dinner, Gabriel had invited him into his study for a drink. Outnumbered in a family of strong-willed women, it was where the two men retired. It was where Jonathan confided in Gabriel, knowing that once the door was closed, it all remained in the small, warm space, preserved by time.

The loud crackle of a record player emitted from the living room. Then the jolting volume of Armenian music. They heard Takouhi's heavy footsteps as she barged in. "Gabriel, did you get the suitcases from our storage unit?"

Gabriel looked up at the cracked plaster of the ceiling as if searching for the answer. Tucked under her arm was a black rectangular canvas pouch. She unzipped it, opened it like a book. Her graying hair was gathered on top of her head with an oversized hair clip. A black claw.

"This side has all the travel documents. I just printed them out. I just put our passports in here," she said, showing them. The holy grail. Gabriel pictured her carrying the black pouch around the airport through the duration of their trip and until they reached the hotel in Yerevan. She would open it and close it obsessively. Triple-check that the contents were still in place.

"I didn't get the suitcases, no," Gabriel said.

"I have to do everything," she said. "Fine. Now let me go do this."

"I can go if you want," Jonathan offered.

"No, no. It's okay, Jonathan. It's kind of a mess down there. There's a lot to go through. The suitcases are buried."

She disappeared down the hallway and into the lobby.

Jonathan waited to be sure she had left. "And please tell Takouhi not to ask Kohar about it," Jonathan said, crushing his cigarette.

He held the camera and stood in the corner of the cramped space. He clicked several times. "How many do you need?" he asked.

"Just one," Gabriel said again. "Why are you taking so many?"

"So you can choose," said Jonathan. "I do this all day. The more you have to choose from, the better. Then just tell me what image, and I'll touch it up in Photoshop."

"Did you always know you wanted to do this for a living?" asked Gabriel. "I wish Azad had more direction. So unpredictable—kids." Then after a moment, "I feel bad we didn't have more," said Gabriel.

"Why? Azad has Kohar and Lucine," said Jonathan.

"Not for her," said Gabriel, smiling. "For myself. I wish me and Takouhi had been able to have more."

Jonathan grew quiet. He leaned against the wall and began scrolling through the shots.

"It'll happen," Gabriel said.

"Yeah," said Jonathan, lifting the camera to his face.

Gabriel could hear the defeat in his voice. "You'll see," he said.

"It's been especially awful for Kohar," he said. "I can't watch her upset again. Over and over like that."

"It's not easy to watch," said Gabriel.

"It's not," said Jonathan.

"Listen, you've done what you can for now. You're doing the right thing," Gabriel said. "Sometimes you have to do nothing."

"I hope so," said Jonathan.

"Are we done?" asked Gabriel. "Stay for breakfast."

"Almost," said Jonathan. "Do something for me. Lean into the camera and give me your best smile."

Gabriel adjusted his gold-rimmed glasses and smoothed out his graying beard. "You know what makes me smile?" he asked as he leaned in the direction of the lens.

"What?" asked Jonathan.

"Peace and quiet," he said.

Gabriel smiled an encompassing smile. One that communicated a childlike happiness, an unburdened man who had all the love to give.

IT WAS AN HOUR LATER, AND HE WAS STILL LABORING OVER RSVP emails to his retirement party. He was supposed to forward them to the manager of the Armenian literary journal, where he had served as senior editor for the past two decades.

"Gabriel! Are you ready?" Takouhi's voice carried from the far end of the apartment to his office.

On days like this, he especially missed the girls' living at home. When he worked at home, there had always been the interruptions for the use of his electric pencil sharpener, a silver Sharpie (for what he was never told), a cigarette (Kohar had started smoking in high school and Gabriel hadn't bothered telling Takouhi), a sympathetic ear during a sibling squabble, and, later on, in matters of young love. It was the other disturbances he minded. Namely, the fights between Takouhi and Kohar.

"Gabriel!"

He leaned back and closed his eyes, rubbing them with the heel of his palm. He groaned softly as he heard Takouhi bounding down the corridor toward his office.

"Are you ready?" she asked.

The room suddenly smelled of perfume and hair spray. Takouhi stood in front of him, her freshly applied lipstick too maroon for his liking, her eyelashes thick with mascara.

"Where are we going?" he asked, bracing himself.

"Lechters is going out of business. We said we would take a ride to Old Country Road early."

"We? You. *You* said. And I told you I have a few articles to finish and the RSVPs—"

"Why can't Nerses do it himself? He's the manager, isn't he? Why are you handling RSVPs for your own retirement party? I don't understand this. We never spend any time together."

Gabriel closed his eyes as if he were about to pray. "Can we go later?" he asked.

"Just forget it, Gabriel. Later will be too late. Traffic. And nothing will be left," she said.

"What are we buying, anyway?" he asked.

"I just want to look. The holidays are coming. Maybe they have something nice. And then I thought we could go to lunch somewhere," said Takouhi.

"I have to do this right now, and then we'll go. Okay?" he offered.

"I hate that you work at home. Do I work at home?" she asked.

"You work at a jewelry shop in Midtown," Gabriel said.

"Which I hate at this point," Takouhi said.

"So quit! I keep telling you to quit!"

"And do what?"

"I don't know!" Gabriel was almost shouting.

"You know what—forget it. I was going to leave the dishes from last night's dinner until later, but I'll do it. And the laundry. And everything else."

Without giving him a chance to respond, she closed the door behind her, as if she was punishing him, and disappeared.

Gabriel quietly prided himself in his innate ability to understand Takouhi. Sometimes it felt as arbitrary as catching a vase before it tipped over or carrying an umbrella before dark clouds gathered. At other times he could predict her eruptions as though they depended on the day or season; an idle weekend with no definitive plans sent her stalking through the house in a cleaning and reorganizing frenzy, the gentle shift from winter to spring left her catatonic in bed for a string of weeks. Alternately, in her brighter moods she would throw the windows open and play her collection of Armenian folk songs at a deafening volume while cooking a dizzying array of dishes in the kitchen. As he pored over a difficult passage in his study, he would hear her heavy-footed dancing through the foyer in time with a song she would repeat four, seven, nine times on the record player.

For all the hours he spent in his study, and despite how early he woke to begin his work or how late into the evening he toiled over the last of what he needed to complete, it had not occurred to Gabriel that Takouhi's erratic moods were a reaction to how indisposed he seemed to be. Every time he found her sleeping in bed on a beautiful afternoon or banging and shutting the kitchen drawers with apparent venom, the only thought that crossed his mind was that Takouhi needed, desperately, something meaningful to occupy her time.

Unlike other Armenian husbands, he had encouraged her to pursue a variety of interests, but none seemed to hold her attention for very long. Her talents ranged from cooking to interior design to sewing elaborate gowns to singing and piano playing, and yet she had continued staying home after they enrolled Azad in elementary school. Takouhi had wasted her days idly watching soap operas, going to the mall, leafing through catalogues that came in the mail. Gabriel supposed the boredom had finally gotten the better of her when she started perusing the classifieds. When she accepted the first job she had been offered as a receptionist at a real estate agency within walking distance from their apartment, Gabriel was dismayed. He wavered between expressing enthusiasm and confronting her for not finding something more suitable. But he worried that she would interpret his reaction negatively, accuse him of being discouraging.

Takouhi was unhappy working at the jewelry shop. Now, she returned home irritable and tired, reminding him how she carried the weight of a job as well as having to cook dinner every night. And for the times she didn't prepare Gabriel lunch or cook him meals, or the evenings she turned her back to him without kissing him good night, Gabriel did not bear this as the punishment for the crime of neglecting her. It was her own personal crisis, for which she was solely obligated and responsible. Though he could not even admit to himself that perhaps he took on the literal volumes of work that he did to avoid her existential dilemma. And so, without ever question or protest, Gabriel left Takouhi to her moods. Through the passing years, he wished desperately that the girls, mostly Kohar, would do the same. It kept life simple.

It was at an Armenian lecture in the city that he had first seen Kohar, then ten years old, lingering by a display table lined with books that were to be sold at the conclusion of the evening. Her hair was plaited in long braids, lending her the appearance of a younger child, and she stood aimlessly, shifting back and forth, swaying on her feet. Though Gabriel was mostly listening, he grew distracted by her in an amused way. It was not until his focus shifted fully, a magnetic draw from the front row, where he saw a head turn in Kohar's direction. A head of hair that reminded him of Prell Shampoo commercials in the mid-'80s, radiating bounce and shine, promising a beautiful face which in this instance did not disappoint. The woman's large, honey-brown eyes flashed with intense anger, commanding the girl to return to her seat. To Gabriel's surprise, the girl shook her head and remained standing next to him.

Gabriel looked more carefully after the woman faced the lecturer, and regarded another younger girl, facing forward obediently, sitting next to the woman with an empty seat between her and a man. When the lecture ended, Gabriel moved toward the front row, as if pulled by gravity. Meanwhile, the woman waded swiftly through the crowd to reclaim the girl, who was now walking toward her mother timidly. Only several feet away from her, too distracted with her daughter, Gabriel was able to fully absorb the woman's beauty, her voluptuous figure, her dramatically large eyes, the perfume of her skin. He felt as if he had been struck, shaken, as if waking from a dark and elaborate dream. And as he walked home that evening, he often thought of the older girl, resisting her mother's command, and her younger sibling, whose face he had only seen for a moment.

How little had changed. Although Lucine was the more abrasive of the two, Kohar challenged Takouhi's expectations, unwilling to sequester herself in her room as Lucine did so often. Why couldn't she sleep over at her friend's house? Why wasn't she allowed to apply to colleges with dormitories? Why was she giving Lucine a hard time about coming home a few minutes past curfew? Kohar fought for everyone. It was tiring to watch, to overhear from behind a closed door. It seemed that the proverbial bombs detonated every day, everywhere, for the many years before Kohar moved out. Azad, the tempering entity (how brutally would they have argued without the presence of a child?), the perplexed bystander, hid with Gabriel. He loved them each heartily, fully. Kohar, for naïvely braving too far; Lucine, for accepting his love so easily; Azad, for giving him enduring purpose.

Now, Gabriel sat in the silence of his office, guessing that Takouhi was in the building's laundry facility—for him, a momentary respite. Within the cramped and narrow space of his study, he was able to sustain his two favorite indulgences without Takouhi scrutinizing: Camel cigarettes and peanut butter. He always hid an extra carton in a small desk drawer that wasn't visible. And the family-size jar of Skippy peanut butter (the butter knife fit neatly inside without ever having to be taken out) he kept in a deeper drawer that was meant for filing papers.

It was only recently that he had been hiding a new discovery that he felt was tantamount to nothing. At first it had been a speck. A tiny drop, not even the size of a pebble, but smaller. Every time he coughed into a tissue, he saw bright red droplets of blood. Perhaps his throat was irritated. Perhaps he needed some throat lozenges. He buried the tissues in the wastepaper basket by his desk and eventually tied the plastic bag into a knot and threw it away in the garbage.

Suddenly, the door flew open. The doorknob crashed against the wall. Takouhi stood in front of the fortress of books on Gabriel's desk, only her head visible.

"What is this?" Takouhi demanded. She shook her fist with aggravation, holding the evidence in her hand.

"What is what?" Gabriel sighed, already defeated. He looked up from his computer. "What?"

Takouhi raised a piece of cloth in the air, waved it emphatically. "This."

She opened it up. It was one of the linen napkins from the dinner party. Gabriel gasped inwardly when he saw the three crimson patches, not the microscopic, innocuous droplets he hadn't bothered scrutinizing for some time now. He could feel a cold perspiration gathering at his temples. Still, he wanted to counter by lying. Why would that be *his* napkin, specifically? Maybe it's from when Shant spilled wine on the tablecloth. Maybe someone indiscreetly blew their nose and there had been a bit of blood.

"It's *not* wine," she barked. "And it's yours because you're the messiest eater at the table, and although all the food stains should cover this horrible red, they don't."

Gabriel sighed again and took a sip of cold coffee.

"What is this?" she asked again.

"I don't know," he said, smiling.

They both understood the significance of the smile. It was the smile of surrender when Takouhi would discover that half a block of the Dubliner cheese they had bought from Costco had been mysteriously eaten or the extra pot of pilaf she had made on a Sunday for Monday's dinner had been half-devoured or when a notice arrived in the mail for an unpaid parking ticket Gabriel hadn't mentioned receiving.

"I didn't even notice it," he said, this time telling the truth.

"I'm sure you didn't. Otherwise, you would have thrown it in the garbage," said Takouhi. "Has this happened before?"

"Yes." He wanted desperately to retract his words. An interrogation was about to ensue.

As if in preparation, Takouhi went over to the radiator and rested herself against it and folded her arms against the bosom of her apron. "For how long now?"

"I don't know honestly," he said. "Maybe a few months."

"Gabriel, do you understand that this could be something serious?" Her lips folded into a grimace. "This could be serious," she said, and wiped her eyes of fresh tears. "I'm going to call Dr. Kochabian. See if I can get a referral."

"A referral?" Gabriel wanted desperately to reach for another Camel. "For what?"

"For what . . ." Takouhi muttered and paused, looked at the walls lined with bookshelves. "For an *oncologist*!" she erupted.

Gabriel sucked his teeth and shook his head. "My throat is probably irri—"

"From what?" Takouhi roared. "From your goddamn cigarettes! Every day I tell you—"

When she saw Gabriel roll his eyes to the ceiling she stopped short. "This isn't one of my lectures, Gabriel," she said. "This could be very serious. What are we going to do if there's something wrong? What am *I* going to do? What?"

Gabriel wished she could have spared him her tragic, private thoughts. Her transparency was frightening.

"Fine," he huffed. "Get me an appointment for an oncologist. I'll go."

As he finished speaking, Takouhi had already risen, had already disappeared into their bedroom. He could hear the door not slam completely, but bang several times, like an angry echo of accusation.

Chapter 6

THE ONCOLOGIST'S WAITING ROOM WAS LIKE EVERY OTHER DOC-
tor's office: the identically furnished chairs, the dull blue wall-to-wall car-
peting, the unobtrusive lighting, and, least interestingly, the strangers who
perused out-of-date magazines or their cell phones. The fact that it was an
oncologist's office is not what Gabriel found the most jarring. Rather, it
was the out-of-season, bright-pink tulips that sat in a clear vase at the receptionist's desk. He wondered what kind of flowers people would be bringing
him when he was admitted to the hospital. Gabriel sat in front of the large
window with a book in his hand while Takouhi sat alongside him filling
out a sheaf of papers, her reading glasses perched on her nose. Takouhi had
always assumed the responsibility for their bills, the mortgage payments,
calling the super if there was a leak, and returning and making phone
calls—essentially, any of the tedious details of their day-to-day existence.
Yet watching her fill out his name and address and telephone number and
all the other blanks that he was more than capable of writing in himself, it
felt as if he was already sick and she had asserted her new role as his caretaker.

Even in Dr. Kochabian's examining room just the day before, where
Gabriel, bare-chested, had sat on the exam table, she had stood over him,
repeating the doctor's prompts as if he were a child or incapable of following a direction after only hearing it once. With every breath that Gabriel
drew, as the doctor had told him to inhale deeply, exhale deeply, as he had
felt the cold silver stethoscope pressed against his back and chest, there was
Takouhi. "Breathe in, he said. Breathe out now. That's it. Now breathe in
again."

The doctor's questions, not as interrogatory as his grueling conversation
in his study, felt like an oral examination, the answers to which carried a
great weight and portent for his future. It had also exposed Gabriel not

only to Takouhi, but to himself. The sturdy tarp that had faithfully concealed the portrait was cruelly torn off, the grotesque truth undeniable.

"Still smoking?" It was easier to answer the question with Dr. Kochabian looking down at his clipboard, pen in hand.

"Yes," said Gabriel, wincing as if about to receive a blow. He expected Takouhi's admonishing glare. Instead, he saw that she was looking away toward the drawn blinds.

"You've lost fifteen pounds since your last visit," the doctor noted. Gabriel looked at him perplexed. "July. For bronchitis."

Now he remembered. It was again, upon Takouhi's insistence, when his hacking cough woke up both of them in the middle of the night, that she had dragged him in to the doctor's office the next morning. He had been near to unconscious from lack of sleep. He remembered standing on the scale as the medical assistant had pulled the scale weight across the bar while Takouhi sucked her teeth; 310 pounds.

"Have you been trying to lose weight?" Dr. Kochabian asked.

Takouhi, her gaze still averted, shook her head. "No," said Gabriel.

"Have you been coughing excessively? After the antibiotics, I mean," the doctor asked.

"No . . . not really," Gabriel began. "Not more than—"

"Yes," Takouhi interrupted, finally speaking. "You have been. He *has* been," she said, turning to the doctor. "He had a terrible coughing fit the other day. Should I tell him about the napkin, or do you want to?" She looked away again. Gabriel knew that her anger was too terrible, too violent now, for her to acknowledge his face.

Perceptively, Dr. Kochabian waited. "When I cough, sometimes blood comes up," Gabriel said.

"How much? And for how long has this been happening?"

This is what an execution must be like. Gabriel mulled over the question. Processing the answer, let alone uttering it, was a true test of grit. "Several months now," he said. "It was only a few drops. And then there was a bit of blood the other day during dinner. I guessed it was just from the bronchitis," he offered.

"You *guessed*," Takouhi hissed, folding her arms tightly.

"I'm going to refer you for an upper endoscopy," said Dr. Kochabian.

"Should I be worried?" Gabriel asked.

"We don't know anything yet," said the doctor.

As he continued talking, Takouhi walked over to the closed curtains and turned her back. Gabriel saw her body convulsing in small tremors, her shoulders shaking, as she cried quietly.

". . . areas of irritation and a biopsy. If you call right away you may be able to get an appointment by tomorrow at the earliest. They'll send the results back to me and we'll take it from there."

They rode home in silence after the appointment. As Takouhi drove more erratically than usual, Gabriel sat upright in the passenger seat, as if he were about to be dropped off somewhere, waiting for the intense nicotine withdrawal to subside.

"Don't tell the girls anything," he said finally. It was the only viable way of drawing Takouhi out of her growing mania.

Unsurprisingly, Takouhi stared at the road ahead and gripped the steering wheel with both hands.

"I'm serious. Not Kohar. Not any of them. Let's wait. This could be nothing," he assured her. Timidly, he reached over and touched the back of her neck. Like she'd been snakebitten, she thrashed out her arm to repel his touch.

Finally turning off the highway, Takouhi turned left sharply as the yellow light changed to red. Gabriel's chest tightened. He sighed and looked out the window. There would be no mitigating. He knew for that evening—to begin with, anyway—he would be surrounded by walls of silence. No matter where he went, Takouhi would abandon the space he settled himself into, and when he lay in bed and turned his back to her that evening, he would fall asleep suffering her indomitable reticence.

And it happened so fast. So very quickly. Like a film that cuts from one scene to the next, one more dreadful than the previous: Gabriel went for the upper endoscopy the following afternoon (in the midst of imploding, Takouhi had made sure of making an emergency appointment). Dr. Kochabian called later that evening with the results and the name of an oncologist on Long Island. And the very next day, Gabriel was staring at a vase filled with fresh, clear water and tulips that were bizarrely pink, suspiciously spray-painted, and he wondered to himself: *Do they change the water every morning, or every other morning?* Gabriel, who carried a book at all times—for distraction or work or amusement—could only stare at the worn cover of *Confederacy of Dunces* he held in his hands, as he waited to hear the receptionist call his name.

Chapter 7

IT WAS BY CHANCE THAT JONATHAN HEARD KOHAR'S PHONE VI-
brating on the kitchen counter; usually she was the first to wake up and
make coffee. Kohar, most likely recovering from a *Lost* marathon and several gin-and-grapefruit cocktails, was still sleeping. Now that she had returned to work, he let her sleep in on the weekends.

Ignoring the phone, he reached for the coffee grinder and put up a
kettle of water to boil. But seconds after the buzzing stopped, it resumed.
Jonathan exhaled. He knew who it was, who would call so persistently, so
doggedly at this hour of the day.

"Hello?" He wedged the phone between his shoulder and jaw as he
opened the cabinet for the coffee mugs.

"Jonathan. Hi. Is Kohar there?"

"Hi, Takouhi. She's still sleeping," he said, now measuring teaspoons of
coffee into the French press and trying not to lose count as he spoke.

"It's nine-thirty. Is she sick?" she asked.

Any measure of unpredictability had to be accounted for. "No. She's
sleeping in," he said and heard the bathroom door pull closed from upstairs. "I'll tell her you called, though."

Without waiting for an answer, he hung up the phone and went upstairs. "Kohar," he called to her softly. "You okay?" He turned the doorknob, hoping she hadn't locked it. He found her resting against the bathtub
holding a cloth in her hand. She looked up at him vaguely. "Are you okay?"
he asked again.

Kohar nodded weakly. She was wearing an old Metallica T-shirt of his
from high school. "I don't know what happened. I just got sick."

"How many drinks did you have last night?"

"Two," she said.

"Did you eat anything weird? Indian food?" he asked.

She felt too weak to remind him that Indian food wasn't weird just because he didn't like it. She managed a smile. "No . . . not Indian food. I don't think I ate anything, actually. I'd say maybe I'm nervous about going back to work, but I still have time."

Although she was approaching her fourteenth year of teaching, Kohar sometimes felt the usual anxiety about returning to work. The back-to-school jitters, she and her friends called it.

He helped her back into bed and brought her a glass of club soda. "Do you have anything going on today? You should stay in bed. Rest."

Kohar eased under the covers and closed her eyes. Jonathan didn't want to have to tell her. "Can you bring me my phone?"

"Your mom called. Several times." He reported the grim news with the gravity of a news anchor recounting the death toll of a hurricane. He looked away. Kohar had slipped beneath the sheets and covered her face with a pillow. "It sounded urgent, though."

Now she ripped the pillow off her face and cocked an eyebrow. They both knew that as far as Takouhi was concerned, anything ranging from running out of nail-polish remover to not being able to get in touch with Azad to unreturned phone calls from Lucine classified as something urgent.

"She seemed oddly insistent this morning, though," Jonathan offered, always wanting to mitigate the tension that gripped Kohar at the slightest provocation when it concerned Takouhi.

"I'll call when I feel like it," she said flatly and aimed the remote control at the TV set and watched it spring to life.

From beneath her bedsheets they both heard her phone vibrate yet again. Kohar scrolled through the channels, waiting for the persistent ringing to end. Then her phone bleated plaintively. Kohar finally grabbed it and saw four missed phone calls from her mother, one from Lucine, and a text message as well. *Pick up the phone. Idiot.*

"I have to call Lucine," she said.

Before she could dial the number, another wave of nausea swept over her. Springing out of bed, she pushed past Jonathan, who was now staring at her, and raced back to the toilet. More vomiting. Moments later, she emerged and slipped back into bed, where Jonathan was waiting with a damp cloth.

"You may have a virus," he said, as he cooled her forehead with the cloth. "Stay in bed and I'll call your mother to tell her you're not well. I'll text back to Lucine. Let's go to a walk-in clinic later when you're feeling better."

Kohar watched as he closed the door behind him, as if he were a prison guard leaving her in a cell from which there was no escape. So he would call Takouhi and tell her Kohar wasn't feeling well. All that would do was to amplify Takouhi's anxiety, her irrepressible impulse to call persistently—or worse: come over unannounced. As Kohar slumped back into her pillow and rested her eyes on the television screen, she felt the beginnings of a dull headache at the base of her neck and mercifully fell asleep.

"Mom left me two messages to call her back."

Kohar was sitting upright in bed nibbling on a Ritz cracker, with her phone on speaker mode. Lucine's voice filled the air.

"And what did she say?" Kohar asked. "She called all morning, but I wasn't feeling well."

"Did I say I called her back?" Lucine snapped back. "Fuck no."

Kohar smiled. Lucine, so quick to anger, amused Kohar.

"I'm seeing my therapist again," Kohar said.

"Good for you."

Kohar wondered if Lucine's snide tone was really one of envy for Kohar having the time to see a therapist, or if Lucine thought it was a frivolous pastime tantamount to that of crocheting or joining a book club.

"She has nothing to focus on but me," said Kohar. "I know how self-absorbed that sounds, but it's true. Both you and Azad don't live in New York, and I feel like she expects me to see her on the weekends. And I'm not saying this is your fault or Azad's fault. I just don't know how to deal with her."

"Join the club."

Lucine, for all her hard-heartedness, seemed also obtuse to Kohar's on-going plight concerning their mother. Kohar sensed that in Lucine's mind, she had been rehashing the same platitudes for over a decade.

"Have you heard from Azad? I wonder how her trip went." Kohar braced herself for the inevitable hostile reply, that guiltily (and only inwardly) would extract a chuckle.

"Who the fuck knows what she's doing. *No,* I haven't heard from Azad. She probably got her earlobes tattooed in some shaman's tent."

"You okay?" Kohar asked. "You seem . . ."

"What?"

"I don't know. More pissed off than usual," said Kohar. The empty silence that followed felt as if Lucine had disappeared. "Hello? Did the call drop?"

"No," Lucine spoke up. "I'm here. What's wrong with you, anyway? Why're you feeling sick?" Lucine asked.

"It may be something I ate. I had a headache the other day, and it came back before I passed out. I'm going to leave in a few minutes with Jonathan to go to the walk-in place around the corner," said Kohar.

"Get some rest," said Lucine before she hung up.

Lucine was chronically unsympathetic, specifically, it seemed, to Kohar's possible stomach virus, the ongoing drama regarding their mother, and all Kohar's banal dilemmas in between.

KOHAR HEARD JONATHAN'S TALL STEPS, TWO AT A TIME, RISING from the bottom of the stairs. He walked in and crept across the room toward his bureau.

"I'm awake," Kohar said, through half-closed eyes. She had been trying, unsuccessfully, to sleep.

"Hey." Jonathan stood at the foot of the bed. "How're you feeling?"

Kohar's eyes grazed over him, admiring how attractive he was in a pair of worn jeans and a heather-gray thermal. His beard, favoring more pepper than salt, was fully grown in.

"Fine, I guess," Kohar said, wondering if she assumed she wasn't well enough or if she was actually too sick to get out of bed and go downstairs. She wanted to ask if her mother had called again.

"I have a question for you."

"What?" Kohar pulled the covers off and sat up.

"Have you thought of taking a pregnancy test?" he asked.

"No. Why a pregnancy test?" she asked.

"You had a headache, you're tired and nauseous. Maybe you're pregnant. When was your last period?" he asked.

Kohar shook her head. She didn't know. "I don't do that anymore."

"Do what?" asked Jonathan.

"Track my periods. I stopped doing that in June." June had been that horrible day on his birthday.

For almost three years, Kohar's wall calendar in her office had served as more of an ovulation chart, with one *P* for each month that was spaced out within twenty-eight days, a chronicle of her regular menstrual cycle. If the *P* was written on the top half portion of the box, it meant that her period had started in the morning. After her last miscarriage, Kohar had stopped tracking and counting, a liberating denouncement that had left a residual bitterness, thick like tar, which could not be reasoned with.

"I'm trying to think when you had it at the beach house . . ." He stared off, his eyes averted in concentration.

Kohar endured this for a moment, and then: "Jonathan, I'm not pregnant. And I don't have a pregnancy test."

"I'm going to get one." Swiftly, he grabbed his sneakers from the closet and walked toward the stairs.

"I'm not taking it. So don't bother," she shouted.

She waited. She heard him pause in the hallway, laboring with thought, four seconds if she had counted. Then twelve seconds later, the dull metal thud of the storm door closing had silenced the house.

Kohar pressed her back against the pillow so sharply that she felt the imprint of the iron bedframe. She would not be able to deny Jonathan. Jonathan, to whom she would be forever grateful, for loving her so purely that she could never bear to be cynical. Kohar closed her eyes, unable to keep them open.

Minutes later, the sound of the storm door startled her awake. Kohar sat up in bed, remembering why he'd left, and wiped off the sudden perspiration gathering in her palms. She heard his footsteps again, gaining momentum as he climbed up the stairs. He walked into the bedroom and kicked off his Converse and threw off his shirt. Once more, Kohar found herself admiring his back, how the smooth and toned muscles rivaled those of swimmers she had known in college. For a moment, she was too consumed to remember her dilemma.

"Are you bribing me by undressing?" she teased. She scanned the room to see where he had put the bag from the drugstore.

"Why would I need to bribe you?" he asked without facing her. "I'm just changing my shirt."

"Where is it?" she asked.

"In the bathroom," he said after a particularly long pause. "I figure I'll bum-rush you while you're peeing and just stick in the test midstream. It'll be a surprise. That's my plan," he said, and headed out.

"Yeah," she called out to him. "Funny." But he had left so suddenly that she was talking only to herself in her empty bedroom with the television on mute.

She was annoyed at his doggedness; it was a quality she generally loathed, although she could only recall two or three times in the past that he had insisted on his point. Each time, there had been a significance, only clear to him. But now it became clear to Kohar. She remembered the first time she had brought Jonathan over to her parents' apartment for dinner, Gabriel emerging from his study and shaking Jonathan's hand amiably, inviting him into the parlor and their having a drink together. Their animated voices carried into the kitchen, where she went to help her mother with dinner, and afterwards, when they stole into Gabriel's study for another cocktail. It was as if they had known each other long before they had become acquainted: an immediate friendship bloomed.

Shamefacedly, Kohar suddenly understood why Jonathan wanted so much to have a child: to become a father. Moreover, his own father, with whom he had spent so little time, had disappeared after his parents' divorce. The divorce, though amicable, had driven his father away for a span of years, during which time he would unpredictably appear and vanish. Despite it all, Jonathan flew to Florida when his father was put in hospice and stayed by his side until his passing. And despite their conversation that night at the beach house, Jonathan carried the small hope that perhaps he would be a father after all.

Kohar finally left her bed and headed toward the bathroom. A plastic Walgreens bag was hanging off the back of the bathroom door. It was a First Response test. One she hadn't used during their years of trying. She wondered if this was one of Jonathan's superstitious purchases—a new test for a different outcome, not Clearblue or e.p.t., which, though obviously not responsible for the long string of negatives in the past, somehow implied negative results.

During the last few minutes from when Jonathan had returned, Kohar had the irrepressible urge to pee. Perhaps Jonathan's theory had triggered panic, or maybe she did need to use the bathroom; but, regardless, she had held it in and waited for the test. Kohar struggled to open the box. She found the cuticle scissors from the cabinet, cut open the cellophane wrapping, then the top of the box. There were two tests. She extracted one of them from the sturdy plastic casing and slid off her underwear. As she crouched over the toilet seat to survey the stream of urine and place the applicator midstream, she reminded herself that her life, before this very moment, had been a wonderful life. Yes, she had been upset. And yes, to give up on having a baby had felt impossible. But she had given up. It had been a choice. In the long run, not being a mother meant not being *her* mother. Nothing could rival the relief in knowing she would not have to confront that possibility.

She would not know that Jonathan had been quietly waiting at the bottom of the stairs, listening to her leave the bedroom and close the bathroom door behind her. She would not know that he had come back upstairs and was waiting for her in their bedroom so he could see the shock register on her face. Because exactly two minutes later, when Kohar emerged from the bathroom holding the pregnancy test in her hand, he would see the pink plus sign from where he was sitting on the bed. He would give her a smile, a small one. A smile that said *See? I told you.* And Kohar would nod and smile back, let the tears gather in her eyes, the words form on her lips, *Yes. You did, didn't you?*

Chapter 8

DR. KOCHABIAN HADN'T GIVEN TAKOUHI THE DETAILS OF THE endoscopy when he called her with a referral for an oncologist. He had said the biopsy came back abnormal and that she needed to schedule an appointment immediately. How swiftly Gabriel's world had cleaved into two distinct halves: his life before Takouhi's discovery of the stained napkin, and now an abnormal biopsy. There were no blurred lines, no gray crevasses in which to nestle himself with hope in his heart.

This thought occurred to him as he followed Takouhi down the corridor, the short procession led by the receptionist. Instead of walking into an examination room, they stepped into a doctor's office with two empty chairs across from an empty desk.

"The doctor will be right in," said the receptionist as she closed the door behind her, leaving Gabriel and Takouhi sitting alone in silence.

Gabriel sat back and began scanning the walls of the room with his eyes, grazing the diplomas and certificates for lettering and punctuation errors, although all he read through were mostly plaques declaring excellence for various achievements and medical degrees from expensive universities. It was a nervous habit of his, proofreading anything written in sight, which absorbed his attention for short spurts of time. It left him feeling tired and fruitless in his endeavor.

Takouhi had begun reorganizing the contents of her purse. Gabriel watched from the corner of his eye as she laid out her reading-glass case, cell phone, lipstick, pen, pencil, mascara, brush, and a small paper-clipped stack of coupons. She opened her purse, now fully absorbed in the trivial task of reallocating the items in a better-purposed designation of the inner pockets. He shook his head, not amused for once by her eccentricities.

The door opened quietly. Takouhi swept everything inside her purse and sat up expectantly. The doctor flashed a cordial smile as he entered the room. He was a middle-aged man with dark, thinning hair. Takouhi noticed his large, gentle eyes behind the horn-rimmed glasses and guessed that he was Greek.

"Hello. I'm Dr. Ariti," he said and sat behind the desk. "Dr. Kochabian sent me the results of your upper endoscopy as well as your medical records."

"Can you tell us," Takouhi began, "anything. . .?"

"As far as. . .?"

"How far the cancer has spread," she said. "He said the results were abnormal. I'm assuming it's cancer."

"We can't assume anything yet. We're going to do a CT scan today. It's a computed tomography scan. It's going to scan your body," he said, now speaking directly to Gabriel, "and it will give us a clearer idea of what is really going on."

"And what if it's stage four cancer? What happens then?" Takouhi was rocking back and forth in her chair.

The doctor shook his head emphatically. "Let's not talk about things in such specific measures. We don't know anything—"

"How long before we get the results?" Takouhi asked.

"Usually twenty-four hours," Dr. Ariti said. "But given the time of day, since it's early morning, we may be able to call you back in by tomorrow."

Gabriel absorbed this with mild interest, aware that he was intentionally keeping his anxiety at bay by hearing the doctor's voice without quite listening. In a few hours' time, he would be back in his study. It would be early afternoon. He pictured the sharp sunlight that peered through the windows at that time of day; it reminded him of the lazy afternoons in the odd towns he traveled through, when he didn't wear a watch because time was as weightless as the air he breathed.

". . . prepare you for the scan. Someone will be here in a few minutes to walk you there. Please have a seat in the waiting room."

Gabriel turned to Takouhi and watched her as she zipped her purse and stood up. He stared at her wonderingly as she headed toward the waiting room; and right before he was able to find his voice and ask her where she was going, Takouhi turned around for a fraction.

"I'll be in the waiting room, okay?" she said. "They're sending someone for the scan."

He wanted to ask why she couldn't at least wait with him until that someone arrived. "Takouhi—" he started to say.

"I'll be waiting for you, okay?" she said. He saw in her eyes the guilt of his impending abandonment choking her.

"Okay," he said.

He watched as she headed out the door, her footsteps muffled by the carpeted hallway. And for the first time in the many hours and months that would follow, Gabriel sat alone in the accusing silence.

His thoughts were interrupted by a young woman in a white lab coat.

"Mr. Manoukian, you can follow me," she said.

Gabriel stood up, clutching his windbreaker, and followed her further down the hallway, away from the waiting room, into an examination room. After changing into the hospital gown, he sat alone again, waiting. His eyes scoped the walls for something to read. Then another knock. This time it was Dr. Ariti.

"How are we doing?" he asked. "Before I take you to the CT scan, I want to explain the procedure. All you have to do is lie still. That's all there is for you to do. You're going to lie on a long bed, so to speak, and lie still. The bed moves. The scanner looks like a large donut. The bed—exam table—moves you through the scanner. The entire procedure takes ten to fifteen minutes. The radiologist may ask you to hold your breath at certain times. Sometimes movement from breathing can blur the images." The doctor paused for a moment. "Do you have any questions?"

Gabriel shook his head. "No," he said. "You said everything."

Weeks later, Gabriel would look back at the day with no recollection of his conversation with the doctor or the procedure or getting into the car with Takouhi after as she bounded home in paralytic silence. It was not a day, in fact. It was a moment, a horrid crossing from his predictable world into a vast wasteland of the unknown. He would not remember lying still on the moving bed, willing himself not to imagine his dead body in a coffin, or Kohar, Lucine, and Azad, and how to tell them and who would be the one.

Or the paradox of missing them if he died, as if he was bound somewhere far and distant, where his consciousness still existed. Memories of each of them swam through his mind, playing out unpleasantly as if the conjurer of these recollections were a disembodied entity. One of Azad at eight years old, barely sure-footed on her bicycle, insisting on riding well over a mile into a neighboring area when Gabriel had warned her that the return would be too strenuous. As he predicted, she had tired easily, and the image of them walking back, on either side of the bicycle holding a handlebar, came to him like a snapshot, the fall afternoon sun behind them.

Then one of the many afternoons when Lucine had sat on the arm of the sofa that faced the front window of the apartment building as she waited for her father to pick her up and take her to the amusement park. Gabriel had gone into the kitchen to head back to his office with a cup of coffee, and had noticed her sitting there. Knowing that she fell into silence as her patience waned, he had said nothing. And when he left his room again, he had noticed Lucine still there, nearly two hours later, the sudden anger that had seized him, an irreconcilable anger that made his heart hurt.

Kohar, guitar in hand, leaving the apartment to play a show in the city, a solo performance. He and Takouhi were sitting on the couch watching television when she had walked past them.

"Are you going to wish me good luck?" she had asked, looking specifically at Takouhi.

Takouhi, holding the remote control in her hand, had stared at the television screen. "Good luck," she had said, so dispassionately that it had been difficult for Gabriel to not look at her questioningly.

"Good luck," he had said, hoping his voice gave enough encouragement without betraying Takouhi.

At Takouhi's request, and unbeknownst to Gabriel, it would be Kohar that would tell her sisters that Gabriel had cancer. A detail that, had Gabriel known, would be much to his relief.

Chapter 9

WE'RE WAITING AT LEAST THREE MONTHS," SAID KOHAR AS SHE reached for the seatbelt and settled into the passenger seat.

"I'd rather wait until you're in labor," said Jonathan.

There was no humor in his sarcasm. They both remembered all too well what had happened the first time she had been pregnant. Naïvely, they had announced it too early on. Kohar had only been six weeks. Really, though, it had been her mother's awkward reaction that had alarmed both her and Jonathan. They had told the family during breakfast at Takouhi's, and Jonathan's mother had been there as well.

Once Takouhi had recovered from the shock, she had looked at Jonathan's mother, Mary, who was still flushed from the happy news. "So, Mary," Takouhi had said. "We're going to be grandmothers. Are you getting ready to fight, or what?"

She had continued by telling Kohar it would be best to take a five-year leave of absence from work so she could stay home with the baby, and that Kohar and Jonathan would eventually have to buy a larger house since the one they were living in, although adorable and charming, was rather cramped.

Kohar tried to forget the memory as they headed to the obstetrician's office. Her stomach turned over as each terrifying possibility swam through her: it's an ectopic pregnancy, it's a false positive, there won't be a heartbeat (but maybe also too early), her progesterone level is too low—a clear sign of an inevitable miscarriage, she's a high-risk pregnancy and the chances of carrying the baby to full term are low. Jonathan gently rubbed her knee, startling her.

"Stop," he said. Kohar sat back and closed her eyes. "It's going to be fine," he said. She wanted to ask him how he could be so sure.

When Kohar took off her clothes and changed into the paper gown, it felt the same as opening the pregnancy test: she was humoring Jonathan. Now she was humoring the results of an over-the-counter pregnancy test. She was thirty-eight. *You're going to need help*, one of her co-workers had told her, rather officiously, once. She had continued by ticking off, on the fingers of both hands, how many of her friends, who were younger than Kohar, had undergone IVF treatment.

She sat on the thin examination paper and swung her legs back and forth like a small child riding the subway, impatiently waiting for her stop.

"Hi." Dr. Morgan breezed in. "So you're pregnant," she said. "Congratulations."

Kohar, puzzled, looked at her.

"Your urine sample? When you walked in?"

Kohar had forgotten about the urine sample. She had been seeing Dr. Morgan for years, years before she and Jonathan had started trying. It was such a perfunctory routine, as routine as signing in when first walking into the office. "Really? I'm pregnant? Since when are the results so fast?"

"They are." The doctor wasted no time. "Now lie back so we can see how far along you are. Maybe we can even get a heartbeat. Come," the doctor motioned to Jonathan, who had been standing by the wall unit. He walked over and stood by Kohar.

Now dizzy and elated, Kohar leaned back as the doctor coaxed the lower half of her body to the base of the table. She watched as the doctor squeezed the gel on the tip of the ultrasound wand and placed it on her bare stomach. She watched the monitor as the doctor pressed lightly along her stomach. At first it was all gray matter. Then a large black circle with a small sac in the center.

"There," said the doctor. "There it is. Do you see it?" Kohar nodded. She saw. She felt Jonathan's comforting grip as he held her hand.

"When was your last period?"

"I don't remember," Kohar said.

"Do you want to hear the heartbeat?" the doctor asked.

"What?"

"The heartbeat." They watched the doctor adjust a knob. Then they heard the soft steady pulse. A gentle, persistent beating. It filled the room. "You're at least eight weeks," the doctor said. "Congratulations."

Only miles away, Gabriel and Takouhi sat with Dr. Ariti as he placed the black-and-white images against the white X-ray light. He explained, with great care and measure, the visible white mass at the base of the esophagus, the small white accumulated masses throughout the larger skeletal images. He explained, as he removed his glasses and tucked them in his shirt collar, that stage three esophageal cancer was inoperable. It was strange to Gabriel, how disembodied he felt from the images glaring brightly at him in the dimmed room. He could not reconcile that he was looking at his bones, his skull, his throat, his entire being glowing meanly with accuracy. Yet they belonged to him. He was them.

Takouhi began asking questions about chemotherapy and radiation. Her voice floated above Gabriel, behind him. He did not belong to himself anymore. Dr. Ariti's words trailed in and out of Gabriel's consciousness. They would do what they could to prolong his life. They would begin treatment immediately. All this could mean to Gabriel was not the end of his life. But rather, that his freedom was to be taken away. Brutally and systematically. There was little to do now.

Chapter 10

THROUGH THE ARCHED WINDOW, THE DIM MORNING LIGHT shone through the tops of the trees while Takouhi scrubbed the teapot with a Brillo pad. She ignored the near-scalding water that had turned her hands raw and pink. The dish drain empty, the floors mopped and dried, the counter bare and clean, the dishes safe in their cupboards, the black stovetop clear of pots and skillets—the kitchen was a gleaming spectacle.

Takouhi's eyes burned with the familiar weariness of one who rarely slept more than five hours a night. Her mind swarmed busily, menacingly: Gabriel's first scheduled chemotherapy appointment, Azad's flight that would be arriving in the afternoon, Lucine's inability to answer the phone, and Jonathan's maddening insistence that Kohar was too sick to talk. What's more, she had called up the man who had organized their trip to Armenia and canceled, avoiding all his questions. The retirement party, now only a week away, was still scheduled. The invitations had been sent and the RSVPs received.

Takouhi had been awake since the day before. She lay at night, listening to Gabriel snoring. She listened for the sounds of cancer (*what does cancer sound like?*) warbling in his throat. She wanted to throw open the bedroom window and scream into the night. Instead, she dug her nails deeply into the soft flesh of her forearms, pressed them in hatefully because there was no one left to punish.

Late in the evening, the smell of burning wood drifted through the crack of their bedroom window, an upstairs neighbor lighting their fireplace. Takouhi had wanted to nudge Gabriel then, to say that maybe they should call the girls over during the weekend to light the first fire of the season and sit in the parlor. Instead, she turned over and watched his back facing her, listening to his persistent snores. She wanted to throw her arm over him, pull him toward her in his unconsciousness. Since her discovery of the stained napkin, she hadn't once touched him. Not a caress, a kiss, a semblance of affection that would reassure him.

In the middle of the night, she had dozed off for a few moments finally. Then there was an empty space next to her, and Takouhi realized with a start that he wasn't in bed. Without calling out to him, she had left the bedroom; and as she walked down the corridor past his office, she had smelled it—the freshly lit tobacco and sulfur from the lighted match. Usually she saw the sliver of light from the base of the study door, but she knew he was sitting in his chair in the dark smoking a cigarette. She fought every impulse to rage through the door. She imagined him sitting in his underwear, his face naked without eyeglasses, smoking pensively in the darkness. After several minutes, he had returned to bed and settled in beside her. She had pretended to be asleep and lay awake as he fell back into a deep slumber. And then a dam burst within her. Gabriel lying on his side in their empty apartment, sleeping intently as the disease crept through his insides, silently, insidiously. He was helpless. More helpless than a child. While he slept on, his body was being consumed. At what rate Takouhi could not know.

Again, a wisp of burning logs slipped into the room with the cold evening air. There had been many evenings to reminisce when the family had gathered around the fireplace. Specifically, New Year's days. After her divorce and moving into the apartment with Gabriel and the girls, Takouhi had decided one year to carry over her family's tradition by celebrating New Year's Day as a special holiday. The girls would wake up to find Takouhi in the kitchen, cooking the traditional Armenian dishes that Takouhi often referred to as *tzerk-purnogh*—labor-intensive. They were dishes Takouhi would spend hours preparing that would disappear in seconds once served. The large square-shaped coffee table in front of the fireplace would be covered with one elaborate plate after another.

Takouhi still didn't know when it all shifted, when her darling girls began to sour, one after the other like converts of her eldest. From her memory she pictured all three of them sitting with filled plates of food as the fire glowed beautifully against their faces. Kohar with her long brown hair pulled back in a high ponytail; Lucine's large, dark eyes (they belonged to Takouhi, but she would not claim so); and Azad with her little round belly bulging deliciously in her one-piece pajamas. They giggled as one snuck food off another's plate when one wasn't looking, or conspired to watch two movies instead of one after dinner. And then one year, a year she can't place, they were magically older, taller, aloof. They grumbled about not having slept enough or missing the New Year's Eve party they had been invited to (Takouhi had claimed New Year's Eve a family holiday as well), as if spending time with her was a chore they had no choice but to carry through.

What Takouhi would have given to spend time with her mother aside from the cleaning, cooking, washing, and hanging laundry—all the household tasks that either her younger sisters were incapable of doing or her older brother and sister were too busy to help with, given their studies. For many years Takouhi had grown isolated and wedged uncomfortably between two sets of siblings as the middle child, her mother's helper who fit in nowhere.

No memories of this came to her as she stood over the metal sink, scouring the dirt with a sponge and baking soda. Her purpose in life had been so conditioned and ingrained that it was a part of her being. It was the reason why she was immune to the high praises of her cooking and entertaining throughout her experienced lifetime. Rarely did she indulge in anything she cooked, feeling oddly detached from the staggering array of dishes she had planned and toiled over with diligence, like a spider having spun another web. It was her job. As for the cleaning—she had finally given up her pride at cleaning the house on Saturday mornings and, with relief, had hired a cleaning woman. And with only her and Gabriel's laundry to tend to, the task didn't feel as menial as her many years by her mother's side.

What she had always longed for was an unrealized dream, which now lay like a corpse within the recesses of her heart. For years it had lain dormant with hope. And one day she had just known it was as far and distant as the sun disappearing into the horizon. She should have known the day it had happened, like a door slamming shut and then sealed.

"Takouhi!"

Her mother's voice carried down toward the end of the alley where Takouhi knew to stay, within earshot. Under her breath, she hummed a song she had only heard once. Having forgotten the melody mid-tune, she began at the beginning, adding broken phrases from her memory.

"*I am sixteen going on seventeen . . . hmmm . . . it's time to . . . hmmm . . . beware that . . . —*"

"Takouhi! Luvatsguh!" *The laundry.*

For a moment, she paused, then broke into a sprint, passing her two younger sisters along the way. They were bouncing a half-deflated soccer ball back and forth on the crumbling pavement of the alley. They regarded Takouhi for a moment as she raced past them, then resumed their game.

Racing up the steps to the back yard, Takouhi heard another distant cry. "*Leb-lebi! Leb-lebi!*" Sugar-coated chickpeas. Frantically, Takouhi shook her dress pockets for a few coins, although she knew that on every other corner on the streets of Bourj Hammoud was a leb-lebi cart. Besides, the beating she had caught for her last disappearance wasn't worth it.

She found her mother in the back yard, clothespins affixed along the rim of her apron and a straw basket filled with white underclothes by her feet. Takouhi observed her father's and brother's white undershirts hanging limply on the long clothesline. From the alley, her sisters' plaintive squabbling erupted and then subsided. She heard their running feet charging on the asphalt. Then laughter. Expertly, Takouhi extracted an undershirt from the basket and continued along with her mother as they both hung the family's wash under the early-morning sun.

She began humming to herself again, trying to fill the tedious drawn-out silence during these long mornings with her mother.

"What is that you're singing?" her mother asked.

"A song from the movie Aram and Mariam went to the other night. *The Sound of Music*," she replied.

The previous evening, while Nevart and Zabel fell asleep in their cots, Mariam had described the movie to Takouhi in great detail, outlining the Nazi invasion in Austria; the exuberant Julie Andrews frolicking against the green majestic mountains was a superficial portrayal of the film, as far as Mariam was concerned. It was like filming a movie in Bourj Hammoud with a marginalized emphasis of the Genocide, she had explained. Takouhi knew this was a secondhand analysis passed down from their brother Aram, who had expounded about the film during their walk home from the cinema.

These moments were rare, Mariam and Takouhi staying up past bedtime. Moreover, Mariam and Aram, only a year apart, were inseparable entities; they went to the same school, stayed within the same circle of friends, and remained separate and above the rest of the three sisters.

"Sing me one of the songs," Takouhi had pleaded.

Mariam was terrible with retaining words and melodies. Even now, from time to time, she would have to follow the hymnbook with the church choir where she had been singing before Takouhi had been old enough to join. Although Mariam was older by five years, it was Takouhi's voice that pierced through the chorus of girls and women during church service. The parishioners' ears perked when Takouhi sang the small solo the choir leader had begrudgingly given her; by virtue, it was meant to be sung by a more seasoned chorister, though it was evident that twelve-year-old Takouhi's range was formidable. After service, Takouhi would overhear her parents' friends and their relatives compliment her singing effusively. "Abris," they would say. "Akhcheegut erkchoohi tartsereh." *Bravo; your daughter has truly become a singer.* Her father would nod politely, seemingly unmoved. It was during family gatherings and after some coaxing that her parents permitted Takouhi to sing. Someone would nudge him and say, "Vartabed, tsukheh mekad togh yerkeh." *Let the girl sing.* And though Takouhi sang for the room, eyes closed, her eyes always rested on her father, who smiled. And perhaps it was her imagination, but she would notice a glint of tears in his eyes as everyone cheered for a second song.

But they would see things differently all too soon. Mrs. Soghomian, her English teacher, had called Takouhi to her desk and handed her the envelope the day prior. "Give this to your parents," she had instructed. The envelope had been sealed, implying, Takouhi knew, that it was not meant for her to open. But she had anyway.

Mr. and Mrs. Stepanian, as you may be aware, the annual student recital will be held two Saturdays from this coming weekend. On behalf of the Bourj Hammoud Secondary School for Excellence, we invite you to join us on this occasion. Takouhi will be asked to perform with the orchestral ensemble. Most importantly, Mr. Bedros Hartunian, the director of the Lebanese-Armenian Conservatory in Beirut, will

*be attending the recital. We have been notified that one student will be
granted a scholarship to the conservatory for the upcoming school year.
It is our hope that Takouhi will be awarded this opportunity.*

The letter had been handwritten and signed by her school director and
principal, Mr. Sarkissian. Takouhi had planned on giving the letter to her
parents that evening after dinner as her sisters were getting ready for bed
and Mariam and Aram had left for another outing to meet with friends.
While she washed and dried the dishes in the kitchen, they would read
the letter. She pictured her father, his tired face, sunburned from another
strenuous day of tarring roofs, beaming with a smile. And her mother sitting next to him in the living room, rereading the letter over her father's
shoulder. It was either Mariam with her high marks in school or Aram's
leading roles in the school plays that seemed to draw her parents out of
their everyday concerns; her father was an out-of-work carpenter with five
growing children, and her mother managed to feed and clothe them hand-
somely with admirable parsimony. She was a skilled seamstress and cook,
and, despite their meager living conditions, Takouhi and her siblings never
suffered from hunger or the shame of threadbare clothes.

Anoush and Vartabed's life remained an ominous mystery to their
children. Both were from Musa Dagh, a small province of Turkey occupied by Armenians during the Armenian Genocide. There was too much
to divulge and too many reasons to leave the past where it belonged. For
Vartabed it was the desolate childhood of being raised by his grandmother
while his older sister lived in an orphanage, the cost of raising both children too much of a burden for the old woman. His mother had died giving
birth to him on a French ship headed to Port Said from Musa Ler, where
five thousand Armenians had been saved during an ongoing battle with the
Ottoman army. As for Anoush, she had never known her father. He had
joined the Musa Ler resistance and died in battle. During her teenage years,
her mother had died of consumption, leaving Anoush with two younger
sisters to raise on her own and no family to take them in.

Vartabed and Anoush's marriage precipitated from a general fondness
they had for each other, but above all it was a union for practical purposes:
they were both old enough to marry—Vartabed seventeen and Anoush

sixteen—and Bitias, the village in which they were born and raised, was dwindling in population. It was time to leave. Droves of Armenians were migrating to Lebanon. After marrying, Vartabed and Anoush followed. The heart of their marriage beat to the thrum of sensibility and diligence, and they raised their children accordingly. They did not know from expressions of love and affection, but that those very things were implicitly communicated by the long hours Vartabed worked, the evenings Anoush's eyes strained under a single lamp to sew Easter dresses, the school tuition they scraped together for each of their five children, the rational decisions they made for their future.

That evening, after Takouhi cleared the table and her parents settled on the couch with a newspaper each, she slipped into the room and stood in front of them.

"Baba?"

Her father was sitting on the couch, shirtless. His bare chest was red and raw. Takouhi winced. She knew he would have to endure another long day of working under the sun the following morning, despite her mother's disapproval that he had recently agreed to take on working Sundays.

Her father glanced up at her, peered over his reading glasses. "My teacher told me to give this to you," said Takouhi, handing the envelope to him. She hoped he wouldn't notice that the ink with which his name had been written was blurry from the steam she had used to open the letter. She stood watching him as he pushed his reading glasses against his face. "I'm not in trouble," she added. She tried not to rock on the balls of her feet, a bad habit her mother had been discouraging since she was a child.

Her father looked up at her sharply. "Go," he said. "Whatever you were doing to occupy yourself—do that."

Takouhi knew this was his way. It was not bred of meanness or contempt toward her. Her father was a terse man. He only spoke when necessary. She disappeared into the kitchen and began filling the sink with lukewarm water and soap suds. She couldn't eavesdrop even if she wanted to. They would know right away when the kitchen grew quiet and they could no longer hear her scrubbing the dishes.

Takouhi worked slowly and quietly, straining to hear the conversation between them. She imagined again, her father smiling—a rare moment of any day—and calling her in. She imagined her mother sitting next to him, letting him speak and smiling with approval. The minutes went by like any other evening. She slowly wiped each dish and fork dry and placed them back in the cabinets and drawers, but did not hear either of them call her back into the living room.

Before getting ready for bed, she stepped back into the room. Both her mother and father were reading their newspapers in silence. Takouhi scanned the surface of the coffee table and the small end tables, one on either side of the couch. She could not spot the envelope.

"I wanted to ask what was in the envelope," Takouhi asked.

They both looked up at her as if broken from a trance. As usual, only her father spoke. "Was your name on it?" he asked.

"No." Takouhi cupped her hands behind her back and gripped her fingers.

"It doesn't concern you, then. Good night." He went back to reading his paper. Time beat inside Takouhi's breast like an impatient metronome. She stood still, five seconds, ten seconds, she counted to thirty. Both her mother and father continued reading the paper in the unbearable silence of the living room. She knew if she stood a second longer, her mother would finally reprimand her. Having little choice, Takouhi left to her room and got ready for bed.

As the days passed, Takouhi was certain her father would bring it up to her. Or perhaps her mother during their long afternoons together after school or on Saturday, which was laundry day. But neither of them did. Takouhi could feel a tight knot gathering in her stomach as the day of the recital grew closer and closer. She wished she hadn't read the letter. For many years after, she would wish she hadn't. The only way it would all change, she decided, was if she sang well enough to receive the award and the scholarship. Mariam and Aram put together wouldn't be able to rival her victory, the promise of her new future.

ANY OTHER TWELVE-YEAR-OLD WOULD HAVE TREMBLED AT THE sight of the audience gathered in the auditorium that Saturday afternoon. Every seat, five hundred twenty-five in total, was filled. The conservatory's scholarship had been written up in the local newspaper and had attracted an unexpected turnout. More than half the recital's attendees did not even have their children enrolled at the Bourj Hammoud Secondary School; they were there to savor the spectacle of children performing, which was held in especially high regard in Armenian society.

When Takouhi was called onto the stage, she wasn't moved by the immense crowd, who were now shifting in their seats waiting for the last performance of the program; they knew it was meant to be the denouement of them all. The hot stage lights pressed above Takouhi's head and blinded her for the first few moments. She dared not look for her family, for her parents. It was for them that her stomach twisted and turned, her tremors of unease. Not the other five odd-hundred bodies crowded in the sweltering auditorium.

The orchestra erupted with music, and within seconds Takouhi sang. Her voice, as if no longer hers, floated out of her body and across the stage. She could feel the vibrations of the melody as the microphone carried her voice into the air. She closed her eyes and felt the weight of the crowd's attention, their rapt silence as the piano trilled against the slow and plodding violins. But something was wrong. Takouhi sang but could no longer hear her voice within the melody of the instruments they carried. The musicians stopped playing one by one until one last violin echoed awkwardly and stopped. The audience shifted in their seats. Some stood up and peered at the stage. Takouhi froze as confusion filled the room. It was the microphone. It had short-circuited.

Behind the curtain, Takouhi heard the frantic footsteps of the music director racing across the stage. She could only guess that the recital would have to end prematurely. But before she herself understood what she was doing, she stood on stage and raised both her arms in the air and gently lowered them, silencing the crowd. Takouhi waited for pure silence. She waited for the crowd to be still. And finally they were.

Takouhi closed her eyes. She was hanging laundry. She was washing dishes. She was in the alley hiding from her mother. She began singing. *Who needs violins?* she thought. *Who needs a piano?* The music teacher called it "a cappella." For Takouhi, it was her pastime for as long as she could remember. Something that made it matter less that she didn't fit in anywhere. That she was her mother's sole helper. That she was lonely. That she saw no future for herself and didn't know better to aspire to something. Finally, she had nearly reached the end of the song. The highest note had yet to be sung. Her voice rose high and clear and before she could even open her eyes, she heard the thunder of vibrations shaking the floorboards of the stage. The audience were on their feet clapping, whistling.

Takouhi bowed slightly and then scanned the room, knowing how impossible it was to catch sight of her family. If only she could see her mother and father. But too late, too late, because she was surrounded now by teachers, the school director, and a short, corpulent man wearing a sweaty smile shaking her hand. Then beside him was a taller man wearing a dark three-piece suit and a pair of burgundy wing-tipped shoes. He seemed to be waiting patiently, allowing the audience's raucous applause to subside. Finally, after quite a length of time had passed, the man stepped forward.

"Good afternoon," he called out. Suddenly the microphone squealed sharply, and the man pulled back. He tapped on its mouthpiece hesitantly. "I'm three times this girl's age and I'm only here to say a few words, but somehow I need the microphone more than she does," he joked. The audience laughed appreciatively. "That was a fine performance," he said, turning directly to Takouhi. "Do you know who I am?" he asked her. It was odd, Takouhi thought, how he was carrying on a casual conversation in front of hundreds of people, as if they weren't there. She shrugged her shoulders.

"Maybe," she offered.

"My name is Bedros Hartunian. I'm here on behalf of the Lebanese-Armenian Conservatory. I'm the director," he said and extended his hand.

Takouhi held his hand and shook it, trying to reciprocate his strong, firm grip. "It's nice to meet you," she said. She jumped a little when the audience laughed again.

As the man continued speaking and congratulating her for her "breathtaking performance," Takouhi looked at the audience again and saw them finally, her mother, her father, her sisters, and her brother on the left side of the sixth row. She saw her mother's set chin and her father's stern, unmoving eyes. She understood right away. In that small momentous occasion of her life, which would be rare occurrences in her memory, Takouhi would not remember the director of the conservatory awarding her a music scholarship or the audience rising again to their feet or being whisked away to say a few words to a local journalist for an article in the newspaper that would run the very next day. All she would remember was the face of her parents, unmoved and detached as if it all meant nothing.

After the reporter had left, Takouhi sat alone backstage listening to the herd of footsteps disappearing out of the auditorium. Within moments it would feel as ephemeral as a dream. The faded voices of her music teacher and Mr. Hartunian grew clearer from behind the curtain. Takouhi listened, straining to hear the words. Then a third voice, deep and terse, came through in short bursts. It was her father. Hesitantly, Takouhi tiptoed toward the far end of the stage and listened.

"Mr. Stepanian, I'm not sure if you understand completely. This is a very special opportunity for someone with Takouhi's talent. After graduating from the conservatory, students move on to the music school in Beirut—it's the sister school of the conservatory. Talent scouts frequent both establishments, always looking for a fresh new voice, they—"

"We understand the opportunity," Takouhi heard her father's voice like a gavel, firm and resounding. "Takouhi is a twelve-year-old girl. We are not interested in sending her away. The matter is settled."

Takouhi stood petrified, her heart pleading for the director to conjure the magical words that would change her father's decision.

"Have you considered moving with your family? To Beirut? It would be a wonderful change. Again, please understand what a special opportu—"

"Don't underestimate my ability to understand. I'm not uprooting our entire family on the whims of talent scouts. Our daughter isn't going to be a traveling singer. She's not going to be a vagabond gypsy singing in nightclubs. I've explained myself more than I care to. If you please, excuse us now."

Takouhi went back to where she was sitting. She could hear the director's footsteps vanishing down the aisle and then the dull slam of the auditorium's swinging doors. The auditorium echoed an emptiness that felt as if the entire day had been a dream. Like a dark seed that would root and grow and fester, a sense of doom cast its first shadow on Takouhi. She would feel this shadow, unpredictably, appear throughout her life, assail her senses, leave her more and more broken and undestroyed.

Many years later, after her mother's death, her father, addle-minded with dementia, would die in his sleep. On his burial day, Takouhi would gather with her brother and sisters in front of the closed casket. She would say a last prayer. She would stand in the first pew with her family and feel the sick grief spreading through her. The memory of the day would come to her, the smell of the sweltering auditorium and the wilting lilac bouquets on either side of the stage.

"Get up!" Takouhi screamed at the coffin. "Get up! Let me sing for you one more time! One more song! Get up!"

The echo of her screams filled the church as her brother and Gabriel carried her away with visible force.

When Aram sold his parents' house after their passing, he faced the arduous task of cleaning the three-story home and donating whatever was salvageable. On his father's nightstand he found a dusty tape recorder with a black unlabeled tape inside. When he pressed the play button, Takouhi's voice came bursting through, as if she herself had been contained within the recorder for too long. There would be no one to tell him how his father used to play the recording of Takouhi's performance that hot afternoon in June. That the music director, for the sake of posterity, had given their father the tape. He had made many copies. Aram would find them unexpectedly as he continued cleaning the house. During the last year of their mother's life, when the onset of Vartabed's dementia had begun corrupting his reality, he would play the tape of Takouhi singing over and over and wander through the house asking Anoush, "Have you seen Takouhi? Where could she be? I hear her, but I can't find her."

For years Takouhi stopped singing—even to herself—to pass the time, to escape as she had as a child. Inevitably, she would sing during special occasions—a family wedding, a christening. Her sisters and brother would listen, tears gathering in their eyes. It was too beautiful a voice to be heard once or twice a year. It was cruel to hear the irony of her life within those rare moments when she was allowed to shine.

Takouhi had been running away for so long that she could not look back on her adolescence in Beirut, her impulsive acceptance of marriage to her first husband Antranig, her abrupt divorce and remarriage to Gabriel as anything but solutions to dire circumstances. Although the latter, she knew, was a plight from which she had been saved, the savior whom she adored for his kindness and depth of empathy, boundless compassion. Never did she need to explain her behavior to Gabriel, who understood the burden of being the middle child among her siblings—overlooked by her parents with little encouragement for doing more than marrying and bearing children, or the ill-fated marriage to a man whose father had been orphaned during the Genocide, the inheritance of violence and abuse that had plagued her husband, who had been conditioned to live in fear and who was the sole benefactor of his family's name, his ancestors having perished in the hands of the Ottomans. Though Gabriel's father and her deceased father-in-law endured a similarly unfortunate past, their offspring were radically contrary in nature and disposition.

Years later, when Gabriel told the story of the first time he had laid eyes on her and how he had consulted the *Armenian Reporter* for announcements of upcoming lectures in the hope of seeing her again, it was difficult for Takouhi to fathom that she was significant to anyone or could leave any memorable impression. No, she had not experienced adoration from anyone as she had upon meeting Gabriel, who was as gentle and kind as her husband had been coarse and erratically violent. It was her fire, her beauty that had moved Gabriel, and as they began meeting secretly, before she left Antranig, he fell in love with her vulnerability and her sense of humor—a combination that he found helplessly endearing.

During the moments they stole away together, Gabriel would slip a piece of paper in her hand with words written in his handwriting, quotes from poems or novels he especially loved. She would hide them in an envelope in her nightstand marked "bills" on the off chance that Antranig would bother looking through her belongings. Sometimes he was home in time for dinner when they all ate together as a family; or he arrived late in the evening after the girls had gone to bed, Takouhi's preference of the two. His moods ranged from quiet and resigned to irritable and terse. During the sixteen years of their marriage, Takouhi was deeply disturbed at how seemingly accepting Antranig was of these grimly monotonous evenings and the sterile, unloving life they all lived.

It wasn't until she had married Gabriel, with Kohar, then twelve, and Lucine, seven, that she experienced for the first time in her life a sense of peace and ease; Friday Night Movie Night they called it, Make Your Own

Pizza Night was how they spent their Saturday evenings, and then the spontaneous car rides to Jones Beach before sunset or going to the circus when Gabriel had seen a commercial on TV. It was so foreign to her, so un-Armenian and untraditional, yet Gabriel was surely Armenian, fluently speaking the language, and well-versed in Armenian literature and history.

On some weekends when the girls visited their father, she and Gabriel would spend afternoons in bed, eating cheese and bread and listening to his collection of Motown albums on old 45s. Sometimes, overcome by the music, he would stand up in the middle of the bedroom wearing only his underwear, snapping his fingers and hollering the lyrics loud enough that he could be heard by the neighbors in the stairwell of their building. *"Ain't no mountain high, ain't no mountain low, ain't no river wide enough, baby . . ."* he would lip-sync and hold out his hand gesturing for Takouhi to get up and dance with him. Awkwardly, she would join him, unfamiliar with American dancing, shuffling her feet in rhythm with the music.

THE RINGING PHONE BROKE THE SILENCE IN THE KITCHEN. Takouhi raced over to the counter with wet hands and wiped them frantically on her apron.

"Mom?"

Takouhi felt her heart constrict. She leaned her elbows on the counter and hung her head. "Yes, Kohar." *What is it.*

"Did I call too early?"

"No. I thought it was Azad."

"Sorry. I didn't mean to disappoint you." Already her voice hedged with sarcasm.

"I'm not saying anything about you," Takouhi said. "I don't know where she is and I need to talk to you girls."

"About what?" Kohar asked, tired and impatient.

"About Gabriel," said Takouhi. "We've been to doctors."

"For what?" Takouhi took small satisfaction in hearing the sudden worry in Kohar's voice.

"For . . . for the fact that he's sick." Takouhi paused, unsure of what words to use.

"What kind of sick?"

"Cancer. Stage two esophageal," she lied. Inside her, Takouhi could feel a balloon slowly deflating. It was the first time she had said it out loud. It would have felt worse if she had told her the truth, that the diagnosis had been stage three.

"What are you talking about? When did you find out? I spoke to you a few days ago, and you didn't mention—"

"Seven. Seven days ago. That was the last time you picked up the phone."

"Did you tell Azad or Lucine?"

"Not yet. I tried calling you before, but Jonathan said you were sick."

Takouhi was yet to understand how someone could come back from vacation and get sick so quickly. All that fresh air and sunshine was supposed to be reviving. "Did you enjoy your vacation?"

"Where is he now?" asked Kohar.

"In bed, sleeping."

"Would you mind telling me everything so we can stop playing twenty questions? Jesus . . . *Christ*." Takouhi was almost certain Kohar had muttered the word *fucking* in the pause between words. "Are you going to get a second opinion?"

"There's no need," said Takouhi. "I need you to tell your sisters for me."

"Lucine and Azad? You want *me* to tell them? Azad just got back."

Takouhi remained silent.

"Can I ask—how are you doing?"

"Me? I'm fine. I'm taking him to his first chemo appointment soon." Takouhi could hear Kohar sniffling and then the tears that gave way. "I have to go," she said finally.

She leaned against the kitchen counter, regarding the sunlight streaming through the tall window. A wren perched itself on a leafy tree branch and fluttered off. And several feet away, Gabriel stood behind the closed French doors, where he had been standing since the phone had rung. He waited until the tidal wave of sobs that pressed against his chest had subsided before returning to the bedroom. Within the walls of these empty spaces, there was no room for his private grief.

Chapter 11

Silence. Lucine's days began and ended with a pervading silence that was too familiar. It was the last days of autumn. And Steve had not returned. Lucine thought that perhaps he would eventually sneak back to pack up some of his belongings while she was at work. She dreaded returning home, when the sky darkened by five o'clock; she would wander through the house, peeking into the spaces Steve used to occupy. To see if he had come and left. She could not afford to change the locks. During the first weeks of his disappearance, she lived in a state of unease, wondering if he would return while she was sleeping.

She was more anxious on the days Max would come over. Though they would inevitably have sex, the thrill of those moments was short-lived. She knew she was avoiding what she had dreaded for as long as she could remember: being alone. A quiet house. The silence of negligence. Her mother asleep or catatonic in her dark bedroom, hiding under a pillow. Her father working from dawn until late evening.

Now Lucine spent her days at work or at home living within the frugal means of a paycheck-to-paycheck income. There was no one to call. She could not fathom asking her mother for money—an admission of failure, and questions raised. Kohar—what would she really know of struggling—with her summer vacations and near-to-perfect husband? And Azad? Please. She didn't even know her zip code.

Lucine had just changed out of her work clothes when the doorbell rang. She snapped open the living-room curtain, knowing that if it was Steve he wouldn't bother ringing the bell. There was a tall middle-aged man wearing a parka and wool hat standing on the porch. Lucine went to the door.

"Who is it?" she called out.

"I'm from the summons and complaint department of the New Jersey eviction court. I am here to serve you a notice of eviction for the day of December 15th."

Lucine opened the door. Dusk had colored the clouds magenta, and the silhouette of the man stood before her. "Are you Lucine Garabedian?" he asked. Hers was the only name on the lease. She wondered now if she had kept her maiden name because she knew the marriage would not last.

"Yes," she said.

The man handed her a manila envelope. Her name was written on a white label affixed in the center.

As she began unsealing the metal clasp, the man had already reached the sidewalk. Locking the door, Lucine tore the envelope open and unfolded several sheets of paper. As the man had said, it was an official eviction notice.

She threw it on the floor. She was four months behind in rent. During these moments, she tried to avoid the obvious answer to her dilemma. Calling her father. Asking for money. She had never done so. And for that reason, it felt as foreign as the thought that he was her father.

Her father, the son of a Genocide survivor who had been orphaned and displaced. Her father was the last to carry the Garabedian name. For years he had toiled with the enduring conviction that he was meant to memorialize his family's legacy, devoting his time to his work and the Armenian community. It was only years later that Lucine would hear the stories about her father's violent temper and the long hours he worked, for her acute memory narrowed forgivingly when recalling happy times with him.

The terrain of her childhood shifted between a graveyard and a battlefield during the years of her parents' marriage. What she remembered most was the feeling of those precious afternoons, just her and her father, when he would leave the house to run an errand and the thrill of sitting in the passenger seat with him when she usually sat in the back seat with Kohar. He would let her play with the radio dial as if it were a toy, whirring through the stations and raising the volume high and low. Never did it occur to her that Kohar was left behind, most likely with their grandmother.

Even then, Lucine understood that every heart beat to the proclivity of a lifelong desire. For Kohar, it was respect and freedom. For their mother, it was recognition and praise. For Lucine, it was the affection and attention of her father. She understood herself well enough to know why: very simply, she was the middle child. It had happened so swiftly and forcibly; one day she was seven years old, the center of her father's world, and the next her parents had divorced.

Then a new chaos took precedence that upended any semblance of normalcy Lucine might have known. Her father, now with his new wife and new daughter, who all lived in the home she had grown up in, was no longer hers. He belonged to them and with them. It was a complicit betrayal that no passing of time would allow for forgiveness. Yet he was her father. The fact of their natural bond.

Tanté. She hadn't said it out loud in months. It was how she addressed her stepmother instead of her given name, Alice. In a community where everyone seemed to be an interweaving of distant cousins, *Tanté* was affectionately used to address older female friends of the family who were not blood-related. In Lucine's realm, her stepmother—Tanté—was the gatekeeper.

She found her phone and pressed in the numbers. She was his daughter. She mattered. Yet it sounded flimsy in light of the long silent months between them. She rarely stopped by on his birthdays or holidays and she called seldom.

Her mind scrambled, a feeling of regret consuming her. A terrible humiliation. Frantically, she tried to end the call and then a female voice answered.

"Allo?"

"Hello, Tanté?" Lucine's eyes burned with tears. She wanted to hang up.

"Allo? Yes?" Her stepmother's nasal voice came sharply through the other end.

"Hi, Tanté. It's Lucine," she said. She felt as if she were slipping down a steep hill.

"Lucine. Yes?" There wasn't the slightest intimation of surprise or pleasure upon hearing Lucine's voice.

"I wanted to talk to Dad," she said. *Don't ask her, tell her,* she reminded herself.

"I'm sorry. I just laid him down for a nap," said her stepmother.

"It's important," said Lucine. The phone trembled in her hand.

"What do you want me to do? Wake him up?"

"He's *always* taking a nap when I call," Lucine pressed on. She knew she was playing into a game that had been designed from the start, where, ultimately, she was the loser.

"Lucine, listen," said her stepmother, her tone patronizing. "I can't help it if he's tired when you call. When."

Too defeated to take the bait, Lucine relented. "Okay, Tanté," she said. "Thank you."

The phone clattered as it hung up. Lucine guessed her stepmother had answered from the old rotary phone in the laundry room of the basement, where she eavesdropped on conversations when Kohar or Lucine called. Her father was probably awake in his bedroom, either watching television or eating.

She felt again as she had as a child, when her father would forget to pick her up from art class or school. Leaning against the concrete steps, Lucine would watch as her peers were greeted by their mothers or fathers eager to see them and ask about their day. The feeling of desertion left within her a well of disappointment that she would carry. It all came back to her now, and she understood why she had avoided her father for such lengths of time.

Then another memory came to her, like a fresh tidal wave, wickedly disorienting: her father marrying Tanté—that jarring afternoon. Her step-mother's pregnancy and the emergence of Beatrice—bitchy half-sister who Lucine always referred to as *half*-sister, a distinction she never made when referring to Azad, who she loved more than she could stand. Then came the divide of her two worlds: one with her mother, Gabriel, Kohar, and (eventually) Azad, and the other: her father, Tanté, Beatrice, and her grandmother, who would remain a loving and abiding entity in the house until she died before her father's stroke. That both her parents had remarried within several months of each other and both her mother and stepmother had given birth three months apart was a coincidence that had been planned, evilly, by Fate itself, if not her parents. That her stepmother was a classic paranoiac, obsessively jealous of Takouhi and her manipulations (perceived or otherwise), was a stunning detail that Lucine could not negotiate as bad luck.

She blamed it wholly on her father's penchant for marrying crazy women. And her grandmother—meek as she was—nudging her father with maddening persistence to remarry immediately to avoid the risk of tarnishing even further the Garabedian family name in the Armenian community—had manipulated circumstances that would grow beyond everyone's control. Pandora innocently opening an unruly box of hell.

Yet here she was, in an empty home. Lucine lay on the couch and closed her eyes, feeling a wave of exhaustion as she pulled a blanket over her shoulders. She heard her phone ringing from the kitchen. It was her father. That rotten woman had been decent enough to give him her message. She would apologize. She would tell him the truth, or as much of it as she could.

"Hello?"

"Hey." It was Kohar. "You home?"

"Yeah. What's up? Are you still sick?"

"I have to tell you something."

"What?"

"Are you alone right now?"

"Yes. What's going on?"

"It's Gabriel . . ."

"Did something happen?" Her saliva tasted like metal. "Kohar?"

"He's sick. That's why Mom kept calling. They had gone to an oncologist and . . ."

Lucine slumped to the floor. "Just tell me," she said.

"It's stage two esophageal cancer. He's going to start chemotherapy as soon as possible."

"Did they say how . . . like, if he's going to get better?"

"I didn't get that far when I spoke to Mom. She sounded really strange."

"Okay."

"Do you want to talk? I'm not busy."

"No," Lucine said. "I don't. I need to go."

Chapter 12

AZAD STOOD IN FRONT OF HER BEDROOM CLOSET, SURVEYING THE limited possibilities of her attire for the evening. In the corner of the closet was a crumpled turquoise garment; a dress she had forgotten having bought from a South Asian boutique downtown. She sensed that this particular dinner with Krikor was not one of their regular dates. Typically, they had dinner and went out for a movie or had a cocktail. They usually ended up back at her house on the couch, Azad discouraging his advances and resisting the urge to break down and roll a joint. She was certain that his vices were limited to the occasional artisanal beer and too much ice cream. She was not like the other Armenian girls Krikor had grown up with. The ones he still ran into at church, who were vying for the attention of Armenian bachelors at the behest of their parents. Their Ralph Lauren ensembles and Prada handbags, their freshly manicured nails and powder-pressed complexions. Rolling a joint was the tipping point where Azad would lose her footing with him entirely.

All week she had brooded over the evening she had spent with his family. The tension between Krikor and his mother surprised Azad. Moreover, how steadfastly contentious he was, despite Azad's presence. Perhaps it was because she was there. She found it endearing. And she realized that she was looking forward to seeing him this evening more than any other. For the first time, there was the possibility of a relationship that was not doomed. And try as she might, she couldn't help imagining how pleased her parents would be upon hearing that their relationship was going well.

Though dark thoughts accosted her. Azad remembered the old woman's words. Not her cryptic prediction, but her comment about her family being abnormal, an aberration. *Normal che.* It was unsettling for a stranger to pinpoint what Azad had accepted as the typical drama of most families. Namely, the vicious arguments between Kohar and her mother. Azad had taken for granted the disjointed dynamic between them: Takouhi, detached and apathetic; Kohar, bold and forthright. There was never a time it hadn't been this way.

THE GAPING AGE DIFFERENCE BETWEEN HER AND KOHAR BLURRED her memory. Though in Azad's recollection there was a defining moment of when it had all started. The day Kohar had brought home a guitar. Before then, Kohar had played the piano. Music she composed. Some of them were songs she sang. Azad didn't realize until years later that her sister only played when their mother wasn't home, though she never understood why.

From behind Kohar's bedroom door Azad heard the soft strumming of chords, some discordant and others light and lovely. Gently, she pushed the door open, drifted in, and sat on the edge of Kohar's bed.

"Where'd you get the guitar?" she asked.

"My friend. She just bought a new one so she gave this to me," said Kohar. "I'm thinking of playing a show. There's a little café on Avenue B downtown. But first I have to learn to play this," she said, clumsily attempting a chord.

"Can I come?" asked Azad.

"I don't think they let ten-year-olds into bars," Kohar said, leaned over, and kissed her cheek. "When you're older."

She extended the guitar to Azad, held down the strings and let Azad pluck at them.

"How about if Mom and Dad bring me?" asked Azad.

"I highly doubt it," said Kohar. "There's no way."

"Why?"

"Because. Trust me," said Kohar. "I don't even know when it'll happen anyway. I should have started playing this a long time ago. Who learns how to play at twenty-four? I'm too old."

"*I* don't think so," said Azad.

At the end of the meal that evening, Azad decided to test Kohar's theory. "Guess what? Kohar's going to play a show," she said.

"Yeah? What show?" Lucine asked, still fishing out pieces of stewed tomatoes from her bulgur pilaf. "You mean with the guitar? That's cool."

"At a café," Azad continued.

Their mother glanced at Kohar, frowning.

"Which one?" Lucine asked.

"It's nothing," Kohar said, nudging Azad's foot under the table. A warning for her to stop.

Gabriel returned from the kitchen with a second helping of food. "Who's performing?"

"Kohar," said Azad. "Will you take me to see her when she plays?"

Gabriel dove into his meal and shrugged. "Sure," he said. "Where?"

"What show is this, exactly?" Takouhi finally spoke.

"It's nothing," Kohar said. "I'm learning how to play the guitar. I'm going to figure out my songs from the piano and sing."

Takouhi rolled her eyes, scoffing. "You think it's so easy to learn an instrument. What show is this?"

Kohar let her fork drop with a clatter. "There is no show. I didn't say anything was actually happening," she turned to Azad and widened her eyes. *Stop.* "If there was," she said, exiting with her plate, "I don't see what the big deal would be anyway."

"You don't see the big deal?" her mother replied. "Why don't we all grab an instrument and learn how to play, then? You think it's so easy? Who's coming to this show, anyway?"

Kohar, not having left the room, turned around. "I *said* there is no show. This is ridiculous. Azad walked in while I was playing guitar and I mentioned that when I learn how to play, I would sing a few songs at a café. That's it. Okay?" She stopped abruptly and then turned around again. "And if I *was* playing a show, what would be the big deal? What do you care? I barely play the piano when you're home because I know you don't like it."

Azad, sensing her mother's fury, hoped Kohar would disappear into her room. Relieved, she heard the creak of her bedroom door closing.

"Poor girl," Takouhi crowed loudly. "She doesn't get to play the piano."

Kohar's door flew open and she came back in. "I don't. And you kept it in tune when *you* were taking lessons years ago, but once you stopped playing it didn't matter to you anymore. I still play even though it sounds like shit."

"Then maybe it's your playing," Takouhi spat back. She settled back in her seat, wearing a look of disgust.

Kohar, stunned: "Why would you say that? Why do you say such mean things?"

She stared at Takouhi, her face contorted with hurt. Gabriel sighed and left for the kitchen. Lucine slinked away, tiptoeing down the hallway. Azad's chest burned with the longing to hug her sister.

Kohar stood over Takouhi, the moment frozen, sealed. Finally she turned and went to her room. Upon her door closing, Takouhi spoke one last time.

"What makes you think you can sing?" she called out.

"Mom!" Azad burst. She buried her head in the crook of her arm and began sobbing.

All they could hear from the dining room was the strum of guitar strings from Kohar's room.

IT WAS SEVERAL WEEKS LATER THAT KOHAR CAME HOME FROM work early. At the time, she was completing her master's in creative writing and working full-time at a publishing house in the city. Usually she would return home late and no one would see her until the following morning when she was getting ready for work.

They were all sitting in the living room, her mother, Gabriel, and Lucine and Azad finishing their homework. Kohar sat down in the dining-room chair and watched them, silent.

"I want to tell you something important," she said.

Takouhi, sitting on the couch and flipping through channels, did not break her gaze from the television. "What is it?"

"I went to see an apartment today. I'm going to be moving out in a few months," said Kohar. Azad remembers still, how her sister had gripped the sides of the dining room chair as if she expected to fall off the seat.

Silence.

Lucine was absorbed in a textbook. Gabriel took a sip of his coffee and cleared his throat.

"It's not far. Astoria. It's a one-bedroom and about a ten-minute drive away," she said.

Takouhi muted the television and kept her eyes fixed on the screen.

"Mom? Can you say something? I'm hoping it's not as big a deal as I thought it would be. I'm almost twenty-four—"

Finally, Takouhi looked at Kohar and hurled the remote control across the room. It crashed against the wall, scattering batteries under the console.

"If you leave this house, I'll never speak to you again," Takouhi said.

"Mom—"

Azad dared not look up, did not dare to move. She could already sense Kohar's face stricken with shock, her tears.

"If you leave this house, I'll never speak to you again," Takouhi repeated. "This is a family. You are part of this family, and if you leave—"

"It's only ten minutes away," Kohar said again. "How long should I live here? I stayed for college because you didn't want me to go anywhere. I'm getting my master's and working a full-time job. Do you want me to live here until I get married—"

"Yes!" Takouhi hissed. "Yes, I want you to live here with your family."

"What if I don't get married? What if I don't want to? Or what if I do but don't find the right person for a long time?"

"I don't care what you want! You're ruining the family by doing this. You are fracturing this," Takouhi screamed, pointing wildly to each of them, who like statues sat in obeisance. "I'm going to say it one last time: if you leave here, I don't ever want to see you again. Never."

"How could you say this?" Kohar yelled, now standing up.

"How could you leave? Look at the upset you're causing right now. All because *you* want what *you* want and the rest of us have to deal with it."

"I just came in here to tell you I wanted to move out," Kohar argued. "I'm not causing—"

"YES, you are!" Takouhi thundered back. "Yes. You are. Now get the hell out of my face. I don't want to look at you."

Kohar would have moved out sooner, but the apartment she wanted was all she could afford and it wouldn't be ready to move into for three months. For the duration of that time, they all watched in silence as Takouhi's brutal rage unraveled mercilessly. One morning she randomly threw a cup of hot coffee across the kitchen where Kohar was standing. Takouhi cooked only enough dinner for the four of them, removed Kohar's wet clothes from the washer on laundry days, threw away her belongings if they were lying around the apartment, and, worst of all, did not utter one word to Kohar since their awful argument. In essence, their mother carried on as if Kohar did not exist at all. Not one of them, not even Gabriel, spoke up.

It was a Saturday morning, the day Kohar finally moved out. Takouhi, Gabriel, and Lucine had left the house, and Azad was sitting on the couch in the parlor. Kohar was in her bedroom numbering and labeling boxes in anticipation of the moving truck that would be arriving soon. Azad could hear the squeak of the marker against cardboard, and then the screech of packing tape. Then the soft melody of the piano. When she looked over, she saw her sister sitting on the piano bench, running her fingers over the keys. She began playing a song that Azad must have heard her entire life, a song Kohar had written when she was a teenager. Azad sat in the stillness of the apartment, the gentle morning light in the parlor, listening to her sister play the piano one last time. She knew the words but didn't dare sing them under her breath. She realized the irony of the words and the prophecy in them. The song was about their mother, and Kohar had written it ten years ago when she was only fourteen. Azad would not allow herself to cry. It felt shallow in the wake of her sister's leaving; she could only imagine Kohar's pain.

"Hey."

Azad looked up at her sister and tried to smile, the tears bubbling to the surface. She couldn't find her voice. It felt as if the pain in her throat would strangle her. Kohar came and sat next to her. "Just us, huh?" she asked. She put her arm around Azad and drew her near her. She pressed her lips against the top of Azad's head. "I'm sorry," she said. "I know you're upset." Azad managed to nod. "Do you think I'm leaving because I don't love you?" Kohar asked. Azad shook her head emphatically. She felt Kohar's relief as she exhaled. "Good. Because I love you."

"I know." The words croaked out. "I'm just worried . . ." she began. She took a breath. "I'm worried that you don't feel loved," she said. "That you don't think we love you."

"I know you do," Kohar said, her voice now shaking. "I know."

Had she been able to capture that moment in her life, Azad would look upon it as a photograph of her and her sister sitting in the empty parlor hugging each other, bathed in the bright morning light. She would feel as if her love was not enough to make up for anything. After all, what solace could a ten-year-old offer? Azad would never know that in the many years Kohar had lived with them, up to that very moment, she had never truly felt loved.

THE SILK TURQUOISE DRESS STILL FELT WARM AGAINST AZAD'S body as she slipped on a pair of silver flats; she had managed to find the steamer to press out the creases. She glanced in the mirror, admiring the subtle tones with which she had applied her eye makeup. The palette of peacock feathers. Her lips were a dramatic shade of crimson. She looked out the bedroom window and saw that Krikor was already parked in front of her house. A giddiness surged within her as she went down the stairs, her legs shaky with nerves. She threw her coat over her shoulders and grabbed a scarf.

She waved to him as she approached the car. Opened the door and pulled it closed. There was no music playing. Usually Krikor would have the radio on at full volume and lower it during their drive.

"Hi," she said and leaned in for a kiss. He obliged her, and she felt the reserved way in which his lips brushed against hers.

"Hi," he said. His face was tense. He smiled uneasily.

She noticed he was wearing sweatpants and his Penn State alma mater hoodie.

"What's going on?" she asked. "Are you sick?"

Suddenly her purse started vibrating. Azad reached in to silence her cell phone.

"No, not really," he said. He ran his hand over his face as if he were trying to revive himself.

"Did something happen?" she asked.

He looked at her face, then at what she was wearing. "You look so pretty," he said, his voice tinged with guilt.

Sitting across from him, she felt overdressed and foolish. "What's going on? Are we not going out?"

Krikor grimaced. "No." He took a breath. "I was going to take you to the restaurant, but I figured this would be better."

"Krikor, what's going on?"

Azad felt her breath shorten. She pressed her hands on her lap to absorb the perspiration.

"I like you," Krikor began.

"Oh, God," Azad blurted out.

They were silent. She looked away, knowing what was to come.

"I just don't think we have enough in common," he said.

Azad shook her head, incredulous. It was the very thing she had wanted to say to him on their second date, their third. Fourth, even.

"*You* don't think we have enough in common?" she asked.

"Yeah, well. Yeah," he said.

"So, why did you make reservations at that Italian place?" she asked.

"Because . . ." he hesitated.

He stared out the window, his chin resting on his fist in contemplation. He was quiet for longer than she could stand.

"Just say what it is," Azad said. "I know you're not a coward."

Her purse began vibrating again. She pressed the side button of her cell phone to make it stop.

"I wanted this to go in a very different direction," he said. "Like, I know, *khosk-gabs* are outdated . . ."

From listening to her mother's stories about engagements in Beirut, Azad understood the term to mean something along the lines of a pre-engagement. A promise.

"I wanted to tell you that I wanted this," he motioned with his hands, drawing a line between Azad and him, "to go in a direction. But it can't. This is not easy, and I'm probably making a mistake."

"You're breaking up with me," Azad said. "I get it."

"Yes, but you don't—" he began, struggling to find the words.

"Your parents don't approve," she said. "Your mother."

Krikor said nothing and looked out the window again. "She's not entirely wrong," he said, this time not facing her. "We're very different. I'm trying to be realistic."

"I was, too," she said. "And at first I felt the same way. About you. That you were too normal." As she said the word, she berated herself. "Or that I wasn't normal enough . . . or something. What did your mother say about me?" she asked. "I want to know. It's probably the Burning Man thing."

"*That*, yes. You don't have a career path," he added. "Which I don't really care about, but I know she's right in wondering."

"You know . . ." Azad interrupted, "the stereotype is true about Armenian guys and their mothers. I really thought you were different. Especially after you went back at her during dinner."

"I *am*," Krikor said. "I am different. She unearthed my misgivings," he said.

"'Unearthed your misgivings'?" Azad said, trying not to sound bitter. "Did you practice that on your way here? I guess this was better than breaking it off in the middle of a restaurant. You and your mother have great foresight," she said, and before she knew what she was doing, she lifted the handle, got out, and slammed the door behind her. She didn't bother fishing for her house keys, remembering that in her haste she hadn't locked up when she had left.

Azad kicked off her flats, stripped off her dress, and sat on the living-room couch, reached underneath. She extracted an ashtray and lit a joint she had rolled for when she and Krikor returned from dinner. From the driveway, Krikor's car rumbled. She wondered how long he would linger. Within that moment, she heard the crackle of gravel and the sound of his car disappearing down the road.

Again, her purse was buzzing. Azad took a deep pull from her joint, exhaled. Then she zipped open her purse and looked at her phone. Three missed calls from Kohar. She listened to the last message.

"*Azad. Where are you?*" Kohar's hoarse voice murmured softly, as if in helpless defeat. From where Azad stood, she could see the silhouette of bare tree limbs shaking against a violent wind. Her throat gathered into a tight knot, understanding finally that something was wrong. She knelt on the carpet, pressed her head against the sofa. "*You have to call me back. It's about Dad. Make sure you call me, not Mom.*"

And then the words she had haphazardly written and taped to the wishing wall came to her: *I wish it could all disappear. I wish I could start over.*

Chapter 13

THE MOON HUNG CLEAR AND BRIGHT OVER THE SLEEPING ROW OF houses. Dead leaves scattered as mighty gusts of wind blew through the streets. A light flurry of snow circled in a frenzy against the winter night sky. Lucine sat in the driver's seat of a 2002 Honda hatchback her friend Craig had lent her. The car had been running for over fifteen minutes. The back seat and trunk were crammed with old boxes stuffed with everything she had been able to grab before angling her belongings and making them fit, like an impossible game of Tetris. She was dismayed at how quickly and efficiently she had managed to gather and pack her life of seven years with Steve and strategize her exit.

Lucine lit a cigarette and cracked the window open a sliver. Then she dialed Kohar's number.

"Hello?"

Lucine had no idea what time it was. "Hi. I don't know what time it is, so don't ask." A groan emitted from the other end of the line.

"I just fell asleep. I had indigestion all day. What's up?"

"I'm sitting in Craig's car and I have all my shit in it," she said.

"What happened? Did you guys have a fight?" Kohar's voice was now alive and warm.

Where to begin. "Not quite," Lucine said. She glanced at the clock, which read 2:17 a.m. "Can I come over? Is it too late?"

"No! It's never too late. Come over," Kohar practically yelled.

"But it's Christmas Eve," Lucine said.

"All the better. Drive."

"Yeah?"

"Yeah. Drive!"

Lucine shifted in gear and began driving away. "I'm doing it," she said. "I'm doing it. I'm turning the corner." It was like the first time she had balanced herself on a bicycle and unsteadily gained strength and momentum as she rode down her block.

"That's good," said Kohar. "I'll have Jonathan get the futon ready for you."

Lucine turned the corner and drove beneath a canopy of trees. Her windshield shuddered against the wind. As if susceptible to the numbing cold, Lucine hunched in her seat and pressed the gas pedal gently, half-listening as Kohar continued talking.

"There'll be no traffic on the road at this hour. Just drive here. It'll take an hour at most."

"Yeah? Well, how about Christmas morning? I know you and Jonathan exchange gifts—"

"Don't be an idiot. We'll all exchange in the morning and then we'll drive to Mom's. We'll surprise her and Gabriel."

"Will Azad be there, you think?" asked Lucine, surprising herself.

"She has been. She's been there since the beginning of the week. She took an extension from work through New Year's Eve," said Kohar.

"That was nice of them for letting her," said Lucine. "That's nice . . ."

She began crying as she barreled toward the I-95 thruway. "Don't, now," Kohar said soothingly. "You're driving. It's supposed to snow. Just get here. I'll be awake waiting for you."

She'd had weeks to pack her belongings and arrange to find a temporary place to stay. Yet she had waited almost two weeks after the eviction date, asking her landlord for an extension. It was the holidays, she had said. Just give me a break. Steve had not returned.

In an hour's time, Lucine had pulled up across the street from Kohar's house and parked the car. She turned off the ignition, not ready to carry in her duffel bag and ring the doorbell. She looked at Kohar's house and saw the dim glow of light from the bedroom window. Their living-room window was framed with white Christmas lights and, embedded in the ivy in front of the house, the wire silhouette of two reindeer glowed beautifully. Lucine regarded the surrounding houses, each adorned with a care and attention that did not exist on her block in New Brunswick. At most, a random wreath or two hung on the doors, but the neighborhood left the impression that holidays were a forgotten thing of the past, the fuss of decorations a frivolous undertaking.

Lucine sat in her parked car and watched the fine snow falling on the ground. For years, she had watched her father string the colorful blinking lights outside of their home. She would sit by the window, steaming clouds of her breath on the glass as he deftly weaved the long string of lights through the bare azalea bushes that lined the front of the house. Every so often she would knock on the pane and he would look up, wave, and continue working. She would give every piece of what she owned, what she had crammed into her car—and more, to sit inside her cozy house and watch her father in the snow. But it was too late now.

From her periphery, Lucine sensed a frantic motion and looked up at Kohar's bedroom. Kohar was waving from the open curtain. Then she reached for the window, struggling to force it open. Lucine opened the car door and stood outside.

"What the hell are you doing?" Kohar cried from the small crack. "Get your stuff and get your ass in here. Jonathan's on his way down."

Lucine felt fresh tears forming, and a quick sob escaped her chest. The snow fell rapidly, covering her hair and coat with a fine mist. She leaned into the car and grabbed her purse and duffel bag and crossed the street. By the time she reached the porch, Jonathan was holding open the storm door for her. Without asking, he took her things and pulled her inside. Then hugged her mightily.

"Thanks," she whispered.

"I'm glad you're here," he said.

Jonathan. Always trying to balance the unyielding seesaw of their family's existence. Yet she did not know that Jonathan had suffered the ordeal of Takouhi's phone calls, complaining that he and Kohar visiting Gabriel once a week was not enough. Despite Jonathan explaining exhaustively the toll of those visits on Kohar, she had not wavered. He had set aside one evening a week and gone to the apartment alone after work, sitting with Gabriel in the living room, watching a movie, or, more recently, at the foot of his bed where they carried on conversation until Gabriel drifted into sleep.

Lucine stood in the middle of the living room and grew still at the sight—the smell of pine, the dark room illuminated by a glowing Christmas tree and tea light candles bright in their holders.

"Is there a fucking choir hiding in the kitchen?" she joked. She felt the tears again, creeping through. She wiped them off.

"Merry Christmas." Lucine looked up. Kohar was standing at the staircase landing, holding her small belly, smiling. The last time they had seen each other, Kohar's stomach was so flat it was impossible to fathom that she would be carrying a growing fetus inside her. And there she was, her stomach protruding pleasantly beneath an old T-shirt.

Lucine wanted to tell her it had only taken her an hour to get there, just as Kohar had said. She wanted to tell her about Steve, the stupid fling with Max, how she still had to bring in all her shit from the car, that she was hungry because she hadn't eaten since the day before. Most embarrassingly—she didn't have any Christmas presents for her and Jonathan. Her life was sitting in a borrowed car.

"Merry Christmas," Lucine said and, for once, she let the tears come.

SOMEONE WAS CALLING HER NAME, PULLING HER OUT OF A DREAM in which she was walking through a blinding sandstorm, following the obscured figure of a man who was being assailed by gusts of sand. Before her eyes snapped open, she could swear she felt the sharp grains of the storm spraying against her body.

"Azad! I'm rolling out the *lehmajoun* dough."

The digital clock in the bedroom read 7:37 a.m. But it couldn't be. Azad rolled over and lifted the curtain slightly. The sky was gray. The dawn had given way to another dull morning.

"Azad!"

"Takouhi! It's not even eight o'clock!" Her father's voice barked from behind the closed bedroom door.

Azad sat up in bed and slumped over on her side. Then she pulled her robe over her back and headed to the bathroom. From her father's bedroom she heard the opening credits for *Mildred Pierce* on American Movie Classics.

"Dad?" Azad pushed the door open and drew in a breath. Every time she saw the pallor of her father's face, she felt a wave of surprise. She was expecting to see his ruddy cheeks, his oversized belly she loved patting affectionately, his large green eyes hopeful for something—food, a cup of coffee. Instead, Gabriel sat in bed with the covers pulled up to his chin like a convalescing child, his face as ashen and white as his beard. *When did it change from gray to white? Had that happened from the chemotherapy?* At the side of his bed was a bedpan. The last time he had gotten sick from the chemotherapy was at the dining-room table. His nephew had driven in from Philadelphia with his young son, and Gabriel, in an effort to maintain a semblance of good health, had insisted on leaving his bed. Azad had watched with growing dismay as her father's face had broken into a sudden sweat and lost its color. She had helped him race to the bathroom, but not in time.

"What's your crazy mother doing now?" Gabriel asked.

Azad perched herself on the edge of his bed. She yawned deeply. "Making lehmajoun."

Gabriel shook his head. Azad couldn't tell if he was disapproving or admiring her determination to host Christmas again. They had been invited to several friends' homes, but Takouhi had declined. He wanted to ask her if it was because she didn't want him enduring the discomfort of not lying in bed. But he knew it was for another reason. One he could accept only within himself.

"Azad!" Takouhi's voice rang from the kitchen, down the hallway and into the room.

Azad and her father looked at one another, holding each other's gaze. Gabriel gave her a lopsided smile, a smile that hedged on the current dilemma of Takouhi's mania and an acceptance of defeat. The present and the future. Azad went to the side of the bed and crawled under the covers, rested her head on her father's shoulder. The bones beneath his skin were hard and protruding. Instantly, Azad was overcome by a hysteria so acute that she bit her lip until she felt the blood on her tongue. She felt his arm across her, holding her gently. They lay together, watching the black-and-white film on the muted television, drifting back to sleep as soft pellets of icy snow tapped against the windowpane.

SEVERAL HOURS LATER, THE ABRUPT BUZZING OF THE BELL STARtled the house. Gabriel had been sleeping through his favorite Scrooge movie featuring Alastair Sim, something he would have stayed up late watching during the Christmas season. Takouhi and Azad had just settled themselves on the couch and turned on the television; they had just lined the sheet pans with the last lehmajouns and her mother had set the timer.

Takouhi was explaining to Azad about the chickpeas in the pressure cooker when they both jumped at the bell.

"Who is this?" Takouhi rose with agitation. "Who is it?" she yelled into the intercom.

"Santa Claus." The voice reverberated from the entrance of the building.

"Who is it?" Azad called out.

Takouhi didn't bother answering her—one of many of Azad's pet peeves—and went to the door. She heard Takouhi gasp with surprise. Azad loved the foyer for this reason; it was obscured by the living-room wall, and it was a mysterious thing to hear the voices of people being greeted at the door and then having them materialize.

"So early!" Takouhi exclaimed. It echoed through the walls of the building. "Oh! You're here, too!—Azad!" Her volume would have carried across the courtyard. "Come help with the bags!"

She could hear Jonathan and Kohar explaining the contents of each bag, but there was the mystery of the third person.

"What's up, asshole."

Azad literally jumped in her seat. If her mother's jolting early wakeup call and the sudden buzzer hadn't jangled her nerves, Lucine's astonishing presence in the apartment was downright unnerving. Like an oil stain on a new shirt. All hope of having a happy Christmas was ruined.

Utterly dispirited, Azad offered a smile she would have given to the mailman. She nodded. "Hey."

"Don't look so happy to see me."

Now with her back to her, Lucine left the room, leaving her words behind her. The back of her T-shirt read "I'd give a fuck, but I already gave it to your mother last night."

Azad wanted to laugh, but she couldn't. Depending on Lucine's mood, this was either going to be a day of excruciating ball-busting and passive-aggressive comments, which would send Azad into her mother's bedroom inevitably crying and her mother chastising Lucine for, well, for everything, or a more subdued experience punctuated by Lucine's long, drawn-out silences alternated with sarcastic comments that were meant for no one and everyone.

"Jonathan, I need you to get the Christmas tree. Maybe Lucine can go with you." She heard her mother in the kitchen amidst the thud of grocery bags and the clatter of dishes being taken out of the cupboard.

"I'll go with him!" Azad hollered from her seat.

Kohar drifted in and settled herself next to her on the couch. "Hey."

Azad regarded Kohar's small belly with amusement. "The baby's already cute the way it's poking out." She leaned over and hugged Kohar, then rested her hand lightly on her stomach.

"It's a girl," Kohar said.

Azad looked at her brightly. "It is? When did you find out?"

"A while ago," Kohar said. Her entire body seemed to exhale. "Jonathan's delighted." Which meant, Azad could assume, that Kohar was not.

"Do you know I used to change your diapers?" asked Kohar. "All the time. This is going to be a breeze. Remember that picture of you? Your entire body covered in talcum powder?"

"Does Mom know?" asked Azad.

"What?"

"That it's a girl."

Kohar shook her head. "Not only will she pick out the name, but she'll start knitting and embroidering clothes with the initials. No, thanks. Keep it to yourself." She thought of the white booties her mother had knitted at the beginning of her first pregnancy and felt guilty. Now four months pregnant, her mother all but ignored Kohar's growing stomach.

"Does Lucine know?"

"No. She has enough going on. Listen, go easy on her today, okay? She's having a tough time."

"*Me* go easy on her? Are you kidding me?"

"Don't go running to Mom."

"I never run to Mom."

"You run, and Mom runs to you. Either way. Just don't run."

The delicate dynamic among them—Azad had the capacity to understand, but couldn't. Or wouldn't. There was too much at stake for her to see the divide of teams: Kohar and Lucine, their mother and Azad. Takouhi had been the unwitting, or premeditated, wielder of this segregation based solely, in Kohar's theory, on Takouhi's hatred toward their father and her intense adoration of

Gabriel. Perhaps it was also that she resembled her father, his almond-shaped eyes and imperfect nose, and Lucine's crabby and berating temperament was seemingly a hereditary disposition, though Kohar understood otherwise.

Recounting the stark differences in their upbringing left Kohar feeling as if she and Lucine were the stepchildren, an unwanted inheritance that their mother resented yet abided by in all matters of necessity: food, shelter, and clothes. When Kohar had moved out, she had never asked her mother or Gabriel for money. Yet despite their having paid all of Azad's student loans, buying her a car, and the house Azad's grandmother had left her, Takouhi still paying Azad's cell phone bill (it was a family plan, so it didn't really count) and keeping her under her health insurance (it was only a few dollars more per month) and paying for her car insurance, Kohar knew that Takouhi still gave Azad money every month. Kohar was careful to not share these details with Lucine, allowing her to live in the oblivion of ignorance. Lucine's sanity would surely be at stake otherwise. Or she would set fire to the apartment altogether. Kohar tried not to remember all this as she sat on the couch with Azad.

"Ready?" Jonathan was still wearing his coat and wool hat from when they had walked in. There were still beads of condensation in his beard. His black turtleneck framed his face, accentuating the handsomeness of his deep-set brown eyes.

"You're going to freeze in that," Azad said, eyeing his tweed coat skeptically.

"I told him," Kohar said. "Since when do *you* notice anything? You walk around in flipflops until November."

Azad disappeared into the coat closet and pulled out a heavy herringbone coat and threw it into Jonathan's arms. As he slid his arms through the openings, he smelled the faint aroma of cologne and tobacco, felt the hollow space against his narrow limbs, realizing it was Gabriel's winter coat. When, if at all, was the last time Gabriel had left the house and worn it, he wondered. And if Gabriel sensed how his body no longer filled the coat, his frame now considerably less significant.

"Are you—?" *sure*, is what Jonathan began to ask and simultaneously Azad's voice, amiable at first, interrupting.

"—he's not going to wear it for—" And then Azad halted as if someone had clamped her mouth shut.

Jonathan dared not look at her. When he finally forced his eyes to where she was standing, her back was turned, her forehead pressed against the wall. Then she spun around, avoiding his eyes, and busied herself with zipping and buttoning the coat—entirely unnecessary, they both knew—and neither could bear to say what they were thinking.

"I have a lighter," she said finally, materializing a neon green lighter and then flashing Jonathan a pack of Parliaments.

"What kind of T-shirt is this?" they both heard Takouhi exclaiming shrilly from the kitchen. "On *Christmas*, no less! Please go change. *Please.* I can't look at you."

Nothing was as pleasant-sounding to Azad as the echo of the front door closing behind her as she followed Jonathan outside in the falling snow.

Kohar ignored the eruption of bickering and walked down the long hallway toward the bedroom. She could hear the soft bodiless voices from the television coming through behind the door. She knocked gently and entered. A slight wind crept through the old windows, shivering the curtains slightly. The gray winter sky glowering behind Gabriel's bed, the falling snow whispering through the air. Gabriel was lying on his side, his mouth open and his eyes closed in a deep sleep. Kohar sat precariously on the edge of his bed, watching him breathing busily. For every breath he took, she felt a quiet gratitude. Had she not known he was sick with cancer, it would not have been hard to discern from his frame, which, though covered in the thick layer of the comforter, was less round and alive.

Since his diagnosis several months earlier, Kohar talked about her pregnancy less and less. When she and Jonathan visited on Saturdays, Kohar was in the kitchen with her mother, watching her pore through books that were propped open on the kitchen counter. Books titled *What to Eat During Cancer Treatment*; *Anti-Cancer Smoothies: Healing with Superfoods*; and *Natural Strategies for Cancer Patients*. The Ninja blender, a ubiquitous kitchen appliance that was being advertised on infomercials and recently featured on a CBS cooking demo, seemed always to be brimming with a concoction that Takouhi had whipped together after shopping at the farmer's market. While Takouhi compiled the fruits and vegetables and roots and fresh herbs for the day's smoothie, Kohar ignored the fluttering in her stomach. It felt like she was being tickled from the inside. The first feeling of the baby kicking, the doctor told her.

Kohar ignored the merciless pangs of nausea and the unbearable desire to vomit. She knew that once they went home, she would be able to let herself feel pregnant again, to almost enjoy the fatigue that so doggedly plagued her, the inability to look at raw meat because the idea of eating flesh made her want to gag, the craving for cold pink grapefruits, Jonathan rubbing her feet although they weren't swollen yet—she loved it all. Neither she nor Jonathan mentioned her mother's obvious disinterest in the baby or being a grandmother—a *medz-mama*—to the firstborn grandchild of the family. Gabriel would smile at Kohar during the lulls between conversations, nod to her and squeeze his eyes, as if embracing her from afar, as if her sizable stomach was an impressive feat she was responsible for somehow. And when Jonathan began his weekly visits alone, Kohar would feel the sickening guilt as he prepared to leave the house, and then the rush of relief as she heard the garage door open and the car back out of the driveway.

Kohar sat and watched. Desperately, she wanted to know if Gabriel would live long enough to hold the baby in his arms. Just once. Ruby Rose. Little Ruby. She hadn't yet told Jonathan the baby's name, knowing it was unfair to have already picked it out. But she hadn't been able to help herself. She imagined a strong warrior of a girl, her daughter, bright and beautiful.

"You're here."

Kohar had been staring at Gabriel but hadn't noticed his eyes open.

"Hi." Kohar leaned over and touched the silhouette of his leg.

"Who's here?"

"Everyone. Me, Jonathan, Lucine."

Gabriel raised his eyebrows. "Lucine?"

Kohar leaned in for emphasis and whispered, "She packed her stuff and left. Last night."

Gabriel's eyes widened, refreshed by this new bit of information. "What happened?"

"I don't know. I didn't want to ask. Don't tell Mom."

"Where's Jonathan?"

"Azad went with him to buy the Christmas tree."

Gabriel nodded to himself. Neither was going to talk about their tradition of buying a tree together for all the past Christmases. Every year, the two were all but relieved and thankful to leave the intense holiday flurry for an hour and buy the Christmas tree; Takouhi would be pulling out boxes of small Dickens' village houses to decorate the top of the grand piano, and Lucine and Azad would help her carry each of the items to the parlor. Then began the tedious task of arranging all the homes that would comprise a winter village of Takouhi's design. Lucine and Azad would watch her toil over the placement of the church, the skating rink, the villagers, the cobbler's shop, the bakery, the small, frosted winter trees. A miniature imitation of Takouhi's imaginings of a perfect Christmas winterland. Meanwhile, both Gabriel and Kohar would be waiting for the car to warm up, the smoke and their cold breath mingling in the frigid car.

"I'm getting up soon."

Kohar regarded the laptop and a cover-worn book beside Gabriel. "Are you still working?" she asked.

He shrugged wearily. "Sometimes. It keeps me busy. How long can someone watch that," he said, motioning to the television screen, "before going crazy. How's work?" He was in the habit of asking her often, especially interested in hearing stories about impudent teenagers.

"Good," she said, smiling at Gabriel's raised eyebrows. "I've got a few hilarious characters this year. I'll tell you later," she promised. Then she rose to leave for the kitchen. "Do you need anything?"

"Yes," he said, rather officially. "Go close the door." He nodded to the door that was barely open.

"It's closed."

"It's not. Your mother can hear the goddamn snow falling."

Kohar let out a sharp laugh. When she turned around, she found Gabriel propped up in bed, a faint color in his face. She sat back down at the edge of the bed.

"She needs to chill out. She's making me *nuts*," said Gabriel.

"Gabriel! You're funny," said Kohar.

"She needs to smoke some weed," he said. "Can you get your hands on some of that?"

Kohar retracted in shock. "Pot? I can get my hands on plenty. But honestly, there's no way you're going to get her to smoke it."

"She's all over me. She's making me crazy. She needs to chill the F out," he said. He took pleasure, she noticed, in his acute bluntness. "Maybe," he said craftily as he pressed the tips of his fingers together in the shape of a steeple, "Lucine can bake some cookies for her. Put some of that pot in there."

Kohar shook her head. "No. Way. Maybe, though, she can bake them and say it's for you. And then we can get Mom to take a bite."

"Go work on this," he said and waved toward the door again. "Go talk to her. Maybe today or tomorrow. Tell your mother I'm still sleeping. I'd like to be able to wipe my ass without her hovering outside the door."

As she left the room, Kohar caught a glimpse of Gabriel reaching into his nightstand drawer and hearing the sound of cellophane. It was one of many Gabriel's sounds, was how she thought of it. Her memory had compiled a collection: the sharp sound of a fork or spoon thrown into a porcelain sink, the distant hum of jazz or classical music, absorbed silence, the clearing of his throat, the gurgling pour of coffee into a cup, the sound of cellophane unwrapping a pack of cigarettes. Kohar kept walking, leaving Gabriel to his small and mighty freedoms.

"Lucine, why are you sitting there? Get up and help us decorate."

Lucine had been sitting on the couch, watching in horror as Christmas boxes had erupted and spewed what seemed an endless collection of ornaments: wooden-shaped ones that hung from jute twine that were relics of their first Christmas in the apartment when they had sat at a newspaper-covered dining-room table painting with tedious care, flat ornaments in the images of old Victorian Santa Clauses, cherubs, Christmas trees outlined in a gold silhouette, miscellaneous ornaments that were given as gifts—the odd fruits of the bunch that Takouhi hung with persistent nostalgia year after year. And the mantel decorations that Lucine apathetically unwrapped and handed over to her mother or one of her sisters as they stood around the fireplace, strategizing the most tasteful display of the miniature trees, stately candelabra, twigs from the pine tree, as if it had never been done before. As if it really fucking mattered since it would be taken down in a few weeks' time. This year, though, Christmas was being orchestrated within the short breadth of one evening; Takouhi had been too overwhelmed to have any foresight this winter.

"C'mon!" Takouhi turned to her from where she stood on the highest step of the stool. "Why are you sitting there?"

"I hate this shit," Lucine muttered, exhaling with aggravation as she stood up.

Gabriel lay across the other couch, watching passively. He had just finally settled himself after spending much of the day in the bedroom.

Kohar leaned over to her while Takouhi asked Jonathan about their New Year's Eve plans. "Whatever you do, please don't storm off into one of the bedrooms."

"I'm not!" Lucine declared too loudly. She felt her mother turn around briefly and then resume her conversation.

"You do it every year. Don't do it—"

"I don't do it every year, Kohar. I hate when you say shit like this."

She did it every year. It was like being in a perpetual *Honeymooners* episode where Ralph Kramden would eventually threaten to send his wife Alice to the moon. Everyone seemed to anticipate the finale with the exception of Ralph himself. Kohar was going to let it go.

"Let's start packing away the boxes. Azad, why don't you do the angel's hair?" Takouhi suggested and dropped the old cardboard box in Azad's lap. White strands were hanging out of the opening that used to be sealed with cellophane.

Azad went to the tree and started extracting the silky wisps and carefully covering the tree limbs.

"How ethereal," she heard Lucine's mocking voice from across the parlor. "Be careful, the placement. It has to be done just so," she continued. She had taken on the voice of a New York City art curator with a precision so accurate that it literally made Azad cringe as she continued, ignoring her. "That's puuuurfect! I love what you're doing there. That's why I always say: you either have it or you don't. And you, my dear, have *got* it—"

"Fuck off!" Azad whipped around and threw the cardboard box on the rug. Her pounding footsteps followed her to her old bedroom.

"Lucine!" Takouhi glared at her admonishingly. "*Eeleh.* You had to. This one night you couldn't control yourself. Where is Steven? I've been meaning to ask you."

Kohar laughed out loud. That word. *Eeleh.* It was Arabic, she guessed. She loved hearing the word, the word being used, saying the word out loud.

It literally meant "you had to." Like: *eeleh* you went out with your friends although there was a snowstorm coming or *eeleh* you ate a second serving of ice cream when you were already full or *eeleh* you had to upset your younger sister on the last Christmas we would spend as a family together with Gabriel. And once Kohar grasped the subtext of her mother's reproach, she looked over at Gabriel. He was staring up at the ceiling, shaking his head, tsking under his breath.

"Go fix it," Kohar spoke slowly, her words only audible to Lucine. She watched her sister gather herself like someone shoving a tangled knot of yarn in their pocket and watched her disappear into the hallway.

"Where is Steven?" Takouhi repeated, once she heard the bedroom door close.

"He's not here," Kohar said.

"Hello? I can see he's not here. Where *is* he?" Takouhi asked.

Kohar shrugged her shoulders. "She came late last night. I didn't want to ask."

"Something fishy's going on over there," Takouhi predicted, naïvely.

"You think so?" Kohar smiled at her, her eyes feigning innocence.

"Did she leave him?" Takouhi leaned in this time, her voice dropping to a mischievous whisper.

"I hope so," Kohar confided. "We can consider it a Christmas miracle."

As soon as she said the words, it felt as if she had inadvertently misspoken. "Uh-humm . . ." Takouhi murmured. Her eyes fell now. A Christmas miracle. Kohar followed her mother's gaze to Gabriel sitting. His hands folded over in his lap in quiet repose, his eyes were closed and his mouth was open. He always napped on that particular couch. Takouhi exhaled deeply and turned her back.

"Mom—"

"I'm going to start frying the meat beregs."

From the length of the hallway that led to Azad's old bedroom erupted a muffled yell. Takouhi and Kohar turned their heads almost at once and paused.

"You always do!" The words now rang in the air, sharp and pleading.

"I don't. You're so fucking sensitive. You're a fucking baby. I'm sick and tired of having to put a muzzle—" It was a diatribe both Kohar and Takouhi could recite from memory.

As Takouhi gathered herself toward the door, Kohar held her shoulder gently. "Please let me. Just go to the kitchen and finish making dinner." She hadn't meant to sound forceful and was glad when her mother relented, as if she was hoping Kohar would intervene.

Kohar moved too quickly to bother eavesdropping and entered the room, closing the door behind her silently, quickly, as if trying to contain the noise.

Azad was sitting on the bed and Lucine was sitting cross-legged on the radiator. "Oh, *greeeeat*!" she said upon seeing Kohar. She rolled her eyes and threw her arms up in exasperated defeat. "Here we go. Now I have to listen to your bullshit about how I ruin everything."

Azad flopped back on the pillows, splaying her body as if assuming the position of being drawn and quartered.

"Why are you being an asshole?" Kohar asked Lucine.

"Why am *I* always the asshole and she's so fucking sensitive and no one says shit to her about anything. It's always my fault in this family. That's why I hate coming on the holidays and having to deal with—"

Kohar exhaled loudly, exhausted from putting out not fires, really, but volcanic eruptions that Lucine generated with such ease.

Azad sprang up violently (Kohar would have begun laughing on any other given day), as if being yanked up to a seated position by an imaginary cord. "I can't even put angel's hair on the Christmas tree without her making a comment. She always has to say something." She waited, for dramatic pause or summoning the gumption, and faced Lucine. "Why do you hate me?" she yelled.

Lucine did the one thing, the Wrong Thing, that would surely have sent anyone else flying across the room to strangle her. She began laughing. "Oh God. I can't. I can't do this." She buried her laughter in her hands, trying to muffle herself.

"Guys—skip the fight this year." Neither of her sisters looked at her. "I'm serious. Or whatever it is you do every year," Kohar said. "This is not like every other Christmas. Both of you figure it the fuck out."

"Big Sister has spoken," Lucine declared.

Kohar couldn't decide what was more irritating—Lucine's obnoxious, unfounded comment, or the fact that she hadn't recognized her bigger point. Instead of taking the bait, Kohar turned to both of them and said something unanswerable.

"Maybe by playing out your yearly Christmas drama—and I'm feeding into it by coming in here—you're trying to convince yourself that this is like any other Christmas Eve. When you know it's not. Don't make me say it."

Without waiting for a response, she walked out, half-expecting to feel the heel of a shoe landing on the back of her head. Instead, there was only the onset of a growing silence in the room.

LUCINE WAITED UNTIL KOHAR WAS OUT OF EARSHOT AND DE-cided to bypass the elephant in the room. "So, what's up with Krikor?" she asked. "Did you meet the family yet?"

"Yes," said Azad, scowling.

"Well, what's going on? Are you guys still together?" Lucine asked.

Azad flopped on her back and threw a pillow over her face. "That ended before it started. I went out with him for like three months and then when I got back from Burning Man he asked me to have dinner with his family and that's when everything was going on with Dad. It was just too much."

"Like you'd be dating him if Dad hadn't gotten sick," Lucine specu-lated, not meaning to come across as sarcastic.

"No. I wouldn't be," Azad said. "I wasn't into him."

"I bet not," Lucine said. "Oh, well for Mom."

"Oh, well," said Azad. "I feel bad though."

"Don't," Lucine said. "She's so disappointed with us already that it won't matter really. Has she asked?"

"Not specifically," said Azad. "She hasn't brought it up, which means she may have given up hope."

"That's good," Lucine said. "You should do what Kohar did. Years be-fore Jonathan, she told Mom she was never getting married. That lowered the bar. Now look how happy Mom is."

"Yeah. Happy," Azad said wryly.

"You know what I mean," Lucine said.

"So, where's Steve?" Azad asked.

"Not here," Lucine said.

"I can see that. Why?"

"It's a long story," Lucine said.

"Let me guess: you caught him with another girl," Azad said.

"No. And I don't want to talk about it."

"Did you tell Kohar?"

"No, I did not tell Kohar," said Lucine. "And I don't feel like talking about it."

"So, what're you going to do?" Azad asked.

"Nothing. I don't have anything to do."

"Azad!" Takouhi's voice carried from the kitchen. "Jonathan needs you!"

Azad stood up to leave the room. She turned and looked at Lucine. She was sitting on the radiator, her back already turned away. "Don't be a dick to me, okay?" said Azad.

Lucine looked up at her. Her hair was gathered in a sloppy bun and her eyes, dark and tired, made her seem helpless and defeated. "Okay. No more dickish behavior tonight."

Azad lingered for a moment, suddenly wanting to hug her sister, to tell her she loved her. The thought held her there awkwardly, until finally she turned away and pulled the door shut behind her.

She found Jonathan kneeling in front of the fireplace, struggling with a bundle of firewood.

"Azad, grab me a pair of scissors, would you? I can't open the casing for the firewood. The stupid mesh thing is indestructible," Jonathan called over.

"Jonathan! Come to the kitchen!"

Takouhi's unnerving ability to call or request for things at exactly the *wrong* time didn't irritate Jonathan as it did the rest of the family. Despite Kohar and Takouhi's unusual dynamic, Jonathan managed to tolerate his mother-in-law, setting aside many misgivings: most obviously the stress-inducing phone calls, comments, backhanded compliments that Kohar had to suffer, Takouhi's passive-aggressive teasing and mocking of his mother, which occurred in Jonathan's mother's presence, her criticism of their home ("The ceilings in our apartment are higher." "The kitchen counter should be longer since it's such a small kitchen." "The back yard isn't big enough for entertaining."), Jonathan maintained his good-naturedness somehow. He felt he saw through the barbed-wire fortress of Takouhi's disposition and understood her better than Kohar or Azad or anyone else in the family.

But not because he was less judgmental than any of them or because he was posturing as an abiding son-in-law; more so it was because he believed at heart that Takouhi loved her family and wanted always to be surrounded by them.

"Come taste this," said Takouhi, holding a meat bereg she had fried from the first batch.

Jonathan smiled and gently bit into the piece, reminding himself that he always burned his mouth, too eager to eat Takouhi's food. The taste of paprika and cumin and savory dough and beef melted in his mouth. He smiled wider.

"It's good?" she asked, knowing already that it was.

"One more," he said, which he knew delighted her.

She laughed. "One more, but finish eating it in here. There will be nothing left for later once they find out."

He watched her drop another meat-filled bereg into the frying pot. The chaos of food on the kitchen counter communicated a mania similar to Kohar's when she was cooking for a large gathering—a plastic bag that was reserved for all the vegetable shavings that would be frozen and then used to make stock, the mysterious bowls filled with various vegetables, liquids, dressings, marinades that would be added to specific dishes as the cooking for the day progressed, an assortment of knives already used and left out for another hour or two of preparation. It was organized anarchy that fatefully came together in an orchestrated parade of dishes for the special meal of the evening.

"How do you think Gabriel looks?" Takouhi asked.

"He looks pretty good," Jonathan said. He had to.

"You think so?" Takouhi asked. "I was thinking the same thing this morning. His face has more color. He left the bed several times this morning. Usually, he gets up once to use the bathroom and then he stays there. He leaves the TV off most of the day because he's still translating."

With each Saturday Jonathan and Kohar visited, Jonathan noticed the waning of Gabriel's being. And more so when Jonathan visited alone, as if he could only allow himself to see Gabriel through Kohar's eyes in her presence, less sick, more alive.

"It's not at all what the doctors had told us in the beginning," Takouhi said. She lowered her glasses and looked at him. "I'm going to tell you something, but you have to promise not to say anything to Kohar or the girls."

Jonathan was familiar with these requests; it wasn't the first time Takouhi had told him something in confidence. He waited.

"Well," she said and exhaled. This was also familiar to Jonathan—the exhaling. As if to say *I'm about to admit a deceit.* "When we found out Gabriel had cancer, he was already diagnosed at stage three. But we—"

"Kohar told me it was stage two," Jonathan said.

"I know," Takouhi nodded. "That's what I told her and that's what she told the girls. Gabriel didn't want you all to worry. But what I'm trying to say is that at this point it's almost a miracle that he's here. They told us we would be lucky if he survived through Thanksgiving. And look. Look. Here he is. I called my sisters and they're coming for Kohar's baby shower. I'm thinking by the spring if he's still doing well and with the baby due in May he's going to make it to see the baby."

"The baby shower? When is that supposed to happen? Kohar didn't mention—"

"I haven't told her yet. She said I could plan it. I think the weekend of St. Patrick's Day will be perfect."

"So, a surprise?" asked Jonathan.

"Yes. I'm sure you're capable of getting her here without giving away the surprise," said Takouhi.

Jonathan hesitated. If it were a miracle that Gabriel was still alive, would this miracle sustain itself for another, say, three months? Four? Hope was a dangerous thing. Hope could thrive and flourish to heights of self-delusion and magical thinking. Jonathan would experience none of this much later in time when he alone would stand over Gabriel's dead body and hold his hand over Gabriel's eyelids to close them for the last time.

"I'm sure I can," Jonathan said.

TAKOUHI SETTLED HERSELF ON THE COUCH, RELAXING FOR THE first time since the morning. The egg timer would go off in thirty-five minutes. The pork loin would need to rest for at least ten minutes after that. Gabriel, just having taken his pills, was resting in the recliner drowsily.

They were all sitting in the living room, watching half-heartedly as Takouhi skimmed through the onscreen guide for a good film. Azad was hunched over her cell phone, busily texting.

"Mom, Stephanie and Tara are in town. I told them they could stop by later on tonight. I hope that's okay," said Azad.

"How nice!" Takouhi said. "Of course. I haven't seen those girls in so long. How are they doing?"

"Did they get married and pop out a baby yet?" Lucine asked.

Azad rolled her eyes. "*No*, not yet."

"That's a shocker," said Lucine. There was no trace of sarcasm in her voice. "Wasn't Stephanie the slut? I'd figure she couldn't *help* getting pregnant."

Azad let her fork drop. "Seriously, Lucine!"

Gabriel, listening with his eyes closed, shook his head, and sucked his teeth, trying unsuccessfully to suppress a grin. Kohar let out a snort.

"Sometimes such gosht things come out of your mouth," Takouhi said. *Crude.* "Where did you learn to speak that way? Not from me." Then she turned to Kohar. "You know who you haven't mentioned in a while?" she asked brightly, proud to have remembered a name from Kohar's friends. "Jackie—that friend of yours from high school. The one who became a children's doctor."

"Obstetrician," Kohar corrected her, too disgusted to hide the sourness in her voice. "Jackie Shapiro."

"Yes! Jackie Sha*piro*. You haven't mentioned her in a long time. I always wondered why you never brought your friends home. Azad has such a nice group of friends from high school. It's so nice that you all still stay in touch and now they're coming over."

Takouhi turned her gaze to the television screen and sunk her hand in a bag of salted watermelon seeds and cracked one between her teeth. Kohar felt the immediate pressure of Jonathan's hand massaging the back of her neck. She struggled between the visceral urge to lunge across the room and grab her mother by the throat and the pending explosion Jonathan was attempting to mitigate. It felt like she had opened a bottle of seltzer too quickly, releasing a surprising pressure of water that sputtered before twisting the cap closed. Too late.

"You didn't *let* me have friends—Jackie being one of them. I had dinner with her recently. And she told me that she stopped calling the house because you told her not to." Facing her mother now, Kohar could feel her face quivering. She wondered if her mother would offer an apology or forfeit the gesture, given that it had all happened decades ago.

Takouhi froze for a moment, as if silencing the room to make sure she had heard clearly. Her face retracted and puckered in disbelief. "Jackie said I did *what*?"

"That the last time she called the house, you told her not to call again," Kohar repeated, her words now feeble-sounding and silly, as if she were repeating a preposterous lie.

"What?" Takouhi asked, drawing out the length of the word. "Why would I do that? No," she said, shaking her head. "Maybe we're talking about the wrong person."

"Why?" Kohar asked, now pulling away completely from Jonathan's hand, which had been poised on her shoulder. "Were there any other friends who you told not to call me anymore? Jackie told me—" And then Kohar caught herself. Not because she was unwilling to rehash the painful memory, succumb to all the painful memories of her adolescence—they seemed to be all strung together in angry, tight knots—but because she could see the reflection of the Christmas tree lights twinkling behind her from the living-room window and sense that her family was holding their breaths: she was holding the lighted match.

She wanted to tell her mother that she had reconnected with Jackie Shapiro on Facebook three years ago—Kohar's only reconnection from the small private school which she had attended for six years. They had met at a bar near Jackie's apartment on the Upper East Side and recounted the lost years between them. Kohar had remarked in passing, not awkwardly but for lack of remembering, why it was that they had lost touch. Jackie had grown quiet then, taken a longer sip of her wine, before setting it down and telling Kohar: the last time she had called, maybe it was her third year at Colgate, Kohar's mother had told her not to call anymore. No, her mother hadn't given any explanation, but said that she didn't want her calling. Jackie apologized, admitting that perhaps she shouldn't have let it go at that, should have called again and that she was still sorry. Kohar remembered then, leaving messages for Jackie that were left unreturned and convincing herself that the demands of pre-med had ultimately dissolved their friendship.

Many of Kohar's friendships had ended at the hand of her mother's moods, disapprovals, and whimsies. In the seventh grade, she had brought home Amanda Greenbaum for the first and only time. A nervous introvert of a girl who was being groomed by her parents to audition for the High School of Performing Arts. Takouhi had made fun of her to her face, mimicking the girl's muffled speech and pigeon-toed gait when she clumped through the front door in her stiff Doc Martens, humiliating her so thoroughly that she hadn't accepted any of Kohar's invitations afterward. Then there was Jennifer Weiner with her frosted lipstick and fluffy Benetton socks, who left horrified when Takouhi had stormed into Kohar's bedroom, screaming at her in Armenian for not taking the garbage down to the incinerator. Within Kohar's first year at Seton Academy, news had circulated that her mother was, for lack of a better term, batshit crazy—a verdict so final and absolute that it forever condemned Kohar as a social invalid, although the facts pointed more to her mother than herself.

Kohar sat stiffly with her hand over her small, round belly tolerating Jonathan's hand stroking the back of her neck now, knowing that she could not confront her mother. She would claim not to remember, as she did for so many unaccountable cruelties that left Kohar feeling as if she had imagined it all. It was similar, although Kohar could not know firsthand, to living with an alcoholic parent who blacked out during the most toxic moments. For Kohar, the moments were a compilation of years that she looked back on and detailed with an emotional precision that her therapist had praised her for many times. One question vibrated within Kohar with a fierce intensity that she could not reconcile or rationalize, try as she might: *If you can't even remember what you did, what was the point of it at all?* There had to be a reason for suffering. It had to come full circle, didn't it?

She grasped for reasons. There were circumstances, Kohar explained to her therapist, beyond her mother's control that had created, mutated her mother from her true self—the deprived and isolated childhood, the dream of fame that had been stolen from her, being married off to her father when she had been only nineteen years old and the sixteen years of neglect and arguments she had endured—it had ruined her mother, broken her irreparably. In truth, her mother's insanities were solely her father's fault.

Kohar reasoned that it was why her mother had disowned her; she had felt like the abandoned child all over again. Until her therapist pointed out that it had not been the last time. She reminded Kohar of her mother's same reaction when she had moved in with Jonathan, not having been engaged yet. Then she handed Kohar a book, suggesting that it would, perhaps, give her insight. *Will I Ever Be Good Enough? Healing the Daughters of Narcissistic Mothers.*

Kohar's thoughts were interrupted as Gabriel began coughing. She watched him convulsing in the recliner, his body bent over and his cheeks pink with perspiration. Guiltily, she let her anger slip away, aware that it would reappear again without warning, as it always did.

"Drink some water! There's a glass of water right there." Takouhi rushed over from the couch and patted Gabriel's back and handed him the glass.

The soft bell of the egg timer sounded from the kitchen.

"I'll get it," Lucine said and left the room.

"This happens," Takouhi said. "One of the pills makes your throat dry. This happens," she said, looking up at Jonathan, Kohar, and Azad, who all sat watching quietly. "Start setting the table," she said. "Azad, when you open the china cabinet, take out the Christmas place settings. Kohar, go see what's going on with the pork loin," Takouhi directed.

Once she left the room, there was only Jonathan. His eyes were smarting with tears. He wiped them away when Takouhi turned back to Gabriel.

"Do you want to go lie in bed?" she asked him.

Now, mostly recovered from the coughing fit, he shook his head. "I'll wait for dinner. After."

It seemed impossible to Jonathan that he would be able to chew, let alone swallow anything. Takouhi's divulgence in the kitchen now left him feeling utterly dismayed. In what reality Gabriel would live past the New Year was more than one could hope for. Takouhi's optimism, he realized, bordered on delirium. He felt as if he were standing on a subway platform, observing from a far distance the glow of the train headlights steadily headed toward a terrible crash. Gabriel's impending death, for all its tragedy, would barely eclipse Takouhi's unraveling when it was all over.

"Can someone help me?" Azad called from behind the swinging door.

Jonathan sat on the couch, not occurring to him that he should help, and watched the bare table transform into a Christmas dinner as Takouhi laid out the cream-color linen tablecloth trimmed with ivy leaf embroidering and Azad arranged the luminous place settings, and then the procession of food emerged from the kitchen one by one. By the time all the dishes were placed strategically on the table, there was barely an inch of space left when they all sat down.

"Open the wine, Jonathan," Takouhi said. "You give the toast."

They were settled now, waiting. Gabriel was at the head of the table and Takouhi opposite him on the other end. Azad and Lucine sat facing Jonathan and Kohar. The smell of the burning wood from the fireplace filled the room, and from behind the curtains dusk had imperceptibly slipped away into night. Jonathan stood over the bottle of red wine and tried to uncork it, the corkscrew slippery in his hands. He managed to peel off the capsule and clumsily drove the screw into the top. The cork was forgiving, and, gently, Jonathan pulled it out with only slight effort. As he poured the wine into each of the glasses, a growing silence filled the room.

He lifted his glass and looked at each of them, sensing their complicit patience. "This is so special," he said. He could feel again the tears gathering in his eyes, and swallowed hard. "We are so special." He felt Gabriel's eyes on him and now looked at him directly. Gabriel's eyes were wide and alive, his face slightly damp and pale. Jonathan had never smiled so bravely in his life. "Merry Christmas," he said. "Merry Christmas to my beautiful family. Thank you for this beautiful evening. Look at this feast. Look at you all. This is a picture to be remembered. Let's always remember it. Merry Christmas."

Jonathan leaned his glass over to Gabriel's and cheered him first. "That was good," Gabriel said. "Sentimental, but good." He winked at Jonathan as he took a small sip of wine. The silence had broken. Jonathan sat back and ignored his empty plate, watching as everyone began passing around the platters of food. He had no appetite. But it was, after all, a beautiful evening.

Part 2

Chapter 14

KOHAR BLINKED ONCE, TWICE, THREE TIMES AND OPENED HER eyes to an early dawn. From the open window in her bedroom came the chitter of birds, their cries sharp and distant. She lay awake, listening in amusement as if she could understand their banter perfectly. She knew she would smell the lilac trees now, with their perfumed flowers, if she were to sit in the back yard. The forsythia bushes were bursting with buds the evening before, and she wondered if by today they would peep open. It all meant that spring had come.

She gently slid out of bed and crept to the bathroom. Her hope was to use the bathroom without the baby hearing and make coffee before Jonathan woke. She longed for several quiet minutes in a house that for now seemed to be breathing with sleep. As she crept down the corridor, she remembered to walk narrowly in the center to avoid creaking the floorboards.

What she needed, she knew, was to drink coffee in the growing light of the morning and do nothing but look out the window. She stood over the sink, forcing herself not to look at the sink full of baby bottles and oddly shaped attachments for the breast pump that should have been scrubbed and steamed the night before. Under the bright lights of the kitchen countertop, Kohar would not have to look at the hamper of dirty baby clothes that sat in a corner of the living room, the bags of maternity clothes that she had meant to donate—all mercifully obscured in the darkness of an early morning. These days, her sanity seemed to rest on the neatness of the house and a general orderliness that had lost its rhythm entirely since she had had the baby.

Her friends from work teased her about the timing of the pregnancy, as if she and Jonathan had planned for a late spring due date, the time of year when one ideally used hoarded sick days to bridge the gap until summer so there were no paycheck interruptions. Jonathan had encouraged

Kohar to take an extended maternity leave. At first, she was hesitant to notify her principal and tell her that she wouldn't be returning in the fall; most teachers in her building were eager to find a caretaker or drop off their newborn at a daycare and return to work. One of her colleagues who had finally gotten pregnant after several IVF trials was also of the mindset that it served her best to go back to work as soon as the six-week maternity leave expired. But none of this deterred Kohar from finally sending her administration an email, less concerned about how she would be perceived by her colleagues and more worried that she would be given a difficult schedule whenever it was that she decided to go back to work.

But it was of no matter to her now. She leaned on the marble counter, feeling the cold hard surface numb her elbows unpleasantly. Then a snore burst from her bedroom; Jonathan was sleeping on his back again. She went to the living room and sank into the couch and closed her eyes. She strained to hear sounds from the baby's room. She sipped from her cup and smiled at the silence that surrounded her. A small gift.

A dull buzzing sounded. She remembered that she had not brought down her phone, an attempt to start her day unencumbered with the impulse to check her messages. She raced upstairs on the balls of her feet and prowled through the dark bedroom, looking for her phone. It glowed in plain sight on her nightstand.

"Hello?" she whispered and looked over at the bed, where Jonathan was still sleeping. Kohar found her way to the bathroom and closed the door behind her.

"Did I wake you? What time is it?" Takouhi's tired voice made Kohar's heart turn inward. Between feeding the baby and the nap soon to follow, there was no way she would be able to get to her mother's apartment in the morning.

"No. I've been awake," she said.

"The baby's awake?"

"No, just—"

"Jonathan?"

"No, just me."

"Why? You said last night you were tired—"

"I just woke up," Kohar said. "I made coffee. I was sitting on the couch."

The questions would stop once her every move had been detailed and accounted for.

"Oh."

"Is everything okay?"

"Oh. Yes. I didn't sleep last night. I'm okay."

Kohar hoped her mother couldn't hear her need to exhale. She gripped the phone mightily as if she meant to crush it. Instead, it shook in her grip.

"The baby's crying," she said, trying to make her voice jump with urgency. "Are you stopping by after work?"

"No . . ." Takouhi's voice faded as if someone was lowering the volume. "I think I'm coming down with a migraine. I already left a message saying I wasn't coming in."

"Do you need anything?" Kohar pressed.

"No, I'll be okay."

She hung up the phone. Another snore erupted from the bedroom. This time, Kohar jumped. Then the soft plaintive cry of the baby.

"Babe?" Jonathan's voice, weak from interrupted sleep.

"I'm up," Kohar called and went to the crib.

The conversation with her mother had left Kohar with the usual angst that, before having the baby, would have lorded over her throughout the day like a low-grade headache. Now as she held Ruby in the crook of her arms, the feeling left her like a dirty robe she slipped off and kicked into a dark corner. Kohar pressed her face into the baby's neck, inhaled deeply. She had never known a smell so sweet and delicate. She looked at Ruby's face, observing her large eyes and simple nose, the cleft in her chin—Jonathan's, and gazed at how innocent, how reserved, and how unto herself she was from the complexities of a temperamental world.

"Did your phone ring before?" Jonathan stumbled over with half-open eyes and kissed her and the baby.

"Yes."

"Your mom."

"Who else?"

He groaned and closed the bathroom door behind him. "Should we invite her over for dinner?"

Kohar wanted to pretend she couldn't hear. "Do we have to talk about her first thing in the morning?" When she heard silence from the other side of the door, she added, "Can we make that a rule or something? To not do that?"

The door breezed open. "Sure. I was just trying to help." Easygoing Jonathan. He kissed her again and then the baby and headed downstairs.

Sleep, an uninterrupted movie, a leisurely shower—Kohar and Jonathan had taken these freedoms and many more for granted during their years together. Since Ruby was born, they checked in with each other. "I'm running to the store." "I have to make a quick call." "I'm about to take a shower." In the autumn and spring evenings they had sat in the back yard and had cocktails. Now they sat, Kohar drinking club soda and Jonathan with a beer, the baby monitor perched on the patio table. They took turns running up to rub Ruby's back or hold her until she fell back to sleep.

Kohar followed him to the kitchen; before she could call out to him to fix her another cup, he was already pouring coffee into her mug.

"Let's sit in the back yard," Jonathan said, reading her mind.

The sky had now opened and a brilliant gold light brightened the distant clouds. A flurry of wrens fluttered on the edge of the shingled roof. A neighborhood cat poked his gray head under the garden gate and regarded them for a moment, disappeared.

"It's going to be a nice day," Jonathan said. He rested himself on the cement steps. Kohar leaned back on a lawn chair and laid the baby on her chest. She closed her eyes for a moment, feeling Ruby's weight against her, the cool chill of the morning raising goose bumps on her bare legs. She could indeed smell the lilac flowers.

"Five weeks old," she said and looked down at the tiny person. Ruby's eyes were closed.

"I was thinking that, too," said Jonathan.

"I was so lucky. Nobody believes me when I tell them fifteen minutes," said Kohar.

For all the heartache of the two miscarriages and the laparoscopic surgery, Kohar's pregnancy and delivery was every mother's wild hope. During the last several weeks before giving birth to Ruby, Kohar had felt energized.

Her ankles hadn't swollen, she'd continued taking one-mile walks through the neighborhood, and on most evenings she'd managed to go to the supermarket after work and make dinner. One morning, she woke up to use the bathroom and felt a dull pressure on her bladder. The baby had dropped, her obstetrician told her. That had been, to Kohar's amazement, the only physical discomfort during the last few weeks of her pregnancy. And her delivery had lasted as long as the Chopin nocturne that Jonathan had played over several times as he let her grip his hand with each exhale and push. Fifteen minutes.

"Easy pregnancy, too," said Jonathan.

"Now that it's over, we can say it: yes, easy pregnancy," Kohar said.

It was a mantra of sorts; something she was willing to be grateful for since having discovered she was pregnant last fall. Because the world as she knew it had collapsed, piece by piece, around her. She imagined herself in a burning city clasping a jewel to her bosom and racing through the blazing streets to save and protect the one thing that mattered most to her amidst the imminent wreckage.

Less than two months ago, Gabriel had still been alive. It had been the morning of her baby shower; the one Kohar wasn't supposed to know about. She had humored Jonathan when he told her he was taking her to a "surprise" restaurant she had mentioned months ago and forgotten about. She had humored him when she wore her mustard-yellow dress—the only pretty item of clothing that still fit her bulging stomach—applied two coats of mascara and bright red lipstick, and rode in the passenger seat as he tried to cleverly explain why they were going to Jackson Heights, but not to her mother's house.

Then his phone had rung while they were driving. What were Kohar and he doing right now? Really? Would they mind stopping in, because her mother had bought too much yogurt from the Indian grocer and wanted to give two containers to Kohar?

When her mother had opened the door, Kohar had felt the wave of murmurs in the apartment. Standing in the foyer were two aunts and their respective husbands. They had flown in from San Francisco and Fresno. Behind them, more faces appeared. Her dearest friends, her family, more relatives who had traveled from far distances.

"Are you surprised?" her mother had smiled. Her mother, whose world had succumbed to weekly chemotherapy appointments, concocting smoothies that were said to eradicate cancer, researching cures from overseas gurus, while Gabriel died slowly and measurably with each passing week.

Kohar could only smile and nod. She knew if she spoke, she would begin sobbing. Her mother had smiled back and hugged her, a rare gesture. Kohar would remember it for the rest of her life.

What she would not let herself remember was the terrible morning and the weeks before. It all seemed too far and distant, like a voice calling from afar, perhaps to shake one out of a dreadful nightmare. She would not succumb to those memories. That fragment of time in her life would come to her all at once soon enough.

It would be years later, both drunk on wine and after a late-night party, that Jonathan and Kohar would piece together their recollections. What they would always remember about that morning is that the phone rang at exactly eight o'clock. And when Kohar struggled to prop herself up in bed, barely able to reach for the phone on her nightstand, what came through from the end of the line was a shriek. A wild caw. They had looked at each other and in an instant of freakish synchronicity began getting dressed. What neither would say aloud, to protect the other, was how close Gabriel had come to holding the baby, even once; Ruby Rose was born two weeks after Gabriel's burial.

The car ride on the Grand Central Parkway, Jonathan would remember. Not Kohar. The four-car jam of commotion and the two police cars double-parked behind the ambulance, Kohar would remember. Watching Kohar throw the car door open and jog heavily toward the apartment building while holding her belly, Jonathan. Kohar would only remember the solid weight of the baby pressing down on her bladder. And then walking into the foyer, hearing the deep voice of men, strangers who did not belong where she found them—standing by the defunct grand piano. Two police officers.

BOTH SHE AND JONATHAN AGREED THAT KOHAR SHOULD TAKE time off from teaching for at least a year. Now, Kohar's daily routine with Ruby was a mechanized schedule of feedings, naps, and diaper changes.

Though some of her friends with older children described the early months of motherhood as mind-numbingly tedious (and Kohar passively agreed by not remarking at all), she thrived on the predictability of her small world with Ruby. She wasn't waiting for anything to happen anymore. She had Ruby now. And Gabriel was dead. The fraying rope had finally snapped. And her mother, the kite from which the rope had been tied, had all but flown away. There was no tether.

For Jonathan, the irony of being a father in the midst of losing Gabriel, the only true father figure he had known, and the sickening vacillation between hysterical grief and the elation of Ruby's arrival, had not been lost. In Kohar and Ruby's presence, he was consumed by the baby, marveling at her while she slept or cried or sighed or burped or closed her eyes. And in the evenings, there was that moment in the night when Kohar had gone back to sleep after having fed Ruby for the first or second time, when Jonathan lay awake. He could feel his body shuddering uncontrollably as if he might explode, as if he could not cry enough and never would. The mammoth of a man he had loved so dearly had vanished.

"What was your mother saying?" he asked.

Kohar exhaled as if she had been trying to lift a heavy box and couldn't get it off the ground. "She's not going in to work today."

"Anything else?" Jonathan sensed he was already pushing Kohar past the point of aggravation. "Do you want to go there? Check in on her? Ruby will be fine with me."

"I'm breastfeeding," Kohar said. "She needs me."

"Azad and Lucine haven't seen her, have they?" Jonathan asked.

"No." Kohar's voice was flat. Disgusted.

"Have you spoken to them?"

"Not really," said Kohar.

"Do you want me to go? I can drive over after work—"

"She's *my* mother. I can go."

"But you just said—"

"What choice do I have? It's on me. It's always on me. Whether it be me visiting her because those two are checked out or planning her sixty-fifth surprise birthday party or swallowing her shit to keep the peace. It's always on me. I'll go."

She put her hand behind Ruby's head and gently leaned forward. Then placed her in Jonathan's arms. She was seething.

"I'll be right back to feed her. Then I'll go over there before you leave for work. I won't stay long. I can't anyway," she said, relieved that her breasts would be full and heavy and aching for release within an hour or two.

Before Jonathan could protest, Kohar was pounding up the backyard steps into the kitchen. He considered calling Azad and Lucine. To say what? *Visit your mother.* No. *Get your head out of your ass and visit your mother because Kohar can't take care of a newborn and your depressed mother.* It wasn't his place. It was Gabriel's.

IF TAKOUHI HAD DRAWN OPEN HER BEDROOM CURTAINS, THE early morning light would have filled the room. If she had opened the refrigerator, she would have seen the expired container of milk that had curdled repulsively into gelatinous globs. If she had walked through the apartment, room after room, she would have commended herself for the orderliness, the cleanliness, the mausoleum-ness of what her impulses demanded of her. The air was dead and sour. A window had not been lifted open, despite the lovely spring air and budding trees that emanated a ripe awakening of a new season. The apartment lay dormant in a gathering gloom that had settled heavily in all its unoccupied spaces.

Takouhi lay on her side, her eyes staring blankly at the wall. When she opened her mouth, her lips parted sourly. They were parched and dry and cracked, and the corners of her mouth hurt. Forming a smile would be physically painful. On her nightstand was a half-opened sleeve of Ritz crackers. The glass filled with water was old and cloudy. The answering machine blinked with twenty-seven messages that Takouhi had heard, but not listened to. The phone rang at erratic times of the day, but most often in the morning between nine and nine-thirty. Her supervisor calling to find out if she was running late or coming to work at all. Takouhi had given Gabriel's name and number as the emergency contact. His cell phone sat on his dresser, uncharged.

It was possible that Takouhi no longer had a place of employment; she had not gone in to work since the burial. They had given her a seven-day grievance period. But Takouhi didn't know from weeks or days. She didn't know from morning or afternoon or evening as she lay dormant in the darkness of her room. She lay awake on her side of the bed with her back turned to the empty space next to her. She waited to hear Gabriel's deep snoring. She waited to hear him shuffle into the bathroom in the middle of the night. She waited to hear the click of the front door unlock and listen to him walk down the hallway. The sound of music from his closed office door, the smell of a matchstick striking sulfur, his breath against her neck as he fell asleep at night.

The one person she called was Kohar. To check in on the baby, she told herself. In the mornings when her brain felt as if it were being set on fire, her skull burning with the numbness of insomnia, she managed to call her. Yet she was too tired to tell Kohar the truth: she had not left the house in a long time. She put off her sisters' phone calls and eventually picked up the receiver only to be greeted with an urgent voice—she couldn't tell whose—asking her all sorts of questions: How was she feeling? How was it going back to work? Were the girls visiting? Was she eating? Sleeping? Takouhi emitted one-word answers, claimed fatigue and sleepiness until one of her sisters, unsatisfied, had no choice but to hang up.

Takouhi pulled herself up in bed and slowly let her feet find the surface of the rug. With eyes half open she went to the bathroom, not bothering to flick on the light. From the closed window she heard a baby's cry from the courtyard. At once Takouhi felt a cold shudder grip her insides. She thought she would vomit, though there was little that would come up. Ruby Rose had not occurred to her until now, not as a real entity, as she sat on the toilet, where she continued sitting hunched over, and felt the edges of the seat pressing into the backs of her thighs.

When Kohar had gone into labor and been admitted into Katz Women's Hospital, Jonathan had called Takouhi once the doctor told him it was only a matter of hours before the delivery. Takouhi could not know that Jonathan had waited as long as he had to spare her the extra hours of sitting in the hospital. As the GPS droned loudly through the Bluetooth speaker, Takouhi had almost pulled over when she realized—she was driving back to the same hospital where she had taken Gabriel for his chemotherapy treatments. It was a different wing, but the exact same route.

Kohar had lain writhing in her hospital bed, gripping Jonathan's hand as the waves of contractions grew closer and closer. Azad and Lucine were still on their way. Mary, Jonathan's mother, had sat anxiously on the small couch in the delivery room, waiting. Takouhi had stared out the window, unmoved, transported to another room where Gabriel would have been administered treatments. Treatments that Takouhi found difficult to believe were meant to kill the cancer ravaging his body. As Kohar had whimpered with labor pain, all Takouhi could remember were the tedious drives back and forth from the hospital, the attendant wheeling Gabriel out of the cancer-treatment wing to the car where Takouhi had been parked waiting for him, watching with utter horror as he was eased and buckled into the passenger seat, and then Gabriel's white trembling face as he gripped the plastic bag shaking in his hand for fear of vomiting.

"Hello?" A thin voice called from several feet away.

Takouhi's bedroom door creaked open. Still in the bathroom, Takouhi stood up unsteadily. "Who's there?" she barked.

Kohar was by the television set. "I called out when I walked in. I guess you didn't hear me," she said. "What are you doing?"

"Am I allowed to use the bathroom?" Takouhi asked, her voice trapped in the hollowness of the bathroom.

She ignored Kohar's startled eyes upon seeing her and then looking away, the expression on her face—as if she'd caught a glimpse of roadkill—and walked out of the room.

"I'm sorry," Kohar said, following her.

"Where's the baby?" Takouhi asked. She kept her back turned to her as she filled the coffee pot halfway with water and positioned it under the brewing funnel.

"With Jonathan. At home."

"How is she sleeping?"

"She's only five weeks old, so not so great."

The coffee measurer shook in Takouhi's grip. She counted six scoops under her breath.

"Mom," Kohar started. "What's going on?"

Takouhi tossed the measurer into the sink. Coffee grounds sprayed across the granite counter. "What's going on?" she demanded. "What am I doing? I'm making coffee."

"I came to check in on you—"

The silence between them, a thick pane of glass, for Kohar was all too familiar. She did not exist. Or, rather, her existence was insignificant.

"No need," Takouhi snapped. "No need to check in on me. You have a baby to take care of. I can take care of myself."

"What did I do?" asked Kohar. "You're angry."

"I'm not. I'm not anything," Takouhi shot back.

"Why are you being like this?"

Takouhi knew the tears were seconds away. She knew Kohar's helpless tone; how quickly she gave way to crying, for some reason, in her presence. It irritated Takouhi all the more.

"I was resting in my room and I wasn't expecting you. You scared me when you walked in. At least you could have called," Takouhi said.

"I've never called before coming," Kohar countered.

"Well, call from now on," said Takouhi.

The coffee maker dripped tiredly. Before Takouhi could stop her, Kohar reached to open the refrigerator door. After a few seconds she opened it wider. Takouhi heard her draw in a breath from where she was standing. Then watched as Kohar bent over and opened and closed the produce drawers, slowly speculating. She reached for the milk carton and shook it, put it back on the shelf without bothering to open it.

"Are you eating?" Kohar's stricken face stared at her with accusation.

"Yes . . . Kohar . . . I'm eating," Takouhi replied testily.

"The food in there is rotted. What are you eating?"

"Crackers. And cheese. Who's the mother and who's the daughter?" Takouhi asked, oblivious to the irony of her question.

The coffee maker sounded.

"Can we have some coffee and talk?" asked Kohar as she reached for two mugs from the cabinet.

Takouhi exhaled sharply. "Coffee and talk. Yes."

Kohar sat at the dining-room table, where Gabriel usually sat, and let her mother settle in on the couch. She tried to concentrate *not* on Takouhi's gray roots that had grown out at least two inches, her overgrown toenails that were a chipped red from a pedicure, the white and purple paisley nightgown that was covered in unidentifiable stains, and her sallow face that seemed to have aged preposterously.

"Before I start talking, I want you to just listen to me from beginning to end," Kohar began.

Takouhi nodded and rolled her eyes. Kohar pressed on. "Do you remember when Gabriel got sick and I told you that if, God forbid, something happened you should see a therapist?"

Takouhi's eyes were now glued to the ceiling. She nodded.

"Mom, I spoke to Tamar Hartunian—she just opened her own practice. And she recommended several therapists who are actually walking distance from you. Two of them are women, which I'm guessing you would prefer, and one of them is a man. And close to your age, which I think you would prefer also. And they're under your health insurance plan." She paused for a moment, trying to shirk her growing irritation at her mother's fixation with the ceiling. "Mom?"

Takouhi nodded without breaking her gaze. "Uh-huh . . ."

"I think you should see someone," Kohar said.

"For what?" Takouhi asked and finally looked at her. "My husband just died. What do you expect from me? I'm not allowed to be sad?"

"Mom, I'm not criticizing you. Is it fair to say you've always been a little depressed?" Kohar asked. She wanted to continue by suggesting medication, perhaps an antidepressant or antianxiety medication. Already she had trod too far.

"Again, Kohar. What do you expect from me? Your father was a terrible husband. I was the middle child of the family—too young to be with my sister and brother and too old to play with the younger ones. Then they marry me off to your father, and that was my life."

"Nobody is blaming you. I'm saying that with Gabriel not here anymore, that maybe this would be a good time—"

"*Kohar*—" Takouhi interrupted and leaned in. Her eyes were as fiery, ferocious as the day Kohar had told her she was moving out. The color of hatred. "I am fine. There is nothing wrong with me. You don't have to take care of me. I am fine taking care of myself."

She ignored the pools gathering in Kohar's eyes. She ignored the pleading look on Kohar's face as she placed her coffee on the table and walked out.

Kohar could hear the definitive slam of her mother's bedroom door. On her drive to the apartment, she hadn't considered the condition in which she would find things. Now, sitting in the living room, she looked around, her eyes grazing the Persian rug, the grandfather clock, the sweeping green pastel curtains that hung drawn closed. A slant of sunlight glowed between where the curtains met. The room was lifeless.

It was the first time she had entered the apartment since the day Gabriel had been buried. After the service, family and close friends had been invited over for the traditional Armenian *hokeh-jash*, the meal for the spirit of the deceased. Her mother had ordered kebab from Gabriel's favorite restaurant; and after the priest lit the frankincense and spoke the traditional prayer, it felt as if it were all over. But it never was, Kohar realized. It was never really over. There was the forty-day mourning period, where everyone gathered at the grave with the priest. Then the one-year memorial at the church. And then the rest of her life.

Kohar stood in the center of the living room and looked over at the parlor. She saw herself sitting on the couch with Azad, each of them holding back tears. A sad memory that Kohar immediately abandoned. Then a cold fall evening came to life. Five of them sitting by the fire, eating French onion soup with toasted hunks of bread that had already been sawed off and deliciously buttered. She knew well enough not to reminisce. Not now. She peered down the hallway that led to her mother's bedroom. The apartment was eerily silent. How did her mother wander through these spaces that had once been alive with human sound?

An unfamiliar dampness crept across her torso. Kohar glanced at the mirror in the foyer and saw dark patches near her nipples on her gray T-shirt and realized her breasts were already full and leaking milk. She breezed toward her mother's bedroom and knocked lightly on the door.

"Mom? Can I come in?"

"What is it?" It sounded as if she were speaking through a funnel.

"I'm leaving. I have to go feed the baby."

She opened the door slightly and poked her head in. Takouhi was lying propped up with her eyes half open, her graying hair in a disheveled mass against the pillow.

"See you later."

"Why don't you come over?" Kohar asked. "One day after work?"

Takouhi let out a breath. "We'll see."

Kohar glided down the hallway, overcome by a strange relief. The new task at hand would be calling her sisters or at least texting them a message to ask how often they spoke to their mother and when they would be visiting. She walked past Gabriel's office. She had reached the foyer and stopped a moment to survey her reflection in the mirror. The dark patches had spread and it looked as if someone had splashed her with a cup of water. Upon looking away, she caught another reflection, one which had been there for so long, she had forgotten.

A photograph of Gabriel. It was one of the candid portraits Jonathan had taken of him. He had framed one and given it as a Christmas gift. It was Gabriel in his most quintessential habitat—his office. He is sitting in his worn leather chair, the backdrop of floor-to-ceiling books nestled in their shelves, holding a half-burned cigarette in his hand, and smiling over a stack of dictionaries. His green eyes smiling behind gold-wired spectacles. A guileless grin. His full beard streaked with gray.

Kohar collapsed against the wall and struggled to stand up. Gabriel was as good as alive, his kind, beautiful face hanging inches away from her. Across from her, the baby grand piano, which she had so often played, was covered in framed photographs. She recognized the small faces from where she sat. One was an absurd picture of her mother and Gabriel wearing peasant costumes. They had acted in an Armenian play together that summer, and someone had snapped a picture the last night of the production.

And then, try as she might, it pushed itself through anyway and Kohar could not move. The memory of that day returned like a terrible phantom, no longer submerged in the underworld of her grief.

MAYBE IT HAD BEEN THREE POLICE OFFICERS AND NOT TWO, but it didn't matter. When she walked into the apartment only half an hour after her mother's phone call, Kohar was expecting to find her mother in the parlor. Instead, the officers approached her quietly, wearily, and began talking, asking questions that Kohar might have known the answers to. *Who was she? Who else was there to contact? Who else had been contacted?* Kohar had seen it many times in movies: the voices are slow and indiscernible, confusing to hear. And there she was, standing, surrounded by officers, being spoken to about her stepfather, who was dead. Somewhere.

"Where is my mother?" she finally asked. "Where is my stepfather? Just please one of you speak," she said. "I can't concentrate."

One of the officers, now noticing her pregnant stomach, pulled her toward the front door. His eyes were large and blue. He was younger than the others. His perspiring face reminded her of her seventh-grade science teacher—a shy young man who couldn't have been older than twenty-five, Kohar thought in retrospect, as the officer spoke to her.

"Your stepfather died in his bed this morning. Your mother . . . she won't come out of the room. We tried. She's in there."

Kohar nodded numbly. Slowly, she crept down the hallway. She prayed the door wasn't locked. When she turned the knob, her heart lurched with relief and dread as she opened the door. Music. She thought it was coming through an open window that faced the courtyard. No. It was from somewhere in the room. Without thinking, Kohar looked over at the bed. Through the parted curtains, sunlight streamed through the window. Gabriel lay unmoving, his face haloed in light.

There was a humming with the music, a humming of a song. And when Kohar turned around, she found her mother, legs splayed on the rug, with a tape recorder in her lap. She was singing along to an old song Kohar hadn't heard in years.

"Mom?" she tried to kneel over her heavy stomach. She touched her mother's wrist lightly. Takouhi kept singing, not seeing her. "Mom."

"Please," Takouhi spoke. "Just leave me for a while. I'm not going anywhere."

"Mom—"

"Please." A low, hollow moan.

When Kohar returned to the parlor, Jonathan was talking to the police officers. "I can't get her out," she said.

The two EMTs were standing in the foyer now. "We have to go in soon. We can wait another ten minutes. But we'll have to go in."

"Are you going to force her out?" Kohar's heart rose with alarm.

"No, but it's better if she's not there when we remove the body," one of them explained.

They all heard the bedroom door open and Takouhi's footsteps. Then another door closing behind her; she had disappeared into the study. The EMT workers started toward the bedroom.

"Wait," Jonathan said. "Just give me a minute. I'll be right back."

Kohar looked at him, perplexed. She would not be there to see Jonathan standing over Gabriel in the empty bedroom. Or that Gabriel's eyes were open, his mouth covered with blood. She would not hear Jonathan cry softly and hold his hand over Gabriel's face, touching it for the last time.

When Jonathan entered the bedroom, he felt the immediate lifeless gloom in the air. The red toile wallpaper was obscured in dark, stalking shadows. The oscillating fan still as a statue. Jonathan had taken for granted how the room perpetually vibrated with the gentle breath of music, the whir of fan blades, the muted television alive with human motion. Stillness now.

At first he stood by the door, as if an intruder about to be chided for trespassing. He stared at the mass of human form under the bedsheets. Slowly Jonathan stepped forward, approaching the bed, his heart clamoring manically. There was nothing to fear, he knew. And yet. What he feared was the savagery of death. Too late now, too late. It had come and gone and there was Gabriel not sleeping deeply, not sick with a vigilant cancer or chemotherapy or resting his eyes from a long day of poring over hundreds of pages of text.

Jonathan prodded himself now, forced himself to stand next to Gabriel's body, knowing he would be carried away, taken. No one would be able to stay as near to him as Jonathan was now. He tried not to look, to not see what he would always remember: the olive greenness of Gabriel's open eyes, the fleck of gold in his pupils—so indiscernible that Jonathan would wonder afterward if he had imagined it—the pale lashes like those of a small child.

"Goodbye, dear friend," Jonathan said. "You were the best of all of us." Gently, he lowered Gabriel's lids closed, kissed him on the forehead, and left the room.

Kohar knew there were phone calls to be made. Just as she had called her sisters to tell them about Gabriel's cancer, she called to tell them he had died. She wondered briefly what she preferred: to be where she was now, with Gabriel and her mother and Jonathan and the police officers and the EMT workers in a house that would no longer feel like home, or to be either one of her sisters—several hours away by car, arriving after it had all been handled, disconnected from everything but their grief.

Kohar's breasts ached. Her chest ached. As if she could literally feel her heart in pain. She knew her mother was still in bed, unaware that she hadn't left yet. Slowly, Kohar stood up and slipped her purse over her shoulder. As she swung open the heavy iron doors, the sun was strong, blinding. As if she had stepped out of a movie theater. Before pulling out in her car, she sent Jonathan a message. She was on her way home. She didn't think of when she would be going back to visit again. Kohar drove and didn't turn on the radio. She hoped that if she drove far enough away, the feeling would not linger.

Chapter 15

AZAD WANTED THIS RITUAL TO WORK. ARIEL, WHO COULD NOT be relied on to go around the corner to buy a carton of milk, had said it would. She had seemed different after coming back from the retreat. Less scattered, less frivolous, more *grounded*—a word Ariel must have picked up at the retreat—that made Azad picture a hot-air balloon secure on the ground only because it was being anchored by foot ropes. Azad didn't want to be grounded as much as she wanted to feel like a capable human who did not sleep through her alarm or cry at the supermarket while walking past the ice cream aisle or forget to shower until Kaitlyn would kindly tell her she smelled like a vagrant. She felt like a clock with malfunctioning arms that continued ticking. Her insides rattled disharmoniously. The broken part, impossible to locate.

Azad boarded the bus at the downtown station with a duffel bag. Pack loose-fitting clothes, a journal, and have your intention, was what the instructor, Hunter, had said to her. She wanted to ask Hunter if he had, by any chance, been handing out animal crackers at Burning Man last summer. *Toxic*, is what Kaitlyn had called it. *You're very toxic right now.* Azad wanted to remind Kaitlyn that she was living in *her* toxic house rent-free, eating her toxic food and taking showers in her toxic bathroom. She wanted to tell her to go fuck herself, knowing it would only prove Kaitlyn right.

Ariel and Kaitlyn occupying most of their time in the living room, binge-watching episodes of *Three's Company* on Hulu, while eating their way through Azad's purchases from Trader Joe's (mostly mochi ice cream and falafel chips) and drinking whatever was on sale at Acme, left Azad feeling less connected, more estranged from her life. It was questionable as to whether the two lived with Azad. After Gabriel's passing, they would arrive, unannounced, to check in on her, like a nurse checking the pulse of a patient in a coma. They decided to interpret Azad not telling them to leave as an invitation to stay for an indeterminate length of time. And so their visits grew more frequent and drawn-out until eventually it would be too late to drive home, and the sleepovers began regularly. When Azad, upon seeing Kaitlyn and Ariel asleep on her grandmother's imported Tibetan rug (despite Grandma's Armenian-ness, she had a peculiar fondness for the *Oriental*, as she favored calling it), walked past them into the kitchen in the morning, it left them with the impression that Azad needed the comfort of companionship for the time being. She was certain Krikor and his family had learned of her father's death, but she had not heard from him. And didn't know if she wanted to.

Although she had been waiting for the assistant position to open at the gallery, nothing had materialized. She had no mortgage, but other monthly expenses that added up quickly, Azad realized. Panicked, she had checked her bank account and realized that quite mysteriously, money was being deposited into her checking account in the amount of two thousand dollars on the first of each month. Her mother. Who she hadn't been calling. Azad felt too vulnerable now, too transparent in her sadness, knowing that her mother would struggle to fix instead of just listen. It was too burdening to feel like a burden. What Azad didn't realize was that Takouhi's monthly deposits were her way of communicating a recognition of both their plights: living all alone in an empty house.

Kohar, now completely absorbed with Ruby, hadn't called Azad. And who the hell knew what Lucine was up to. The last they had all seen each other was the day the baby had been born. By the time Azad had showed up, Kohar was passed out from labor and Jonathan was holding Ruby in the delivery room. Her mother had been standing at the far end of the room by the open blinds of the window, looking far away and foreign. A person looking at the ocean for the first time after boarding a ship that was pulling away from land.

"What did you name her?" Azad had asked.

"Ruby. Ruby Rose," Jonathan had said, smiling down at the small, wrapped newborn in his arms. The baby slept soundlessly.

Azad had glanced at her mother, jarringly stoic, and then the baby. Her niece. It seemed familiar, the strange juxtapose. And then she had remembered: something ending. Something new for everyone. A blessing.

A flower. A brilliant red budding flower. It will happen at the same time. Almost simultaneously. Apocalypse.

The old woman had been right.

AZAD SETTLED HERSELF AT THE FRONT OF THE BUS AND TUCKED her duffel bag under her seat, pulled out a book she had been unsuccessfully trying to finish, and looked at the window. She was scheduled to arrive at the Hudson bus terminal in several hours, where she would be picked up by one of the retreat coordinators. The ceremony would begin that very evening at eight o'clock. She wanted to forget what Ariel had told her. Some rules of thumb. But if she wanted to forget what Ariel had told her, then she might as well get off the bus and drive back to her sad life in Newtown Square, where Ariel and Kaitlyn were, probably still sleeping or consorting over weekend plans. She should ask them to leave, Azad knew. But she was too lonely. And what ate away at the base of Azad's self-worth was the knowledge that she would rather live with a couple of brainless hipsters who were sponging off her, than be alone.

Remember that it's not a drug, it's medicine, was the first thing Ariel had told her. *Go there with an intention. But don't have expectations*, was the next annoying paradox. *Take a personal object of power.* An uncontrollable grin spread across Azad's face. If only Lucine had been sitting across from Ariel, listening to her gems of wisdom. Azad couldn't even imagine Lucine's retorts, her innocuous-seeming questions that hedged on patronizing if not blisteringly insulting. Ariel, though, too dim to notice, would have indulged Lucine with answers.

Azad thought of this as the bus gently lurched forward and the doors sighed and sucked closed. She plugged in her earbuds and started skimming through playlists on her phone. The bus weaved its way through the dense city streets, yielding and racing through traffic lights. She felt a light tap on her shoulder. When she looked up, a young guy her age was standing over the empty seat next to hers. He was asking her a question, but she couldn't hear him through the blasting music. The blue bandanna he wore around his neck reminded her of pubescent boys in '80s summer-camp movies.

"Sorry. Yes?" she said, removing an earbud to dangle in her lap.

"I'm guessing no one's sitting here?" he asked. "This three-hundred-pound guy just sat next to me back there," he explained, jerking his thumb toward the back of the bus, "and I can't even *breathe*. Mind if I sit here?"

Azad nodded. "Sure."

She went to face the window and turned the volume so high that music vibrated in her brain unpleasantly. Then a voice came from the loudspeaker. By the time she lowered the volume, all she heard were the groans and sounds of disgust from the passengers.

"What did he just say?" she asked the guy.

"That the GPS said it's going to take us close to an hour longer to get there," he said.

"Ugh. Whatever. As long as I get there by eight o'clock, I don't really care," Azad said, and began scrolling through her phone.

"Are you by any chance going to the Ayahuasca retreat?" the guy asked.

Azad looked at him with slight alarm. "Yes," she said, lowering her voice. Ariel had mentioned it wasn't entirely legal, Ayahuasca. That it had originated thousands of years ago and most people went to Peru or the Amazon for the true Ayahuasca experience.

"I guess you are," Azad said.

"My fourth time," he said.

"Fourth?"

"I know a guy that's done it over twenty times," he said.

"That must have been interesting," she said, a half-hearted effort to sound polite. She wasn't in the mood to hear war stories about psychedelic experiences.

"He said it's different every time," he continued. "My name's Luke, by the way. And that every time you do it, after you purge, it leaves you feeling different, changed."

Azad didn't bother giving her name. She continued listening, growing steadily bored with all the details. There's a shaman. Most people experience a rebirth. Some people change their entire lives after the Ayahuasca ceremony. Leave their families, shift careers, divorce or get married, move overseas. It's like condensing ten years of therapy into one experience.

"I hope you don't mind," she interrupted, sensing a lull in his expounding, "but I've had a bad night's sleep and need to close my eyes." Without waiting for a response, she balled up her sweatjacket and rested her head against it.

Why was she listening to Ariel anyway? She glanced at Luke from the corner of her eye. He resembled the art students from college. Particularly the freshmen who strolled through campus in the early semester utterly wide-eyed and enchanted as if they had just landed on Earth. It unnerved her. What's the big fucking deal. Nothing. This guy's good-naturedness, his wholesome black Converse sneakers (so clean they were fresh out of the box), his "Nevermind" T-shirt (he had definitely never listened to Nirvana) and camouflage shorts were off-putting.

When Azad woke up she realized the bus was not moving. They had pulled over at a rest stop, somewhere in between Philly and Hudson. The seat next to hers was empty. As she stood up and stretched her arms, she saw the top of Luke's dark head waiting in line to get back on the bus. She settled herself immediately and opened her book.

"I grabbed a water for you. In case you didn't have," she heard him say; and before she could say thank you, he held out an oversized bottle of Poland Spring water.

"Thanks," she said. "You didn't need to."

"Apparently, we're going to really hit a shit ton of traffic now. Always in New York."

"I know," she said. "I used to live here."

"Me, too," he said.

Her impulse was to ask him where, but she didn't.

"This traffic is obscene," she said, when the deluge of cars appeared before them on I-95.

"So, have you done the ceremony before?" asked Luke.

Azad glanced at him again, noticing the large scar on the base of his chin. It was shaped like a horseshoe.

"No," she said. "I haven't."

"Don't be scared," he said. "I was, the first time."

"I'm not," she said. She wanted to tell him she might not go through with it at all.

"Why are you?" he asked.

"What?" she asked

"Doing it? The Ayahuasca?"

"I don't know."

"That was personal. Sorry."

The bus sat in a sea of angry cars, their brake lights glowing in the coming night.

"I hope we get there in time," Luke said finally.

I hope not, Azad wanted to say. She'd rather miss it because of bad traffic than choose to not go. Kaitlyn had asked her to write it all down. *Please.* She wanted to know all the details before actually doing it herself. *You're so brave*, Ariel had told her when they dropped her off at the bus station. Azad had wanted to slap the smarmy grin right off her face. *Will I be as cool as you then?*

"I'm going because my father died two months ago and I feel like shit all the time," Azad blurted out.

Luke puffed out his cheeks and blew out an audible breath. "That sucks. I'm sorry."

"Thanks."

"Are you from New York?" he asked.

"Yeah. Queens. I moved here over a year ago," she said.

"You know Forest Hills, then?" he asked.

"Yes." Azad looked at him curiously. "My sister lives there," she said.

"I used to live there years ago," he said. Azad was about to comment on the unusual coincidence. "Do you remember years ago, when there was this guy going around attacking women?" he asked.

"Not really," Azad said. "Wait, yes. I do." She had noticed the article her father had cut out and left on the dining-room table. It had been meant only for her mother to see. Kohar and Lucine's father lived in Forest Hills with his wife and newborn at the time. After seven assaults, the police had finally arrested the man, and he had been sentenced to prison for life. It had been on the front-page cover: *Forest Hills Killer Apprehended*, and the black-and-white photographs of the Gardens in Forest Hills where the last attack had taken place.

"The papers didn't give exact details—probably you don't remember that part—of the attacks. Like, how he attacked women. But he came up behind them and cut their throat."

He was about to say his mother had been one of the victims, Azad guessed. Or that his father was the killer.

"I was one of the victims," said Luke.

Azad cocked her head back. "I had long hair at the time," Luke explained, and ran his hands through the shaggy mass of hair that fell into his eyes. "And I was walking home at night—through the Gardens—you know how dark it is around there at night?"

Azad nodded. Several times, Kohar had driven her through the dark, beautiful depths of the Forest Hills Gardens. Medieval-looking manors wrought with iron trimming and chestnut doors framed with black Gothic hinges, huddles of cottages mottled with bright moss and inlays of slate path, Gatsby-reminiscent mansions with semicircle driveways, brilliant green lawns, and azalea bushes, fuchsia, red, white, and pink. In the evening, the streets were hushed and cavernous, visible by streetlights that cast a candle-like glow along the narrow, winding sidewalks. After nightfall, the austerity of the gardens lent itself to the mood of the seasons and weather.

"...and he came up behind me...thought I was a woman. He'd already cut my neck and when he realized I wasn't a woman he ran off. That's how I survived."

"And that cut on your chin?" Azad stared at him in complete horror. Then she looked again at the bandanna around his neck. It was a paisley royal blue, soft and faded.

He broke into a grin. "That?" He pointed a finger at the scar on his chin. "That's from a skateboarding accident. *That*," he said, pointing to the bandanna, "is mostly faded now but I'm still self-conscious about the scar."

Azad leaned back in her seat, engrossed in her thoughts. "Sorry!" she heard him say. "Did I just scare the shit out of you?"

"No," she said. "You didn't."

For once she wasn't living in her thoughts, too bored with everyone around her to be distracted. It was the first time in weeks that she hadn't thought about herself.

"So, why am I doing it a fourth time—you probably want to know. It makes me feel better. That's all. That's it. Without all the psychological analysis," he said.

"Is it really like an intense therapy session?" she asked.

"It's like whatever the hell you figure it as being for yourself. Vague, I know," he said.

"I don't want to. I don't want to do it," she said.

Finally, the bus began riding smoothly down the highway. The passengers emitted a hearty sigh of relief. The air itself felt lighter.

"Then don't," said Luke. "Why do you have to? If you don't feel like it."

"Because," said Azad. "I don't know what else to do."

"Then do nothing."

"I have been doing nothing. And it's not doing anything. I feel like shit all the time," she said.

"I'm sorry—what's your name?"

"Azad."

"Azad—your father died. You're supposed to feel like shit." It was so obviously true. As true as the sun setting at the end of every day, yet Azad did not know it.

Her father dead now and her sisters as far away as they had ever been, and her mother grinding through each moment of her life like a rusty wheel, creaking fitfully. On most mornings the physical task of getting out of bed had felt impossible to Azad. Like an invisible force was pressing on her, bearing down with all its weight. Lifting her arms pained her. At odds with gravity. A dull throbbing radiated across her shoulders when she tried moving her head side to side. She knew, in the unconscious way that a person knows they are being watched, that she was living in her father's old bedroom. That she was living in the very house where her grandparents' rigid expectations of her father had yielded unpleasant results: a son wandering along a desultory path who somehow became an autodidact and one of the most renowned translators of his generation. Of his former life, Azad did not know. More keenly, it was the awareness that her father had run up and down the same chocolate-brown oak wood staircase as she did now, hundreds of times, laid in the same room and stared at the same four corners of the wall, now chipping and flaking, had driven up the same steep driveway that led up to the entrance of the back yard and kitchen. She was entombed in his past life.

When she was drunk or stoned or both, a stealthy masochism would overcome her and she would play a terrible game with her memory, remembering pictures of her father from family photo albums that spanned years. And in that game, she imagined her father walking up and down the staircase, allowing time to slowly and perceptibly age him. First, a raucous boy of five or six, scrambling up the steps in a pair of scuffed black-and-white oxfords; and then an older boy returning at the foot of the staircase, with a more reserved face, serious, measured steps, that was surely heeded by great lengths of discipline and lecturing. Then a teenage boy, her father in a short-sleeved button-down shirt and a pair of black slacks (a hint of his predilection for pot-smoking and budding friendships with outcasts and beatniks) sauntering up the steps. Up and down, Time moved swiftly through her father's life until the last semblance of Gabriel, shuttered in the confines of her memory: receding hairline, sparse beard completely white, unsteady hands grasping for the banister to steady himself, his unsmiling eyes enduring what was left of his life because he knew he was going to die soon, very soon . . . Does he climb up the steps, climb down? Of the answer, Azad could never be sure. All she could know at the end of these evenings as she fell asleep under the hush of the ceiling fan was that never, not ever again, would she rest her head on his shoulder. That she would not say "Dad" out loud to him, to call for him, to even refer to him.

Now, sitting on the bus, watching the curving road stretch ahead of her, a strange quiet settled in her. As if a turbulent plane had changed its course toward a milder path. A new thought bloomed in her mind: thus far, she had lived her life painlessly, soaring uninhibitedly with no obstacles or tragedies. Unlike Lucine and Kohar, whose symbiotic lives were wrought with disappointments, broken childhoods, a mother who reverted to senselessly harsh means of withholding love and approval, a chronically ill father who they rarely visited because of his paranoid wife. Yet somehow they thrived. They moved forward. As if the cruelness of their sharply erratic past had shaped the trajectory of their future. And here she was, floundering. Purposeless. Like being in the desert, she realized, vast and unpaved, where she could go in any direction. There was no resistance. Was it unhappiness that made one stronger? What is the grit of life that pulled us forward? The clamor in our hearts? As dusk illuminated the pale sky that was now shrinking into darkness, Azad understood finally that she had never been happy or unhappy. There had been nothing until now that had roused within her the distinction between the two.

She glanced at Luke, who was now busily scrolling through his phone, reading intently. *What does a shaman look like?* she wondered. Already she pictured the scene of the coming evening: sitting in the darkness of a hut on her mat, in a circle with other people, lighted candles casting a glow of ritualistic aura, the vomit bucket by her side, her intention (of course, she had no clue what that was), and then drinking the potion that was given to her. Like Ariel with the animal cracker. It was not the same. But it was. *This is all the same. Like Burning Man. There's no point.* She wanted to bolt out of her seat and ask the driver to pull over. *I wish it could all disappear. I wish I could start over.*

Yet it all felt the same way: that the world around her was moving, like a machine indifferent to her existence, and it didn't matter whether she was alive or not. And the world without her father felt like a barren place, where there was no small nook in which to curl up and feel warmth.

Chapter 16

To spite her father, and herself—she supposed—Lucine had driven past her father's house on many occasions. She had driven past without slowing down, although every time it felt as if she was walking past an unmarked grave. It was an elusive place, her childhood home. Elusive with the melancholy of phantoms and shadows, it emanated an overall non-corporeal past of a general awfulness. During the rare times that she had visited her father (upon the invitation of her stepmother), Lucine braced herself uneasily as she entered the house, as if a ghost was bound to jump out. Those memories, the ghosts that they were, slithered through her unconsciousness and resurrected flashes of time that she had forgotten: the rising sobs of her mother's muffled crying from her parents' bedroom, her grandmother making breakfast on winter mornings while Lucine and Kohar waited at the kitchen table with sleep in their eyes, the groan of her father's truck backing into the driveway hours after dinnertime.

Sitting in her car parked in front of her father's house, Lucine pondered this morosely. There was no knowing if Tanté would come to the door; she could easily peek through the kitchen curtains and scurry to the back of the house and pretend no one was home. Unlike all the other times she had visited, Lucine didn't bother trying to work up the nerve of ringing the bell. Steeling herself was too exhausting now. She also hadn't a clue what had propelled her out of her apartment in New Brunswick into her car for the hour-and-a-half drive to her father's house. Especially since the last time she had called. At first, she had reasoned she would call Kohar for a visit. Kohar and Jonathan lived in her father's neighborhood, only a fifteen-minute walk from each other. But then as she exited off Jewel Avenue, she found herself not crossing Queens Boulevard, and instead making three lefts until she reached her father's block.

Lucine breathed heavily, her palms moist with anxiety. Beatrice would most likely be home. She was the sitcom character, forever unchanging, a caricature of laziness and an overall inchoate being who sat on the couch grazing on boxes of Cap'n Crunch and sour cream American-cheese sandwiches, a ghastly combination that had Lucine inwardly retching upon first glance. She had once watched Beatrice bite into a ball of mozzarella cheese like someone eating an apple and proceed to consume the entire mass without pause. Lucine could overlook Beatrice's sloth-like existence. But her deep-set eyes, steady with apathy and a truculence so disarming that even Lucine was flustered in the girl's presence—it put her on edge.

In the far recesses of the house, in her father's bedroom that her mother and he had shared for the first seven years of Lucine's life, was her father. Her father, who had shrunk from Herculean proportions to a paralyzed invalid, solely relied on his wife and trusted her explicitly. A misplaced trust, really. Relying on her questionable medical background as a temporary nurse in Romania, Tanté had ignored the doctor's orders for Lucine's father to stay in the hospital for physical therapy and brought him home months earlier. The doctors had been confident that he would have had a seventy-five percent recovery after the stroke. Yet her father's mobility declined. And it dawned on Lucine that Tanté, who endured the tremendous undertaking of caring for her father, had orchestrated this dynamic because it served her. Absolute control was a paranoiac's delirious fantasy realized, even if it meant allowing oneself to be worn down with bathing, feeding, primping, emptying catheters and bedpans, massaging deadening nerves, maintaining and administering an extraordinary supply of medication, and the rest of the mind-numbing dreariness of caring for a disabled person.

As if Beatrice's purposeless predilection wasn't bad enough, her mother had let her take several years off from going to college. This meant that at her mother's behest, Beatrice drove her from one random destination to another and ran errands for her at any hour of the day. There could be no protest on Beatrice's part; the bargain was most in her favor.

Feeling once again transported, Lucine pressed the glowing button of the rear door and heard the doorbell sounding faintly from within the house. From her periphery she saw the quick-handed flash of the kitchen

curtain opening and closing. Footsteps pounding in and out of rooms.
Lucine began counting backwards from fifty, refusing to languish on the
backdoor steps of a house that was rightfully hers. She was determined to
turn on her heels and get back into the car, phone Kohar as she drove over
to her house: she hadn't seen Ruby since Kohar had given birth to her in
the hospital.

She wasn't prepared just then as the door opened slowly, as if someone
were turning the heavy crank of a drawbridge.

"Hey."

A young woman appeared before her, dressed in oversized jeans that fell
past her underwear, revealing a meaty stomach that half-concealed pink
Victoria's Secret stitching; cork-screw hair pulled back in a severe ponytail; and a broad, heavy face that shrunk her facial features, resembling a
Cabbage Patch doll. Her skin, though, was pockmarked and faintly scarred
with teenage-acne trauma. Upon first glance, it would be difficult to esti-
mate her age.

"Hi," Lucine said curiously.

"Come in," the girl said and turned away, moving toward the living
room.

Beatrice. It was to Lucine's advantage that Beatrice's back was turned to
her so she had a second to recover from the shock of not recognizing who
she was. She dared not stare at her openly, but watched as she sunk back
into the couch with a flourish of one who had been wrongly interrupted
from an afternoon of relaxation. Lucine drew in a breath at Beatrice's man-
nish hands as she thrust them into a bag of Doritos, unblinkingly fixated
on the television screen.

"Is your mom home?" Lucine asked.

"Yeah," said Beatrice matter-of-factly. "She's with Dad."

"Does she know I'm here?" asked Lucine. "I didn't call first."

"She probably knows," Beatrice replied. She pulled out a sizable chip
from the bag and nibbled on it absently.

"I'll just wait in the kitchen then," Lucine offered. "I wanted to see
Dad."

"He usually naps around now," said Beatrice, her eyes pinned to the
screen.

"Could you tell your mother I'm here? Just in case she doesn't know? Kohar's expecting me soon. I wanted to swing by here first and say a quick hello."

Peering now into the bag of chips, Beatrice huffed. "Hang on," she said, rooting through the bag and extracting another large chip. She placed the entire piece into her mouth and crunched loudly, then stood up and plodded down the hallway. Lucine heard Beatrice knocking on their father's bedroom door and then speaking Armenian. Her grammar was atrocious. Lucine grimaced, wondering if Beatrice was speaking Armenian on her account or because their father preferred it.

Her stepmother's sharp, nasal voice came through from the other side of the room, but it was too low for Lucine to hear the words. Sitting up anxiously now, Lucine tried to remember the exact time that she had last seen her father—or Beatrice, for that matter. It was several years after she and Steve had married; she had passed by afterwards to tell him. Beatrice hadn't been home. It occurred to her that during the rare times she had visited, Beatrice could have been home, but hiding out in her bedroom or in the basement, which had been refinished as Beatrice's new space—her "she shed," she had called it. Lucine realized that she probably hadn't seen Beatrice in nearly eight years. The last time she had visited, her stepmother, as usual, had been curt with her and had not bothered to congratulate Lucine after she had shared the news of her marriage.

The topic of their father was one that Kohar and Lucine rarely broached. Each of their relationships with him were vastly different; despite their stepmother's aloofness, Kohar had persisted calling to visit or speak to their father, but Lucine had abandoned all desire to see him.

"You're letting her get her way. Don't let her keep you from seeing Dad," Kohar had once said to her.

"She hates me," Lucine had said. "She's always telling me he's not feeling well or that she's coming down with a migraine or she just put him down for a nap or some shit. I'm sick of it."

"She tells me the same thing," Kohar had replied. "I call anyway."

Kohar, so good in her intentions. It was so simple for her. But for Lucine it felt impossible to sort through it all, like a book where some of the pages are stuck together. *I don't want to see Dad*, she wanted to tell Kohar. When she did see him, sitting across from him, watching him propped up in bed, his mouth moving slowly with enunciation, the rolling table beside him with a box of tissues and the sectional pill box, the left side of his body limp and dead, she could not locate or name a single emotion that reverberated through her. Numbness. Nothing. The concoction of guilt, anger, pity . . . it was too heady a potion.

"She'll be out in a minute," Beatrice announced, and leaned back into the couch on the mound of chintz pillows.

"What kind of car are you driving?"

At first Lucine didn't answer, not realizing that Beatrice's question was directed to her, although there was no one else in the room.

"A Honda Civic," she said. "My car's in the shop. It's my friend's."

Her car had been seized and impounded the morning of Kohar's baby shower. When she opened her front door to leave for the shower, she almost walked into a New Jersey police officer who, judging from the oversized clipboard and stack of papers in his hand, was about to ring the doorbell and inform her that her car was being towed.

Before Lucine could politely reciprocate Beatrice's question, she heard her father's bedroom door open and close quietly. Then another door, the hallway bathroom, opened and closed. The intense gush of faucet water. Lucine's distaste for her stepmother shifted in her stomach to something akin to dread. Now the dull stomping of footsteps grew louder, carrying the weight of fatigue and aggravation.

When her stepmother appeared in the living room, Beatrice briefly looked up at her mother and began fiddling with the remote control. The woman's presence, all four feet and eleven inches of her corpulent frame, was as mythical as a leprechaun's. Wearing an eggshell white housedress that stopped below her knees and her white-socked feet tucked into a pair of open-toed sandals that displayed a cheerful spray of pink flowers, it was laughable—impossible, really—that her presence could evoke such a feeling of wretchedness for anyone.

"Hi, Tanté," Lucine said, aware that the weariness in her voice was transparent.

"Hi, Lucine."

Instead of sitting next to the open space on the couch next to Lucine, Tanté nudged Beatrice's legs off the couch and heaved herself into the narrow space.

"How are you doing?" Tanté asked.

"I'm fine. How are you?" asked Lucine.

"*Pahn muhn eh, gertankgor,*" Tanté responded. An expression in Armenian that conveyed the sentiment that every day was more of the same, banal, and monotonous.

"I just wanted to stop by and see Dad," Lucine said.

There were so many replies she was anticipating—*It's about time*, or *How long has it been now—a year?* or *He's stopped asking about you*, or *Thanks for doing us the honor of stopping by*. All things that Tanté would rightfully be able to express, given her life's toll of being her father's caretaker.

"He should be up in a few minutes," Tanté said.

She sat up and hoisted herself off the couch, laboring to stand on her feet. "Can I get you something to drink? Or eat?" she called out and disappeared into the kitchen.

"No, I'm good. Thank you."

One Thanksgiving, her stepmother had presented a platter covered with pieces of fried meat, mysteriously gray-colored. She had placed a piece on Lucine's plate, assuring her that it was fried chicken. It was only after Lucine had bit into the spongy texture that she heard her stepmother's staccato laughter, announcing that Lucine was eating calf brains.

"How's the baby doing?" Tanté asked, returning with a plate of headcheese and pita bread.

"Ruby? She's fine. I'm going to stop after I leave here, to visit Kohar."

"She's so skinny! I couldn't believe it when she came here last week," Tanté said as she lifted a thick slab of cheese and took a sizable bite.

Lucine regarded the pieces of pink, fatty meat embedded in a revolting gelatinous substance that she could not name. Tanté's skinny remark, she knew, was an underhanded insult toward her. This had been another one of her stepmother's tactless tendencies—remarking on someone's weight gain or weight loss. Lucine knew she was Tanté's easy target, but it got the better of her every time anyway.

"Yeah, she looks good," she offered.

"Good? She looks great!" Tanté exclaimed.

A bit of the headcheese stuck at the corner of her lips. Behind her thick-lensed glasses, her eyes recessed in her head, she resembled a mole.

The day after her father and Tanté's wedding, Lucine had locked herself in the bathroom with a Sharpie and a framed snapshot her father had given her. Clutching the marker, she had scrawled BITCH across her stepmother's face while Kohar pounded her fists from the other side of the door. Lucine was seven.

"Yes!" Beatrice sat up wildly.

Lucine glanced at the screen and saw the credits for another *Full House* episode.

Beatrice pumped her arms to her sides as if she had scored a goal. "Syndications ruuuule!"

It was the most animated Lucine had seen her since walking through the door as she watched Beatrice sprint into the kitchen. The abrupt banging of cabinet doors reverberated sharply.

"Let me check to see if your father's awake," Tanté said and left the half-eaten plate of food on the coffee table. "Help yourself."

Lucine sat, now poised on the edge of the couch. Moments after closing the bedroom door behind her, her stepmother flung the door open. "Lucine! He's up."

As Lucine left the living room, Beatrice returned from the kitchen with a box of Lucky Charms. Lucine wondered if she could leave without having to say goodbye to her. Beatrice wouldn't notice.

It had been so long since she had last visited that it felt as if she were walking through a different house altogether. Her mother's traditional Armenian décor from years ago had transitioned into a display of gaudy European-ness; she walked past a long and narrow gold-framed mirror in the hallway and noticed the pink and yellow flowery fringed rugs that lay on the hardwood floors. The doors of the coat closet were now mirrored. Matching lamps with copper brown lampshades in the living room displayed marble lions looking away from one another. The house was foreign. Overly adorned. An ugly museum where she did not belong.

Her stepmother walked out of the room as Lucine entered and closed the door behind her. Lucine felt heavy, uneven breaths leave her body.

Breaths she could not control. She was grateful that the shades were half open and the afternoon light brightened the space. The acrid smell of disinfectant, Febreze, and Bengay lingered in the room. The mustiness of a closed-in room, shuttered from life.

Positioned and reclined against propped-up pillows, Lucine saw the silhouette of her father's face and torso. His mustache familiar, yet unevenly trimmed. He wore tinted spectacles, lending himself the uncanny appearance of a retired mobster. As she moved toward him, she saw the sloping trace of his left side, slackened from his chronic paralysis. Sensing a presence in the room, he glanced at the doorway; and then his eyes seized on Lucine with wonder, magnified by his eyeglasses. He watched her as she lowered herself into an old living-room chair that had been placed across from the narrow rolling table.

"Hi, Dad," she said.

Her father cleared his throat and pulled his body toward her direction. Then, a lopsided grin stretched across the right side of his face. Disappeared. As if his facial muscles could only form a smile for brief, spasmodic moments.

"How've you been?" he drawled.

"I'm okay. Just wanted to say hi," she said.

He nodded with a mechanical repetition. Lucine wasn't sure if this was an effect of the stroke, or if he were absorbing her sudden presence in his room.

The faint sound of the doorbell rang from the other side of the house. Then the gawky pounding of footsteps. Beatrice.

"How's your husband?" he asked.

Lucine found it within herself to shake her head. "Not so great," she said. "I mean, he's fine. I moved out a while ago."

Her father's eyes widened. "I'm sorry. To hear that. Too bad."

He would not, Lucine knew, ask questions as to why she and Steve had separated. The two had never met.

He lifted his right arm and placed it on the rolling table, opened his hand. Unconsciously, Lucine placed her hand in his.

"Where are you living?" he asked.

Lucine felt his strong grip encasing her hand. "With Mom for now," she lied, wanting to reassure him that she was safe and secure.

Her father nodded. "He should have moved out. Not you."

The eviction notice, Lucine's temporary arrangement of living with her friend and having to work more double shifts—she wanted to spare her father the ordeal of those details.

"It worked out better this way," she offered. "I can start fresh."

"New Jersey's a piece-of-shit state anyway," her father said, trying to offer her solace. "If you ever buy property, buy it here. In Queens."

Property. During the height of her father's financial success, he established his own construction company and maintained four properties he owned throughout Queens in Woodside, Sunnyside, Astoria, and Ridgewood. Every other weekend the family drove three hours upstate to his two-acre property in Hunter Mountain, and in the winter they flew to Florida, where he owned a condo in Boca. He was the exemplary model of the American Dream, arriving in New York with no more than a suitcase and going to trade school for licensing in locksmith, plumbing, and electricity. It was difficult for anyone to fathom that her father, who returned home from work in a grease-stained utility uniform and washed the caked dirt from under his nails with Lava soap, owned a business and property and real estate that was worth over seven million dollars. Kohar and Lucine's childhood memories of him were tantamount to a kiss on the cheek in the twilight hour before sunrise and Sundays of going to church and eating at IHOP for breakfast.

"How's work?" he asked.

"It's okay," she said. "I like this place. I've been there for a while."

"You look tired," he said.

"I work the morning shift," Lucine said. "How are you doing?" Compelled, whether it was necessary or not, she knew he deserved an apology for her years of absence. "I'm sorry I—"

He released her hand and held his up in protest. "I'm just happy you're okay."

Lucine understood, in this moment that would haunt her for the years to come, that her father could not be angry with her absence because he no longer felt worthy enough. He knew he had disappointed her. He knew the man he was and what life had reduced him to, and thought he was no longer fit to be deserving of anything.

As she sat in what was once her parents' bedroom, she remembered the bureau draped with her mother's embroidery, the picture frames and jewelry boxes. Lucine felt delirious in her memories that began to unfold. She and her father. Her father paralyzed now for so many years, sitting across from her. *Do you remember when we used to race down the block? How you would let me beat you every time?* she wanted to ask him. She remembered the hard pavement beneath her feet, the sharp air in her lungs as he ran alongside her, threatening her victory just long enough to propel herself past him and to the edge of the crosswalk. What she would do to run with him one more time.

"Do you need money?"

Lucine snapped back to attention, aware of the stilled silence in the room. She looked at her father's blank face.

"Do you need money?" he repeated.

The opening and closing of doors came through from the other side of the wall. Lucine could imagine, if not sense in all possible breadths of reality, that her stepmother was eavesdropping. A staccato of laughter carried from down the hallway.

"No," she lied, feeling the heat rise from her neck to her cheeks.

Her father stared at her briefly, nodded, and scrunched his chin, assessing her.

"I should go," she said. "I'm going to see the baby."

Another grin flashed across her father's face. Then it disappeared so quickly she thought she had imagined it.

"Have you seen Ruby yet?" she asked.

Her father nodded. "Once. Kohar said something about shots and then she'll bring her back. Why all these shots?" he asked, half to himself. "A little baby and all those needles." His face quivered with disgust. Lucine had forgotten her father's squeamishness at the mention of blood and needles.

As she stood up, she realized he was still holding her hand. She felt his grip tighten around her wrist, drawing her to him awkwardly as she leaned over the table between them. Though he could not throw his other arm over to embrace her, he leaned in and pressed his face to her cheek.

"I love you, *akhcheegus*. Thank you for coming to see me," he said.

The sweet detergent smell of his shirt flooded Lucine's nostrils. She wanted desperately to tell him she loved him, too. She pressed her lips together in a tight line, so painfully tight that her teeth shuddered against the rising sob in her throat. She wiped the tears from the corners of her eyes, hoping he didn't notice. "Me, too," she managed.

When she tried to pull away, she realized he would not let go. "You're a good girl," he mumbled into her hair, the strands caught on the scruff of his face. "You're a good girl."

Finally, he released her, and Lucine turned toward the door. Then she turned briefly before closing it behind her and waved.

Disoriented, she walked down the hallway. The sound of a young male voice came from behind her grandmother's old bedroom. Then Beatrice's bursting laughter.

"Stop! Stop."

"Isn't she doing laundry in the basement?"

"Sshhhh!"

"I can be quiet as long as you can."

Lucine grimaced and sped toward the door.

"Tanté! I'm leaving," she called down to the basement.

Without waiting for an answer, she flung open the door and raced toward her car, which was parked in front of the house. Immediately she pulled out of the spot and headed up the street toward Kohar's house. The car seemed to wheeze for a moment, deciding whether it would idle or chug along. The needle of the gas tank paused precariously above the "E" mark. Lucine hoped the car would make it to the nearest gas station, although she wondered if ten dollars of gas would get her back home.

With only a hundred seventy-five dollars in her bank account and another week before getting paid, Lucine would be playing another game of making ends meet. She would not dare ask her mother for help; she had helped well enough during her marriage to Steve. The fifty-two-inch television set was still hanging on the living-room wall in New Brunswick. The dining-room set, Steve's first point of contention concerning Takouhi, was probably covered in a film of dust and nearly new from lack of use; not once had they entertained friends or celebrated a holiday in their house.

Regardless of Takouhi's motives—perhaps her distaste in Lucine's décor—her mother had been generous. When she called her now, the conversations between them were stilted, scripted exchanges. Her mother's voice came through as if she were falling very slowly, perceptibly. Takouhi's chronic depression had marched in and out of Lucine's—and everyone's—life, unannounced. A boorish guest, refusing to leave. And then, one day, vanishing until the next visit. A different kind, a fiend of immeasurable proportions, was, ostensibly, camping out. Lucine could not consider visiting her. When she imagined her mother, what came to mind was a specter, floating through the rooms of a cobwebbed apartment.

Given that she was only a few miles away from the cemetery, she knew she should visit Gabriel's grave. She hadn't gone since the forty-day blessing, where she and her sisters and mother stood over his headstone while the Armenian priest chanted over wisps of frankincense that hovered above their heads. Even then, she had thought of her father. Her eyes blurred with tears. In her purse was a photograph of her and Gabriel when she was nine—only two years after her parents' divorce—sitting on Gabriel's lap with her arm draped around his neck. So casually, so playfully. As if he were her father. As the priest sang that afternoon, Lucine wondered if she would feel her heart ache for her father the way it did for Gabriel. Since his death, she had spent more time mourning his absence than she had missing her father during five years of his illness. She did not allow herself to feel guilty; not for the evenings Gabriel had sat by her side going over her algebra homework or helping her proofread a term paper, or entertaining her unannounced tirades in his study while he was working, or eating her experimental creations before she knew she wanted to be a pastry chef—or for the pure love that he gave so willingly.

Turning onto Kohar's block, she wondered how much or how little she would tell her sister. As she backed into a parking spot, her phone buzzed with a message. It was Max, she knew, yet to be deterred by her unanswered texts and phone calls. It was callous, to ignore his messages, to avoid telling him that although their trysts had been rather magical, in the long run it wouldn't work out between them. Though he would not want to be, Max belonged where she had left him.

Chapter 17

As Kohar let herself into her mother's apartment, she dropped her purse by the foot of the door, wondering how long she would stay. She hadn't realized how alienated she had become from herself and her family until she walked toward the kitchen and heard their voices, light and easy as if it were just another afternoon together. She sensed within herself a feeling of intimidation, as if standing in the foyer of a party before entering a room. She found her mother rolling dough in the kitchen and Azad and Lucine slathering a mixture of olive oil and za'atar on the small floury disks that their mother was generating with impressive speed.

Kohar had finally given up breastfeeding after six difficult months of producing very little milk. During that time, she had exhausted herself (and Jonathan), going to great lengths to increase her supply, but nothing had worked—fenugreek supplements, consultations with multiple experts at the La Leche League, brewing lactation teas, baking lactation cookies. Her obstetrician suggested that her body was too stressed to produce milk. Now that Jonathan was able to bottle-feed Ruby, he told her to take the day for herself, spend time with her sisters and mother.

"Hey!" her mother called out on the sight of Kohar. "Pull out the baking trays and let's put the manaeesh in the oven."

Takouhi was wearing a housedress—as Gabriel used to teasingly call it—but it wasn't the drab gray one that resembled a dying sheep (this was the unfortunate image that came to mind when Kohar saw her mother wearing it). Rather, it was a dress of thin fabric covered in a damask pattern of fall colors. She had pulled back her hair as she usually did when cooking, but Kohar noticed how smooth and straight it shined, like gray silk.

Ever since her mother had announced to the three of them that she had decided to go away on a trip by herself, her disposition had shifted noticeably. The destination was a small country in West Africa that Kohar had never heard of and hadn't bothered looking up. She wondered with passing curiosity why her mother would choose to fly such a distance, but was too relieved with her mother's plans to bother asking.

"You look good, Mom," she commented.

"Thank you!" Rare was the moment that Takouhi received a compliment begrudgingly.

Azad and Lucine, both looking unlike themselves in a way Kohar could not place, blew her kisses from where they stood. Kohar felt guilty for not calling them more often, but neither of her sisters seemed aloof with her. The frequency of Lucine's phone calls had tapered to once or twice a month, and Azad sent half-hearted texts, communicating in her passive way that she was alive.

Since Gabriel's passing, Kohar tried to visit Takouhi once a week, usually on Saturdays. In the first few months, she sat on Takouhi's bed with Ruby in her arms, talking to her as if she were a convalescent, bedridden and confined. Kohar would ask all sorts of questions—how was work? had her mother spoken to her sisters? her aunts? was she going to stay on board with the co-op's gardening committee? Twenty minutes later, Kohar would collect herself and Ruby to leave. It did not occur to ask her mother if she wanted to hold the baby. The dull glaze in her mother's eyes, the odd way in which she didn't shift her body as if she were in a cast, her averted gaze— Ruby might as well have been a doll Kohar was holding.

On other days, her mother was alert, irritable. Kohar would find her in the kitchen reorganizing the pantry and the contents of the freezer—bags of dried lentils, bulgur, flour, spices, strewn all over the counters and the kitchen floor. She would regard Kohar and Ruby with an aggravated hello, their presence interrupting her organizational tirade, and continue with her task while Kohar tried for another impossible conversation.

She broke away from these thoughts as they all huddled on the couch together, poised with fresh anticipation as the MGM lion roared to life on the television screen.

"This is an excellent movie," Takouhi remarked for the third time that afternoon. The girls leaned back and looked at one another, rolling their eyes.

"We know," Azad said.

"I set the timer for the manaeesh. Kohar, before you pull it out of the oven, touch the top to make sure the crust isn't too soft."

"I know," Kohar said.

The smell of dough and herbs permeated the apartment. "How much longer?" Azad asked.

"About fifteen minutes," said Takouhi. "I just put it in the oven—Watch." She nudged her and drew into silence. A brief caption appeared on the screen, and then a piano playing as the closeup of a microphone opened into the expanse of a radio station.

"I saw this movie with Gabriel. It was like this outside," she said, pointing at the narrow French doors that overlooked the street from the living room.

The sky was white, the sun blotted out by a canvas of clouds. Though it would not rain, it was exactly the kind of day that kept people, happily, indoors. The gray weather darkened the unlit room, and the four of them pulled the thin comforter against them, consumed in the pleasure of this rare afternoon.

COLIN FIRTH WAS STUTTERING INTO A MICROPHONE WHEN THE timer rang. As Kohar rose to leave the room, Takouhi shot up from her seat. "I'll get it."

A few seconds later, they heard the clatter of the metal baking trays. Azad sat up at full attention.

"Do you want us to pause it?" Lucine called.

No answer.

"Mom!" Lucine hollered. "Do you want us to pause it?"

Silence. As Lucine reached for the remote control—"No."

The sound of their mother's heavy-heeled footsteps disappeared down the hallway.

"I'm going to stop it," Lucine muttered.

"She probably went to the bathroom," Kohar said.

"I'm going to check the manaeesh," said Azad and sprung to the kitchen. "Should I bring you guys some?"

"Well, duh!" said Lucine.

Azad returned with three plates, one in each hand and the other balanced awkwardly on her forearm like a waitress. "Grab it before it falls."

The three sat in silence, Colin Firth frozen in mid-sentence. Steam rose from the fresh bread as they tore off small pieces and blew before chewing.

"Where the hell is she?" Lucine growled.

Azad glanced at the empty space at the far end of the couch, absorbed in her last bite of food. "Maybe she's still in the bathroom."

"She's going to miss the speech—this is her favorite part," said Kohar.

The long gaps of time between visits manifested in odd ways to Azad; the reorganization of drawers and their contents occupying a new space, the coat closet sparser-seeming after her father's passing (his gray wool herringbone still hung on the far right, obscured and present), the tobacco-less air, and, most startlingly, the repurposing of rooms. Instead of calling out for her mother, Azad swung open each closed door, absorbing the unexpected transformation of each. Kohar's room had a seamstress's bust and sewing machine that overlooked the window to the courtyard and a small china cabinet filled with French antique place settings Gabriel's mother had given to Takouhi before she had died. Her and Lucine's bedroom was now entirely emptied, save the queen-size bed and a demure nightstand, as if it were a humble guest room for a passing traveler. Azad paused in front of her father's study, listening to the benign silence of a room where once was a place of enchantment, like a rarely visited attic filled with overlooked treasures.

Gingerly, Azad nudged open the door and stepped into the shadowy room. She sighed with wonder. It was all in place: the revolving leather chair with the sagging, worn seat, the books in their shelves, now nobly retired. The amber ashtray was where her father had kept it. Now clean and polished, it resembled a precious stone. And a half-empty pack of Camel cigarettes with a book of matches rested on top. The frayed edges of the hand-knotted rug felt ancient and inviting beneath Azad's bare feet. How often did her mother walk into this room, Azad wondered. She closed the door behind her and returned to the hallway, heading to her mother's bedroom.

Azad leaned her ear against the closed door. She knew to knock before entering; surely the door was closed for a reason. Yet there were no sounds coming from the other side. She heard Lucine huffing into the kitchen and the abrupt opening of the refrigerator door. Kohar's voice asking for a glass of seltzer. Laughter then. An unfamiliar trickle of laughter from behind the door. It carried with it a secretive intonation, like someone cupping the receiver of a rotary phone is how Azad pictured it. As if dialing a combination lock, Azad turned the doorknob and entered the room. She glanced momentarily at the clothes draped over the plush red velvet chair and the unmade bed, and then hedged toward the closed bathroom door. She felt scandalous now, knowing she should be with her sisters in the living room, waiting.

"I can't either," her mother's voice echoed within the narrow confines of the bathroom. "Me, too." Then a pause. "I will." A promise. "I will." Another pause. "Okay. Yes. Bye."

Azad could have raced out of the room on her toes and slinked back into the living room, but she didn't. She waited for her mother to open the door and see her reaction at her standing there.

Takouhi yanked the door open, refreshed with giddiness, and saw Azad. She drew in a breath and clutched the phone behind her.

"We were wondering where you'd gone," Azad said. "Who were you talking to?"

"You could have kept watching," Takouhi said.

For the first time since that day, she saw that her mother had let down her hair. It was salt-and-pepper now, straightened and hanging long past her shoulders. A vague sheen of glamour emanated from Takouhi, as if she had gone to a party the night before and not bothered cleaning off her makeup.

"Who were you talking to?" Azad asked again.

"Who? A friend," Takouhi said.

She started walking toward the door.

"Is it someone you're meeting on your trip?" Azad wasn't sure what had prompted her to ask.

"Why all the questions, huh? Kezee chee kharnuveer." *It's not your business.* This was one of several of her mother's notorious lines. She was fond of using it, Azad knew, when she was keeping a secret.

"Come off it, Mom. This isn't me walking into Kohar's bedroom and catching you reading her diary."

Takouhi's eyes flashed with sudden outrage. "I never did that."

"Yeah, okay. Whatever. Who were you talking to?"

"Azad, I said it's none of your business," Takouhi said coldly. "Did I ask you who you were texting with, all through dinner last night?"

"You're traveling thousands of miles away. If you're meeting someone there, don't you think it would be a good idea if at least one of us knew who you were with?" Once in a rare while, Azad was able to squirm through the fissures and gaps of Takouhi's erratic emotionality and appeal to her logic.

"Are we watching the end of this movie, or what?" Lucine's yelling traveled across the apartment. Both Azad and Takouhi rolled their eyes.

"His name is Ray," Takouhi said. "Don't ask me any more questions."

"That's not enough," Azad protested. "Where does he live? How did you meet him?" Takouhi exhaled again. But Azad would not be held off with impatience. "Is he from there?" It was too ludicrous. She was preparing herself for the trials of intensive guesswork.

"Yes."

Azad's mouth fell open. Not fully recovering, "Did you meet him online?"

"Yes."

Azad slowly shook her head. "Did *you* find *him* online, or did *he* find *you*?"

"He found me."

"*Moooom*," Azad's voice rose with alarm. "How *old* is he?"

"He said he has never seen such beautiful eyes. And he could tell from looking at my picture that I had lost someone in my life," Takouhi replied, not answering her question.

"Mom. Seriously. Mom, are you listening to what you're saying? Do you even know what he looks like?"

"Yes, Azad. I know what he looks like. We've been FaceTiming."

"From here to *West Africa*? Seriously?" and then, "Have you told Kohar? Lucine?" Azad asked. "Anyone?"

Takouhi shook her head. "Please don't say anything. I want to tell them when I get back."

"Do you remember what you said to us when you told us you were going there?" Azad didn't wait a beat and continued, "'I want to prove to myself that I can go somewhere alone,' you said, 'I'm sixty-five and have to learn to be independent' and then went on about the beautiful beaches and how a co-worker had told you it was a French-speaking area like Beirut," she finished.

Takouhi pursed her lips now, defiant. *Haven't you gotten enough out of me?*

"Just don't tell them anything yet. Please. I'm asking you. They're not going to understand," said Takouhi.

"Then you have to promise to contact me every day. There's an app they have now. It's free. I want you to download it and promise me you're going to contact me every day. Do you promise?" Azad was breathless now, out of her depth, grasping to harness the heedlessness of her mother's plans.

Takouhi's eyes softened. "I promise," she said. "And please, I'm asking you, don't tell anyone. Especially Kohar."

Before Azad could ask why Kohar especially, Takouhi had marched out of the room. "Sorry! My cousin Zevart called from California!"

Azad heard her voice ringing down the hallway from where she stood. She looked around the room again, noting the small, significant changes since her father's passing. But most especially, there was less order in the room. The bed was unmade and covered with various piles of paper. Dresses and skirts were limply piled across the seat of the red armchair. The lids of the jewelry boxes on the bureau were open. The room breathed with contentment. Azad had been accustomed to manic anxiety and physical order, how they tangoed in precise unison. Sparse perfection.

"We're putting it on! There's popcorn!"

Azad settled into the couch, wedged between her two sisters, sensing their complete absorption in the film. Distractedly she checked the time, relieved that the movie was almost over. She contemplated the new, forbidden knowledge of her mother's true intentions about flying to West Africa. A needling indignation grew within her as she recalled Takouhi's passing remarks regarding her upcoming trip, and within moments she felt such an acute outrage that she fought every impulse to spring up from her seat and leave the apartment.

The lengths she had gone to to lie, when none of them had hinted or even provoked her with questions. How nonchalantly, how egregiously her mother had lied. And Azad had to keep the lie to protect her mother. But from what? A seed of guilt burst within her. How would she manage to lie to Kohar and Lucine for the next two weeks? And then again, outrage. If it wasn't bad enough to feel the chronic isolation that only she felt from her sisters, Azad dreaded the possibility of their both finding out that she was lying for Takouhi. She was, as the family had joked throughout the years, terrible at it. Red-faced, stuttering, avoiding eye contact—she exhibited the telltale characteristics of a very bad liar.

Azad would brood over her uncomfortable predicament as she drove back to Philadelphia. Her mother's absence would sound a timer, perpetually ticking and growing louder as the days passed until her return. In her conscience, she was only liable for withholding the truth for fourteen days; once Takouhi returned, Azad was no longer culpable. Until that time, she would avoid conversations about her mother and only answer her sisters' phone calls half the time they called. And hopefully, she wouldn't hear from them.

Chapter 18

Takouhi's friends from work, rather hesitantly, had suggested the idea of online dating. There were so many men—single, like herself, who were lonely and looking for companionship. She was still visiting Gabriel's grave before and after work, kneeling on the cold earth and talking to the massive headstone that read:

In Memory of Gabriel Avedis Manoukian
Loving Son, Father, and Husband
June 4, 1946–April 17, 2019
You will be cherished in our hearts forever
Takouhi Manoukian
1950–

Dating someone seemed as wild as anything she could have imagined. Besides, where on earth would she find another Gabriel? Or an Armenian man, no less. Takouhi understood now, from her quarantined and sterile existence, her daughters' aversion to marrying an Armenian.

Gabriel wasn't the typical Armenian man. For all their modernism, the Armenian community Gabriel and Takouhi had become acquainted with, some of whom they considered close friends, was still conservative and traditional. Though most of the women certainly had careers, those of Takouhi's generation still catered to their husbands in most domestic matters and were largely in charge of all facets of the home as well as raising their children. When Gabriel's friends came to visit, they would gather in the parlor while Takouhi brewed *sourj* and poured them into demitasse glasses. Through the growing fog from cigarettes and cigarillos, Takouhi would place the tray on the coffee table and return to the kitchen to bring out the usual assortment of appetizers and return again with plates and forks and napkins. As if a humble caterer, unacknowledged, were trying to enter and leave without disturbing the intellectuals in the midst of their important discussion about the state of Armenia, American politics, a new translation that had recently been published. It was downright oppressive. It would be one of *those* men that Takouhi would have to suffer.

Perhaps Kohar's generation was more progressive, but Takouhi thought not. She would regard Kohar's old friends from the Armenian school at church now, all grown with families of their own, abiding their parents' single-minded desire for their children to continue the lineage of a nearly lost Armenian population. Though she would never admit it to Kohar now, Kohar who had declared in her early twenties she would never marry an Armenian, Takouhi (wryly) understood Kohar in an uncomplicated way.

Now she tolerated Kohar in new ways that Takouhi would not have expected: her obsessive need to keep the child on a nap schedule, the parenting books that were strewn open all over the house, as if prepared for an impending disaster, the pureeing of organic fruits and vegetables that were frozen into plastic, sealable ice-cube trays, the bedtime ritual that entailed the reading of *three* books, the colorful foam letters of the alphabet during bath time. This was Kohar's indirect, accusing way of telling Takouhi, *This is what you should have been doing with me. I'll show you how it's done.* But what did she know, really? Did she know of a husband who backhanded her in the middle of her daughter's birthday party? Or knocked over an entire china cabinet because he didn't like the dinner that had been made? Or locked her out of the house one winter night because he suspected her of having an affair? Takouhi had borne this and more. Her parents, counterparts of the staunch belief that divorce was a shameful thing to bring upon a family, a tragedy to be avoided, were no help: Takouhi hadn't the gumption to turn to them for solace. Kohar's easy life was a bitter thing to witness. Less and less did she reach for the phone to call her. Kohar always seemed to be in the *middle* of something, yet would stay on the phone with her while the baby wailed from her crib or while Kohar changed her diaper, expecting Takouhi to *hang on* or *give her a second. You don't have your old life anymore*, Takouhi wanted to tell her. *You can't just keep me on standby.*

Takouhi hadn't much time, she knew, but wanted to spend the years she had left the best way she knew how. It had all started with a link her friend Josephine from work had sent her. Takouhi had been wary. She wasn't ready to even have a conversation with another man, let alone meet someone face to face. You're just talking, her friend Josephine had said. You can talk to someone once and never speak to them again. You can delete your account immediately if you haven't the heart for it.

Hesitantly, Takouhi had clicked on the link. The screen sprung open to the backdrop of a tree-lined lake and a bright sun. Sitting by the lake was an older couple, a blond woman and brunette man, with their backs half-turned, the man's arm slung over the woman's shoulder in amiable companionship. *We find comfort in each other*, the photo seemed to say. *We enjoy each other's company and that's okay.* Takouhi scanned the rest of the page. *Silver Singles*, it read. *Exclusive site for 50+ singles. Dating and friendship.* Then two boxes underneath. *I am a woman/man. I am looking for a woman/man.*

Takouhi ticked off the boxes, which led her to a membership page promising a three-month trial with no fees. Minutes later, Takouhi found herself grappling with the Describe Yourself section. Questions she had never considered or known the answers to, gave her profound pause. She deliberated over each question with more attention than they deserved.

What is your favorite place to go out for dinner? "My house. I don't know anyone that cooks as well as I do," Takouhi chuckled as she consulted the keyboard with each hunt and peck.

What are two or three things you enjoy doing during your leisure time? Takouhi glared at the screen. After a few sips of coffee and a few minutes staring at the bedroom curtains, she returned to the keyboard. "Gardening, spending time with my daughters, and cooking." She read it back to herself, pleased.

How happy are you with your physical appearance? She rolled her eyes, glowering at the ceiling. "Are these people serious, or what?" she said aloud. "Very happy."

If your best friends had to pick four words to describe you, what would they be? Friends. Like who? The Armenian wives she seldom spoke to, now that Gabriel was dead? Their polite, distanced sympathy as if death were contagious. The American women at work who strained to understand her English through her thick Armenian-Lebanese accent? "Creative, passionate, beautiful, and straightforward."

The questions, hurdles of a confounding magnitude, seemed to become less and less so as Takouhi waded through them. By the time she reached the last one, her shoulders ached from hunching over the computer screen, but she felt triumphant. She lay in bed that night, renewed. Her mind spun with anticipation.

When she awoke the next morning, the luster of her mood had disappeared. Instead, she felt bedraggled as she sat on the edge of her bed, her slacks hanging off her calves, contemplating calling in sick again despite having just returned from medical leave. It had been granted by her supervisor not begrudgingly, but Takouhi's months of catatonia—in which although she arrived to work and managed to carry out her responsibilities—resembled a mental convalescent.

On this particular morning, somehow, again, Takouhi felt the futility of living. Looking back on her effort of conjuring words and creating her new self—it seemed a maudlin, pathetic undertaking. A moment of idiocy. As she sat frozen in the coming daylight, she felt Gabriel's eyes boring into her from the framed photograph of their last Christmas together. He was sitting at the head of the dinner table, with Takouhi poised next to him. Gabriel smiled tiredly. Takouhi's smile spread too wide, too happy. They had both known it would be the last Christmas. She remembered their conversation that evening with grim accuracy.

"Have I made you happy?"

They had both retired to bed together that evening, leaving the cleanup to the girls and Jonathan. Even from the far end of the apartment, Takouhi knew they were gathered in the parlor and Jonathan had thrown another log onto the fire. Kohar had her legs propped up in Jonathan's lap, and Azad and Lucine were pouring Grand Marnier into snifters.

"Why are you asking me this, Gabriel?" Takouhi had spoken in the darkness. She had found his hand and put hers in his.

"Have I made you happy?—I want to know."

"Yes. Go to bed, Gabriel, now. It's late."

"It's not late," he had said tiredly. "I just need to rest."

Takouhi wanted to ask if she had made him happy. But it had sounded too painfully like goodbye. He would die tomorrow, she thought, if she asked him the same question. She would never ask him. Whether Gabriel interpreted that as apathy, Takouhi would not know, nor did she care. She refused to reminisce about anything. But also, she did not want to know the answer. She wanted to assume that she had made him happy, that they had tolerated each other's unpleasantness with love and acceptance, and that the unpleasantness was reciprocally equivalent. She would not revisit this consideration again.

Before she could ask him if he had enjoyed Christmas Eve, he began snoring, consumed by sleep.

Takouhi stared at the framed picture now, hesitating. "I did a strange thing, Gabriel," she said to the photograph. Her slacks had slipped to the floor, revealing her pale legs that were covered in fine, unshaven hair. Takouhi glanced at her reflection, assessing the sag of her cheeks—jowls, really—her eyes starving from lack of sleep, her wiry hair streaked with white against her ashen face.

"Who would love me, anyway?" she asked, speaking to the photograph again.

Half an hour later, Takouhi struggled into her coat and walked to the subway, leaving behind all the complications of emotion and conflict for her return, perhaps. And when she did return that evening, she undressed, tied up her hair, reheated a few stale falafels, and watched the first episode (of many) of a British show about royalty that Azad had insisted she would *love*. With utter abandon, Takouhi plunged herself into its depths, for once not thinking of anything but the lives of strangers, with whom she found an immediate kinship. That evening when she fell into a deep sleep, she did not think about the singles website or Gabriel or who would not love her. She was grateful to be tired enough for her mind to rest for once.

Several weeks later, while she was on the phone with Azad, the conversation shifted from Azad's new job to a food-recipe website Azad had sent her.

"Have you opened it yet?" Azad wanted to know. "I sent you a link to this website that has Armenian recipes. You never write anything down. Can you take a look at it and tell me if the ingredients are similar? I want to make mantuh."

"Mantuh? You need more than just you for mantuh," Takouhi countered.

"I'm going to have my friends over and we'll all do it together," said Azad.

"You're going to have your friends over? For all the afternoons you grumbled about helping me make mantuh, now you're throwing a mantuh party. Unbelievable."

"Mom, open the link," Azad demanded.

"Later. I will," said Takouhi.

"No, now. You never check your emails. Just open it. I want you to look at the recipe and tell me yes or no so I can go buy the stuff."

"Give me a minute." Takouhi went to Gabriel's study and carried the laptop back to her bedroom. "I have to charge it. It's dead," she said.

"So, charge it now. You're so out of touch, Mom," said Azad.

The laptop flickered to life and finally Takouhi managed to open her emails.

"How often do you go online, anyway?" asked Azad.

"Not often," said Takouhi.

When the screen first opened, Takouhi thought she had accidentally signed into Gabriel's old account; there were over thirty messages in her inbox.

"Did you find it?" Azad asked.

"I'm looking," Takouhi said testily. "I have all these messages in my account."

"Probably junk if you don't go in often," said Azad.

But they weren't junk emails. Not all of them. *Silver Singles*, they read. Notifications from matches that had contacted her. She scrolled through and randomly opened an email. A picture of a man with thinning brown hair and a ruddy complexion appeared. Tom Binckes. *I liked your profile and we have a lot in common. Write back. I'll be waiting.* Takouhi drew away from the screen, scrunched her face.

"Mom??" Azad's voice pierced through the phone.

"I have another call." Takouhi hung up abruptly and muted her phone.

She clicked on the emails, observing the faces of men whose desperation was uncomfortably palpable: their casual language, aloof smiles, offhanded postures—all trying to convey the same allure. After scanning several profiles, Takouhi grew bored; these men were each and all the same person. An image of pomegranates came to mind. All lined up in a neat pyramid in the grocery store, all of them dull red with dark spots of premature rot.

Takouhi scrolled through the significant queue of emails until she came across an email address she did not recognize. The subject read "Hello, this is from Ray." When she clicked to open the email, there was a letter one paragraph long and signed with the sender's name:

Dear Takouhi,

You don't know me, but I saw you on Facebook, which is where I found your email address. I don't know you either, but I can tell from your profile picture that you are a beautiful person. So much has happened in my life that has led me to this place of me contacting you. I can tell from your eyes that you have lost someone dear to you and I know the pain you carry. If you'd like to talk on instant message, I'll send you my profile name on Facebook. Or you can just write me back here.

Hoping to hear from you,

Ray

Chapter 19

Look what I found!" Azad's voice called over from the foyer between the living room and the kitchen. "I didn't know they made this."

She was standing in front of two rows of liquor and wine bottles that her parents kept on a shelf below the cabinet of china. The thick-glassed bottle in her hand gleamed with an orange liquid, nearly fluorescent. *Saffron Gin.* "Kohar—you should try this. I bet you'll love it," she said.

Lucine and Kohar were in the kitchen pressing their oiled fingers into a tray of dough dimpled with olives. It was Kohar's first visit to the apartment since the three of them had spent the afternoon with their mother watching a movie. To both Kohar and Azad's wonder, Lucine had suggested they meet at their mother's apartment and spend an evening together since Takouhi wouldn't be home until very late.

"What is it?" Kohar called out, carefully wiping off a stray hair from her brow with the back of her hand.

"Saffron gin," said Azad. "We are drinking, aren't we? I'm definitely sleeping over."

"I'm not driving back to New Jersey," Lucine said. "Were you planning on going home tonight?" she asked, turning to Kohar.

"I don't know." She hadn't spent an evening away from home since giving birth to Ruby. "Is Mom staying over at her friend's house tonight, or is she coming back here?"

"What difference does it make?"

Takouhi had left for the evening to meet a friend in the city for dinner and a show. Her flight was scheduled for the day after next, and she had only agreed to plans at the insistence of her friend, who had an apartment on the Upper East Side. To Kohar's recollection, her mother had never stayed over at anyone's home for any reason. She was about to say that she couldn't fully enjoy the evening if she was expecting their mother's imminent return.

"Don't be a loser," said Lucine. "Sleep over. Jonathan can take care of Ruby." Her tone, flat and dismissive, made Kohar more anxious.

"I've never been away from her overnight," she said. "I have to see."

"See about what? It's shit outside," Lucine said, cocking her head in the direction of the window. An angry spray of rain spattered against the panes that revealed a black sky. They heard the dull thump of empty garbage bins falling over onto the pavement. "And you told me you found a spot right in front of the building."

"I brought us some treats," Azad announced as she walked into the kitchen. She opened the double doors of the refrigerator and then placed a blue-lidded Tupperware container on the counter. "If we have this first, then *that* is going to taste extra delicious when it's ready," she said, eyeing the focaccia that was ready to go into the oven.

"Seriously, Azad?" Lucine groused as she leaned in to inspect the contents. "Brownies. How imaginative."

Azad sucked her teeth and grabbed the container off the counter. "Kohar?" she said, edging an elbow in between the two of them and holding the brownies under Kohar's nose.

"Definitely not," said Kohar as she peered at the contents.

"Why?" Azad lamented. "You and Jonathan used to smoke all the time. Just take a bite."

Surprising both herself and Azad, Kohar broke off a small piece and began chewing.

"Lucine?"

"It's just pot, right?" she asked.

"I didn't even think about that!" Kohar's eyes widened as she swallowed. "Azad—"

"Just pot," Azad said. "I'm not that crazy."

"Aren't you, though?" Lucine asked as she broke one of the more sizable squares in half and began eating.

"I guess I'm sleeping over," Kohar said. "Where'd you put that gin?"

A strange, unsettling elation had taken hold of her as she went to the foyer to find a cocktail glass. Similar to the times she had broken curfew beyond the point of return, emboldened somehow and not terrified. It was her mother's house, after all, and she was standing in the kitchen eating a pot brownie and about to mix herself a strong and much-needed drink. Jonathan had told her that morning that she should stay over at her mother's house; he and Ruby would be fine, and his mother was stopping over in the late afternoon in case he needed help.

"How long before it kicks in?" she called out as she extracted a tumbler and headed back toward the kitchen.

"It depends. Half an hour? Forty-five minutes?" Azad said.

"Did she really want us to check her mail? She said something about it before she walked out," Lucine said. "And why does she need us to check it? She's home all the time. Who's supposed to get it while she's away?"

"That would be me," Kohar said. In what righteous universe would her sisters be given the responsibility to do anything when Kohar's proximity was most convenient for requests like stopping by the apartment to collect the mail? "And no. I haven't had a chance to drive over. Also, the mailman usually puts her mail in a stack and rubber-bands it. Check," she said as Lucine left for the lobby.

"I wonder how she'll do, away for so long," Kohar said. The kitchen was silent as she busied herself with measuring the orange liquid into a shot glass and pouring it over the mound of ice in the tumbler. "I hope she'll be safe there." She tipped the bottle of pink grapefruit juice until it met the edge of the glass, and then she grabbed the end of a spoon to stir with. The house was quiet. "I wonder if she'll check her email."

Azad stood in the hallway next to the portrait of her father and held her breath, listening. She could not tell if her mouth was dry from the premature onset of the brownies taking effect or if it was her nerves. The moment would pass. Or she hoped so. Like those screeching catfights she would hear in the middle of a summer night through her open bedroom window, the sensation of imagining claw tearing through flesh. The moment would pass.

The front door thudded closed. Azad jumped. "Who's that?" she barked. Her stomach lurched.

"It's me, stupid," Lucine's bored voice breezed past her to the dining room. "Mom has a ton of mail. Jesus. How long has it been sitting there, and why? She hasn't even left for her trip yet."

She plopped the stack down that the mailman had bundled with a thick rubber band and began separating the envelopes.

"What are you doing?" Azad asked.

"Separating her shit. She loves the catalogs," she said, holding up a Soft Surroundings magazine in the air. She tossed it on the dining-room table. "Hopefully there's a Chico's and J. Jill in here. She'll be a pig in shit then."

"Do you think she'll try calling us while she's away?" asked Kohar. She ran her tongue along the crevasses between her molars, the aroma of marijuana in her mouth.

"No!" said Lucine. "Why is she calling us from Africa?"

"I'm just saying. We'll have no way of getting in touch with her. Do you know where she's staying?" Kohar pressed.

"Relax," Lucine said. "You worry too much. This is why she's up your ass all the time—because you're up in her shit."

"I'm not up in her shit! I just want to know that she'll be okay," Kohar said. Lucine had a way of making her uneasy, defensive. "I didn't create this relationship," said Kohar. Lucine continued flipping through the mail and sorting it into several piles. Whether she was deliberately ignoring Kohar or hadn't heard her, Kohar couldn't tell. She watched Lucine narrowly, aware that she had the dangerous urge to walk over to her and slam her against the wall.

"Since when did Mom—" Lucine broke off.

Kohar was waiting now: for what, she did not know. Another passing comment, obnoxiously apathetic. And then, the way snow begins to drift and fall on a mild winter night, she could feel a dullness in her limbs softening her senses. The pot had already started to take effect. Her eyes, though still fixed on Lucine, lost their focus.

"What is it?" Azad went to Lucine, who was now holding a piece of paper, staring at it in consumed silence. "What is it?" she asked again, standing over Lucine's shoulder, knowing she might snatch it out of her sight.

"It's from my dad," said Lucine, her voice thick. "It's from Dad," she said and looked over at Kohar, who was sitting on the couch.

"Dad? What is it?" asked Kohar. "*He* sent you something?"

Lucine put down the sheet of paper and looked in the envelope. She extracted a check, drew in a breath. "It's money," she said.

She turned her back, faced the wall, and covered her face with her hands. Kohar knew she was crying. As a little girl, she would oftentimes find Lucine in the very same posture and knew something bad had happened. Kohar, her anger now dissolved, went over to her, put her arm over her shoulders. Lucine's entire body shook, sobs racking through her. Finally she turned around, red-faced, and wiped her eyes.

"He wrote me a check," she said. "He knew. He even asked me if I needed anything and I said no." She stared at the check in her hand, her eyes pooling with fresh tears. "I don't deserve it."

"You saw him?" asked Kohar.

Lucine nodded as she put the check and the letter back in the envelope.

"When?" asked Kohar.

"Like two weeks ago. I don't even know how he wrote this out. It's definitely his handwriting," she said, remembering that he was a lefty.

"He's probably learned how to write with his right hand," Kohar said.

"When shit like this happens, I feel guilty," Lucine began; and before Kohar could interrupt, she said the unexpected: "Because when he dies, I'm not going to feel as awful as I do without Gabriel here. Dad was never around, even when he was." Whether or not she was also thinking of her soon-to-be ex-husband, neither Kohar nor Azad asked. "I don't deserve this," she repeated, now placing the envelope on the dining-room table.

Azad perched herself on the edge of the couch, watching her sisters. Her eyes, too, were filled with tears, an angst of sadness expanding in her chest. She dared not rupture this rare moment.

Since her discovery of her mother's romance, Azad had been unable to think about much else. For the first time she could remember, there was no one to turn to. Sometimes she would lie in bed and talk to her father out loud, as if he was sitting in the room listening. "How ridiculous is she being?" she would ask. "Can you please talk some sense into her?" And as she spoke the words aloud they hung in the room, the reply of silence reminding Azad that she was utterly alone.

She fell into a rabbit hole of Google-searching "African scams," "African romance scams," "Nigerian Internet scams," and all the variations that came to mind, knowing her mother was not in Nigeria and aware of the ubiquitous cliché that, regardless, frightened her. She watched videos on

YouTube, read articles in the *Huffington Post*, had even found a cautionary African scamming page on Facebook. All of them young African men, hanging out in Internet cafés and preying on women. Despite her aversion to daytime talk shows, she watched a Dr. Phil episode where a family of children similar in age to Azad and her sisters sat across from their mother, also similar in age to her mother, explaining with inarguable soundness that she was being scammed by a young Nigerian man for thousands and thousands of dollars. She countered with herself that her mother was too clever to succumb to being hustled, especially to such proportions. She imagined her mother strolling along a beach, arm in arm with an African man, his graying sideburns and good-natured smile putting Azad at ease, as if he already existed.

She stood in the dining room, watching Kohar smooth Lucine's hair, a gesture so intimate that it left her feeling out of place and odd-seeming until it occurred to her why; she had never seen her mother so tender with her sisters as Kohar was with Lucine at that very moment. Azad felt the injustice of the imposed alliance between herself and her mother—a collusion Azad had been obviously a part of, for longer than she realized, until now.

"The reason Mom's flying out to Africa is because she met a man online who lives there. She's flying out there to meet him."

Both Kohar and Lucine looked up, their faces still. Azad braced herself, as a numb quiet settled in the room. "Did you say to meet a guy from the internet?" Lucine was the first to speak.

Azad felt Kohar's eyes on her, an unrecognizable glare of hostility she had never seen before. Then Kohar's eyes snapped, her attention diverted as she glanced around the room, looking for her drink. It was sitting on a place mat on the far end of the table. She strained to reach over and pull the place mat toward her until the glass was within reach. She took a short sip and sat down in Gabriel's seat at the head of the table.

"Yeah, this guy on the internet. He lives in Africa and—"

"Yeah, we know she's flying to Africa—weird—but where? Where in Africa specifically? I thought she was going to Johannesburg. Don't fucking tell me Nigeria," said Lucine, her tone threatening.

"Johannesburg—what? That's in South Africa. And no, she's not going to Nigeria. It's some area near there—Lomé, Togo." Azad rested her gaze on

Kohar, who sat in silence, taking sips from her drink. Her hair was pulled back in a high bun; her face was clear and smooth, startlingly composed.

"Let me guess—she told you like, yesterday. So that it's too late to talk her out of it," said Lucine. They all knew how resolute their mother was, once plans had been put in place—unchangeable, as if carved in stone. Before Azad could reply, she was spared by the delay of another question. "How did she meet him online? Like, how? Was she on a dating site? Did this guy contact her?"

"I don't know," Azad said, her face reddening.

It reminded her of the time her two friends had been caught cheating on a chemistry exam and the dean had questioned her afterward, as if she was an accomplice because she had been sitting a row behind them. But this felt grotesquely worse. She had stepped into darkness. How far and for how long would she be inadvertently pushing each of them away, she couldn't fathom. She pictured her sisters' love for her as a fraying rope that would eventually break, remain unmended. "I don't know anything."

"So she's going to fucking Africa to run around with some guy she met online? If we did something like that—"

"We'd never do something like that." Kohar stood up, holding the drink in her hand. The ice had watered the vibrant orange down to a pale amber. "The rules apply to everyone but her. She's special."

Lucine and Azad watched Kohar disappear into the hallway, leaving a residual air of frost in the room. Their eyes met as they exchanged wondering glances, a telepathic harmony between them. Then they heard the freezer door open, ice being thrown into a glass, clinking in the silence. The freezer door slammed closed and they both winced; for years, their mother had conditioned them to catch the refrigerator door and close it gently. Kohar's footsteps grew closer. Now she was in the foyer, topping off her glass with more gin. She returned to the dining-room table and took a fresh swallow from her glass.

"How long have you known?" she asked, looking up at Azad, who was standing by the piano now.

The silence stilled between them.

"You've known all this time. You didn't just find out," said Kohar. "She told you weeks ago, right?"

"You have?" Lucine asked.

"Tell her," Kohar barked.

Azad jumped, and then her face crumpled. Before she could wonder how Kohar had known, Lucine began. "Jesus Christ. Are you fucking kidding me?" Her voice rose to a near-scream. "How long have you known?"

Azad shrugged. "But I had to get it out of her. It's not how you think it is. She didn't pull me aside and confide in me. It wasn't like that."

"Well, that's refreshing," Kohar announced. "And you've been keeping her secret for her?" she angled.

All Azad could do was nod.

"Why? Why would you do that?" Kohar sat eerily still, her face white, her eyes dark and looming.

"I don't know," Azad stuttered. "Maybe she thinks you won't understand."

"Because you do?" Kohar countered.

"No . . . I don't. I don't understand it any more than either of you," Azad gasped through her tears, trying to explain. "But I'm telling you now. Before she leaves." *Isn't that worth something?* she wanted to ask. She could not contend with Kohar's intense hostility; their mother hadn't left yet. There was still time for something to be done.

"Don't you know her by now? How she thinks? In her mind, if you're complying, then it means what she's doing is not wrong. She has the moral development of a six-year-old. She rationalizes, she equivocates, she vilifies others and gives herself the pass card over and over again. Anything either of us did was a crime," she said, pointing to Lucine and then herself. "But she got away with murder. You're here, though," Kohar spoke, looking directly at Azad, "and now *you're* holding the buck." She knew her vagueness would confuse Azad all the more, and she didn't care.

Kohar threw her head back and tossed the remains of the drink down her throat. Before they could stop her, she had grabbed her coat from the sofa in the parlor, thrown the front door open, and walked out. Both Lucine and Azad, suspended in shock, stared at the front door, neither of them moving. It wasn't until they heard the sound of a car turn over and looked outside the facing window that they realized it was Kohar, backing out of her parking spot and driving off.

ESCAPE. THE FREEDOM TO LEAVE. KOHAR DROVE DOWN THE block and made it past the yellow traffic light before it turned red, pulled over, and parked by a hydrant. There was nowhere to go. She stared grimly into the street. The very street that she used to walk along to school every morning, the elation of being away from her mother for a stretch of time lightening each step. The dread of returning home to the flat, joyless space of the apartment. She would have done anything to get away from her mother. Just about.

One afternoon in the eighth grade, Kohar had come home and swallowed a bottle and a half of extra-strength Tylenol pills. She remembered, as the light-headedness had set in, that her mother had told her once of her own suicide attempt after marrying her father. In recalling this, Kohar thought of sticking her fingers down her throat, wrenching her insides, picturing the undigested white tablets spilling out of her into the toilet, slimed in bile. Then she had looped into the living room with the aplomb of a serenading Broadway dancer, and announced what she had done. Gabriel, who had been sitting hunched over a manuscript, pen in hand, looked up with astonishment. Her mother had been on the couch watching *Guiding Light*, drawn into her afternoon ritual.

At first, her mother had muted the television. The brightness of the afternoon sun crept through, a blinding brilliance. Silence. A silence that began to dull with each passing second, expelling the intensity of what Kohar had said, until all that was left was a brittle weariness. Perhaps they had misheard her, or she hadn't said anything at all. Kohar, her face now so hot and damp that she could no longer stand, had ejected herself from the living room and went to lie down. When she had closed her eyes, she could hear her mother and Gabriel from the other side of the wall, conferring. Then her mother's final word—whatever it was, Kohar could not hear— and her footsteps bounding down the hallway past her room.

Mercifully, it took only hours before Kohar was hunched over the toilet, spewing and coughing up the white, chalky bitterness, where she would be until the next morning. She had stared into the toilet, the contents of her insides foaming. She wondered if her mother had thought she was lying. She wondered why she had done such a thing. Hours later, half-asleep with her head resting against the tiled wall, she had heard the bathroom door being thrown open. She had felt the heat of her mother's presence, her figure standing behind her. Kohar dared not turn around.

"Let this be a lesson to you," her mother had yelled. "Next time, think before you do something stupid like this again."

She had woken the next morning and gone to school. The day came upon her with jarring disconnectedness, hard and bright and surreal. A numbness had set in from which she would not recover. Was it then that she had stopped feeling love for her mother? Or was it the sharp and inarguable truth that her mother did not love her and never would? To come upon this moment again would be tantamount to resetting a dislocated shoulder that was now healed and disfigured.

As the rain sprayed across her windshield Kohar accelerated her wiper blades and began driving. They swished back and forth maniacally. The streetlights ahead blurred in the torrent that was beating against her car. Kohar drew into herself, leaned toward the windshield, squinting. The intensity of the downpour was so preposterous that it made her laugh suddenly, if for a second, remembering watching the behind-the-scenes of a movie production where the set designers were literally dumping buckets of water over a car for rain effect.

Slowly, she drove down 34th Avenue toward the street where she could make a right and get on the Grand Central. But really, there was nowhere to go. Not home. She imagined walking through the back door and finding Jonathan half-asleep on the couch, a Star Wars marathon glowing in the darkened living room. And his disappointment when he realized she had been drinking and driven home. Maybe find another bar, she thought. Or park the car and sit until the rain ended. Or go back to the apartment, but someone had surely taken her parking spot already. She would be circling and circling and there was no telling whether she would get pulled over.

A few blocks ahead she saw a cluster of spinning lights, realizing with immediate alarm that there were four or five police cars that had blocked off the street. Behind the wooden barriers was a fire truck that had barricaded the street. The rain continued pounding against the car, relentlessly, as Kohar continued driving, peering carefully to make a right turn, far and away toward Northern Boulevard. But too late. Twenty feet in front of her was a policeman holding two glowing sticks in his hand, motioning for traffic to make a left U-turn. There were no cars in front of her or behind her as Kohar paused to follow the signal of the officer. Upon seeing Kohar's car, he stopped and held up his hand. Kohar could see him clearly through the rain-soaked windshield.

She put on the brakes, too scared to shift the gear into park. Her head pulsed with the flood of gin she had consumed before leaving the house. Her heart beat with the steady resonance of a brooding drum. The officer motioned downward with his hand; he wanted her to lower her window. *Ruby*, thought Kohar wildly. *I wish I was with her right now, holding her, feeding her. Ruby.*

The officer, now several feet away from her car, called out. "You're not supposed to be on this street. They shut it down twenty blocks back. Where are you going?"

"I'm headed home," she called back, terrified that he could smell the liquor on her breath.

"Where's home?" The officer did not relent.

"Eightieth Street," Kohar said.

"No wonder. Just a few blocks back. Make a U-turn and head back. This isn't going to let up, and we have a fire down this block," said the officer.

Kohar, wilting now, slowly maneuvered the car and circled back to the apartment building. As she turned the corner and drove down her mother's block, she saw a figure standing near the middle of the street. Upon seeing the car, the person raised their arms, waving frantically. It was Lucine. Kohar pulled over to her. She rolled down her window.

"Get out of the car. Go inside," Lucine shouted over the rain.

Her Guns N' Roses T-shirt was plastered against her body, and her long hair clung to the sides of her face. Kohar wondered how long Lucine had been standing in the downpour, waiting, hoping for her to return.

Lucine reached for the car handle, unable to open it. Kohar unlocked the car and got out. "I'll park it," Lucine said. "I have a friend two blocks from here who's away and said I can use his driveway. Just go inside," she said as she climbed into the driver's seat and closed the door behind her. Despite the rain, Kohar watched as the stoplight turned green and her car disappeared around the corner.

Glancing up at the first-floor window, she saw Azad's silhouette rustle behind the opaque curtains; by the time Kohar stepped into the lobby, Azad was holding the front door open for her with a large towel in her arms.

KOHAR TREMBLED UNCONTROLLABLY AS SHE UNDRESSED IN THE bathroom, her bare wet feet planted on the cold tile floor. Her teeth chattered. She let her clothes fall off her, the mass of her sweatshirt and damp jeans gathering around her ankles. She clamped her mouth closed, trying to quell the shaking, only to feel the uncomfortable pressure in her jaw. A deep breath and then another, until finally a sigh gave way to stillness. She dried herself with the plush towel that Azad had given to her, and then slipped on a waffle-print robe that was hanging on the back of the bathroom door.

The sudden thud of the front door was followed by plodding footsteps in the hallway. Then they stopped short.

"Where is she?" Kohar heard Lucine's voice half-whisper.

"Changing in the bathroom." Azad.

"Did she say anything to you?"

"Just that she was freezing."

"Kohar? You okay in there? Do you need anything?" Lucine's voice cried out.

"I'm okay," Kohar called back through the closed bathroom door. "I just need a few minutes."

If only another drink. As if her wish had been magically conjured, there was a soft knock on the door.

"Do you need anything?" Azad's worried voice came through.

"Can you bring me a glass of water? And maybe half of one of those brownies?" Kohar asked, embarrassed by her meekness.

The strange familiarity of it dawned on her: her hangovers, so many of them, that Azad had seen without knowing: during her late teen years, when Kohar had started college, asking Azad to bring her a glass of seltzer and two Advils; she couldn't have been more than five or six years old at the time. So innocently, obligingly, Azad had fetched these items, then crawled into bed with Kohar, her arm, light as a bird's wing, draped over Kohar's shoulders.

She heard the knocking again. Kohar opened the door, too sheepish to face her sister, and held out her hands to receive her request, a piece of a brownie placed in one hand and a glass of cold seltzer in the other.

"I love you," Kohar called out after she closed the door.

"I love you, too," Azad called back. Her voice was not weary, not haggard or beset with impatience, irritation. Just like Gabriel, her tolerance for bullshit and waywardness was frighteningly infinite.

"I'M GOING TO CALL JONATHAN," AZAD SAID, REACHING FOR THE phone.

"No, you are not!" Lucine walked over to where Azad was lying on the couch and sat on top of her.

"Get off of me!"

Azad, now prostrate on the couch with Lucine on her lap, her head hanging awkwardly off the side, had the phone in her hand.

"Why can't I call him?" she croaked.

"Dummy," Lucine chastised. "Fucking dummy. Think about it."

"Get off of me."

"Here, I'll draw you a picture." Lucine's voice, now light and dreamy, began. "Jonathan sitting in Ruby's nursery, circa Pottery Barn Kids' 2018 catalogue, page thirty-two. Mozart's Opus whatever the fuck is playing on volume three. He's giving her a bottle and reflecting on his amazing life, being the perfect guy that he is; and then, out of nowhere, he gets a phone call from your dumb ass. What's that, you say? Kohar ate a pot brownie and slugged two double gin cocktails and then ran out of the apartment and drove around in a rainstorm? And then we dragged her back into the house and she's okay?" Her voice now hostile and condescending, "Certain truths can remain untold. How about that? Like today—"

"You're hurting me," Azad moaned. Lucine repositioned herself and leaned across Azad's torso, settled the heft of her body with more weight.

"Did you have to tell us that Mom was meeting some African guy on the other side of the world? Maybe we didn't want to know. Maybe I don't give a shit and glad she's getting the hell out of here. That's her business—"

"Yeah," Azad yelped. "Let's just stick our heads in the sand and waste seven years of our lives being miserable."

Swiftly, Lucine felt the unexpected blow. "What?" She sprang up and Azad tottered to her feet. "What did you say? Are you talking about me and Steve? Is that what?"

"You and Steve. You," Azad said.

"While you live in a house that was handed to you and a car that you didn't pay for and a college tuition that Mom paid off for you—but you're giving me advice about sticking my head in the sand," Lucine yelled.

"Why are you yelling?" Azad yelled.

"Why can't I?" Lucine yelled back. "You are so out of touch with reality. You're not even a fully formed adult. You haven't struggled one day in your life. Maybe some people have real reasons to stick their heads in the sand. What's your reason?"

"I don't stick my head in the sand. I don't avoid life by not spending time with my family and working seven days a week. I—"

"You don't even have a job! What are you talking about?" Lucine hollered, now utterly exasperated. "Oh, my God! You don't even know what you're saying. You're a child. It's like white privilege—for years it's been that. Or rather, *Azad* privilege."

Kohar bit into the brownie and sat on the bathmat with the door cracked open, listening with amusement. It felt satisfying to have her sisters tell each other what she herself had wanted to say to each of them, for a long time now, but had never found the courage. She took a sip of the cold seltzer and felt a peaceful stillness come upon her, the pot brownie from earlier now in full effect.

"—*my* fault she says I love you to me or hugs me. What am I supposed to do? Tell her not to say I love you?"

"So, say, when you were in high school and saw some kid being tormented in the hallways—you're saying you just walked by and thought nothing of it?"

"That's not the same thing."

"It *is*, though. It is the same thing. The fact that you haven't even had the passing thought to tell Mom how fucked up she's been to Kohar and me—that is some *shupatzadz*, self-involved bullshit." *Shupatzadz*—spoiled and privileged—was one of Azad's least favorite Armenian words and one that their mother used with loathing when referring to some of their cousins who lived in Los Angeles. "By being passive, you're allowing everything to stay the same. All those classes you took in college—did they ever teach you about being an upstander? Do you know, even, what that is?"

Kohar laughed quietly. For all of Lucine's crassness and vulgarity, her socially conscious vernacular was heartwarming.

The protracted silence that followed left Kohar wondering if they realized how much she could hear. But had she been in the room, she would have seen Azad sinking to the floor and crossing her legs with guilt-stricken contemplation.

"Let's not get into it now," Lucine finally spoke. "Just fuck the whole thing."

"Let's not get into it *now*?" Azad practically howled. "We just got into it. What are you talking about? What do you consider getting into it? Like, beating the shit out of each other?"

No sooner had the words left her than the apartment door suddenly swung open and slammed shut. Takouhi never bothered catching the door; it was in this way, for years, that she had announced her return to the apartment.

"Hello?"

They heard her keys dropping into the copper dish by the foyer. Then her footsteps appearing and disappearing into the kitchen.

Lucine and Azad, sitting on the living-room couch, did not call back out to her. Kohar, now leaning against the wall in the bathroom, took deep breaths, as if preparing to dive from a treacherous height. As she walked down the hallway toward the living room, she heard her mother's voice and then the dull voices of her sisters.

"Hi," she said.

"Oh," her mother, a bit startled, turned to her. "You're still here? Who's taking care of the baby? And why are you wearing a *robe*?" she asked dryly, eyeing Kohar.

Takouhi was wearing a square-necked dress of cotton turquoise, the cuffs and hem embroidered in gold, as if she was about to board an Aegean Sea cruise. Kohar wished she could laugh.

"How was the show?" Kohar asked. She could feel Lucine and Azad's eyes on her and realized that what lay in question now was whether or not she would bring to light what Azad had told them.

"Eh," her mother said. She was notoriously dissatisfied with Broadway shows. "It was beautiful, but the singing not so much."

A collective silence fell among the sisters. Either ignoring them or unaware, Takouhi went to the piles of mail on the dining-room table and began going through the stacks. The girls watched her, a halo of anticipation.

"What's going on?" Takouhi looked up from a piece of mail she was tearing open. "Why are you all so quiet? Who had a fight?" A rhetorical question. She went back to unfolding the paper.

"Nobody," Kohar spoke. Then, "All of us."

Takouhi huffed, her eyes scrutinizing the paper she held in her hand, and then discarding it absently to begin a throw-away pile.

"Why didn't you tell Lucine and me that you were going to meet someone in Togo?" Kohar asked. She could feel her stomach jumping frightfully, as if something inside her was about to claw its way out. Her chest ached.

Without looking at Azad, Takouhi, now fully aware of what was about to transpire, regarded Kohar with a look of contempt. She stared at Kohar stonily, as if contemplating an articulate answer. "Because. I don't need to explain myself to anybody."

Though she had not slapped Kohar across the face, the sting of her words left a sharp mark.

"Just to Azad," Kohar replied, refusing to give her mother's response the import of silence.

"Azad can tell you that that's not how it happened. And like I said—I don't need to explain anything to anybody," Takouhi said and began walking toward the hallway.

"So that's it?" Kohar called to her turned back. "It's none of our business and you're going to bed?"

Her mind scrambled awkwardly to find a way of snagging her mother back without following her around the house like a simpering idiot.

"I'm not talking about this," she heard her mother's dismissive reply halfway down the corridor and then the closing of her bedroom door.

Kohar looked at Lucine and Azad, who were both gaping in utter dismay. As if a runner sprinting before the blow of the whistle, Lucine sprang up from the couch and bounded toward Takouhi's bedroom. Wordlessly, they slowly followed her, aware that shrapnel would be flying from all directions within seconds.

"—think you are?" Lucine's voice boomed. "You tell *her*? You tell her and not *us*? Why? Why do you do this? Why does she get to know and we don't?"

At first, all they could hear was Lucine's screaming and, alternately, their mother's cool replies, her voice at such a low register that her words were unclear.

"Because *I* am entitled to do whatever *I* want to do!" Takouhi's voice rose as Kohar and Azad walked into the room. "I'm living my life, finally, the way I want to."

"You haven't been living your life the way you've wanted to up to this point?" Kohar asked, redirecting Takouhi's focus. "What have you not been doing, exactly? You left your husband and married Gabriel and you had a happy marriage for almost thirty years."

"Kohar—please. You don't understand," retorted Takouhi.

"I *do* understand. When you tell people they don't understand, what you're really saying is that they aren't letting you get away with behaving the awful way you always do."

"Do you see what happens?" Takouhi looked at Azad. "And you wanted to know why I wouldn't tell them."

"Mom, that's not what this is—" Azad began.

"What awful way, Kohar, have I been acting?" Takouhi challenged.

"Where does one begin?" Lucine asked.

"So awful that Gabriel never wanted to deal with you," said Kohar.

"I was the perfect mother," Takouhi replied. "Gabriel never wanted to interfere and make you feel like he was trying to replace your father. I sent you all to private schools, you always had nice clothes, I made dinner every night, you had a roof over your head—"

"You're talking about basic necessities. And you've said so often that you sent us to private school because it was a block away and you could keep your eye on us," Kohar said. "Do you understand that you're congratulating yourself for providing us food and shelter?"

For all the times Kohar had carefully constructed her imaginary response for this exact moment in her life, a moment that she'd thought would never present itself, she could not find the words. Where to begin? The alienated, friendless years as a teenager, the backhanded criticisms of her physical looks or her cooking or her house or her ability in any scope of personal interest, her dramatic and poorly executed suicide attempt that her mother made her suffer, her lack of encouragement to improve academically or musically. It felt as if after driving to the same location for years upon years, her memory could not summon the names of the streets and where to turn.

"I'm realizing that no matter how much I do, you'll never be happy. That's why I don't bother anymore," said Takouhi.

"The only thing I ever asked for was respect and freedom," Kohar said. "Not anything else. And it's the one thing you haven't been able to give me."

"What respect, Kohar? What are you talking about? How have I not shown you respect?" Takouhi stood up at complete attention now, her eyes burning with the same rage and haughtiness from when Kohar was a teenager.

"When I moved out—"

"Oh! Here we go again? That I disowned you? Is that what you told your American friends? I was upset and I needed time to cool off. Get off this, already, with me disowning you. You like to make yourself feel miserable," said Takouhi. "Try living my life and then come talk to me."

"A year? A year to cool off? After I told you I was moving out I still had to live at home for another two months—you didn't look at my face! You ignored me at the dinner table. You had the girls set the table with four settings instead of five. You pretended like I didn't exist! Your love is conditional. My having freedom was at the cost of not having your love."

"I never did that!"

"You did! And Gabriel sat there and said nothing. Nothing. And that's why you continued behaving the way you did. Nobody in this house stood up for me!" Kohar yelled, now turning to her sisters. "And how could either of you—the younger ones? And Gabriel didn't either. Because he didn't know how. He couldn't even defend himself. How was he going to defend me? And then again when I moved in with Jonathan—you didn't speak to me for over six months. And you apologized to him to leave a good impression, but you never apologized to me. Am I not good enough for an apology? Why are you so willing to let go of me? To throw me away? To not fight for me? Because you know I'll never turn away from you. You've managed, somehow, to surround yourself with very forgiving and tolerant people, and it's given you the illusion that you are entitled to behave the way you do. And this divide," Kohar continued, pointing to herself and Lucine and then her mother and Azad, "*you* created this. Not us."

"Mom, please don't go to Togo," Azad broke in. "It's a really bad idea. Please."

"She's going to do whatever she wants anyway," Lucine said, the disgust in her voice so penetrating that her mother broke her gaze from Kohar to look at her.

"Me doing whatever I want?" Takouhi said. "How about you? Marrying that loser?"

"He *is* a loser," Lucine said. "And I married him for the same reason you married Dad—to get out. Of this house. You think I was going to move out and get my own place? After watching you and Kohar? I was terrified. I lived here until I got married—just like you wanted us to do. It still didn't make you happy. And it got me nowhere anyway."

"What is this? *Blame Mom for my mistakes?* You see how Azad has nothing to say? That's what I'm talking about. The two of you have had something against me for years. You blame the divorce on me—"

"It's *you* who have something against *us*," Lucine said. "All these years you've told us 'I'm not the huggy-kissy type of mother,' yet even now when Azad walks through the door you're all over her, telling her how much you love her and how you're proud of her—"

"I tell you I'm proud of you!" Takouhi's voice rose again, now exasperated. "What do you want from me? Azad is the youngest; I remember my mother being the same with my sister Zabel. I can't keep up—"

"Do you know how hard it's been watching Azad get love and attention? And me standing by and watching it all?" Lucine interrupted. "And that's why when I wake up every morning I think of Gabriel and I miss him. I look at that picture I have of him—too big to sit in his lap, and he let me anyway. Not you or Dad could ever show me love the way he did."

Lucine turned her back to them, as she had when reading her father's letter just hours ago, and cried mightily, her face pressed into her hands. Kohar stood without going over to her, her heart aching so terribly that she could feel the tears slip down the corners of her eyes. And to her surprise, Azad rushed over and threw her arms around Lucine, who at first would not receive her embrace and then turned to her.

Takouhi, her face rigid with disgust, began taking off her shoes and pulling open a drawer for her nightgown.

"Please don't go, Mom," Kohar said. "It doesn't sound like a good idea."

She couldn't tell if her mother's silence was one of contemplation or resolution. She disappeared into the bathroom and closed the door behind her. They heard the sound of running water, the flush of the toilet. When she stepped back into the room, they waited. Ignoring them, she draped her clothes on the small chaise longue and turned to them.

"I am going on this trip," she said. "You've said what you've had to say. I'm doing what I want to do without having to worry about taking care of anyone but myself."

"No one is saying you shouldn't. You've been through a lot. I just don't know why you're in such a hurry to fly all the way out there and not tell us you're meeting someone."

"Because I wanted to make sure he was who I thought he was," said Takouhi. "Which he is. And it's not about sex or anything—"

"Mom! We don't want to know. Please."

The last time she had heard her mother use the word *sex* was when Kohar had told her she was moving out: "You're getting an apartment so you can bring boys back with you to have sex." To which Kohar had responded "I thought that's what cars were for." In her early teen years, Kohar had cobbled together the confounding science of sex and pregnancy by watching episodes of *Diff'rent Strokes* and *Family Ties*.

"Well, I'm just telling you. He said he has too much respect for me to expect something like that, and because he loves me."

"*Jesus* Christ," Kohar whispered.

"I deserve happiness."

"Your depression—the ups and downs—it's part of this whole thing." Kohar was fumbling through her thoughts now, reaching for the fine line between sensibility and tact. "You have a chemical imbalance, or . . . I don't know, because I'm going off what I've learned in school, but maybe if you took medication—"

"When I met Gabriel, I was down in the dumps," Takouhi shot back. "Your father was abusing me, and I had tried to commit suicide twice after having you. And then Gabriel came along and pulled me up, lifted me back on my feet. And now he's gone. And I like this guy, for whatever it is."

"And that's fine," Kohar said. She had learned long ago not to react to her mother's dramatic overtures. "We don't want to see someone taking advantage of you—"

"How stupid do you think I am, Kohar? You think I'm some idiot? You're insulting me."

"I'm not," Kohar replied, tight and firm. "You want me to say yes to everything you do. To just agree."

"I don't give a shit what you agree with. I'm going. End of story."

Chapter 20

AZAD LAY IN THE MUTED DARKNESS THAT REVEALED SHADOWS and gray silhouettes, thinking of the war that had exploded around her. She realized that little had changed. Or rather, that her mother had remained the same.

She turned to Lucine, who was sleeping next to her, and it occurred to her, now that it was too late, all the possible rebuttals, missed opportunities when she could have redeemed herself to Lucine before their mother had barged in. She wanted also to confront her sister, but without the risk of another explosion.

Like at Kohar's baby shower in the early spring. Lucine had arrived later than expected, and it was Azad fumbling through all the silly baby shower games when it had been Lucine's job. "It's about time you got here," Azad had joked. They were placing a ridiculous hat covered with pastel-colored ribbons on Kohar's head. "Go fuck yourself," Lucine had shot back and disappeared into her old bedroom.

At Gabriel's burial and after, during the hokeh-jash, Lucine was distant, aloof, occupying herself with clearing tables, plates, washing platters and trays in the kitchen while the guests convened in the parlor and living room. Azad had watched, burning with envy, when Kohar walked into the kitchen and shut off the running water, wiping off Lucine's hands with a towel, and insisting she go rest in one of the spare bedrooms. Kohar could do that so naturally, with no hesitation. Azad missed the closeness she and Lucine could have had. She admired her sister's unapologetic demeanor and her gumption to tell anyone and everyone to get lost. The boyfriends and friends galloping in and out of Azad's house, taking full advantage of her open heart, as her mother called it, was a shameful thing.

She wanted to tell her about the Ayahuasca retreat, but knew that Lucine would laugh in her face, add it to her list of Stupid Shit that Azad Does

Because She's a Fucking Idiot. She hadn't told anyone what had happened, or rather not happened, when she had arrived in New York.

After the bus had pulled into the Hudson terminal the evening she was supposed to have signed in with the Ayahuasca retreat coordinator, she stepped off the bus with her backpack and headed toward unfamiliar streets.

It wasn't until after the bus had sighed into the station that she had turned to Luke and said she wasn't going to the retreat.

"I don't think you should, not that you asked," he said. "Take this." He handed her a torn piece of paper that looked like it had been ripped out of a book. "It's my phone number."

Azad waited for him to stumble over his words, overexplain himself. He looked at her pensively, trying to hold eye contact. Azad smiled at the piece of paper and placed it inside a book she had brought with her for the ride.

"Thanks," she said, standing up and gathering her backpack, slipping past him although the bus had not pulled in quite yet.

Had she turned around, she would have seen him following her with his eyes, down the steps and out the retractable door, past the length of the bus where only the top of her brown-haired head bobbed up and down and then vanished.

All night she walked through the town, in and out of bars, bookshops, their doors propped open invitingly. She spoke to no one, relishing the anonymity of being an outsider, for there was a general camaraderie wherever she seemed to find herself; the people in town seemed to know one another, greeted each other heartily or, at the very least, with general recognition.

She stayed awake until twilight, fell asleep at the Hudson station waiting for the next bus back to Philadelphia, and almost missed it. She slept through the early-morning traffic, drove home from the city where she had parked her car in an overnight lot, half-dazed, and back to her home. On her sofa, finally, she pulled a blanket over herself and fell back asleep until the evening.

Upon her waking, a golden light filled the room. Azad squinted, disoriented, wondering what time it was. And as the sun sank into darkness, the home in which she lived revealed itself in a light she had not seen until

that moment: the house and its surfaces had been living in the filth of neglect. The piano, which had not been played since years before her grandmother's passing, was covered in dust so thick that if one could sign their
name across the top surface, the words would be discernible. The thin Persian rugs that Azad had chosen not to part with were embedded with a
fine powder, too ancient-seeming to regard as dust. The walls, once a bone-
white, were matted with gray fingerprints along the doorframes and light
switches; the cracks in the ceiling trailed and branched out from one side
of the room to the other. The longer Azad's eyes combed over the surfaces,
the deeper she fell into a trance of scrutiny.

It erupted in her the wild impulse to scrub and shine anything she
could touch, to uncover and unearth the decades her father, her uncle, her
grandparents had lived in this intricate space that she had taken, so egregiously, for granted. As she thrust herself into the undertaking of a task she
was determined to see through, once and for all, her mind faded in and out
of monotony and then realizations, small epiphanies.

The morning she decided to attack the kitchen floor, it occurred to
her, as she lowered her gloved hands into the soapy basin of water, that her
mother's monthly deposits, which neither of them openly acknowledged,
was her mother's way of saying *We are both alone now, living in large spaces
without anyone to love us.* And then the more significant realization—that
her mother had designed this co-dependence, whether cognizant or otherwise, so that Azad would always need her, and her mother would always
feel needed. When the thought formed itself on that particular morning,
an angry rain pounding against the panes, Azad clenched the sponge in her
fist and threw it against the window.

After several days of cleaning the second and first floors of the
house (she was too exhausted and daunted to excavate the basement or
attic), Azad walked through the rooms, admiring her toil, eyeing the
obscure corners that she had dusted and scoured. If only she had someone with her to admire how she had transformed the house, someone
to commend the marvelous fruition of what she had accomplished.
But then, with little reflection, she recognized that what seemed an
extraordinary feat for her was, for the rest of human civilization, a
mundanity. An indication of a functioning person, in many ways.

That she had lived in squalor for all the time the house had been given to her was not a thought she had considered.

She imagined her retort to Lucine in the middle of their argument: "That's what you think! You know what I spent three days doing last week? *Cleaning*—that's what." Lucine would have stopped yelling mid-sentence, paused with amusement, and burst out laughing, fallen on the floor, unable to contain herself.

What came to Azad as she drifted to sleep that evening, listening to Lucine snoring with her back to her, was a feeling of autonomy. It felt like a distant thing that she could see. A silhouette in the fog. A harbinger of hope drifting toward her.

Lucine cupped her hand against the flame of her lighter that kept snuffing out from the wind. Between her pursed lips was a joint she had brought with her, anticipating a calamity or two where she would be in dire need of a few hits. She had woken in the middle of the night to use the bathroom and, after an hour of lying awake, unable to go back to sleep, had crept out of the apartment and headed to the courtyard.

It was a beautiful expanse that ran the length of the block, residing in the center of the surrounding co-ops. The area was lush with greenery and flowers, meandering paths; and at the far end was a grassy clearing with swings and a play yard for children. It was where Lucine had spent much of her time playing with Azad when Kohar was old enough to take a part-time job and their mother was preoccupied.

In her teen years, she would take a book with her and go there after dinner, isolating herself in a quiet nook once the kids her age from the neighboring buildings showed up. They usually hung out on the swings, passing around a bottle of liquor and a joint. Lucine found it depressing, revisiting a place from one's childhood and corrupting the memories of innocence with alcohol and drugs. She preferred to sit on the stone bench where a pair of griffin statues stood atop pillars overlooking her with a gaze of austerity while she smoked her joint.

Lucine guessed there wouldn't be anyone in the courtyard in the middle of the night and preferred to sit where she always did. With the world asleep around her, she allowed her thoughts to roam freely, unconcerned that anyone would wake up and discover that she wasn't in the apartment. Mostly, she wanted to walk around the corner where she had parked her car and drive away. But Lucine knew, much to Azad's satisfaction if she were to ever acknowledge her accusation, that she had spent much of her life running away, turning her back on the truths that life had presented her. Namely, the fact that her husband was, for lack of a better word, a loser. And he always had been. He had never constructed pretenses that would have told her otherwise, but she had chosen to focus on what she wanted to see and filter her reality. Marrying him and ignoring the degeneration of their relationship was a testament to how deeply and stubbornly Lucine could not accept what was in front of her.

Her father was another painful example. As she inhaled deeply and held the smoke in her lungs, Lucine reached inside the pocket of her denim jacket, grazing the corners of the envelope he had sent her. She hadn't told Kohar or Azad that her father had written a note on a small piece of paper he had enclosed with the check. *I'm sorry. Love, Dad,* he had written. She wished he was strong enough to hear the truth about the last year of her life. That she had been sleeping on her friend's couch and working double shifts at the bakery to save money and buy a used car. Perhaps it was she who wasn't strong enough to tell her father the truth.

As for Steve, for all she knew he was somewhere else, still jobless, drunk, and high. She had not heard from him since he had taken off with her money. Even after she had the divorce papers served. It pained her in the same way it did to see her mother lavishing her affections on Azad: she didn't have to contend with extricating herself from a toxic person who would slowly deplete her. And yet, his willingness to let her go so easily hurt her heart. That a person as broken as Steve couldn't love someone like her. *We accept the love we think we deserve*—a line she had read from a novel a long time ago, a phrase that revisited her time and again during her darker moods, its truth stark and undeniable.

So much of this she had not shared with anyone, not even her sisters. Including her newfound pastime, which had come to her unexpectedly. It was on an afternoon she had spent with her friend Emily helping her set up her booth of homemade candles at an arts-and-crafts fair. While walking through the narrow paths with booths on either side of her, Lucine had come across a table displaying used cameras. Without consulting the man standing behind the table or knowing anything about cameras, Lucine had impulsively bought one. It had grabbed her attention on first glance. It was an old Nikon. From the approving look on the man's face who sold it to her, Lucine felt a newfound elation as she immediately placed the strap around her neck, pleased with the tugging weight of the camera that she would soon be carrying with her everywhere.

The images she snapped with little thought were not what she had expected to be drawn to: an obscenely pregnant woman who looked like she was ready to give birth, a dead baby bird lying next to a fire hydrant, a stray cat with a missing eye, the back yard of an abandoned house overgrown with tall weeds and stalks of grass, a cake she had finished decorating that had accidentally tipped over and smashed upside down on the kitchen floor. The heft of the camera in her hands, the way she could control and adjust the focus of what she wanted to capture invigorated her.

Sometimes she would walk around her neighborhood at night while she took photographs. She was tempted to call Max, but knew better for obvious reasons. Lucine preferred the simplicity of her life now, unburdened and free. With the money her father had sent her, she had enough to find an apartment near the bakery and pay the first month's deposit, with money left over to put her mind at ease. For the first time in a long time, Lucine felt taken care of. Loved. Like the warmth of sunshine on her shoulders.

Though she would never admit it to Kohar, who had stressed to her the importance of living alone before getting married, Lucine enjoyed it more than she thought she would. When Kohar had first moved out, Lucine imagined letting herself into an empty apartment with no one to talk to, the sad loneliness of such a life. She found it odd, and Kohar selfish for creating such unnecessary tumult in leaving. For this reason, Lucine had decided to live at home instead of reliving the drama of Kohar's departure. Now she realized that her mother's unhappiness was a chronic condition that she had little control over.

Lucine stubbed out her joint and stood in the center of the courtyard. If there was a moon, it was hiding behind the clouds. She closed her eyes, pleasantly overcome with sleep. As she walked back toward the entrance to her mother's apartment building, she felt the crinkle of the envelope in her breast pocket and thought of her father again. She would drive to him in the morning, she decided. To tell him she loved him. Just the thought of sitting beside him made her feel complete. As if the last puzzle piece had been found and placed where it was meant to be.

NEARLY DAWN, KOHAR WOKE WITH A START, FORGETTING WHERE she was. She was in Azad's old bedroom, which resembled a vacated apartment with empty bookshelves and bare walls, the low-hanging curtains giving the room a semblance of a well-planned evacuation. Given how much she had drank and the torrential rain that continued through the night, Kohar had decided to stay overnight.

Half-awake, she crept out of the room, passing her mother's bedroom toward the front door to make her escape; her mother hadn't woken and she didn't want to take the chance of seeing her. Her purse was sitting by the foot of the sofa, and her coat was lying on top of it. As she knelt over her boots to carry them with her out of the apartment, she saw the piano in the parlor. Before she realized, she walked toward it, regarding its austerity despite the thin film of dust on the fallboard.

The worn fabric of the piano bench felt inviting as Kohar settled herself onto the seat. In the living room, Azad and Lucine lay with their backs to each other; they had decided to open the sofa bed at some point in the evening and were still asleep, and had forgotten to shut off the television. From behind her, Molly Ringwald was on the screen designing her prom dress in *Pretty in Pink*. Although the volume had been lowered, Kohar could still hear the familiar '80s new wave, charged with aliveness and barely audible, filling the silence. Kohar couldn't remember how long it had been since she had been in the apartment alone. And she found herself once again sitting in front of the piano, where she virtually always seemed to be when she was alone; she always sensed that her mother found her piano playing intrusive and rarely played when anyone was home.

Inside the piano bench were old piano books, the front covers missing or barely attached to the spine. For many years, her mother had taken piano lessons; when Kohar had shown interest, her mother had made arrangements. The woman's name was Anahid, one of her mother's friend's sisters, who Kohar was convinced hated her. Kohar's natural assumption of all teachers was their patient and encouraging temperaments, neither of which Anahid had possessed.

"Do you practice at home?" Anahid had finally asked her, after several weeks of lessons.

At nine years old, Kohar had not understood that it was her responsibility to practice every day for a given amount of time. When Anahid wrote down page numbers in the little red instructional book that Kohar kept in the small front zipper of her backpack, Kohar had assumed it served as an inventory of what she played during the lessons. It had not occurred to her then that perhaps her mother should have designated a time during the day and reminded Kohar to practice. In fact, her mother had seemed unconcerned with her lessons; never did she ask what she was learning or if she liked her teacher. Looking back, Kohar remembers the gray building on the corner of an unnamed neighborhood, where her mother dropped her off at the lobby and where Kohar waited to be picked up after the lesson was over.

Kohar pressed her hands on the smooth curved wood that covered the piano keys. The dark amber still gleamed invitingly. She glanced behind her. Through the open curtains, a wisp of light illuminated the sky. Dawn was slipping through. Quietly, she lifted the cover and ran her hands over the white keys. She pressed the middle C. It clinked dissonantly. When her mother had stopped taking lessons, she had also stopped calling the piano tuner. A beautiful antique dress left in the closet for moths to devour. A thing of wonder aging from disuse. A sense of remorse plagued Kohar, though she was not sure who or what she had betrayed.

Though she could not see the framed pictures arranged on the lid of the piano from where she was sitting, Kohar could remember them well: a photo of her extended family with all the cousins and aunts and uncles at a wedding in California, her wedding picture, Azad's graduation picture from art school, a photograph of Lucine and Steve in front of City Hall (taken by Steve's brother on his phone, which he had forwarded to Lucine, who'd had it printed out at Walgreens), the infamous photo of Gabriel and her mother dressed up as Armenian peasants when they had acted together in an Armenian play. For all the times Kohar had walked past the baby grand piano, the photos a fixture she rarely looked at, she had not thought for a moment that her family would ever be so fractured, that they would be so isolated from one another.

When she had considered the inevitability of Gabriel or her mother's passing, her assumption had always been that Gabriel would have suffered without her mother more than she without him. She had been thinking only of the daily practicalities of laundry and dishes and meals, and envisioned Gabriel, wasting away without the necessities that her mother provided. But as she sat on the worn piano bench, envisioning her mother and Gabriel in their peasant costumes—her mother, an indomitable presence wearing bright red lipstick and a green floor-length dress, and Gabriel standing next to her, humble and honorable in his meek shirt and trousers—Kohar realized that it had been Gabriel who had kept them all together. Because he himself was a whole person. And all the while, Kohar had taken it for granted that her mother was the heartbeat, the foundation on which their closeness rested. But she understood now, as dawn filled the room with a dull, ashen light, that it had always been Gabriel.

Chapter 21

As Takouhi toweled herself dry in the bathroom, a cool wind gusted through her bedroom windows, carrying the sweet smell of detergent from the laundry room in her apartment building. The sun rays shone brightly through the opaque curtains, casting light on the red toile wallpaper. On the rug was a large black hard-shell suitcase that had been zipped open. The king-size bed, already made and covered in its extravagant bedspread, had piles of clothes in neat stacks, which had been folded the evening before. A passport, wallet, house keys, and lipstick—Red Passion, the girl at Sephora had told her—were sitting on her bureau alongside a black purse.

Takouhi drew her robe over her and stepped out of the bathroom, regarding the piles, and the empty spaces she would fill, with anticipation. She stood in front of the standing mirror and unraveled her hair from the complicated towel. Her hair hung limply to her chest, and she began combing through the knots to prepare for the ordeal of blowing it dry and straightening it with the expensive hair iron she had purchased earlier in the week.

She had stopped dyeing it after Gabriel had died. To her sisters' dismay, who had all encouraged her to maintain the light brown color, Takouhi hadn't listened. Eventually the color faded, and she let it grow long past her shoulders. Retiring from life, from looking beautiful, from being told she was beautiful—at first that had been the impetus for the graying hair. If she could have seen herself: the shock of her white, wiry hair tied behind her head in an untidy knot, her pale, wan face that nearly matched the whiteness of her hair, and the oversized black sweater she wore with black bell-bottom sweatpants and a pair of worn black suede clogs. A dying flower that was still breathing.

SHE LOOKED IN THE MIRROR AND SAW A GLIMPSE OF HERSELF that had never fully come to life: her younger self at nineteen, before her betrothal to her first husband, Antranig. But it had been stolen from her, forever changing her future. She had disappeared. Marrying Gabriel had resuscitated her. Now alone, she could still feel the youth of those lost years. It was impossible to think it had all vanished.

THE DULL BUZZING OF HER PHONE VIBRATED AGAINST TAKOUHI'S hip as she walked through the narrow aisle to her seat. A smile spread across her face. Unzipping her purse and reaching for her phone, she knew it was him.

"Hello?"

"Are you on the plane yet?" The deep, husky intonation carried the exotic smells of the tropics, warmth, pure freedom.

"I'm finding my seat," Takouhi said.

"I can't wait."

The thrill of flattery coursed through her flushed face. "I can't wait either," she said, radiating a smile to the young woman sitting next to her seat.

"Long flight, I know."

"It's going to be worth it," she said.

"I'm about to send you a picture."

After hanging up, Takouhi settled herself in the seat and looked out the window. The exhaust of the turbine engines blurred patches of the tarmac and the flat, uninspiring landscape of the runway.

Her terror of flying danced fretfully in the recesses of her mind. What she sensed, though not immediately, was that there was no one accompanying her on this flight. Not Kohar, as she once had when they had flown to a cousin's wedding in Fresno. Not one of her sisters, who would return with Takouhi to New York. Not Gabriel. But two strangers sitting next to her, nameless and remote. This certainly was her first trip alone anywhere.

Before Takouhi shut off her phone, she looked once more at the screen and saw a new image in her texts. A tall young African man of twenty-nine smiled at her, headphones over his ears, the cord dangling haphazardly off his shoulder. He was waving as if to say *Hi there, beautiful.* Takouhi smiled back at the image. And as the plane rumbled and charged, Takouhi's heart leapt with relief and exhilaration. She could feel her old life shrinking away in the distance behind her. The gravestone she would no longer visit. Her sisters' phone calls, wrought with prescriptive advice. Her daughters, who no longer needed her. Her failed life. It was all behind her now.

Chapter 22

"Mon oiseau chanteur, voulez-vous café?"

Though his back was turned, the young man's voice resonated across the hotel room to where Takouhi was sitting up in a king-size bed.

"Mais, oui," she replied.

The pale blue curtain, drawn against the open balcony door, billowed like a parachute canopy.

"You speak French so beautifully," he commented.

"I learned as a young girl in Beirut," she said.

"Are you hungry?" the young man asked, his back still turned. From his gestures, Takouhi saw that he was pouring coffee into a cup and had measured exactly one teaspoon of sugar, as she preferred her coffee, and stirred.

"You did not tell me," he said, now turning around and walking with deliberate steps, as to not spill the coffee, toward the bed, "that you sang so beautifully."

"Thank you," Takouhi replied to both the compliment and the cup of coffee he gently placed into her hands.

He sat poised on the edge of the bed, wearing the navy blue jeans and white undershirt from the night before. His smile revealed a row of white teeth, and his eyes, the color of honey, radiated a generosity and kindness Takouhi had only known once before in her life. Although he wore his hair similar to his friends, shaved close to his scalp, it lent him a boyishness that made her succumb to him all the more. Despite their mutual affection, he had maintained a respectful distance between them—holding her hand, a gentle touch on the shoulder, a soft kiss on her cheek—all to express to her that his desire for her transcended the sexual impulses of a passionate young man.

For weeks they had communicated through video chatting, and she'd thought she had the advantage of fully taking in his person. She had even grown accustomed to his daily schedule, anticipating where he would be speaking to her from, depending on the time of day. Some afternoons he would be shouting over the blast of honking cars, the spare few minutes between picking up a passenger from the airport and their arrival. Other times, mostly in the evenings, he would call her from his studio apartment, where to his left a white refrigerator was visible, the light of the table lamp illuminating his face.

Although having spent many days with him now, his physical presence still disarmed her, his tangibility unreal. A fictitious person come to life.

"I had never been to a club before," she said.

Despite having just woken, her hair was unruffled from a long night's sleep; it spilled past her shoulders, shiny and smooth. She was wearing a coral-pink robe with wide, sweeping sleeves that moved in harmony with her gestures, trailing behind her with dramatic flair when she would walk across the room. Takouhi had seen the robe at the market, the Grand Marche, as the locals called it, and Ray had insisted on purchasing it for her as a gift.

"You don't want to open your wallet here. They will follow you around for hours. Look."

He had pointed to a group of small children, wearing threadbare clothes and flipflops, trailing behind a female tourist who had left one of the kiosks with a friend.

"It's not them, though. Not the children. It's the father who puts them up to it, begging for money. Don't come here without me," he had advised.

Takouhi sipped her coffee pensively, considered sitting on the balcony to spend her last afternoon gazing at the ocean. Since her arrival, she had spent many mornings on the balcony, sometimes before dawn, watching the hotel staff begin their daily rounds of cleaning and maintaining the grounds. She watched, unbeknownst to them, and felt as if she were spying. As the mornings drifted into early afternoon, she bided her time this way, sometimes urging herself to stroll along the beach; Ray had encouraged her to leave her hotel but stay within its perimeter, to go only as far as the private beach that was overseen by the hotel.

Though hesitant at first, Takouhi would step outside the hotel and follow the narrow pathway that cut through the swimming-pool area toward the beach. Mostly, it was empty of people. The hotel provided no umbrellas, but instead there were straw-roofed structures supported by what resembled a tree trunk. Beneath these were lounge chairs where Takouhi sometimes sought refuge from the sun. She sat and watched the ocean, observing the waves that on some days gently lapped toward her. On other days, days when the sky was shrouded in a gray haze, the ocean roared with high-crested waves that rose and fell tirelessly. Despite the monotony of these empty afternoons, when Takouhi glanced at the clock too often, she did not think of Gabriel or New York. It was too distant a place for her mind to reach. An echo so far away that it could not be heard.

Somehow, two weeks had passed. She would be flying back to New York very much alone.

As if reading her mind, Ray put his hand over hers. "I know what you're thinking," he said.

Takouhi gave him a rueful smile. "Do you?"

His eyes, dark and soft, rested on her face. He nodded. "I understand you," he said. "It will all be okay."

"Are you going out for very long today?" she asked.

"For a bit," he said. "For as long as it takes you to pack, and I'll be back soon after. Then you'll be headed to the airport."

Takouhi pulled her hand away from him, just slightly. "Are *you* not driving with me to the airport?"

Ray let out a sigh, expressing that the circumstances were beyond his control. "I will, yes. But I will be staying in the car—Jean-Pierre doesn't have a driver's license, but he'll be coming with us. You saw the airport. It's a madhouse. Similar to New York, I imagine. And I'll be going back to work around the time your plane is scheduled to depart."

Takouhi had no choice but to accept the fact that her days revolved around Ray's work hours as a cab driver, which consisted of an early-morning shift with a late-afternoon break and then sundown until nine o'clock. That was his allotted time, he had told her. A much coveted one, considering he had the evenings free to do as he pleased. It was also for this reason that he did not work for *LoméTaxi!* and preferred a lesser-known car service because it offered such flexible hours. He had explained this the first time he pulled up to the circular driveway in front of her hotel to take her out on their first evening together.

Takouhi braced herself, as he expertly navigated through the city, motorbike taxis flying past them on the empty, dimly lit roads. "Would you prefer one of those? You can hold on to my back," he said teasingly as he lowered the windows all the way down. In the past, Takouhi would have complained about her hair whipping around her face and the harsh gust of wind blasting from all directions. But sitting in the passenger seat of the maroon Buick that smelled vaguely of an ashtray, she didn't mind.

On the dashboard was a wallet-sized picture of a young boy who was close to Ray's age now, Takouhi guessed. The photograph was bordered white and sepia-toned. The boy was leaning against a spray-painted stone wall, holding the handlebars of a bicycle with a missing seat. He wore a black tank top and jeans that were too short, his ankles visible. His jaw was set with impatience, as if the person holding the camera was taxing his time for the sake of a mere memory. Ray would tell her later that it was his cousin Emmanuel, who lived in Vogan, an especially impoverished area less than a two-hour drive away. They had been raised as brothers when the boy's mother had passed away, and he was later reclaimed by his father, who he had never met until then.

"I hear from him when he wants to be heard, but I don't have a way of contacting him," Ray said on one evening they were driving through Lomé. "I know he has several brothers from his father's mistresses. We used to run around together on these streets," he said, pointing to nondescript, narrow alleyways that were only illuminated by the headlights of passing cars. "We are still like brothers, although I don't hear much from him."

When they neared an area of significance, Ray would slow down the car, leaning toward her side by the window.

"This is our sacred cathedral," he said that first evening, on the first of many tours. "It's the Sacred Heart Cathedral."

She stuck her head out of the lowered window, taking in the cathedral, its eggshell-white exterior, the terra cotta-colored embellishments and three ornate pinnacles. Though dusk had quickened and the sky was only faintly lit from a distance, Takouhi regarded the emerald-green roof of the cathedral, noting the unusual juxtaposition of colors. When she leaned back into her seat, she felt Ray's arm drape behind her. She felt his hand against her bare shoulder and said nothing. She had thought of this moment many times and, despite her adoration of him, she expected to cringe or pull away; it would have been her first encounter with another man since Gabriel's passing. Instead, she allowed his hand on her shoulder, wondering if it would go any farther. It never did.

During the day, they wandered through the various marketplaces. Holding hands, they kept a distance from the vendors unless Takouhi saw something of interest. Women wandered through the streets wearing brightly patterned dresses, sometimes balancing large baskets covered in cloth atop their heads, most likely to protect the contents from the dry dust that kicked up from the hot wind. Takouhi watched them with admiration, how regal and poised they were under the perpetual and unforgiving heat, sometimes with a small child strapped to their back.

Oftentimes, when her eye came across a kiosk, she would sense the immediate gaze of the vendor, like a magnetic force pressing upon her.

"Once you buy something from one vendor, the others will try to coerce you to buy what they're selling," Ray said as they passed a long row of tables covered in what Takouhi understood to be Togolese artifacts. Upon closely looking, she realized they were displays of animal skulls, grotesque arrays of petrified eye sockets and gaping jaws, their teeth gnashing at her menacingly although they were dead. Rows of calcified reptiles and amphibians covered a large blanket a few feet away. Tortoise shells, leathery brown and hard. Heads of primates, which Takouhi could not name, sat in rows, the fur on their heads the color of copper.

"Marche des Feticheurs," Ray remarked. "This is the voodoo market."

"We're near a church," Takouhi pointed out.

"It's no matter," Ray shook his head matter-of-factly. "It's part of Togo. Hundreds of years," he said.

Takouhi looked ahead and around her as they continued walking through the market. Tables, exhibiting animal skulls, stretched before them. The wind carried a sour stench, like the smell of boiling bones that Takouhi remembered from her childhood in Beirut, when her mother returned from the butcher and made broth. But here the air reeked of rot. Flies bristled in the air. Dust and sand whipped through the market, precipitating a feeling of barrenness, a desert wasteland.

On either side of them were empty streets, locals strolling in the direction of what Takouhi guessed to be the fringes of neighborhoods and, consequently, escape. Without asking Ray, she turned sharply toward a narrow street and walked rapidly away from the market.

"Where are you going?" he asked, his voice panicked.

"Away," she said, "from this. I don't like it."

"You don't know where you're going," he protested.

She waved her hand in the air, as if swatting away his concern. "It's fine. I want to go back to the hotel. Let's just walk through here first. You know how to get back to the car, I'm sure."

"Takouhi, this is a residential area. It's all homes where people live," he said.

"And? Everyone is so friendly here. Is it because I'm not from here?" she asked and stopped walking.

"No, no," he said. "On the contrary. If we continue walking, you'll surely be invited into someone's home for lunch."

Before he could finish speaking, Takouhi was already walking ahead toward the direction of the maze-like, foreign streets. As they navigated through the paths that narrowed and widened unexpectedly, the din of the marketplace faded to a silence, punctuated by the stray voices and conversations coming from behind them or afar. The drowsy lull of the afternoon fell upon Takouhi and Ray, as he continued his quickened pace toward where Takouhi assumed he had parked the car.

Takouhi treaded with slow deliberation, taking in the novelty of her surroundings. She realized that she was not walking past homes as much as quaint hovels with open entrances, where, upon entering, one would find themselves in a kitchen or a living room. There were no doors, rather drapes that hung above openings, which lent Takouhi a feeling of safety; if the residents had nothing to fear, neither did she.

To the right of her, Takouhi saw a woman in white sitting beneath a wooden sign covered in letters; the words, though once decipherable, now resembled haphazard marks scratched across the surface of the plank. As Takouhi moved closer, she saw that the woman was old, her eyes weary and passive, as if the weight of expectation or boredom had burdened her for too long. Upon seeing Takouhi, the old woman shifted with mild interest until Ray appeared ahead of her. Like a dull spark brought to life, the old woman sprang up from her stool and pressed her hands to her hips.

Her head was covered in a white cotton hat, and she wore a matching white cotton dress that seemed more like a loose bedsheet wrapped around her frame. From her neck hung long, elaborate strings of brightly beaded necklaces studded with shells, meeting the length of her torso.

"*Cent cedis!*" the woman hollered. She gathered the hem of her dress in her tightened fist and stepped out of the entrance. "*Cent cedis!*"

One hundred cedis, the currency of Togo.

Ray quickened his steps, lurching forward, taking Takouhi's hand. "This woman is mad. Walk."

The woman stood in front of her hovel now, not following them, but continued yelling. It was not in French, as it had been upon her initial utterance. Takouhi looked behind at the woman, who, in the distance, resembled nothing more than an agitated grandmother.

She was chanting now, a word Takouhi could only assume was in Ewe, one of the local dialects she often heard Ray speak when communicating with his dispatcher. Her rich, deep voice carried through the alleyway, the exotic enunciation of her words incomprehensible: *foomnaya, foomnaya.*

Takouhi saw Ray's figure disappear around the first vacant turn. And the old woman's voice halted abruptly.

"Rest loin de lui!" the woman then yelled out.

Takouhi turned and saw the woman, still further away by the entrance of her home. The afternoon sun now sank away behind a cluster of clouds, and the alleyway was obscured in shade. It was only Takouhi and the old woman, swaddled in white, standing in the desolation of silence.

"Rest loin de lui!" the woman called out again, more with concern.

She paused and stared at Takouhi. Takouhi stared back, awkwardly, unsure if there was anything to say. As she considered this, the woman shook her head, muttered, and clucked with aggravation, returning to her stool.

"What is that woman? Who is she?" Takouhi asked once they had found themselves back on the street.

When she had finally caught up with Ray, who had gained a considerable distance on her, he was reticent. Sensing this, Takouhi had followed him the short distance back to where they were parked.

Ray, now busying himself with inserting the key into the ignition, did not pause to look at her.

"A fetishist priestess," he said finally. "A witch."

"She works for the market?" Takouhi asked.

Ray shook his head, peeled out of the parking spot.

"It's voodoo," he said curtly. "People go to them for their services. My family is very opposed. If you met my father, he would put the fear of God into you for even walking where we just were. We don't believe in such things, but as my father says: you have to fear, even a little bit, the darkness you don't know."

Takouhi thought of this as they drove back to the hotel in silence. She thought of the old woman, her caramel skin and stern countenance. *Rest loin de lui*, the woman had called out. *Stay away from him.*

"How far a drive is it?" asked Takouhi.

It was her last evening in Lomé, and Ray was preparing to take her out for dinner where they would be meeting his friends. She leaned into the mirror and squinted as she applied her mascara. It seemed impossible without her reading glasses, as she steadied the wand in her hand to meet her eyelashes.

She heard his voice from another room and thought to call out again. "I asked how far a drive—?"

When she turned around, she saw that the bathroom was now closed, his subdued voice coming from the other side of the door. Takouhi inched toward the door and leaned in, her ear nearly pressing against the door.

"I don't know . . . *je ne sais pas.* I can try . . ." His voice rose with staccato in another language and then, "Em, where is that father of yours now, eh?" A protracted silence followed, leaving Takouhi thinking that the conversation had ended. As she stepped away from the door, Ray's voice exploded with rage. "Tu te fous de moi?" *Are you kidding me?* Takouhi jumped. His words now, mingled in French and his native tongue, strung together provokingly, were incomprehensible to Takouhi. She raced back to her bed and grabbed her cell phone, intent on seeming absorbed and occupied in his absence.

When he finally walked out of the bathroom, she saw that he had changed into a pair of jeans and a freshly pressed button-down shirt. She noticed the bracelet he wore around his wrist that she had bought him several days before when they had strolled past one of the hotel boutiques in the lobby. It fit perfectly around his wrist, the smooth, brushed silver against his dark skin. Oftentimes, when they left the hotel together Takouhi would glance at their reflection when the elevator doors opened to the gilded-framed mirror on the main floor; how young she seemed alongside his tall frame, her long flowing hair and stylish clothes, the makeup she applied so expertly, hinting at long-lost youth, now fully recovered. She could not help sense the glimpses of strangers as she and Ray held hands walking through the lobby, their eyes reflecting a sense of fascination—how paradoxically, yet well-paired they were.

"Almost ready?" he asked.

He went to the full-size mirror by the door and pulled back his shoulders, pressed his hands against his shirt to smooth out the wrinkles, pretending to study himself, though Takouhi knew his mind was elsewhere. Despite how seamlessly he was trying to compose himself, Takouhi thought, his distress was transparent; his temples trickled with perspiration, his smile more put-on than genuine. She did not want to ruin his efforts and decided not to bring up what she had overheard until later, perhaps.

Jean-Pierre, who she hadn't seen since the airport when she had first arrived, was waiting for them outside the hotel. She was surprised to see another man in the driver's seat with Jean-Pierre, who was sitting on the passenger side.

"Where are we going?" she asked as she slid into the back seat with Ray next to her.

"It's a bar. A restaurant also with dancing," said Ray.

Jean-Pierre turned around and reached over toward the back, fumbling to where Takouhi was sitting. "So good to see you again," he said, shaking the tips of her fingers lightly. "This is Charles," he said, nodding to the driver. The man, slightly older than Jean-Pierre and Ray, kept his eyes on the road and nodded at their reflection from the rearview mirror.

The car sped down a long, broad road that was dotted with arbitrary streetlights. The oversized mop-headed coconut trees flopped back and forth on either side of the road. The only sound in the car was the radio, turned down so low that it felt as if it were only meant to be listened to by Charles and Jean-Pierre. Minutes passed. Darkness stretched before them, a tunnel guided by the car's headlights. Charles and Jean-Pierre continued to stare ahead in silence. Takouhi felt Ray's hand take hers. A group of motorbikes zoomed past them with startling speed. She heard Charles swear under his breath, unflustered and irritated. Within the breadth of their surrounding darkness, the car swerved and pulled over, as if making an unplanned stop.

"Jesus," Ray remarked. "Are you trying to kill us, Charles?"

"Sorry," the man shook his head. "This place sneaks up on me every time."

The three of them stepped out of the car and closed the doors behind them, only for the car to pull back onto the road and disappear. As Takouhi repositioned the purse in her arm, she looked up and saw a stone-paved driveway that led up to a patio. From the foot of the path, she saw glowing lights strung up across the entrance of the restaurant and heard the amplified strum of an acoustic guitar.

"French," Ray said, turning to Takouhi. "You'll like it."

With Jean-Pierre behind them, Ray took Takouhi's hand and led the way as if entering a party, where all the guests were already gathered in expectation of one's arrival. They walked past the bar, which was in part constructed with dark wood pillars and cemented natural stone, with a sign hung beneath that read *Brasserie*. To their left was a makeshift stage constructed of planks of wood and an old Togolese man sitting on a patron's chair with a guitar in his lap. A sixty-inch television screen hung in the main dining area, which led to a smaller room in the back mostly reserved for larger parties.

"There they are," Ray said, nodding to a group of men Takouhi recognized from their evening outings. They were sitting around a long, narrow table covered with platters of food that looked as if they had just been brought from the kitchen.

Upon glancing at them, the men raised their glasses of beer and cheered. They found three chairs and placed them at the table, and greeted the three of them. Each man shook Takouhi's hand with dutiful courtesy. An empty white plate was placed before her with a set of utensils. Platters floated above her head, food placed on her plate although she hadn't requested anything: sautéed prawns in tomato sauce, a bed of yellow rice speckled with diced red peppers, a portion of grilled fish, its skin charred and doused in lemon juice.

Takouhi began eating, taking in the conversation the men had been absorbed in before their arrival. Between snippets of English, French, and Ewe, she was able to gather a debate of some sort. The naysayer, the youngest looking of the men, would interrupt hotly, litigating his contentions as he counted them off, shaking a finger in the air with each point he raised. She watched in amusement as she began to eat, sensing Ray's full attention shifting away from her. He leaned in toward her and told her they were arguing about boxing champions. Then he interrupted and looked at the younger man, made a wry comment, and winked. The table exploded, as if a new pair of dice had been thrown into the game.

From the main room, the sound of music erupted too loudly, silencing the table. Within seconds, the volume was adjusted. The song sounded similar to the music at the club Ray had taken her to several nights before. In the spirit of the evening, Takouhi had taken it all in, danced to the pulsing lights alongside the half-naked, overheated bodies that moved with disturbing delirium. Amid the deafening beat and the bass vibrating through her, in her chest, she had heard something familiar: a Madonna song that had been popular when her girls had been in high school. Oddly, the song was distorted, the chorus appearing and disappearing, weaving in and out of another song altogether. Takouhi had sung anyway, shuffling her feet and raising her arms in the air, snapping to the rhythm, and letting her voice rise as high as she wanted, shouting "Just like a dream! You are not what you seem! Just like a prayer!"

She was disappointed now, remembering the old Togolese man with the guitar and the *Brasserie* sign by the bar. She continued eating and endured the music, hoping the next selection would be to her liking. The more she tried to decipher the conversation at the table, the more removed she felt, as if she were a stranger watching them from afar.

Again she felt Ray's hand, now on her knee, his attention shifting. She swallowed her food and leaned back with the glass of red wine that had been poured for her. He pulled his chair away from the table slightly and moved toward her. She thought he might kiss her.

"I know this is going to be crazy to you, *oiseau chanteur*," Ray's tender voice filled her ear, "but it would be an honor to marry you."

Takouhi expected him to pull away for dramatic pause, join back in the banter that he had broken away from so unexpectedly. Yet he remained near her, his face raptly fixed on hers. "I cannot imagine you leaving here. My life without you. I can come to you afterwards. You don't have to come back."

Though she had not fully expected it, Takouhi felt unsurprised, as if she had read this script and had known all along how it would play out. Bursts of laughter resounded around her. She flinched slightly, disoriented by how boisterous it all felt, grazing against her skin uncomfortably. Where she sat, Ray's friends continued their debate, which had escalated from a friendly banter to a mood more contentious, and the jukebox boomed with a new song, which was just as unpleasant as the previous selections.

"Let's go outside," she said, standing up. "There's a lot going on here. I want to go outside," she said again, and waited for him to get up from his seat and follow her.

There were as many people outside as there were in the bar. Young girls clad in shorts and bikini tops danced in the center of small circles, which had attracted both men and women who clapped as the girls danced obscenely, gyrating in the center of the open space. Takouhi grimaced with revulsion as the gathering crowds howled and shouted with perverse delight.

She grabbed Ray's hand, pulled him away from the scene to a far corner. The desolate streets surrounded them. She walked to the end of the block and would have walked farther if he had not stopped. Without hesitation, Takouhi began.

"Who were you on the phone with at the hotel?" she asked.

"When?" Ray asked. She watched his face slacken.

"You were in the bathroom. I could hear you yelling," she said.

"It was no one. Just a misunderstanding—" he began to explain. Takouhi held up her hand and regarded him with intent. "My cousin Emmanuel. The one I told you about," he said finally, his eyes looking away.

"You sounded upset," Takouhi said.

"He wouldn't tell me everything," Ray said. "Which is in part why I was getting so angry. He's been badly hurt—he won't tell me how. He's in the hospital, and there's all sorts of other trouble he won't tell me."

"Can't you go to him?" Takouhi asked. "We can drive there—"

Ray shook his head. "No. No, no. It's dangerous there. As it is, I tell you not to leave the hotel without me. Only because I don't want you to get pickpocketed or harassed, but where *he* is—no."

"So what can you do? Can he come here?" Takouhi asked.

"I've told him to, so many times. But he won't. And he needs money now. It sounds like it's for more than just the hospital bill. When I told him I didn't have it and asked him where his father was, he hung up on me."

"How much does he need?" asked Takouhi.

"Five thousand dollars," said Ray. "A lot. What you can buy with five thousand dollars here . . . that's why I know he's in some other kind of trouble."

They stood in obscure darkness, the distant cries and music now part of the fading scene behind them. And then it struck Takouhi how truly far away she was from home. How starkly different a world she had traveled to. And when she looked at Ray in the shadows, amidst the clamor of chaos, a surge of pity overcame her. He would live this life, year in and year out, the same as any other. How easy it would be for her to pluck him out, reciprocate the happiness he had given her in such a short time.

"Well?" he asked. She knew he was still waiting for an answer to his question.

The silence between them grew; and with each passing moment as she smiled intently at him, her response became clear.

"How do you expect this to happen?" Takouhi asked; and upon doing so, she felt Ray slip into her arms, lift her up from her feet. He pressed his lips to her cheek and smiled.

"Jean-Pierre," he said.

"Jean-Pierre?" Takouhi asked. "What about him? Does he have an uncle he can wake up in the middle of the night to marry us?"

Ray laughed and shook his head. "No. He has the authority. How do I explain it—I'm not finding the words . . . He's an ordained minister.

Online. He received his certificate. We do what we can to make some money around here. But Jean-Pierre—he'll marry us at no cost."

"Tonight, then?" Takouhi asked. The air around her felt suddenly electric. She could not stop smiling. She felt as if she could burst.

"Tonight," said Ray.

When looking back what Takouhi would remember was standing on the balcony of her hotel with Ray beside her, the salty smell of the ocean, and the palm trees swaying behind her. She would remember the sound of Jean-Pierre's resolute voice, reading the short script that he had brought with him that evening as Ray slipped a gold band around her finger. Then Ray kissing her softly on one cheek and then the other, his calloused hands holding her face and brushing back her hair. *"Mon chanteur,"* he said. "My beautiful songbird."

Takouhi would fall asleep that night with Ray beside her, his soft breath on her neck. All the while, she would clasp her hands together, press her right thumb and index finger across the gold band on her left hand, slowly circling it back and forth, waiting for sleep.

Chapter 23

FROM WHERE KOHAR WAS SITTING, SHE HEARD A PULSATING VI-bration from the depths of her purse, which was in the dining room. Jonathan, perhaps. She rummaged through the annoying jumble of her wallet and keys and a nipple guard and lipstick until she extracted her phone. It was a text. She scrolled up to read through the messages she had most recently sent her mother.

Hi Mom. Are you awake? I'm just texting to say hi.

Mom, I don't know what time it is there, but let me know how you're doing when you get a chance.

Mom, please call or text me, was the last message she had sent.

Just now her mother had finally written back. *what is it*

Kohar could never be sure if her mother's lack of punctuation deliberately or coincidentally communicated her emotionality.

I'm sorry. Did I wake you up? We haven't heard from you and I wanted to make sure you're okay.

I'm okay

What's going on? Where are you?

I told you where I was going I'm fine

Kohar paused, deliberating. A small child came to mind, clutching matches in her hand.

I can't wait to hear about your trip. You must be having a great time.

Her eyes fixed on the screen, Kohar waited. She knew not to write more. After several minutes, she placed the phone next to her on the counter. Then suddenly it came to life.

I have something to tell you

She would pretend to be surprised. She would assure her mother that the most important thing was for her to be happy. *Okay . . . Is everything okay?*

I'm going to send a picture

More than anything, Kohar was curious. Aside from her father and Gabriel and her mother's long-standing crush on Tom Selleck, who her mother had recently declared unattractive—"He didn't age well"—Kohar could only wonder about her mother's taste in men. Perhaps the man was Armenian. Some widower or divorcé from Glendale, California—Ashod, Armen, Veeken, who had flown to West Africa to meet her mother.

The phone vibrated in the grip of her palm. When Kohar pulled up the screen, she drew in a sharp breath. Below the body of her mother's text was a close-up photo of a young African man, smiling playfully, wearing earbuds.

"Holy shit."

Before she could write back, her phone shuddered, displaying her mother's phone number. She swiped against the screen to accept the call, aware that her hands were now damp with perspiration.

"Hi, Mom."

"Did you see the picture?"

"I did."

"How come you're not saying anything?" Her tone was abrupt, accusing. Kohar could hear her mother's breathing, too loudly, from the other end of the line.

"Well . . ." Kohar cleared her throat, preparing to negotiate with insanity. "If you're wondering if I think his age is weird, I don't."

"Uh-mmmm . . ." Kohar pictured her mother rocking back and forth on the soles of her feet, staring at the ceiling, as was her habit when she was anxious.

"How old is he?" Kohar asked. Preemptively, she winced.

"What difference does that make?" her mother asked, and before Kohar could answer—"twenty-nine."

"I think you need to be careful. Because . . . he looks pretty young. And you're almost seventy—"

"That is an insult to me!" her mother's scoffing voice exploded from the receiver. "Do you know I went out to a club with him and his friends? And I danced? And his friends thought I was in my forties! They couldn't believe how much energy I have. For once in my life, I want to do what *I* want to do."

Without warning, the line went dead. A stone falling down a bottomless hole.

"Everything good?"

Takouhi put the cell phone in her purse and zipped it closed. "Yes," she replied, turning to Jean-Pierre.

"Your daughter?" he asked, extending the chamomile tea she had asked for half an hour ago.

It felt lukewarm in her hand. "Yes," she said. She grimaced slightly, unwilling to confide Kohar's misgivings to someone as guileless as Jean-Pierre. There would never be a way to articulate to Kohar the simplicity of the people she had met in Togo, their generous nature, their humble and unpretentious disposition.

"Takouhi," he said, "I have to go. He can't stay parked for too long. Have a good flight." He took her hand and pulled her toward him, hugged her politely. "I can't go with you any farther anyway. The rest is security."

"Thank you, Jean-Pierre," she said. "Please tell him goodbye for me again. I know he's waiting—go," she urged him, picturing the anarchy of cars and taxis and police vehicles clustering around Ray, as he sat in the driver's seat waiting with growing anxiety. "And thank you for *this*," she said, lowering her eyes to her hand, to her finger that displayed the simple gold band.

"It is nothing," Jean-Pierre said, offering a moderate smile. He nodded to her, half-saluted courteously, and turned toward the automated doors.

Though Takouhi watched him leave, it was only seconds before his head disappeared out of the terminal and back into the throng of chaos. Takouhi took a breath, a parting breath that she always took before leaving one destination for another. All the girls, Gabriel also, had noted this about her upon arriving or returning from a vacation together: she released an audible breath as if to say *Here we go again*. For Takouhi, traveling did not merely entail the packing and unpacking of personal items, the transportation from one location to another and back, the experience of wonder and curiosity from one unexpected moment to the next. Rather, it involved the anticipation of checking off a tedious to-do list, from beginning to end.

It began in its most nascent phase—the conception of the trip—and saw itself all the way through to returning home, unpacking her belongings, washing and folding every item of clothing, and arranging her entire life back into its original order, the last vestiges of her travels found only in photographs and shared memories.

And so, as Takouhi zipped her purse and arranged the long strap across her body and pulled up the retractable handle of her suitcase, she drew in her parting breath and headed toward the security checkpoint. It had only been moments since Jean-Pierre had left her. Amidst the usual hum of airport busyness, several feet in the distance Takouhi saw uniformed men, heading in her direction. Three men, stoic faces, walking swiftly toward her. Takouhi looked behind her, for a thief, perhaps, racing through the crowd. She strained to listen for an announcement through the loudspeaker. Her mind ran wildly. A bomb. Or a bomb threat. An impending disaster.

Before she could move aside to clear a path for the officers, the three had surrounded her. She stared at their black boots, all identical. Three pairs of laced boots. Three pairs of long legs. Around their waists were holsters and no weapons. Takouhi felt herself shrinking, ignoring the clusters of people surrounding them now. The sound of a child's plaintive whine. An announcement in French, garbled words. Meaningless in the wake of what was to come.

One of the officers finally spoke, his voice quiet and subdued. "Please come with us," he said.

Takouhi could not find it within herself to protest, to call out to anyone. For there was no one to call out to. One of the officers took her suitcase, which she was gripping with such force that she felt the imprint on her hands after it was taken. Two stood on either side of her. The one who spoke stepped in front of her. Takouhi began walking, to where she was unsure, all the while twisting the gold ring tirelessly around her finger.

Chapter 24

"There's no fucking way you're doing that." His tone was forbidding. Jonathan walked past her toward the side of the bed where he had laid out a stack of T-shirts to fold. He stared at the pile. "There's no fucking way you're doing that. And if I have to explain to you why, then that's more fucked-up than anything else."

He had tried, for all their time together, for all the years he had known Kohar, to mitigate. Jonathan had managed to walk the treacherous tightrope of getting along well enough with Takouhi and empathizing with Kohar's unusual, and oftentimes disturbing, relationship with her mother. He recognized with the passing years that Kohar was not all of who she once had been: passionate, decisive, optimistic, confident. Slowly, Kohar had depleted herself in the persistent tug-of-war that she had fought for as long as she could remember: tolerating her mother in all that she was to her, and Kohar still trying, with exhausting effort, to maintain her best self. But she was slipping away. Irritable now, when he dared to ask for something as simple as whether they had run out of milk. She hadn't made any effort to continue writing her novel, claiming that it wouldn't get published anyway and that she couldn't write because she was too sleep-deprived. When Jonathan would arrange for his mother to babysit so he and Kohar could go out for the evening, she was only agreeable, not appreciative for their time together. The animated woman he had married, who would be excited at the idea of trying a new recipe or planning their next trip, had dulled with the burden of Takouhi's mere presence in her life.

"But I am," she said. "I have to."

She was leaning against his bureau, wearing the baby-pink robe, now oversized, that he had bought her when she was pregnant. Jonathan wanted to point out the irony of her words, how deeply they resonated as the mantra of her relationship with Takouhi. But he couldn't be sure she would listen, clear-headed as she seemed. So matter-of-fact in her decision.

"Why?" he asked. "Why you?" He paused for a moment, closed his eyes as if harnessing the patience necessary, and took a breath. "We need you. What don't you get about this?"

"I'm not trying to save her—" Kohar began.

"You think she needs you more than I do? Or Ruby?" Jonathan asked. He sensed the humiliation registering in Kohar's face. "If you keep telling yourself that, you'll be chasing your mother until she dies."

"Then who's going to get her?" asked Kohar.

"What would any of them do if you weren't here? They'd figure it *out*," Jonathan said. "Without Gabriel—" and ever so slightly Jonathan turned away, took another breath to level his voice. "What are we doing, now that he's not with us anymore? *This*. And it's always on you."

"I know," Kohar replied, her eyes clouding over for a moment, now less adamant. And yet still, "I just feel like I have to."

How could Kohar explain to Jonathan, her mother's strained voice coming through the other line. *Kohar . . . Kohar . . .* calling out to her as if she were wandering through a wasteland, blind or lost or both . . . *Kohar?*

It was only five hours ago that she had been woken up by the buzzing of her phone, the neon blue lighting up on her nightstand.

"Yes. I'm here," Kohar had replied, sitting up in bed with her hand cupped over the mouthpiece, staggering in complete darkness from her bedroom to the office.

"*Kohar?* Can you hear me? *Kohar?* I need to talk to you," her mother had called out to her, her voice panicked with desperation. An unearthly static crackled on the other end of the line, an outer-space quality as if her mother were speaking through radio waves.

"Yes, I'm here. Can you hear me? I'm here." Kohar had stood frozen in the middle of her office, on the edge of a horrifying precipice. "Mom!" she had cried out sharply. "Mom!"

"*Kohar?*"

"Mom, I'm here. Can you hear me? Where are you? What's happening?"

"I'm still in Togo. I didn't get on the flight." Her words expelled in gasps.

"But why? Where are you?"

An eerie silence had pressed between them. Knowing her mother was still listening, Kohar waited.

"They apprehended me," her mother had said.

"'Apprehended'? Who? Arrested, you mean? Who did?"

Another uneasy silence settled. "I need you to come and take me back," her mother had finally spoken again. "It's the only way. And don't tell the girls," she had added.

"Mom. Seriously. What is going on? I'm not flying to the other side of the world when you're speaking in code," she had said. Her irritation had given way; she knew her mother well enough to understand that she only left out information to avoid being implicated. "I'm not doing anything until you tell me the whole story," Kohar had replied flatly. "Tell me now."

"Fine." Her desperate pleas, with all its ephemerality, transmuted now with an ugly coldness. "They arrested me because I married Ray."

Kohar had leaned toward the floor lamp and pulled the chain and glanced into the mirror as if she were looking at a live audience. *Can you believe this shit?* In spite of herself, she had smirked, shook her head.

"Why would they arrest you for marrying someone?"

"I don't know," her mother had answered peevishly now, as if none of it, including her plight, had anything to do with her.

"So why do you need me to fly to Togo? Why can't they just let you go? I can talk to them if you want," Kohar had offered.

"*Talk* to them? These are *police* officers who work for the Togolese *government*. They don't give a shit about me or you," her mother had heaved her words, one by one, like rocks in her fist.

Kohar had sat heavily in her armchair, pressed the phone to her ear. When enough time passed, her mother continued. "They'll keep me here for two days. For someone to come get me."

"And then what?" Kohar had asked.

"'And then what'? I don't know, Kohar. I didn't ask. You have to come get me."

As Kohar opened and closed her dresser drawers, throwing random clothes into her carry-on, she could not even explain it to herself; Ruby would always be her daughter. She was forever. But her mother, an untethered kite. That Kohar had raced toward, zigzagged as if across the glassy sheen of wet sand. The kite wanted to dance with chilling ferocity, manically alone. Kohar knew she wasn't grounding the tether anymore for the sadness it carried; but that, rather, she wanted to believe that she was whole enough. To acknowledge her mother's raw strength and depravity. That her mother did not hate her and that mothers treat their daughters the way they feel about their own selves. She could not remember if that was once told to her or if she had known it all along.

When she looked up, she saw that Jonathan had left the room. Her eyes wandered to a bright patch of light on the bedspread. There was no accusing silence in the room as she had expected. She thought of the last phone call, the broken stream of their conversation. Only bursts of soft static interrupting. *Kohar . . . you have to come get me . . .* In her mother's mind, Kohar knew, this was the first time she had turned to Kohar, asked for help. But Kohar understood otherwise. She had always been that person. The person who thought to throw their mother a surprise sixtieth birthday party, which her sisters now only hazily recalled; the person, as the eldest, who had stood alongside her mother and witnessed the long, hard years of marriage to her father—more than even Gabriel or anyone else; the person who had endured her mother's apathy after her parents' divorce because she was damaged from the years of abuse; her mother had loved Gabriel too much and pitied Lucine too dearly to have anything left for Kohar but austerity and hatred. And now Kohar was that person again.

From Ruby's room she could hear the crinkle of a diaper being changed. Ruby with a beauty mark on the left side of her upper lip, her unusual hazel-green eyes, her fine brown hair, her smooth, sweet face. The irony of motherhood came upon Kohar with clarity now, as if a clock whirring forward uncontrollably; she was scared of being a mother not because she was scared of turning into Takouhi; rather, it was because she thought that by being a mother, she would understand her mother better, that she would find less fault in her brutality. But now that she was carrying this lovely creature in her arms, her Ruby, humming to her, bathing her, loving her more wholly in the small span of time than Kohar had ever felt her mother's love in all her life, Kohar realized that she understood her mother less. It had not occurred to her that in her sudden absence Ruby would look for her, miss her—cry, maybe. She could not fathom being so significant to anyone besides Jonathan. What would Ruby's life be without her? And what would life be without Ruby? And how could Kohar leave? She wasn't going to tell Jonathan he was right. Not yet.

Kohar opened the phone and dialed.

"Hey." Lucine's haggard voice came through.

"Were you sleeping?"

"Duh. What time is it? What's up?"

"It's about Mom."

"Is she okay?" Kohar heard the tousling of bedsheets and then the metallic clicking of the lighter. Exhale.

"Not really."

"Not really? Why? Have you spoken to her?"

"She's been arrested. In Togo. She wants me to go get her."

"Are you *fucking kidding* me?" her voice shifting from lethargy to alarm. Kohar could practically hear Lucine spit into the phone.

"No. I'm not kidding you. And I can't go."

Lucine puffed into the phone. "Well, *I* can't go."

"Okay, then. Call Azad and see if she can go."

"Can you call her?"

"No."

"Why?"

"Because I can't. *You* call her. *God*," Kohar couldn't tell if a scream or a sob or something hysterically horrendous was quaking within her. "I can't do this anymore."

"What if Azad can't go?"

"Oh. Well."

"Are you mad at me?" A rare question from Lucine.

"No. I'm just not flying to Togo to bail out our mother who married a twenty-nine-year-old guy."

"*What?*"

Perhaps her mother would wallow in a Togolese cell for a few weeks before Lucine and Azad flew to her. Perhaps two days later Lucine and Azad would fly out on a plane together to bring her back. Kohar could already feel the safety of distance between herself and her mother, picturing her disoriented face upon seeing not Kohar, but her two youngest daughters.

As reality would have it, Takouhi was released several hours after speaking to Kohar. She and Ray had never really gotten married. A ruse, the officials theorized, to create an illusion of love and extract more money from Takouhi once she returned to the States. She would sit in the sparse room under an unshaded lightbulb gaping at an array of black-and-white photographs of Ray and the man who had wed them—Jean-Pierre—one of the café boys, as the officials referred to them. Takouhi, blinking at the photographs in the dizzying, stultifying heat of the closed-in room, would at first glance not recognize Ray in the high-gloss shots and then retract with shock; snapshots of him, his affable smile with his arm around various women in the same marketplaces that he had taken her on those afternoons. Women younger than her, more attractive. Women older than her and less attractive. By which Takouhi felt more insulted, she could not tell.

The officials, two of them, would rattle through a long string of questions, which Takouhi would answer as obligingly as possible, hoping to avoid being incriminated. She would be more forthright and honest with these strangers than she had ever been with anyone in her life. No, they had never had "relations." As she spoke, Takouhi could almost feel the hot, dry wind pushing through the open sliding door of the balcony as she lay in the darkness of her hotel room with Ray lying next to her and holding her for all the nights she had spent there. He had asked for money, yes, which she had given him—five thousand, to be exact. No, he had not asked her to carry a package anywhere. No, upon her arrival he had not picked her up from the airport, nor had he dropped her off for her departure that afternoon. It had been Jean-Pierre, his best friend, who had been holding a sign with her name on it as she had walked through customs, had escorted her to the parking lot where Ray was sitting, in the passenger seat. He had only gotten out of the car upon seeing her, hugged her tightly, quickly while Jean-Pierre put her luggage in the trunk of the car before they sped away from the airport. Takouhi understood now, how all the pieces came together. Ray, whose name was not Ray—Kphatcha Fumnaya, was subverting police officers. For what specific reason, the officials would not tell her.

He is wanted, was all they offered by way of explanation.

"Is there anything you want to tell us about him?" one of the officials asked.

"What can I tell you when you aren't telling me why you're looking for him?" Takouhi replied.

"We are sorry, madam, but there are reasons why we have to maintain discretion," the official replied. "But I am sure you can infer from the photographs why we are searching for him."

How had she traveled so far away, only to find herself where she had always been: alienated from who she was meant to be. Not the compliant daughter, the obsequious housewife, the resilient mother who, at all costs, had made sure her daughters were taken care of. It was the best she could have done. If only there was someone to understand. Because her daughters, not one of them could. Kohar and Lucine resented her for who she had become, when it was no fault of her own. Like a pebble, she had been tossed by the wind through rough terrains, and she had persevered. Takouhi wished they could acknowledge everything she had sacrificed despite it all. And Azad, wide-eyed and vulnerable just like her father, Takouhi accepted her natural disposition and her maternal duty to protect her. Takouhi thought of all this as she sat alone, observing the clouds as her plane took flight. And for once, she quieted the detonations of worry that began to crowd her thoughts, and closed her eyes.

ONE WINTER NIGHT AFTER SETTLING RUBY INTO HER CRIB, Kohar would wake up in the silence of the house. The first thing she would remember was holding Ruby in front of the Christmas tree, the smell of freshly cut pine as her daughter reached over to touch a silver-frosted ornament. Warm and light in her arms, Kohar would hold her there. She remembered this as she kept her eyes closed in the darkness of her bedroom while Jonathan slept soundlessly next to her. And it would dawn on her so unexpectedly, like a shooting star in a cloudless sky that only she could see: it was not Jonathan who had saved her, no. It was not she herself. But her daughter, her Ruby. By giving her motherhood and absolute salvation.

Then, suddenly, Ruby's soft cry interrupted Kohar's thoughts. Quickly, she slipped out of the room before Jonathan could stir. And with every step, Kohar grew closer to her new world, to the marvelous being who she could love freely, openly. Because after all, there was freedom in being loved.

Acknowledgments

THEY SAY IT TAKES A VILLAGE TO RAISE A CHILD. SO MUCH OF IT is true when writing a body of work. First and foremost, thank you to my husband Brian who listened and read countless pages and drafts, encouraging me to continue and write as bravely as I could. Your unwavering faith in me has been the backbone of this long and meandering path. This book would not have come to life without your honesty, your love and your confidence in me. Thank you to my daughter Sophia for wandering into my office again and again, peeking over my shoulder to look at the page count and say "Wow." I had no choice but to make you proud.

My sister Alice, my first fan, used to sit waiting for me to complete my stories on an electric typewriter, eager to read. You took my writing seriously before I ever did. Thank you.

My sister Ani, thank you for loving what I do and understanding me.

My cousins and family have always championed my work and it made me feel less solitary in writing this novel. I thank you all.

Thank you to my mother for inspiring me.

A huge thank you to the talented writers who read my novel and wrote heartfelt blurbs: Nancy Agabian, Arif Anwar, Christopher Atamian, Jared Harél, Arthur Nercessian, and Christine Kandic Torres.

Thank you to Olivia Katrandjian, founder and president of the International Armenian Literary Alliance, for championing Armenian writers and giving me unwavering support in so many ways. I also thank the members of IALA who have helped as my Armenian writing community.

Karen Clark, my book coach: without your bold guidance this novel wouldn't have taken shape and fallen into place. Thank you so much!

My sister in writing, Nancy Agabian: from the days of Gartal until now, I have admired you, turned to you and you have always encouraged me at my most difficult moments. Thank you so much for your wisdom and the gift of your friendship.

Thank you to Christopher Atamian for reading so much of my work, writing splendid reviews and editorials, and making me laugh.

Lola Koundakjian, I thank you for our first eye-opening conversation that I have entitled "How To Become a Real Writer", when you sat with me and explained with care and patience exactly what it takes to truly start from the ground up.

Thank you to Richard Jeffrey Newman, for your writing advice, for your depth of insight and positive spirit.

Alan Semerdjian, all it takes is a cup of a coffee and your open ear for me to feel heard. Those conversations helped me press forward despite my deepest doubts. I thank you for your friendship and your beautiful soul.

Arthur Nercessian, thank you for taking my phone calls, emails at a moment's notice to advise me during times of (perceived) crisis. Your wisdom was invaluable.

Thank you Arthur Kayzakian for our meditative discussions about writing, for your hilarious wit and encouragement.

There is only one person I can thank for the beautiful cover of my book - Amy Kazandjian. Your talent, your exuberant spirit and sense of humor has been a pure delight. Thank you for creating a portrait of my novel that has been sitting in my heart for decades.

I want to thank Turner Publishing for supporting my writing and giving my novel every opportunity to shine. Thank you to Ryan Smernoff, my first editor at Turner, who embraced my novel from the day I submitted it for consideration and through the initial phases of the editing process. Thank you to my editor Amanda Chiu Krohn for her keen eye, enthusiasm, and in helping me continue the process of edits all the way through the publication of this book. Thank you to Makala Marsee for all your energy, help, and insight in marketing and promoting my novel. We did this together and I'm grateful for that.

Lastly, thank you to all my friends who believed me when I said upon my first published piece in 2008, that I wanted to be a writer. You have read more of my stories and come to more readings than a writer could hope for. It has brought me all the way here.

About the Author

AIDA ZILELIAN is a first-generation American-Armenian writer, storyteller, and educator. She is the author of *The Legacy of Lost Things*, recipient of the 2014 Tololyan Literary Award. Aida has been featured on NPR, the *Huffington Post*, *Kirkus Reviews*, and *Poets & Writers*. Her short story collection, *These Hills Were Meant for You*, was shortlisted for the 2018 Katherine Anne Porter Award. She lives in Queens, New York with her husband and daughter.

Printed in the USA
CPSIA information can be obtained
at www.ICGtesting.com
JSHW021521110324
58997JS00004B/163